"Angus," she gasped in amazement. "Is it really you?"
Tears burst forth as she threw her arms around the stiff,
motionless figure. Then, leaning back and holding his
hands, she realized that his eyes were devoid of expression.
"Angus." She shook him anxiously. "Angus, it's me, Flo.
Say something, please." She shook him again gently.
Then another thought occurred. *Gavin.* Where was Gavin?
She glanced around, as though expecting to see him among
the group of men smoking and playing cards. Then she
squeezed Angus's hand once more.

"Angus, you're all right now. You're with me." His eyes flickered
and her heart leapt. "Oh, Angus, darling, please. Please come
back. Please tell me where Gavin is," she whispered, almost to
herself.

"Dead." The voice was flat.

She stared at him, then shook her head. "No. It can't be.
No." She shook her head again, her hands gripping his sleeve
savagely. "Not Gavin." She began shaking, then laughed
hysterically. "People like Gavin don't get killed. They're
immortal."

"It should have been me," he whispered.

**"A thrilling drama of passion and revenge, brilliantly
set against the epic backdrop of the twentieth century."
—Carla Neggers, bestselling author of *The Carriage House***

FIONA HOOD-STEWART

THE STOLEN YEARS

MIRA

ISBN 1-55166-833-5

THE STOLEN YEARS

Copyright © 2001 by Fiona Hood-Stewart.

All rights reserved. Except for use in any review, the reproduction or
utilization of this work in whole or in part in any form by any electronic,
mechanical or other means, now known or hereafter invented, including
xerography, photocopying and recording, or in any information storage or
retrieval system, is forbidden without the written permission of the publisher,
MIRA Books, 225 Duncan Mill Road, Don Mills, Ontario, Canada M3B 3K9.

All characters in this book have no existence outside the imagination of the
author and have no relation whatsoever to anyone bearing the same name
or names. They are not even distantly inspired by any individual known or
unknown to the author, and all incidents are pure invention.

MIRA and the Star Colophon are trademarks used under license and registered
in Australia, New Zealand, Philippines, United States Patent and Trademark
Office and in other countries.

Visit us at www.mirabooks.com

Printed in U.S.A.

As always, for my boys,
Sergio and Diego.

For Daddy,
in loving memory.

This book is dedicated to all the men and women
who gave their youth, their hopes and dreams
and all too often their lives in the name of freedom.

May we honor them by preserving their legacy.

F.H.S.

My deep gratification to David d'Albis for his untiring
dedication in helping me research this manuscript.
To Jean d'Albis, of Limoges, France, for recounting events as
they took place and for the documents he furnished me with.
Many thanks to Laure Kovats, Fran Garfunkel, Frances
Lynch, Carter Parsley, Bonnie Skop,
Miranda Stecyk and Donald Maas, my agent,
for all the help along the way.

Part One

1917–1918

Surely, surely there must be somewhere in which the sweet intimacies begun here may be continued, and the hearts broken by this war may be healed.

—Vera Britain
A Testament of Youth

1

Edinburgh, Scotland, 1917

She waited, tiptoeing along the chilly corridor and creeping quietly into the darkened ward, listening intently as the matron's footsteps faded to a distant whisper on the worn flagged staircase. Except for the occasional muffled groan, the long row of narrow metal beds was quiet, their chipped white paint glittering harshly in the filtered moonlight.

Taking advantage of the matron's absence, Flora Finlay sat down gingerly in the single uncomfortable wooden chair the ward offered, careful not to crush her starched uniform. After casting a covert glance at the door, she finally opened the letter that had been burning her inner pocket since early that morning. As Angus's neat, precise letters swam before her, she chided herself for the twinge of disappointment, aware she should be thankful for any news at all. Unfolding the single sheet of flimsy paper, she held it close to the dim aureole of light escaping from under the battered shade of the solitary lamp and smiled. Angus's writing reminded her of Miss Linton, their old governess, who on more than one occasion had made pointed comparisons between Gavin and Flora's sloppy calligraphy and Angus's perfectly formed loops.

Skimming the text rapidly, she jumped hopefully to the end, knowing it was silly but unable to help herself. Why couldn't

Gavin write something, however short, in his own hand, instead of sending vague messages through his twin? But that was Gavin, she realized with a sigh. Seeing him in her mind's eye, bright-eyed and impulsive, she wondered why she expected him to be any different, when this was the way she loved him.

The letter was dated three weeks earlier and was postmarked from Arras, where the fighting on the western front was at its worst. Terrifying images of the twins, lying buried in the bloodied gut of a shell-torn trench, their features unrecognizable amidst the mass of mangled bodies, flashed through Flora's mind in eerie succession. But she ousted them and instead concentrated her attention on the letter, knowing the matron could return at any minute.

Today it pours and we're up to our calves in mud. The only trees that have survived the shelling are two stringy poplars to our right, but the landscape bears all the scars of war. After the last onslaught things have been fairly stalemate, but it is my feeling there is more to come. How they expect us to fight in this pockmarked, muddied mess beats me. There simply isn't any suitable terrain for the kind of breakthrough we hope for.

But I'm rambling on about the war, when what you really want is news of your beloved Gavin.

We are in a front-line trench now. I know that sounds worse, but you mustn't worry. Actually, it's preferable. Gerry's shells fly over us rather than straight at us—for now, at any rate.

Oh God, Flo! It all seems so bloody futile. We hammer them, they hammer us, and for what? I'm sure the German chaps, huddled in their muddy, lice-infested dugouts across no-man's-land are asking themselves the same damn questions we are. Wishing they could get on with their lives, instead of being burrowed here like moles, for God knows how much longer, waiting to be wounded or die.

But once again I've deviated and I know you must be thoroughly impatient. Gavin is up to his old tricks, hobnobbing with the French, as I told you in my last letter. Now that they know we both speak the language fluently, they've selected us for all the liaison missions! Need I tell you whose idea *that* was? I hate every minute of it, but Gavin loves it. He is utterly fearless, and I have come to the conclusion that he thrives on danger. The other day he went on a reconnaissance mission where he all but got himself killed. I begged him not to go but he listens to no one, and is as determined and headstrong as ever. Unlike me, he is a true officer and leader of men. Even the seasoned soldiers listen to him, which is quite something. You can imagine how ridiculous it makes one feel, giving orders to a man old enough to be our grandfather, who knows much more than we ever will. There's one old fellow in the unit who fought in South Africa and is probably the best man we have. Doesn't it make you question a system that appoints young men like Gavin and me as officers, merely because we are gentlemen?

I have asked Gavin to write but he continues to claim he is a poor correspondent. He sends his love, as always, and says how much he misses you. I miss you too, Flora dearest, but I know that won't make up for his not writing...

He had sent his love. She read quickly through to the end, then let the letter droop. Swallowing her disappointment, Flora reminded herself that to be ungrateful was to tempt fate. Then, folding the page carefully, she prayed that the two men she loved most were still alive. Too often she had witnessed the arrival of these precious letters from the front, seen the relief and joy they raised, only to be dashed hours later when it was learned they were to be the last.

She turned her thoughts to the ward, the smell of antiseptic and the stifled sighs coming from the iron beds, and rose, slipping the letter into her apron pocket. She winced as pain shot relentlessly from her ankles up her slim, shapely legs, stiff and swollen after forty-eight hours on duty. Not that Matron cared, she reflected bitterly. To her, the Voluntary Aid Detachments were nothing more than glorified slave labor. Never mind that many of them, by this stage of the war, were more knowledgeable than most of the young nurses brought in fresh from training.

Resolutely, Flora switched on her flashlight and straightened the intricate uniform that enveloped her diminutive figure like a suit of starched armor. She glanced sleepily at her watch before making her way past the row of narrow beds, her rubber soles squeaking eerily on the linoleum.

She lingered, staring sadly through the shadows at the bandaged remains of a generation. Months before, boys her own age had left for the front as brave young warriors, ready to conquer the world, only to return wounded forever in heart, body and soul. Each time her eye fell on a flat sheet where a limb should have been, her throat clenched, for try as she might she was unable to shut out the smothered moans and the heartrending aura of resignation. Six months of quivering stumps, the familiar hum of agony, and dressing wounds, some so horrific death would have been preferable, should have made her immune to these sights and sounds. But they hadn't, and probably never would. The outer control she displayed was a necessary survival tool, one that she upheld bravely, aware that a calm front helped the suffering patients. But her soul wept, unable to accept so much needless pain and mutilation.

Halfway down the ward she stopped to smooth the forehead of a sandy-haired private, relieved to find him calmer. But his limp pajama sleeve told its own tale, and she wondered for the thousandth time what it would be like if Gavin were to return like this. The thought was haunting. Again she chased away the images of his tall, handsome figure lying broken and maimed at the bottom of a trench, his bright blue eyes dulled by pain and his thick, black hair caked with blood and mud.

Shuddering, she headed toward the screens raised ominously around Jimmy McPherson, a young private brought in yesterday for whom little could be done. She slipped behind the divide and gazed unhappily into a pair of delirious eyes that glittered, bright and frantic, above fiery emaciated cheeks.

With nobody to alleviate his soft moans of agony, Flora lay

the flashlight on the nightstand and realized that all she could do now was pray. Reaching out, she took the boy's hot, dry hand in hers, begging not for his recovery, but for a quick release from this horrendous suffering.

"Allow him to go in peace, dear Lord," she pleaded, holding her other hand close to the young man's feverish brow.

All at once, her body became weightless, as though she were not a part of it, and a strong sensation of energy ran through her. It had occurred several times, always with those patients on the brink of death who seemed unable to let go of life. As on the other occasions, she suddenly felt an invisible presence. The heat from Jimmy's brow abated, his eyes cleared and his chapped lips moved. Flora leaned closer, desperate to catch his last, whispered words.

"Tell Mother I planted the daffodils for her. Tell her..." But the rest was lost as his eyes closed and life ebbed gently away, and Flora watched in motionless awe as two hazy shadows appeared above the bed. She saw him rise out of his body and walk away between them.

Slowly, as the dawn crept stealthily through the Victorian windows, the image faded and she became aware that her fingers still clasped the stiffening hand of the figure in the bed. Gently, she folded his hands over his chest and, with a final look at his expressionless countenance, devoid now of suffering, she pulled the sheet up over him. A rush of exhaustion followed and she clutched the railing of the cot as everything went black.

Gradually she recovered her balance. The ward and its gloomy monotony came back into focus, and she stared as though seeing it for the first time. All at once, the endless rain battering the rattling panes of the old windows, the groans, the sickening scent of death and despondency, swooped down on her like a terrifying specter, and to her horror she feared she could not go on. Shame followed her initial panic as she faced her own inadequacy. Suddenly she wanted to run, escape from this dismal drudgery.

"Nurse?" A harsh call from the door made Flora snap to and hurry to face the starched, disapproving matron. It was bad enough being surrounded by suffering, but the matron's constant censure made matters worse. She never missed a chance to slip in a snide remark about the privileged few, coupled with derogatory reflections on Flora's small frame. Added to that were the woman's disdainful looks. Often Flora wished she were plain and invisible, ashamed of her trim figure, her misty gray eyes, delicate, translucent complexion and chestnut hair that the matron regarded as nothing less than the wiles of a wicked temptress.

"I was just doing the rounds, Matron," she murmured hurriedly, afraid her expression might give her thoughts away. "I'm afraid poor Private McPherson passed away."

"I see. I hope you filled out the chart properly, Nurse. I won't stand for any inefficiency." She peered ominously through a pair of thick, horn-rimmed glasses perched on the beak of her bony nose. Behind them, her small, steely eyes glinted like two metal buttons. "You can finish cleaning the floors before you go. There's to be no slacking. And mind your posture, Nurse. I won't have slouches on my ward."

Mustering her dignity, Flora straightened her sore back and dragged herself to the laundry to get a mop and pail, feeling the matron's piercing gaze boring into her back as she trundled down the corridor. She cleaned the floor with aching arms and sighed with relief when the clock finally struck seven, careful to make herself scarce before the woman found another last-minute task for her to perform.

Flora grabbed her cloak and umbrella, left the drab building and made her way through the heavy rain to a shelter on the street corner. There she waited for the tram that would take her to the end of Prince's Street, where Murray and the car would be waiting to take her home. She leaned against the damp wall, staring at the rising mist still clinging to the flagged pavement, and glanced shamefacedly at the peeling posters with their patriotic appeals. What right had she to complain, when everyone was suffering just as she was? Still, she knew she'd reached the end of her tether and could not stand the ward or the matron's badgering any longer.

At the sound of the tram's approach, Flora went to the curb

and waved it down. The aged conductor gave a tired smile. She sat down on the wooden bench, relieved to be off her feet, and considered her situation. As a solution presented itself, a slow smile and a tingle of excitement replaced the shame and fear. Why hadn't she thought of it earlier? The Foreign Service! Perhaps it wasn't here at home that she was needed but at the front. Perhaps there, in the midst of it all, she could be of true help, offering more than the menial tasks the matron assigned her. She steadied herself as the tram rumbled along, filled with newfound inner strength, elated despite the physical and emotional fatigue. All at once Jimmy McPherson's passing and the strange, recurring experiences made sense.

Then she remembered Tante Constance and Uncle Hamish and her heart sank. What would they say? They were sure to protest. Technically, they could even stop her from going. Like Gavin and Angus, their sons, she had lied about her age to become a V.A.D. Still, her mind was made up. Somewhere deep within, a dogged voice summoned, as though the young private's death had opened a window to her soul, making the months of frustration and endurance—of patiently washing slops and cleaning bowls, rolling bandages and running endless errands—worthwhile.

She gazed out of the clammy window at the drizzling morning, wishing she were a man. Men were simply called up, and neither family nor personal commitment mattered before service to king and country. But for women it was different. The older generation, having so willingly given up their sons, husbands and brothers, considered it the duty of a young woman to attend to them. An ailing parent was enough to call a V.A.D. back from the front, leaving her no choice but to return, wretchedly divided between duty to her family and her country.

Flora leaned forward, pulling her cape closer, anxiously imagining all the arguments her aunt and uncle were sure to put forward. But the more she thought, the more prepared she became to do battle if necessary. No matter how exhausting she found the Foreign Service, it couldn't possibly be worse than the tedious, unrewarding pattern of the present, where the only highlight lay in Angus's sporadic letters, carrying brief news of Gavin.

With her six-month trial period complete, Flora was eligible to apply overseas. The government was appealing daily for V.A.D.s willing to go to the front. As the tram swung round the corner into Prince's Street, a large billboard came into view, exhorting the population to trust in their country and support those brave young men and women at the front. It had to be an omen, Flora averred.

The moment she reached the car, Flora instructed the chauffeur, who was too old for the war or the coal pits, to drive straight to the inscription office. There she waited for nearly an hour in a stuffy waiting room, while an efficient middle-aged woman in uniform sat behind a large desk, writing diligently. Flora stared at the carpet's fading gray pattern, which was probably once blue, and read the announcements pinned on the walls. She fiddled nervously with the buttons of her cloak, convincing herself she'd done right to come.

Finally the woman beckoned and Flora followed her down a colorless corridor to a door that had an opaque glass panel with RECRUITING written on it in bold, black letters. She was invited to sit down by an unusually sympathetic young matron who did not question too closely when she blushingly stated her age as nineteen. She merely filled in the blanks on the form, apparently glad that after three long years of pain, tedium and despair, some gallant souls were still ready to go to the western front. The interview went well, and by the end of half an hour she had been accepted for foreign service.

Flora dropped her bombshell at dinner that evening, a formal affair despite the lack of servants. Tante Constance gazed helplessly down the gleaming stretch of fine Georgian mahogany decked with the usual array of silver and porcelain, silently seeking her husband's opinion in the aftermath of the announcement. Flora fidgeted under the table, about to break the silence, when Tante Constance finally spoke, her French intonation still noticeable after twenty years of living in Scotland.

"But why you, *ma chérie?* They have so many nurses already. The conditions... Angus writes that conditions are appalling." She appealed once more to her husband, who continued eating the meager soup, unusually quiet. "Hamish," she exclaimed, irritated, "did you hear what Flora is suggesting? It is absurd, ridiculous—out of the question. I don't think she should go. You agree, of course, Hamish, yes? It is impossible to permit the child to go. She was only sixteen last week! *Mon Dieu!* What would your poor cousin Seaton have said if he and Jane were still alive? I'm sure they would have been opposed to their only daughter going to the war."

"But Tante, how could they be opposed when they themselves were the first to seek danger?" Flora blurted out. "The missions in Africa were very dangerous. That's why they were killed. For what they believed in," she pleaded, caught between the determination to go at all cost, and the boundaries of an upbringing that placed family considerations before all else.

"That was not at all the same. There was no war at the time and they were missionaries," Tante Constance replied with a dismissive wave of the hand.

Flora bit her tongue, knowing it was useless to point out that her father—a distant cousin of Uncle Hamish's—and her mother had lost their lives in the midst of a tribal feud. So she remained silent, anxiously waiting for Uncle Hamish to answer. Although he ran the MacLeod coal empire like a benevolent nineteenth-century dictator, he often reacted unexpectedly. It was he, despite all Tante's supplications, who had allowed the twins to lie about their age and enlist, saying that in their place he would have done the same. Now, seeing his gray hair and lined face, it was easy to deduce what it had cost him. There must have been days when he rued his decision, wishing only for their safe return, questioning his own sanity for having allowed them to go. But her uncle bore that, and Tante Constance's endless reproaches, in stoic silence.

She waited with bated breath as he laid down the soupspoon and carefully dabbed his thick mustache with a white linen napkin.

"This is a sudden and serious decision, my dear Flora. Are

you certain that you have reflected sufficiently upon the matter?''

"Oh, yes, Uncle Hamish, I have," she responded, meeting his gaze full on. "I can't bear being useless here. I have to go," she said simply.

He looked at her hard, then nodded silently before turning to his wife. "I respect Flora's decision, just as I respected that of our two sons," he said, continuing before Tante Constance could protest. "There is a war on, my dear. The flower of our youth has suffered its consequences, but so it is. And although, like you, I deplore the fact of her going, I can only applaud our dear Flora for her courage. Patriotism will wear thin soon if nothing breaks," he added, tight-lipped. "If it weren't for the endurance of our troops on the western front, their amazing courage and sacrifice, God knows what would become of us all. The future of our nation depends on the effort and fortitude of those willing to sacrifice their personal lives for a bigger cause. Therefore, I believe that she should go if that is her wish." He turned back to Flora and smiled, his eyes filled with melancholic admiration. "We shall miss you dearly, child, but you have my blessing."

"But how shall we manage without her?" Tante Constance's large form sagged before her husband's decision.

"We shall manage, my love, just as everyone else does."

"But it seems so unnecessary for her to join the Foreign Service. I'm sure they have enough girls out there already. The government should deal with it."

"But Tante, if no nurses or V.A.D.s went to the front, what would happen to all the wounded? What if Gavin or Angus were hurt and there was no one to tend to them?" Flora appealed softly.

"I know, *ma chérie.* I…" Constance raised her hands in a Gallic gesture of defeat, lips quivering as she shook her graying head and sighed. "But you are so very young, *ma petite.* There is so much of life you don't know yet, things you are not aware of, ought not be exposed to. Girls should not have to go to the front with the men. It is not at all seemly." She gave another long sigh that expressed better than words all the pain and anxiety, the keeping-up of a brave front while praying fervently that the ominous telegram beginning with those fateful words— *We sincerely regret to inform you...*—would never arrive.

"It won't be for long, Tante." Flora reached across the table and gently touched her aunt's trembling fingers. "I'm sure the war cannot last much longer."

"How can we tell?" Tante Constance pressed a hankie to her eyes, trying to hold back the tears. "How do we know how much longer? They say in France that General Nivelle has all these wonderful plans, but all the while, the army is refusing to fight. My brother Eustace writes that were it not for the astute intervention of a young officer named Philippe Pétain things would be a disaster. And look at this country! Lloyd George argues with General Haig and that Robertson man, and everything remains exactly the same, more young men dead or wounded, more widows and weeping mothers. Have they no hearts?" she cried. "You are like a daughter to me, Flora dearest." She clasped the outstretched hand. "I could not bear to lose you, too. Oh, *mon Dieu, non!*"

"My dearest," Hamish said soothingly, "we must all be prepared to make the supreme sacrifice for the good of the nation. Or there will be no nation," he added dryly.

Flora stroked Tante's tremulous hand, wishing she could offer solace. She hated being the cause of more suffering, yet she knew she had no choice. She glanced at Uncle Hamish, struck all at once by the irony that this war that they all deplored was multiplying his fortune several times over. The need for British coal was overwhelming and Hamish's factory could provide it. But she knew he would gladly have given every last penny to have his sons returned to him safe and sound.

That night they played cards in the drawing room as they had before the war. Little had altered at Midfield, as though defying the onslaught of change that would inevitably come. Here, a few miles south of Edinburgh, the war seemed a remote happening that had afflicted but not yet debilitated. Rationing wasn't felt the same here; Uncle Hamish had arranged for eggs, butter and lamb to be brought from Strathaird, the estate on

the Isle of Skye where the family used to spend a large portion
of the summer holidays before embarking on an annual trip to
Limoges. There Tante Constance's brother, Eustace de la Vallière, and his wife, Hortense, owned la Vallière, one of the
largest porcelain factories in France.

Flora gazed at the green baize of the card table and thought
of Cousin Eugène, Oncle Eustace and Tante Hortense's son, so
serious, spiritual and mature despite his youth, entering the
priesthood. It had been three long years since they were all
together. She tried to concentrate on the game, making sure she
made just enough mistakes for Uncle Hamish to believe he'd
won fair and square, her lips twitching affectionately when she
discarded an ace and his mustache bristled with satisfaction.
He was so dear, and she so grateful that he supported her decision, despite his natural concern and what were sure to be
endless recriminations from his wife.

As soon as the game was over and tea was served, Flora
excused herself and slipped outside. The rain had stopped and
the sky was surprisingly clear. The stars glimmered like the
flickering flames in a Christmas procession seen from afar.
Were these the same stars Gavin gazed at from his trench, she
wondered, sitting on the damp terrace despite Tante's admo-
nitions about catching a chill, her knees hugged under her chin.

The pale satin of her evening gown cascaded down the stone
steps like a waterfall as she searched the gleaming stars, their
sparkle replaced by Gavin's twinkling blue eyes and possessive
smile. She sighed and recalled each precious moment, each
tender endearment and the treasured instant when his lips had
finally touched hers. Before leaving, he had raised her fingers
to his lips, kissing them ever so softly before whispering the
question to which he already knew the answer. She smiled and
bit her lip. How could he possibly have doubted? Of course
she would wait for him. A lifetime, if need be.

Yet he never wrote. Never communicated directly except for
the occasional scribble at the bottom of a page, sending his
love and a hug. It was always Angus, the younger twin, who
kept her abreast of their life in the trenches, sharing anecdotes,

some so tragic they were hard to believe, others oddly humorous despite the circumstances.

Now, at last, it was her turn to experience these things.

She rose slowly and wandered back into the house, gazing affectionately at Tante's stiff French furniture, the paintings and the delicate porcelain on the shelves, realizing how much it all meant to her.

Midfield and Strathaird had been home to her since she was barely four, when the family had taken her in as a surrogate daughter and sister after her parents' death. It seemed a lifetime ago. But then, so did the boys' departure to the front.

She heaved another sigh, feeling worldly-wise and much older than her years. The last few months spent at the hospital had been a shock at first, a revelation. The prim, innocent young girl who had entered its portals with no more knowledge of male anatomy than a nun was now a different person. She smoothed the faded brocade of her favorite cushion, glad that women were taking on new functions, becoming vital to the country's economy, and learning much about themselves and their capabilities. That was about the only positive aspect of this dreadful war. All at once she remembered Tante's veiled remarks at dinner and grinned, wondering if her aunt had the slightest idea of the tasks Flora performed each day—washing the men, dressing their wounds, emptying their bedpans.

At the drawing-room door she paused, smiling at Millie, Gavin's spaniel. The dog wagged her tail patiently, hoping to be allowed into the hall. "Just a minute, Millie," she said, her eye catching a photograph in a silver frame. It had been taken at Chateau de la Vallière, her cousins' home in Limoges, during that last, wonderful summer of 1913.

She picked up the picture, tears welling suddenly. There was dear Eugène, serene as always, and his baby sister Geneviève. René, their younger brother, was slouching behind him and sulking. Uncle Eustace, dressed in a white suit and panama hat, leaned on a walking stick behind his sister's deck chair, while in the foreground were Gavin, Angus and herself, sitting on the grass, their arms entwined. The merry trio—or rather, Gavin and his two faithful followers. What a beautiful day it had been. They had laughed and played, oblivious of what life had in store for them. She replaced the picture with damp eyes, wondering when the friendly banter she engaged in with Gavin had transformed into an embarrassed awareness that left her dizzy, her heart racing whenever he was around. Perhaps it had been that very afternoon. But it was not until last year, when he had returned for a short week's leave, that she knew she was in love.

She leaned against the door, staring into space, recalling that thrilling moment when he'd walked in and their eyes had met and clung. Oh, what heaven it had been. Gavin, so tall and mature in his well-worn uniform. The white and purple ribbon of his M.C., the Military Cross won for bravery at the Battle of the Somme in 1916, was worn with casual nonchalance, although he was the youngest man to have received it yet. For days they had walked, talked and laughed, each too shy or too young to make the first move, yet so aware of one another it hurt.

She wrinkled her nose and stared at the picture once more. If she'd known half of what she knew now, she'd have given herself to him without a second thought, she realized, shocked at her own depravity. But there might never be another chance, unless…perhaps she would be blessed, and one day he would be brought in to her section of the field hospital. Not with a bad wound, of course, but just enough for him not to return to the front and for her to take care of him.

Tante's singsong voice calling from upstairs interrupted her daydreams. She let Millie into the hall, regretting now that all she'd allowed Gavin was one chaste kiss. The thought of his lips on hers made her shiver, and she ran quickly up the stairs and along the corridor to her room. If only she was at Strathaird, she wished. There she had her favorite spot, among the worn chintz cushions of the window seat in the upstairs sitting room, where she would curl up and dream, gazing out over the lawn to the cliff and the churning sea below. Oh, how she missed it. The family fondly called the room "Flora's dreamery," for it was there she spun her yarns, meditated, daydreamed and saw things others didn't, and where everyone always knew they could find her.

But tonight she had to content herself with having achieved her objective. At least now she would be close to Gavin, and truly serving her country. Finally she would be a part of this war to end all wars that would mark their lives forever.

2

Arras, France 1917

"'If you were the only girl in the world,'" an out-of-tune voice warbled.

"Gawd, you've got a bloody awful voice, mate."

"Says who?"

"Says I. We should stick you out in no-man's-land and let Franz 'ear you. 'E'd be off 'ome in an 'eartbeat, 'e would."

Laughter ran the length of the trench, and banter flew as the men moved, ankle-deep in mud, trying desperately to keep their spirits up while they repaired the traverses, piling sandbags near the entrance to secure it before the next rainfall. Those taking a break sat smoking wherever they could find a dry spot, wrapped in their greatcoats, exchanging jokes. Lieutenant Angus MacLeod, of the Fifty-first Scottish Highlanders, leaned over and offered his brother a light.

"Thanks." Gavin shielded it with his palm, took a long drag and surveyed the men, wondering how long it would be before they finally made an advance into the massive defenses, through the endless stretches of mud and barbed wire that separated them from the enemy. There was something big stirring, he was certain, for powerful artillery had been moved in to back them up. He felt sure General Harper's orders would be imminent. Smoking, Gavin silently calculated their chances of success and reckoned they were slim. The German offensive was gruesome. "I hope things will be better than at Ypres," he murmured to himself. There, the Guards, the Fifteenth Scottish, the Sixteenth Irish and several other assault divisions had fought themselves out from August through September in what was known as the battle of the mud at Passchendaele.

"It's one of my last, so smoke it slowly," Angus remarked, referring to the cigarette.

Gavin grinned affectionately, watching the thin ribbon of smoke rise above the damp earth of their burrow, and listened to the sound of the enemy artillery becoming uncomfortably close, noting the occasional flash of flares. Too damn close, he realized. Eyeing Angus, he decided not to share his misgivings with his brother. Although they were fraternal twins, their personalities were as different as their looks. Angus hated it all. They never talked about the war much unless they could help it.

"God, I wish this were all over," Angus remarked gloomily.

"I don't know, it has its moments." Gavin took another long drag, enjoying the scent of the Will's tobacco, which was a dash sight better than the never-ending stench of gangrene and death. "This may be the one exciting thing that will ever happen in our lives. Once we're home, Papa will expect us to follow in his footsteps, enter the wretched coal business and lead life exactly as he did."

"Ha!" Angus shook his red head. "Trust you to consider this mess an adventure."

"What makes you think life will be the same as it used to be?" Jonathan Parker, a young medical student from Cambridge, asked, swallowing tea from his tin mug. "I don't think anything can ever be the same. For one thing, people aren't going to be as complacent as they were. And God knows what will happen if we lose."

"Lose, be damned," Gavin replied. "We can't."

"If the doughboys don't take a hand in it soon, we will, old chap. Look at us, for Christ's sake! Three bloody years and we've only a couple of miles gained and few hundred thousand

dead to show for it. That's not counting the wounded," Jonathan added with a bitter laugh.

"You're right." Angus nodded, pulled his greatcoat closer.
"Who knows how long it may go on?" he added dismally.

With the sound of a courier arriving at the entrance of the
trench, every head turned in unison. The men stopped smoking
and those working laid down their picks and shovels, silently
praying his name would be called. Letters from home were
what kept a man sane. As names were called out and letters
passed down the line, those who received nothing got back to
work, masking their disappointment.

"Angus MacLeod." Angus leaned forward as the letter was
passed down.

"Who's it from?" Gavin asked, stubbing out the precious
cigarette casually, knowing the girls at Paris Plage could get
him more.

"Flora. It's from Flora," Angus replied, blushing, his hands
trembling as he slit open the envelope.

For a second, the sweet softness of her gray eyes and her
mysterious smile replaced the mud, the wet and growing rumble of enemy fire. And for a moment, Gavin wished he'd written, but it just didn't come naturally. He could say the words,
and felt them deep inside. But write them? No. He didn't like
writing letters. He hadn't even written that infamous "goodbye" letter, the one you left for after you were killed. Not him.
Something told him it wasn't a good omen. He shrugged, eyeing Angus impatiently as he read the letter, wishing she'd addressed it to him.

"I think you've got a crush on her," he teased, dying to
hear what she had to say.

"You know she only has eyes for you." Angus scanned the
lines avidly, then frowned.

"Well," Gavin prodded, "what does she say?" Again he
wished that she'd write to him. But then, she had before and
he'd never taken the trouble to reply. Gavin shrugged. Flora
knew he loved her. She would wait. She understood him as no
one else ever could. She was his. He wished he'd kissed her
again that last time they'd been together. But he couldn't. If

he had, things would have gotten out of hand. She was so young, so lovely, so innocent... Biting back his feelings, he nagged his brother again. "Well, come on. What's she got to say for herself?"

"She's coming out," Angus replied in a flat voice.

"What do you mean?" Gavin's head flew up.

"She's asked to be posted overseas. She's being sent here to France." He glanced at the date of the postmark. "In fact, she's probably here by now. This letter is more than a month old."

"Good God. But why would she do that? There's no reason for her to. Surely Papa could have intervened."

"She says here that Father backed her up. She wants to do this, Gavin," he added quietly, handing him the letter. "She's made a choice."

Gavin scanned the lines. Feeling powerless, he kicked a piece of stray traverse angrily, afraid for the first time. He knew how to take care of himself, damn it, but the thought of Flora in danger, without him to take care of her, had him swearing. Why hadn't she stayed at home, where he knew she'd be safe? "You're right about this damned war," he exclaimed suddenly. "It's time we got on with our lives. Do you think she'll be posted near us?"

"She'll probably be sent to Etaples," Angus replied. "That's where most of the V.A.D.s get sent when they first come out."

"At least that's not in the middle of the fighting. Still, I don't like it." Gavin looked up as the sound of shellfire intensified. He glanced at his brother, away in a world of his own, then stared back at the letter. His name had been pointedly avoided. She was angry he hadn't written, he supposed. Well, he'd explain later, clear things up.

"Perhaps we'll be able to see her," Angus said dreamily.

"Maybe. If we live long enough," Gavin answered, squinting upward.

"Oh, you will," Angus laughed, his face alight with sudden admiration. "You're like a cat, always falling back on your feet. We made it out of the Somme last year thanks to you."

"Rubbish." Gavin handed him back the letter then checked his rifle. "We all did our part. Imagine our little Flora at the front, though. It seems so strange. And I don't like it one bit."

"Not so little anymore, and from what I gather between the lines very much in love with you." Angus gave him a fixed smile.

"I don't know." Gavin cocked his ear and tried to identify the exact direction of the increase in shellfire.

"Of course you do. You always have. You've only had eyes for one another for as long as I can remember," Angus replied a touch bitterly.

Gavin gave him a surprised glance. "Jealous?"

"Of you two? Of course not." Angus shook his head. "You're meant for one another. I never stood a chance. She's very fond of me. As a cousin and friend, that is."

"Well, if anything happens to me, I suppose you'd better take care of her for me. Can't have her going to some stranger." Gavin spoke with a flippancy he was far from feeling, and scanned the trench once more. Deciding where to position his men, he ducked as the firing grew suddenly louder and a flare nearly grazed his head. "What in hell's name's going on? I know we're in the middle of a bloody offensive, but it's too damn close for comfort and I've not received any direct orders from H.Q. I hope the telephone lines aren't down." He raised his head aboveground.

"Don't, you fool, you'll get yourself killed." Parker yanked him back.

"We need to know what's happening." Gavin jumped back down into the squelching mud and took charge. "Summers, stand to." He ordered. "Marshall, keep the end bay covered." He shouted orders as the noise increased and the men hastened as best they could, taking up their positions.

Then an eerie hum approached. Too late he realized what was about to happen. "Move," he shouted, pushing Angus down into the mud in the split second before the explosion. Then pain tore through him. His body jerked up before it was thrown into a tangled mass of torn limbs, ripped flesh and horrifying screams.

For a while, he thought he was dead. Then, gradually, consciousness returned and he heard cries, smelled the bitter, acrid smoke. He tried to move but pain shot through his hip and thigh; he tried to open his eyes but they stung. Everything was hazy. He felt about him in a daze, all at once aware that the soft, wet substance he was touching must be flesh, and choked, as horror, gas and blood filled his lungs and he tried vainly to move.

Little by little he extracted his left hand from the sticky warmth below, gripped by nausea when he realized he was lying on Jonathan Parker's dead body. He gasped, trying to catch his breath. Trying to think. He was alive. He had to stay alive. But where was Angus? Making a superhuman effort, he heaved the mangled pile of blood-soaked remains that lay across him, hearing the sound they made as they sank into the mud. The effort left him exhausted. But he focused now, and the rush of relief when he saw Angus staring down at him, apparently unharmed, was overwhelming. Thank God. He tried desperately to speak, but his lips wouldn't move. To motion, but his arm wouldn't budge.

Angus stared at him, expression detached. Gavin shouted but no sound emerged. Couldn't Angus see him, damn it? He closed his eyes against a whiff of gas. When he was able to open them once more, Angus's face still loomed impassively over him, an expressionless mask. Why didn't he pull him out of here instead of just standing there? "Angus," his mind screamed. "Help me, for Christ's sake!"

But Angus made no gesture, no motion. Instead, he crouched beside him, wearing the cold, half-amused, disinterested gaze of a spectator. Desperately, Gavin reached his left arm toward his brother in a frantic effort, daggers searing through his hip and upper body as he grasped the gold chain and cross swinging from his twin's neck, clutching it.

But Angus made no move and the chain gave way. Gavin reeled back, collapsing once more in the mire of blood, mud and misery. As his head sank into Jonathan Parker's open guts and everything went black, his last conscious image was of Angus, watching calmly as he sank into oblivion.

3

Etaples, France, 1917

"Nurse, we need to vacate the facility immediately. There's a new convoy coming in from the front lines. They're bringing in the wounded as we speak."

"Yes, Sister." Flora hurried around the ward, which she and Ana, another V.A.D., ran with virtually no assistance, and helped the patients who could walk to other wards. Once they'd all been shifted to the next building, Flora hurried back to prepare beds and blankets for the new arrivals. As she tucked in the last sheet, she heard the ambulances drawing up and sighed, realizing it would be another long night. Every spare hand was needed and getting to the wounds before they festered and required amputation had become a grilling challenge.

She dumped the dirty laundry in a corner and prepared for the onslaught, forcing herself to stay calm, pushing away the fear that each new batch of arrivals brought. Inevitably she searched each incoming stretcher for his face, praying it wouldn't be there. Flora sighed again. She'd had less news in the two months she'd been here than all the time back home.

She pulled herself together as the wounded began pouring in, and the usual frenzy of dressing wounds, injecting morphine and preparing the dying began. There were plenty of those today, she realized, horrified.

The doctor approached, face exhausted and eyes bloodshot, his white coat splattered with muted bloodstains that no amount of washing erased. He looked at the wound. "Better to put a bullet through the poor bugger," he muttered angrily before setting to work. The priest and the chaplain stood nearby; they had long since stopped bothering about denominations, instead simply murmuring prayers in a desperate effort to bring solace to those last remaining moments, leaning close to catch final messages whispered from barely moving lips.

Flora worked nonstop. There would be countless letters to write to the soldiers' families, she thought sadly. It was the only tribute she could pay to the young men who'd died so valiantly in her arms. At least she could give their loved ones the treasure of their last words. When there were none, she took it upon herself to invent them, sure that what mattered most was that a parent or a wife be given something to cling to.

"Pass the morphine, Nurse. I'm afraid we'll have to amputate," the doctor said above the moans and agitation. Flora glanced at him, his young face prematurely lined, marked by three years of battling disease, death and devastation.

She handed him the bottle as a young orderly came up to her. "Nurse, we have a bad case of shell shock. Where should we put him?"

"Oh my goodness. Is he wounded?" she asked distractedly, preparing for the operation that was about to take place.

"No."

"Then put him in number ten and I'll get to him whenever I can. I'm afraid I can't do anything about it at the moment." He nodded and left, and Flora prepared the patient for amputation, trying to overcome the nauseous smell and increasing heat in the ward. The hospital back home had seemed bad, but here life was hell. There was none of the priggish, ordered behavior of regular hospital life, with the petty rules and hierarchies of the matron. All of that was forgotten in a common effort to save as many lives as they could.

Getting to a wound in time had become an obsession, with heroes and enemy treated alike. And so it should be, Flora reflected, throwing out the slops and taking more bandages back into the ward, for how could you feel rancor toward young men as vulnerable and damaged as any of their own? It was tragic and intolerable to see a generation—whether German, British or any other—condemned to die, drowned in mud-filled trenches, buried under the rich earth of northern France that for over a thousand years had claimed her victims relentlessly. For an instant, she wondered what had happened to the Europe of before the war that all had believed would be over by the time the leaves fell, but that was more than three years old.

It took her five more hours to see all the patients, then Matron came on duty and forced her to go.

"You simply have to get a rest, Flora. You'll be worn-out if you don't. I'll see you back at the hut. By the way, could you take a quick look at that shell shock case on your way out? I don't seem to be able to get through to him at all, and you're so good with those patients."

"I'll see what I can do. I'll be back at seven."

"Right. But you must rest, dear, or you'll be no use to anyone."

"I will." Stepping over stretchers of soldiers whose wounds were less urgent, she walked down the corridor and headed for the last ward, where a gramophone with a scratchy needle played a popular tune. There, some men sat in dressing gowns, smoking and playing cards at a rickety wooden table. They called to her as she entered.

"'Ey, Nurse, 'ow ye' doin'? Goin' 'ome, I am. Back to Liverpool, it is."

"Good, Berty. I'm so glad. How about you, Harry, how's your leg?"

"Oh, fair enough. Never be much good on the football field again, but at least I'll be able to walk, which is more than most."

She nodded, smiling to mask her exhaustion, and looked for the patient. "Have you seen a chap sent in with shell shock?" she asked Nancy, the V.A.D. in charge.

"He's over in the corner." She pointed to her left. "He

seems unable to speak. Perhaps you can do something with him, poor man.''

Flora glanced at a chair that faced the far corner of the crowded ward, then walked toward it, filled with sudden foreboding. Gavin's image flashed before her and she shuddered, her misgivings increasing as she approached the chair. The young man had his back to her, his head in his hands. Mustering every last ounce of strength, she dragged herself forward, dreaming of the hut she shared with three other V.A.D.s and her bunk, longing to crawl into bed for a few precious hours of sleep before it all began again.

She came up behind him, gently touched his shoulder.

"I've come to help you," she said softly. "Will you tell me who you are?" She came around and crouched at his side, seeing nothing but a thick shock of red hair falling over the hand that supported his forehead. At the sound of her voice, he raised his head. For a moment Flora simply stared, stunned. "Angus," she gasped in amazement. "Is it really you?" Tears burst forth as she threw her arms around the stiff, motionless figure. Then, leaning back and holding his hands, she realized that his eyes were devoid of expression. "Angus." She shook him anxiously. "Angus, it's me, Flo. Say something, please." She shook him again gently. Then another thought occurred. *Gavin.* Where was Gavin? She glanced around, as though expecting to see him among the group of men smoking and playing cards. Then she squeezed Angus's hands once more.

"Angus, you're all right now. You're with me." His eyes flickered and her heart leaped. "Oh, Angus, darling, please. Please come back. Please tell me where Gavin is," she whispered almost to herself.

"Dead." The voice was flat.

She stared at him, then shook her head. "No. It can't be. *No.*" She shook her head again, her hands gripping his sleeve savagely. "Not Gavin." She began shaking, then laughed hysterically. "People like Gavin don't get killed, they're immortal."

"It should have been me," he whispered.

Alerted by the tone of Flora's wild laughter, Nancy came hurrying toward them.

"Flora? What is the matter?"

Unable to respond, she sank to the floor, clinging to Angus's limp hands as though she might find some part of Gavin there, refusing to let go, to believe.

It took Nancy and two other nurses to pry her away. Half carrying her to the hut, they put her to bed and forced some pills down her throat. It was only when she woke, twenty-four hours later, from the heavily drugged sleep, that the truth hit home. *He was gone.* Gone forever.

She stared at the pegs that sagged under the weight of various clothes, wanting to cry, but she couldn't. She, who had shed so many tears for all the others, was incapable of weeping for the man she loved. Now that it was his turn, she was numb. She dragged herself up in the narrow cot, pulled the brown blanket up to her chin and sat shivering, trying to visualize him, but her mind was blank, as though her memory had been wiped clean as a slate. She closed her eyes tight, desperately trying to conjure up his image, recall some feature, some peculiar expression that made him who he was, but the harder she tried, the more distant he became.

Duty and training dragged her out of bed. Legs trembling, she dressed, then returned to the ward, where another convoy of badly wounded was being brought in.

"Nurse! Thank goodness you're here. Get this patient ready for surgery." The doctor laid a hand on her arm. "He's going to lose both legs, I'm afraid."

She nodded automatically, senses blunted, gazing down at the young officer about to lose his limbs. Distantly, she felt thankful that Gavin had not gone through this. Their dreams and life were over, but at least he had not suffered the indignity of surviving as half a man.

She braced herself, refusing to allow her personal loss to keep her from her duty, and made her way over to the bed where the young man lay, his head bandaged but his eyes clear blue and lucid.

"I'm sorry to have to break the news, Captain," she began, surprised to hear that her voice sounded calm and gentle.

He smiled thinly. "You don't need to tell me, Nurse. I've been here too long and seen too much not to know. Is it one or both?"

"Both, I'm afraid. I'm so sorry."

His lips tightened and he nodded. "I'm lucky to be alive, I suppose. At least I'll get home. Not like the other poor blighters buried out there."

She nodded and closed her eyes a second against awful images that danced before her. Then silently she went to work, preparing him for the operation. Suddenly she remembered Angus. He would have to wait. She glanced down at her patient with an aching heart, reached for his hand and squeezed it.

"Thank you," he whispered, eyes damp. Then with a brave smile he turned to the doctor. "Better get on with it, Doc. There's plenty more out there waiting for you."

4

Frieburg, Germany, 1917

"*Es gibt einen der lebt noch.*" From far away, Gavin heard voices but they faded again. The next time he gained consciousness he was being rattled painfully to and fro, amid the stench of blood and urine. But it was dark, he was moving and the pain in his thigh and hip were blinding. His eyes closed once more and he dreamed. Of Angus's cold and expressionless face, waiting impassively for him to die. The dream kept repeating and repeating itself.

When he next woke, the pain was too agonizing for him to think, but he realized he was alive and being given an injection. There were more voices, a woman and a man speaking German, but he was too tired to care and drifted back into sleep.

This time he dreamed of Flora, of the rose garden at Strathaird, of a picnic in the Périgord, the delicious sensation of biting into a thick tartine, a sandwich made of pâté and spicy *saucisson,* smelled the sweet scent of freshly cut hay and heard the sound of laughter rippling on the breeze.

As the days went by and he regained consciousness, Gavin realized two things—that people spoke German, and that they addressed him as Angus or *Kapitän.* It was puzzling. But the pain was so sharp and the need to sleep so great he didn't care.

Then one day he woke up feeling hungry and, to everyone in the ward's surprise, he sat up.

"*Mein Gott, der Englander sitzt!*" the matron exclaimed.

"Not *Englander*," Gavin replied with a spark of his old self, "*Shotten.*"

"Hey, do you speak German?" a cultivated English voice coming from the next cot asked. He turned, wincing as a sharp pain shot up his leg and into his thigh.

"Only a couple of words. Did they get you, too?"

"Actually, no." He blushed. "I'm German."

"Oh."

There was a moment's silence while Gavin looked the other man over. His head was bandaged and his arm hung loosely in a sling. "How do you speak English so well?" he asked curiously, instinctively liking him, although he was the enemy.

"My mother's English and my father is German. We've lived in London all my life. My father's in banking—rather, *was* in banking—in the city. Then this mess came down and we had to leave. My parents and sister returned to Hanover. I got called up."

"What a God-awful situation to be in," Gavin replied sympathetically, feeling much more like talking than thinking.

"What happened to you?"

"A shell exploded in the trench. Lucky to be alive, I suppose. Where are we?"

"The army hospital in Frieburg."

"Oh. That's in the Black Forest, isn't it?" he said, calculating approximately how far he must be from his unit. "Any news about what's happening out there?" he asked casually, unsure how far he could trust the man. Perhaps they'd put him there on purpose, to see what they could find out.

"Not much—except the Americans have entered the war."

"Thank God for that," Gavin murmured, leaning back against the pillow, his eyes closing. "How did that happen? I thought Woodrow Wilson didn't want to have much to do with us."

"A U-boat sunk a merchant ship with two American passengers on board. I suppose it was getting too close to home."

"Hmm. Probably. I'll bet you lot weren't counting on that," he added, squinting at his neighbor, who looked pale and drawn.

"They didn't. I think it may tip the balance," he murmured softly.

"Damn right it will." Gavin saw the other patients murmuring suspiciously, and turned painfully onto his other side. He looked into the cot on his left, where a ruddy blond face stared belligerently.

"Zigaretten?" he asked, keeping a wary eye on the others, trying to read their minds. The other man shook his head, eyes filled with resentment. Gavin shrugged and acted as though it was natural to be the only British officer lying among a ward of German soldiers.

"Oh well." He smiled. *"Danke,* anyway. When I get some, I'll give you one of mine." He leaned back and took stock of the situation.

"Kapitän Angus, you must not speak so much." A pretty, blond nurse came to his bed and patted his pillow briskly before whisking out a thermometer and popping it into his mouth, preventing him from asking why everyone thought he was Angus. Then he caught sight of the gold cross lying on the tiny nightstand, next to the bed, and everything flashed before him. Suddenly dizzy, Gavin put his head in his hands.

"Herr Kapitän? Sind sie schwach?"

"I'm all right," he said, removing the thermometer. "But I don't want this damn thing in my mouth."

"Be thankful for small mercies. The other one sticks it somewhere else," his English-speaking neighbor commented as the matron approached with a firm, brisk march.

"Is there a problem with the prisoner, Nurse?" she demanded, eyes glinting.

"No, Sister," the nurse replied quickly, reading the thermometer and writing something on the chart.

The matron looked him over coldly. "I don't want you causing problems in my ward," she barked, her English guttural. "It is bad enough to have to treat you Saxon dogs. So behave yourself or I'll have you sent to the prison camp, ill or not.

It'll be one less for our men to rid themselves of." With that, she turned on her heel and marched off.

Gavin listened meekly, but as she marched off, he stuck his tongue out, causing the whole ward to break into laughter. She turned suspiciously, but found him lying down, eyes closed, the picture of innocence.

A minute later he opened one eye cautiously. A man wearing a dressing gown, who sat reading at the far end of the ward, came over.

"Zigarette?" he asked, offering him the pack.

"Danke." Gavin took the cigarette warily, his eyes never leaving the German's face. Then he heard his neighbor again.

"Jolly good show, old chap. We're scared stiff of her. She's the devil to deal with. That's done more to break the ice than you'd believe."

"Thanks." He leaned forward and accepted a light. "Ask this chap what his name is, will you?"

"That's Karl. I'm Franz, by the way, Lieutenant Franz von Ritter. Who are you?"

"I'm Gavin MacLeod."

"That's odd. For some reason, they've been referring to you as Angus. Something to do with a cross you had in your hand when you were brought in."

"It belonged to my brother." Gavin took a long drag of the cigarette, knowing he was going to have to face his memories of his twin eventually. What had Angus been thinking? God! A sudden thought crossed his brain. Could the shell have blinded him? Maybe that was it.

"Sorry to hear that." The other man obviously assumed Angus was dead.

"That's the way it goes," he replied, wondering where Angus was now. Suddenly he felt ashamed of having doubted his twin. There must be some explanation for his behavior. Gavin immediately felt better, the tightness lifting from his chest. Now he must apply himself to getting out of here, he resolved. His family would be worried to death about him. He could imagine poor Flora, sick with worry at the hospital, and his mother and father back home.

* * *

By the end of the following week, he was recovering fast, and was in good enough spirits to charm the young, blond nurse, Annelise, into sneaking cigarettes and schnapps into the ward. These he distributed liberally among the men, making him the most popular patient there. The matron mumbled, disgusted about lack of loyalty in the present generation, but the men didn't care. They were fed up with a war that never seemed to end, and Gavin had brought new life to a tedious situation. He always had a joke for Franz to translate, a word for someone who needed jollying up. Soon they were looking to him for direction.

Franz turned out to be a decent sort and they spent long hours talking about their lives in Britain before the war, and what their plans were for the future—whatever that might be. Gavin chafed at the hip, which kept him bedridden, but Franz told him not to complain. It was much better to be in the medical station than with the other prisoners. Gavin had to agree. Sitting out the rest of the war in an internment camp was not his idea of bliss.

Despite his newfound comforts and companions, every day he woke with Angus's face as he'd last seen him—devoid of expression, cold. It haunted him and he prayed that his brother was all right. He thought of Flora and wished she'd stayed at home, where he would know she was safe. He wondered if she knew he was alive. They must know by now that he'd been taken prisoner, Gavin reasoned. After a moment, these thoughts depressed him and he got up and joined Franz and Karl, who were playing poker for cigarettes. Pulling up a chair, he prepared to join the game.

"Deal me in," he said with an American twang that made them all laugh. He studied his cards carefully. Karl was easy to bluff. Franz played better, but Joachim, a lieutenant from Mannheim, was the best of the three. He lit a cigarette and the game progressed.

Half an hour later, the matron marched in. She pursed her lips, looked his way and announced with a triumphant smirk that a number of prisoners were to be brought in within the hour. Gavin pretended to concentrate on the game but he was excited. Perhaps he would finally learn some news. There was another fact to face, as well. Until now, he'd been comfortably letting time go by. But his duty as an officer taken prisoner was to immediately search for a route of escape. While he was healing, that hadn't been possible. But although his thigh still ached and his hip hurt like hell when he walked, his arm was considerably better. If there were more British prisoners, then the situation might change.

He glanced at his cards, aware of the nurses hurrying through with fresh piles of blankets, followed shortly by stretchers carrying the wounded. He barely managed to control his impatience, ready to drop out of the game in his eagerness to question the newcomers. Watching as the wounded—more victims of the salient—were carried passed, Gavin realized guiltily that for the past couple of weeks he'd allowed himself to fall into the apathy of convalescence. The war seemed remote without the backdrop of artillery fire. He got up, unable to stay still, and went to the door. A particularly nasty case of gangrene reminded him of just how real the conflict still was. When a straggling group of wounded officers was directed into the ward under the matron's vigilant eye, he moved next to them.

"Where did they get you?" he asked a pale lieutenant not much older than himself.

"In the shoulder, and a scratch on the head. It's a bloody mess out there."

"What regiment are you with?"

"Warwickshire. And you?"

"Fifty-first Highlanders." Gavin smiled at Annelise, and got her to direct the lieutenant to the cot closest to his. The other man nodded and thanked him, sinking onto the bed in exhaustion.

"All hell's broken loose. I hope this time it may get us somewhere." He gave a tired shrug and closed his eyes.

"The Germans are as fed up as we are."

"I'll bet. When were you captured?"

"October."

"You've heard about the French mutiny? They refuse to

fight any longer, except to defend. Can't blame them, poor chaps. Chemin des Dames was a bloodbath.''

"I don't suppose you saw any of the Fifty-first, did you?''

"Only back at Etaples about three weeks ago. There were a couple of fellows wounded at Passchendaele—probably some of your chaps—waiting to be shipped home. The other poor buggers were waiting to die.''

"Does the name Angus MacLeod mean anything to you?'' Gavin offered him a cigarette.

"Thanks.'' The young man smiled his appreciation. "MacLeod. That rings a bell. Isn't he Ghost MacLeod's twin, the chap who braved the lines at Ypres and saved a whole battalion? That was either incredible courage or plain stupidity. He got the M.C. for it, you know. Apparently he was much younger than he made out, too. I think his twin was back at the field hospital waiting to be shipped home. He didn't handle his brother's death too well.''

"Death?'' The lighter stopped in midair.

"I'm afraid so. There was no trace of him, poor devil. Did you know him?''

"They think I'm dead,'' Gavin murmured, horrified. Wiping beads of sweat from his forehead, he sat down on the bed with a bang.

"Are you all right? Was MacLeod a friend of yours?''

"I'll be fine. It's just rather odd to know you've been given up for dead.''

"Oh God. What do you mean? You're—''

"Yes. I'm Captain Gavin MacLeod. Angus is my brother.''

"Good Lord.'' The man looked at him in sudden awe. "I'm Lieutenant Miles Conway, by the way,'' he said, stretching out his hand and smiling from below the bandage. "It's an honor to meet you, Ghost.''

"Thanks.'' They shook hands and Gavin sensed an immediate bond.

Dead. They thought he was dead! Gavin assimilated this news, imagining Flora and his parents. How devastated they must all be. It was bad enough to picture them thinking him missing. But dead... The image of Angus's impassive face flashed before him, but he refused to think of that right now. There were other priorities—such as escape—to be thought of, that took on new urgency.

"Any chance of us getting out of here?" Miles asked, voicing Gavin's thoughts.

"I don't know. Up until now I've been on my own," he answered vaguely. "Difficult to believe one's been given up for dead. Gives one a damn odd feeling, I must say."

"They may know that you're alive by now. Perhaps they've set the records straight."

"I bloody well hope so," Gavin replied, suddenly angry—at the army, at Angus for not helping him and at the damn Krauts for catching him. "Now that you're here, perhaps we can get an escape plan going." He rose and smiled at his new companion. "You'd better rest. By the way, my neighbor Franz is okay. Has a British mother, and lived in England all his life. He got called back here at the beginning of the war."

Annelise approached, hustling Gavin away before attending to Lieutenant Conway. "You want to butter her up," he said over his shoulder. "She's a great girl."

"Everything all right?" Franz asked him anxiously as Gavin flopped on his bed, cold sweat racking his body. He leaned back, his eyes closed, feeling nauseous. Was it possible his twin had left him to die? He squeezed his hands into tight fists, his knuckles white, seized by doubt.

That night he barely slept, tossing and turning, positive one minute that Angus had betrayed him, convinced the next that it wasn't so. To distract himself, he set his mind on ways of escape. Glancing at Franz, peacefully asleep in the next bed with his face etched by the light of the full moon, Gavin wondered just how far the man could be trusted. He seemed to be on their side, but could he be sure?

At 3:00 a.m. in the pitch dark, he rose, stiff and restless, to smoke a cigarette.

"*Wo gehen siehen?*" the nurse asked peremptorily.

"Annelise?" he whispered, offering her a cigarette. She relaxed, smiled as his eyes lingered on her face and he ran his fingers though his hair. The patch that had been shaved was growing back, thick and black as ever, and she was obviously not oblivious to his Gaelic charm, whatever she might have heard about the British.

He motioned for her to go to the far end near the door, where they could sit, the flame from the match lighting her face. She was pretty enough, he considered. Full, round breasts, a trim waist, shapely hips that could only be imagined under the stiff uniform. He went suddenly hard, picturing her skin melding to his. As though reading his mind, she leaned closer. It was a risk, he realized, blood pounding. A big risk, yet an enticing one. If she so much as squeaked, they'd shoot him. But for the first time since arriving in the godforsaken hospital, he felt alive, back in the game, dodging danger.

He raised a hand to her cheek, his eyes mesmerizing. "*Shön,* beautiful," he whispered, hearing the quick intake of breath and sensing no rejection when his hand dropped below the stiff edge of her collar toward her generous breast. He reached her nipple and she shuddered under the many layers of material that separated his fingers from her flesh.

It was exhilarating to peer through the shadows and know that this enemy nurse, decked out in her prim stiff uniform, was hot, wet and throbbing for him. A rush of power, followed by the primeval need to possess her, overwhelmed him, and he wondered where he could take her to satisfy the urgent, consuming need.

Pulling her close, he felt her breasts press against his chest. Then she led him by the hand, glancing about cautiously as they slipped from the ward, out into a muddied alley that separated the buildings. She pointed to a nearby hut some two hundred feet away.

Making sure the coast was clear, Gavin followed her across the alley and slipped inside the hut, closing the door hastily behind him before striking a match. As his eyes became accustomed to the dark, he recognized a bed and what appeared to be piles of clean laundry in the corner. He laid the matchbox on the table, fascinated by the shafts of moonlight lighting Annelise's hair. In one swift movement he reached up, pulled the pins from the neat chignon she wore and watched the thick, silvery-blond mass fall about her shoulders. Then their bodies cleaved impatiently and they tumbled onto the tiny bed, the need for one another too acute.

He was about to undress her, but his hip brought him to a grinding halt. Swearing under his breath, he smiled apologetically, wondering what the hell to do. To his surprise, she turned her back to him and kneeled forward, leaning on the bed. Twisting her neck, she smiled invitingly. Gavin got behind her. Raising the stiff skirt above her waist, he gazed through the shadows at her pert, shapely bottom, encased in the ugly suspenders that held up thick regulation stockings.

Fumbling with excitement, he undid his pajamas, all danger forgotten as she raised her buttocks in a brazen demand for satisfaction, and slipped his fingers between her firm thighs, savoring her need, her stifled gasps, prolonging the moment for as long as he could before entering her with a swift, hard thrust. She moaned softly, writhing as he grasped her waist, and they fell into a frantic rhythm. When he came, he spewed all the pain, doubt and anger of the past months, and let out a sigh of satisfaction as he leaned against her, still feeling her throb. Then, as he opened his eyes, he heard Annelise mutter a strange name in a muffled whisper. All at once, he realized with a shock why she hadn't wanted to look into his eyes. They were the wrong ones.

The sound of boots squelching in the mud had him extricating himself hastily. He pulled up his pajamas, while Annelise straightened her skirt and fumbled on the floor for her hairpins. Retrieving them, she gave her hair an expert twist, and he handed her the cap, laying a finger over his lips and listening carefully as the footsteps came closer. She trembled, and he slipped his arm around her as the sound grew louder. When the footsteps stopped outside the hut, she began to shake. A nurse who betrayed the fatherland would be shot, just as he would, if they were caught. Gavin felt suddenly ashamed for allowing instinct to overcome reason, annoyed that he'd put her in danger. After all, she was just a young girl, suffering the ravages of war.

All was silent now except for their heartbeats. He leaned
forward against the rickety wall of the shanty, ears tuned, and
peered through the darkness for another way out, reluctant to
strike a match. As far as he could see, there was only the flimsy
wooden door by which they had entered, and that opened onto
the muddy path leading to the ward. He couldn't risk letting
her leave alone, he realized, squeezing her close. If she were
caught she might scream rape to save her skin. Damn. He could
tell by the sudden darkness and chill in the air that day was
about to break. He was almost certain there was only one man
out there. Probably the sentry, doing his last round, had stopped
for a smoke. Gavin held his breath, feeling the girl's heart
beating wildly and her teeth chattering.

"Annelise, we must *raus*," he whispered. "If they find us
here, they will kill us." He drew his hand across his throat,
then pointed to her and at himself. She nodded tearfully and
the trembling increased.

As a tiny sliver of gray light appeared, Gavin pressed his
eye between the slats but could see nothing. Withdrawing, he
turned again to Annelise. Then, as dawn broke, he distin-
guished clothing, hanging on hooks on the opposite wall and
piled in a number of baskets. Looking closely, he saw they
were freshly pressed German uniforms. He turned Annelise
around by the shoulders and pointed silently to the baskets,
indicating that he needed something to wear. She nodded, moving quickly, while Gavin picked up a heavy, unlit gas lamp
from the shelf and stood with it raised behind the door, in case
it opened.

Annelise rummaged through the piles, then turned, holding
up a German uniform that looked about his size. He smiled
and their eyes met as he laid down the lamp and took the
uniform from her, putting it on over his pajamas.

"What about boots?" he whispered, pointing to his feet, clad
in felt army slippers. Gavin watched in amazement as she
opened a locker, where several pairs of immaculately polished
boots stood in a symmetrical row. She went straight to the
largest pair and handed them to him, along with some heavy,
gray, knit socks. He pulled the boots on, ignoring the steady

increase of pain in his hip and thigh. Finally, she handed him a cap. Gavin put it on, then grinned and raised an eyebrow. Annelise smiled despite herself, easing the tension as they tiptoed to the door. Gavin pointed to himself.

"*Ich* first. Count to ten *minuten*." He held up all his fingers and she nodded. When she grabbed his sleeve, he saw the fear in her eyes and held her close, then dropped a hard kiss on her mouth. "It'll be okay." He used the universal American expression and raised a thumb. She nodded. Then he edged the door open and sent up a silent prayer that it wouldn't creak.

Peeking through the crack, he saw the sentry's back turned toward the telltale smoke rising above his shoulder. Gavin guessed that he was probably three-quarters of the way through his cigarette. The seconds dragged as they waited anxiously for him to finish. Other than the sentry, the coast seemed clear. All that lay between him and the field hospital was a muddied stretch of dirt.

Finally he saw the cigarette butt tip into the mud, and the sentry tramped off. With a sigh of relief, Gavin slipped outside and walked purposefully toward the ward, realizing he had no idea what rank he held. Two soldiers passed and saluted respectfully. He returned the salute, struck by the humor of it. This was easier than he'd thought. The other uniforms in the hut had set his mind working. As he walked quietly through the silent ward toward the curtain separating the officers from the men, he came to a sudden decision. Reaching Miles's bed, he clamped a hand quickly over his mouth. Miles's eyes darted open in horrified surprise.

"Don't worry, it's me," Gavin whispered. "Just don't squeal, that's all." He removed his hand and continued in an urgent whisper. "I think there may be a chance for us to escape, if we're very quick."

"How?" Miles asked, blinking sleepily at Gavin's uniform. "Where on earth did you get that?"

"A couple of hundred yards to the left, outside the ward, there's a laundry hut full of 'em. It may be our only chance. Annelise will help. She's in there now," he continued urgently, ignoring Miles's raised eyebrow and amused admiration. "If anyone comes around, remember to address her as *Schwester*. Can you speak any German?''

''Not a bloody word.''

''Damn.'' Gavin glanced over his shoulder and ducked when he saw Franz, lying in the next bed, move. He was too late, though. Franz pulled himself up.

''How the hell did you get that?'' he asked, gazing at Gavin. Gavin turned quickly, gesturing for silence as Franz slipped from his bed.

Gavin and Miles eyed him warily. He could save them or sign their death warrants. As though sensing their doubt, he whispered urgently, ''You can count me in. I've had enough of this bloody mess, too.''

''Okay. Then let's get the hell out while we can. Franz, you've got your uniform. Better get it on.''

Franz returned to his bed and silently retrieved his belongings from beneath it, while Miles and Gavin made their way to the entrance of the ward, making sure no one was awake. ''Make a run for it, Miles,'' he said when they reached the door.

Franz joined them. ''Wait. We'd better stick together. If anyone speaks to us I can talk to them and explain we're taking Miles for questioning. Just look haughty, Gavin. You're a high-ranking officer.''

''He's right,'' Gavin whispered. ''Let's go. First hut to your left across the stretch.''

The air was raw as they marched smartly toward the hut, the only sign of life a thin spiral of smoke from the kitchen chimney. Gavin breathed hard. There was still the risk that Annelise might have called someone. But his gut told him no, and silently they slipped inside the rickety wooden hut.

Annelise stood inside still, her eyes widening as she recognized Franz. *''Was machen sie?''* she whispered, horrified. ''Why are you here? What is happening?'' As her voice rose, Gavin clamped his hand over her mouth, then soothed her. ''It's all right. Franz, you explain.''

''We can't.'' His tone was cold and emphatic.

''Why the hell not?''

"We can't risk it."

"Okay, we'll think about that in a minute." Gavin pointed impatiently to the baskets. "You'd better change too, Franz. They'll be on the lookout for you. As soon as the new nurse comes on, she'll wonder where we all went."

Miles was already climbing into a uniform, and Franz joined him, searching quickly through the piles.

"What about her?" Miles asked Gavin, looking doubtfully at Annelise as he buttoned his shirt.

"She'll have to come with us. If they find her, they'll kill her," he replied, peering through the slats and missing the look the other two exchanged. "Do you know the layout of this place, Franz?" he asked.

"Not really. But Annelise probably does." He turned and questioned her quickly in German. "Good. She knows where the Officers' Mess is. We must get hold of a car. You're a *Haupt Kommandant,* Gavin, so you can requisition whatever you like," he added with a touch of humor.

"If we head toward the British lines we'll be shot at," Miles mused as he straightened his jacket.

"The Swiss border's probably the best bet," Gavin agreed, dropping a quick kiss on Annelise's forehead.

"No. Too risky," Franz countered. "But perhaps we can reach a place my parents own in the Black Forest, not far from here."

"We can think of that later. For now, let's just get out of here. Franz, explain to Annelise while I see if the coast is clear." Gavin turned her around and kissed her again. "It's okay," he reassured her, pointing to Franz. "He will tell you what to do." She nodded fearfully and he smiled at her. Then, going to the door, he edged it open just a fraction. It was raining and would get worse, if the dark gray clouds forming overhead were any indication. He glanced back. "This is it. Good luck!"

Gavin strode firmly ahead, the others following. Together they marched purposefully across the muddied road toward the main section of the barracks, Franz and Gavin in the lead and

Miles and Annelise following slightly behind. They headed directly to where she had told them the cars were kept.

"Okay, this is it. It's up to Franz now," Gavin said, letting out a breath he didn't know he'd been holding as they approached the building, a large whitewashed farmhouse with a stable attached. "You stay here with Annelise, Miles. Franz and I'll go inside. Look as if you're flirting. Give her a cigarette."

Miles nodded silently and took the cigarette from Gavin, offering one to Annelise. As he held her trembling fingers to light it, Miles exchanged a quick look with Franz before the two men left.

"Show authority, but don't speak, even if they address you," Franz whispered to Gavin as they marched up the stairs to the building.

It was barely light as they entered the office. A subordinate stood up from behind a desk, sleepily saluting. Franz took command, ordered a car—the best possible vehicle. It was to be handed over to the *Haupt Kommandant* immediately.

"But the orders, sir?" The young man hesitated.

"What orders, you idiot," Franz barked. "Can't you hear me, *Dumkopf?* These are your orders."

Excusing himself profusely, the young corporal blushingly preceded them out of the house and ran to crank up the car. Gavin stood by nervously. Franz opened the back door ceremoniously for Gavin, then got in next to him. Tension was rife as two soldiers passed, eyeing them curiously, but they continued on their way after a prompt salute.

"Where the hell are Miles and Annelise?" Gavin hissed anxiously as the seconds ticked. Finally, after what seemed like hours, Miles climbed behind the wheel.

"Where's Annelise?" Gavin asked, frowning and twisting his neck to see where she might be. Miles didn't answer. Instead, he started the car and began to drive, picking up speed as they moved toward the entrance.

"Don't look at the sentries. Just look straight ahead," Franz murmured. But the guards merely saluted smartly and the car passed unimpeded. The three men breathed a little easier.

"Where is Annelise? Why didn't she come?" Gavin shouted once they were on the road. "We can't just leave her there, for Christ's sake. What happened, Miles?"

"I killed her. I'm sorry, Gavin, but I had to. She was too much of a liability. She could have blown the whole operation."

"You *what?*" The blood drained from his face.

"I'm sorry."

"You bastard. How could you?" Helpless anger seethed through Gavin. Franz held him back as he lunged at Miles across the car seat.

"Control yourself, damn it. It's awful, but he did the right thing."

"How could you? She was my responsibility. I got her into this. Oh God."

He sat trembling, horror and rage battling as he tried to reason, to remain in control. *No liabilities.* He could hear the sergeant at the training center repeating the same thing over and over. No feelings, no pity, no risk. But this was Annelise, a woman he'd made love to only a few hours before, a woman he'd brought this upon. It was his fault she was dead.

All at once he was tempted to look back, to jump out of the car, as though by doing so he could make her materialize through the rain, the trees speeding past.

Exercising every ounce of self-control, he stayed silent, dealing with the shock. The pain in his thigh increased, like sharp dagger thrusts.

"I'm sorry, Gavin," Miles repeated, his voice icy, and for a second, as the car swerved onto a road that led to the forest, Gavin wanted to kill them both.

But a decision on their final destination had to be reached, and there was no time to grieve. Miles suggested the Swiss border again.

"It's too obvious," Franz replied, shaking his head. "We've only got a head start of a couple of hours before they'll be on to us. I reckon we should go to Schloss Annenberg. It's a small hunting lodge that belongs to my father's family. At the beginning of the war we stocked it with provisions in case we needed to hide. My father was worried that my mother, being British, and my sister, might find themselves in danger. Nobody has lived there for years. It's tucked away in the depths of the woods.''

"Where the hell are we, anyway?'' Gavin asked, trying to escape the images of Annelise's body sinking to the ground.

"Slightly south of Frieburg, I reckon.'' Miles leaned across the dashboard and opened the glove box of the Daimler. Sure enough, a map lay neatly folded inside. He handed it to Franz, who opened it and began studying it. "We'll have to head farther south. Now we're going east. At the next crossroads, we'd better make a right.''

"How do you think your parents are going to take the news that you've deserted?'' Gavin asked evenly, directing his anger at Franz.

"It will be a blight on the German half of the family, but I know my parents will understand. They know I feel more British than German and would rather be fighting for the other side.''

"Isn't home the first place the Germans will look for you?'' he asked scathingly.

"Perhaps they'll go to the house in Hanover, but not to Annenburg. They will advise my family. The news will travel fast. But they'll imagine we're trying to reach the British lines or the border. And right now they're too busy to spend much time looking for deserters. It's my father I'm sorry about.'' Franz looked away, his face bleak. "But I don't believe in this war, and neither does he. I don't believe in what Germany's doing, in all the massacres that have taken place, and now this expansionist vision of Ludendorff's. He thinks he can reinstate German culture in the Baltic states and Russia, and I don't want to be a part of any of it. My sister and I were raised in London and I've always considered myself British. I can't change that now.''

"Why didn't you fight with us, then?'' Gavin challenged, noticing that the forest had thickened and the road narrowed.

"The ironic part is that, if I'd offered my services to the British, they would merely have taken me for a spy, and I'd

have spent the rest of the war rotting in a damn prison camp."
Franz sighed. "Of course, you chaps will want to get back as
quickly as you can." Turning, he glanced at Gavin as the car
rattled over a particularly bumpy stretch of road. His eyes narrowed. "Your leg is hurting, isn't it? You can't go anywhere
until you get well, or you'll be caught immediately and expose
the lot of us."

"Maybe you should finish me off, like Annelise. After all,
I'm a liability."

"Don't be ridiculous," Miles snapped savagely as they began climbing a small road that wound its way farther into the
forest, now a dense mix of dark, heavy branches.

He peered through the windshield at the drizzling rain that
was making progress increasingly difficult. Gavin tried to
change positions as the pain in his thigh grew more excruciating.

Just as they reached the top of the hill, the car jolted to a
sudden stop, the bonnet tipped forward and the front wheels
sank deep into a rut.

"Bloody hell," Miles swore. Trying to rev up the engine,
he succeeded only in producing a screeching of tires as they
rotated in the mud.

"What rotten luck," Franz exclaimed. "We're not far from
Schloss Annenberg now, only about twelve kilometers."

Miles tried again, then threw up his hands, irritated. "It's no
use. I'm just making matters worse."

A few straggling houses, their pointed roofs peering out from
above the trees, formed a hamlet bordering the roadside about
a kilometer down the road. "Do you think we should try and
get help?" he asked Franz uneasily. "God knows what will
happen if we're found here by the wrong people."

"We have to be very careful," Franz replied, jumping out
and avoiding the worst of the sludge. "It's just near enough to
Schloss Annenberg for someone to remember me, although I
haven't been here in years, so it's doubtful. But you never
know, and people can be very treacherous in a war. We cannot
trust anyone to protect us." He glanced at the cottages. "We
can't risk them seeing you wounded, Gavin. We're too far from

the front and your rank is too high for anyone to believe that you would not have been immediately transported to a field hospital. We must hide you.'' He glanced at the forest, frowning.

Miles gave the engine a last try, then admitted defeat. ''I think the village is our only chance.''

''Franz, you're right.'' Gavin gritted his teeth. ''The blood on my uniform will make them suspicious.'' He was feeling faint and wondered how long he could hold out. ''I'd better get away from the middle of the road.'' He glanced at the forest on either side of them ''I'll get into the forest and you two go find help together.'' He began heaving himself out of the vehicle while Franz steadied him.

''Think you can manage?''

''Of course.'' Gavin tried his best to walk straight. ''I'll make it. It's not far. Now get going. And if for some reason you can't make it back…well, for God's sake, just go.''

Miles handed him a knife. ''Better have this—just in case.''

''You might need it yourself.'' Gavin gazed at it in horror, his stomach lurching at the sight of the tiny red specks of blood, still fresh on the flashing blade. He thought of Annelise's blue eyes and silver-blond hair, and anger returned in a rush. But he was too weak to do more than hope he'd make it to the trees.

Reluctantly, he took the knife and pocketed it. ''Good luck.''

Franz slipped his hand into his jacket pocket and took out a handkerchief, which he handed to Gavin. ''I've had this since the beginning of the war. My mother embroidered it for me right before I came out, and it's brought me luck. If, for some reason, we get separated, you can always try and reach my parents' home in Hanover.'' He quickly wrote down the address. ''Give the hankie to my mother and tell her I said to hug Bubbles for me. She'll understand. Don't argue, we haven't time. Just take it.'' He thrust the address and the white linen handkerchief into Gavin's hand. Their eyes met, then Franz turned and he and Miles trudged off, squelching through the ankle-deep mud toward the hamlet.

Gavin glanced at the initials exquisitely embroidered by a

loving hand and pocketed the handkerchief, glancing at the backs of his two companions with mixed feelings. Dragging his leg he limped determinedly toward the trees, each agonizing step an effort. Taking deep breaths, he forced himself forward, determined to reach seclusion before any vehicles appeared. It took him awhile—he didn't know precisely how long, for he'd lost track of time—to reach the edge of the forest, where he collapsed in a cold sweat beneath the shadowy safety of the fir trees. He stopped and sat, breathless, before pushing farther, making sure he was well hidden before sinking among the pine needles, exhausted but thankful for the branches sheltering him partially from the rain. He huddled painfully against a knotted trunk, barely conscious, and pulled the thick coat Annelise had handed him with the uniform closer, his delirious mind haunted by her image.

He slept, woke, slept again. When he regained consciousness, it was dark. He could feel his aching body, racked by fever. Somewhere, in the back of his mind, he wondered where the others were, wondered if he was back in the truck, returning to the hospital in Frieburg, but the effort to reason was too great and he drifted off once more.

5

Etaples, France, 1917

The first few days after Angus's arrival were grueling. Endless convoys of wounded packed the corridors, as soldiers and enemy prisoners continued to arrive, day and night. Flora functioned in a numb daze, grief and exhaustion mingling with the putrid stench of flesh that permeated the crude operating theater. Preparing the frightened patients for surgery she strove to quell the terror in the eyes of those aware of the risks they faced. Over and over again she waited for the moment when, even in her weakened state, she felt the change within that warned of the imminent delivery of a soul ready to be released.

Flora saw little of Angus during those first chaotic days. The facility was inadequately staffed, and every hand was needed. There was little hierarchy at these times, V.A.D., nurses and the doctors pooling their energies in a superhuman effort to save as many lives as they could. Occasionally, she took a few precious minutes off, to walk outside and gaze at the far-off fields behind the lines, intrigued by a solitary cottage that stood alone. Like a dollhouse, it was surrounded by a well-tended garden of pansies and columbines. Against the hollow echoes of shell fire, it made her wonder if the rest was all a dream. The tiny cottage somehow made it impossible to comprehend that only a few miles away war raged, cruel and pitiless, and that the body of the man she loved lay buried in the blood-soaked earth.

By two weeks after learning of Gavin's death, Flora's shock had quieted down. She was able to get some sleep at night, and visited Angus occasionally during the day. He continued to spend his days sitting, pale and silent. Distant. And she worried, knowing she must give him some affection, concerned that the shell shock was worse than she had at first believed. She'd been too caught up in her own sorrow, she realized guiltily, and with all the critical cases, there was little time allotted to those suffering from psychological wounds. There was simply no one to help them, except the chaplain in the few moments he could spare.

Walking into his ward later that day, Flora saw the hope that gleamed, for these men knew they were going home. They joked with one another, denying the past, looking toward the future—or a reprieve, at least, from the hell they had left behind in the trenches. But Angus didn't talk; instead, he sat alone and aloof, in a world of his own.

"How are you, Angus?" she asked, touching his shoulder gently.

He looked up with a start.

"Flo."

"It's my tea break." She sat opposite him on a wooden stool, smiling bravely. "Are you better?"

"Fine." But his face was gray, eyes bleary, and he hadn't shaved.

She glanced at him uncertainly then decided to speak anyway. "You know we can't pretend it hasn't happened, Angus dear. He's gone. I know that it seems so strange...unbelievable, in fact." She clasped her hands, forcing back the tears that threatened to burst forth whenever she mentioned Gavin's precious name. "Sometimes I think I'm going to turn round and see him standing behind me," she whispered, swallowing. "The odd thing is, I haven't felt him at all. You know what I mean," she added quickly.

"Do you think he'd come to you?" he asked, a glimmer of hope lighting his eyes.

"I don't know. I don't know enough about it. Just what I feel when the men are dying. The same as I used to when the animals were hurt or something bad was going to happen when we were little. Remember?"

He nodded, his eyes hollow.

They sat, absorbed in their own thoughts as a gramophone droned in the smoky air.

"I could have saved him," Angus whispered suddenly. "I could have done something and I didn't. Why couldn't I move? Why was I paralyzed with fear? I'm a coward, Flo. And because of that he's dead and I'm alive. Oh God." He buried his head in his hands.

"You must stop, Angus. It wasn't your fault. You aren't to blame. Shell shock is as bad as any other wound, it just doesn't show." She pried his fingers from his face. "Angus, please. You can't go through life feeling guilty for something you didn't do. The war is to blame, not you. You must think of poor Uncle Hamish and Tante Constance."

"It should have been me. It would have been so much better if it had."

"Stop it. We all need you, Uncle, Tante—and me," she pleaded, hoping she could reach through the barrier he'd erected.

Angus raised his head, and propped his chin on his hand. "You know, he asked me something just...before it happened."

"Asked you what?" She frowned, her pulse beating faster.

"We were reading your letter, talking about you—" He stopped midsentence, far away once more.

"And what did he say?" she prompted softly.

He blinked, then continued. "As I said, we were talking about you, and...well..." He stopped, focusing on her. "He said that if anything happened to him, I should marry you," he blurted out, closing his eyes.

Flora sat up with a start. "Marry me? But why would he say that?"

"I don't know," he shrugged and glanced toward the men playing cards in their worn, striped dressing gowns and carpet slippers, smoke and two flies swirling around the lightbulb above them. "I know he wanted to marry you himself. He loved you, you know."

"I'll always love him." She swallowed, clasping and unclasping her hands, and realized she'd referred to him in the present tense. "It wouldn't be fair if I married you or anybody else."

"Yes, it would. I don't care. I know I'm more like a brother to you, Flo, but at least we'd have each other. We could share what's left of him." His eyes became suddenly brighter.

"We'll talk about it once you're better. You're in shock just now. We'll see later. Try and rest." She got up quickly, the gleam in his eyes making her uncomfortable. "I have to get back to the ward, but I'll come by tomorrow."

"All right. You really will come, won't you?"

"Of course." She hesitated before speaking. "Are you sure that was what he meant?" she asked, her voice cracking.

"Yes. He didn't want you to…belong to anyone else." He glanced away, cheeks flushed, and Flora felt her own face burning. She had never talked about that, even with Gavin.

"I—I have to run. I'll see you tomorrow."

She turned and almost ran from the ward. The thought of giving herself to anyone but Gavin was unbearable.

That afternoon and evening she worked herself into a stupor. It was only late that night when she lay in the dark, curled under her army blanket, that she allowed Angus's words to surface once more. Tears for all that should have been and now would never be, for shattered dreams and cherished hopes buried, soaked her pillow.

Still, as days passed, she thought more and more about what Angus had said about facing the future together. In some ways, it made sense. It wasn't only Gavin who had died. There were so many others, friends and relations, of their generation. Perhaps the only way to survive in the new world that would emerge after the war was by sticking together through thick and thin. Before leaving her quarters, she combed back her chestnut hair into a neat bun and placed her cap on it. But now was not the time for decisions. First, they had to win the war, only then could they try to heal the scars.

That afternoon when she stopped by for tea, Angus was waiting for her. She noticed immediately that he looked different, neat and shaved.

"Let's go for a walk," he proposed, sounding more like his old self.

"I'd love to. Perhaps we could wander over to that little house, the one I pointed out to you from the window."

Flora wrapped up warm, for the day was cold and windy, and they left the ward behind, walking side by side down the main road that lead toward Etaples.

About a mile down the road, they reached the house. It was a magical oasis untouched by the world around it. Flora gazed at the whitewashed exterior, the blue shutters and the flower beds that would bloom again in spring.

"I thought about what you said," she whispered, eyes fixed on the house, heart filled with Gavin.

"Will you marry me, Flora?" Angus half whispered the question, held out his hand, eyes filled with hope.

"I promise I'll think about it."

Angus clasped her hand. "Thank you, Flo. I don't know if I could go on living without you. It's what Gavin wanted."

She ignored the sudden shiver that ran through her, and blotted out Gavin's image again, as the afternoon died and they made their way slowly back to the ward.

6

The Black Forest, Germany, 1917

Somewhere in the recesses of his brain, Gavin heard a voice speaking German, then shivering and pain took hold as he was slowly moved. He heard a woman's voice whispering to him. "Not a word. Pretend you're out still."

Gavin closed his eyes once more and fell back into a semi-comatose sleep, too weak to think, haunted by Angus's indifference, Flora's smile and Annelise's fear-filled eyes. Frustrated, angry dreams, where his twin became a different being to the brother he knew, were followed by soothing images of Strathaird, standing high above the cliff with the sea churning below.

The next time he woke, Gavin knew at once something had changed. He sniffed, eyes closed, recognizing the subtle scent of crisp, fresh linen and lavender. When he opened his eyes, sunlight poured through a window onto a bright patchwork quilt. Taking stock of his surroundings, he wondered how he got here. The room was low-beamed and filled with heavy, rich furnishings, relics of a past era. He felt weak, but the excruciating pain in his hip and thigh had subsided somewhat. He tried to sit up and winced. For some reason, his arm lay across his chest, bandaged and wrapped in a neat sling. This must be the hunting lodge, he decided. Franz and Miles must have brought him here.

After a while he heard footsteps approaching and warily closed his eyes, unsure of what to expect. It might be someone other than his friends, someone who believed him to be a wounded German officer. The door opened, followed by a whiff of delicate perfume. A soft, cool hand stroked his forehead, lifted a strand of hair, then touched his cheek. A woman's voice whispered something soothing in English before straightening the sheet and placing two fingers on the inside of his wrist. Finally, curiosity won and Gavin squinted warily. He stared in surprise at a pair of bright green eyes and high cheekbones that reminded him immediately of Franz.

"Shh. Stay quiet." The girl stood, looking sad and serious as she measured the beat of his pulse. Gavin watched, fascinated, as the sunlight brushed the golden strands of hair that cascaded over her shoulders down to her waist, glinting like a burnished mane. Her face was youthful, and he guessed that she was no older than sixteen. He swallowed, taken aback by her beauty.

"Your pulse is regular now," she said in perfect English, laying his arm back on the quilt. "Don't worry. You are quite safe here."

"Who are you?" he asked, trying to sit again.

"Don't. You're still weak. I am Franz von Ritter's younger sister," she said. Leaning forward to assist him, she plumped the fat goose-down pillows before retreating a step from the bed. He noticed how slim she was, her gray skirt too big and the woolen sweater too loose.

"Is this the hunting lodge?" he asked, looking at her curiously.

"Yes. You've been here for almost a week."

"Where are Franz and Miles?"

She hesitated, then gave a sigh. "Franz is dead, and Miles has been taken prisoner."

"Dead?" Gavin sat up, shocked, then fell back in pain. "But how? When? It can't be!"

She seemed suddenly frail and he leaned forward as best he could.

"Sit down. I don't even know your name. But please, you must tell me."

The girl reluctantly perched on the edge of the bed, twisting a handkerchief and speaking in a controlled voice, as if trying to suppress all emotion. "The car broke down, they went to get help."

"I know that," Gavin interrupted. "I hid in the woods."

She paused, swallowed, then continued in a trembling voice. "As Franz was about to go and fetch you, he and Miles were intercepted by three army officials called in by one of the locals. I believe someone must have overheard Franz and Miles speaking to one another in English, otherwise it is incomprehensible that anyone would have suspected. But they did. It was impossible for Franz and Miles to keep up their disguise for long. They brought my brother before a military tribunal." Her voice went hoarse and her hands trembled. "He was sentenced to death by firing squad." She swallowed again, tears pouring down her cheeks, while Gavin remained in shocked silence.

"Out of deference to my father," she continued shakily, "the *Haupt Kommandant* allowed Franz to see me and my parents before his execution. They brought him to Hanover before they killed him. It was in those last moments that he told me where you were. He said you had Mama's hankie and told me where they had left you. He begged me to save you," she whispered, choking on the words. Gavin's hand covered hers, horrified. "He...he thought of you till the end. He said you were his responsibility."

"My God. I'm so sorry."

"Sorry?" She turned on him angrily. "Sorry? Do you think that will bring back my brother? Or my father, who died of a heart attack shortly after? And my mother, who put a pistol in her mouth and pulled the trigger? You say you are sorry? Perhaps if it wasn't for you they could have got away. But no. He waited, did everything he could to save you, and now he is dead." She broke down, buried her face in her hands and sobbed, as Gavin sat in helpless shock. He reached out a hand tentatively but, realizing he was doing more harm than good, he leaned back, eyes closed, incapable of assimilating the spectacle of Franz's death that played out in his imagination.

Slowly the girl's tears subsided and she wiped her face with the hankie. "I'm sorry," she gulped. "I know it isn't your fault. But I can't believe they're gone. All of them. Just like that. I can't believe it. And he was so brave, so heroic. He kissed my mother, he…he was the brave one, not me. He went to his death a hero, while we were all destroyed."

"I'm privileged to have known him and called him my friend," Gavin said, throat tight, watching her tear-blotched face. "What's your name?" he asked, gently touching her hand once more.

"Greta."

"I'm Gavin MacLeod."

"I know. He told me in a whisper as we were kissing goodbye. He said, 'Take care of Gavin, little one. I know I can count on you.'" Her voice broke again and she twisted the damp handkerchief into a knot. "It was so terrible, but I knew I had to find you. I had made that final promise to Franz. I left by car the same day. They don't know that I can drive, but Hans, our chauffeur, taught me. I drove to where Franz told me. I made sure no one was there. Sure enough, you were in the exact spot."

"But how did you manage?" Gavin asked, amazed at her courage.

"I dragged you and heaved you into the car. You are quite heavy," she said with the first trace of a smile.

He squeezed her hand. "How can I ever thank you, Greta? You and Franz saved my life. What a brave woman you are."

"No, I'm not. It was not bravery. I was merely fulfilling a last promise to the person I loved most. He told me he will come back." She shifted and sighed. "We used to talk a lot about metaphysics, about spirits and whether, if he died in the war, he could return to visit me as a soul. Do you believe that can happen?" Her face was childlike in its hope.

"I don't know." Gavin hesitated. "I have a cousin whom I

love very much. She believes that people come back. She is convinced of it. Personally, I've never experienced it, though many of the soldiers in the unit said they were certain they'd seen men that they themselves had buried later rallying in battle. Whether it is the truth or just wishful thinking, I can't tell you.''

She nodded, rose and sniffed. ''You must be hungry. I will get you some soup.''

''Uh, I need to use the washroom,'' he murmured, ''but I don't know if I can stand.''

Greta blushed. ''Of course. Allow me.'' She came close to the bed. Gavin heaved his legs over the side and tried to stand, but everything went black and he had to sit once more. The second time was better. ''Thanks. I can probably manage if you tell me where it is.''

''I had better help you.''

''All right,'' he conceded, as embarrassed as she was.

Slowly they made their way across the wooden floorboards, then painfully negotiated the corridor, Gavin leaning heavily on Greta's slim shoulder. As they passed through arched doors, Gavin observed iron braziers and coats of arms, interspersed with boar and deer heads on the walls.

''This is the water closet,'' she said, blushing more deeply.

''Thanks,'' he replied, making a superhuman effort to stand straight and sound casual.

''I'll wait for you here.''

''I'll be fine,'' he answered, sounding more confident than he felt. What if he couldn't manage on his own? He entered the bathroom, sank down on the edge of the tub and tried to regain some strength. It took him nearly ten minutes, but he was finally able to open the door with a semblance of dignity. Greta stood by the window, arms crossed protectively over her chest, pretending not to notice. He felt a rush of pity. She had been through so much, and now she had him to contend with.

He felt stronger as they walked back to the room, and better able to observe his surroundings. The ancient suits of armor standing like sentries along the wide corridor reminded him of Strathaird.

"Is this place very old?"

"Only about eighty years old, though it appears older. My grandfather built it for a visit from the kaiser, who wanted to go hunting. Wild boar, I believe. But my father didn't hunt. He lived most of his life in England—we all did—so it has been closed for many years."

"Where are we exactly?"

"Well hidden in the heart of the Black Forest. The nearest village must be at least twelve kilometers away. Nobody ever comes here, except the odd hunter during the hunting season. Anyway, the men are all at the front, so we're safe."

"Won't anyone look for you?" he asked curiously, relieved they had reached the bed.

"What? Look for the Englishwoman's daughter, and the traitor's sister? No. They are glad to be rid of me." She gave a bitter little laugh that belied her young face.

"You can't assume that. There must be someone who cares."

"Only my aunt Louisa, but she lives in Switzerland. Lie down now. We'll talk later, after I get your food."

He lay back thankfully against the pillows, hating that he felt so damn weak, but relieved that Greta appeared calmer. The sun had gone, replaced by dark shadows that filtered through the diamond-shaped panes. The mention of food made him realize just how hungry he was and helped explain his weakness. He hadn't eaten for days.

Sitting up despite the pain, he looked out through the window at a sea of leaves that stretched for miles, like a heavy green carpet dotted with golden spots. All at once the war and the recent tragedies seemed like a dream. Even Franz's death seemed remote. He thought of Flora, tending the wounded, and wished he were with her and his parents, who perhaps believed him dead. He fiddled fretfully with the sheet, wishing he could turn back time, wishing he hadn't left Annelise alone with Miles, wondering how long it would take him to get back to his platoon, where he could let them all know he was alive and well.

His thoughts were interrupted by a knock on the door, followed by Greta, carrying a large tray loaded with a bowl of steaming soup, crisp fresh bread hot from the oven and a bottle of Moselle wine. His mouth watered as she laid it carefully on his lap, then she perched at the end of the bed, watching him, as he forced himself to take his time and maintain a semblance of good manners. Perhaps it was sheer hunger, but he couldn't remember anything ever tasting that appetizing before.

"It's delicious," he said, wishing he could scrape the bottom of the bowl.

"Would you like more?" She smiled tentatively, a sudden sweetness lighting her features.

"What about you?" he asked, afraid there might not be enough.

"I've eaten. Don't worry, there's plenty. Father made a vegetable plot, and I shot a rabbit this morning." She stood up.

"You're an enterprising young woman," he said, handing her the tray, "and a very brave one." Their eyes met and held for a moment, then she busied herself with the tray.

"This war has made us all into different people." She looked down and sighed. "I'll get you more soup."

"Greta?"

"Yes?" She turned back.

"Just...thank you." He smiled, embarrassed. Her mouth softened and her lovely green eyes shone with unshed tears.

Three days later, Gavin felt better. The rest, good food and companionship had strengthened him considerably, and he woke up feeling energetic and ready to rise. Swinging his legs carefully over the edge of the bed, he dressed in an old pair of gray trousers and a jersey that had once belonged to Franz and headed slowly down the large staircase toward the kitchen, filled with new exhilaration. The strain of the escape, followed by being bedridden and catered to hand and foot by Greta, had been getting on his nerves. At least now he could be of some use.

He reached the kitchen, guided by the smell of freshly baked bread that had become familiar over the past few days, and stood in the doorway. It was low-beamed and cozy. Sparkling copper pots and bunches of herbs and dried flowers hung from the ceiling. A pretty vase of wildflowers that sat on the large wooden table, which was covered in a bright checked cloth, gave the kitchen a homey feel. Greta stood over the immense stove, her back to him, stirring a pot. He watched her, aware all at once of her lithe, slim body, which even the faded blue cotton frock and woolen jacket couldn't hide, and her hair. That amazing hair, like a princess's in the fairy tales his mother used to read to them as children, fell smooth and golden down her back.

He thought sadly of Franz, a man he barely knew, who'd saved him, and realized he was partly responsible for her. Perhaps if he hadn't planned the escape, Franz and her family would be alive. And Annelise. Surely that should have taught him what uncontrolled reactions could end up causing? He moved silently across the kitchen and came up behind her, peering over her shoulder to see what was in the pot.

"Mmm, that smells good."

Greta squealed in surprise and upset the pan. It clattered to the ground, the contents oozing over the flagstone floor in a thick white puddle at her feet.

"How could you?" she cried angrily, fists balled, lips trembling.

"I'm sorry. I didn't mean to frighten you," Gavin apologized.

"I don't care *how* sorry you are. Look at the mess you've made!" she exclaimed. "You're as thoughtless as Franz—" The words died on her lips and she began to tremble. Without a second thought, Gavin stepped over the spilled porridge and put his arms around her, holding her close, soothing her until he felt the shaking stop. Then, gently, he stroked her hair and neck, easing her head against his shoulder and wishing he could give her back what she'd lost.

He gazed angrily over her head at the bright autumn morning through the open window, so serene and far removed from the horrors they were experiencing. He kissed the top of her head and whispered to her as he would a child, while birds twittered and a plump gray squirrel scuttled up a branch. It was impossible to believe that, not many miles away, war was causing such endless grief and destruction. He stroked her hair tenderly, feeling her body against him, trying to keep the inevitable reactions under control. She was so brave, yet so vulnerable, and he raged at her life being so bitterly devastated almost before it had begun.

He felt her stir and eased his arms. As he looked down into her face, he became aware that these were the true casualties of this absurd war. The women, the children, the too young and the too old. He was only seventeen himself, but he felt and looked so much older. The past eighteen months of trench warfare had marked him forever. The naive boy who left Scotland now possessed more experience than most men encountered in a lifetime.

But he pulled himself together and showed none of his thoughts. Negativity was a killer. The trenches had taught him that. "Come on, Greta. I'll clean it up later. Would it be safe to go for a short walk? I would love to go outside. You could show me around."

She stepped back, gulped, then nodded. "I'm sorry. I shouldn't have reacted like that."

"Don't be sorry. You had every reason to be upset, and I'm a damn fool for having surprised you in the first place." He gave her a winning smile. "Let's put it behind us and get outside. It's a beautiful day, and I haven't seen real fresh air for nearly two years."

"All right." She gave him a shy, tremulous smile, then slipped off her red-and-white flowered apron before heading through the kitchen door.

Gavin stood back and looked at the exterior of the hunting pavilion, a heavy structure built of stone and dark wood that was almost medieval in style, its gothic windows and thick walls reminiscent of a fortress. They walked through the overgrown gardens that stopped abruptly at the edge of the forest, trampling over weeds, daisies and grass that stood knee-high, and headed toward two stone benches shrouded by damp moss and clinging ivy. Beside them was a chipped Italian fountain with a dry spout that housed a family of toads.

"I've never seen toads in a forest before," Gavin remarked, picking up a stone to throw at them.

"Don't." Greta stopped his hand. "That's their home. They're happy there. You have no right to hurt them."

"That's true," he conceded, realizing how indifferent the war had made him. "Come on. Let's run to the woods."

"Run? You can't run," she exclaimed, her laugh girlish.

"Of course I can. It's just a silly leg wound. I'm fine."

"Really?" She arched an eyebrow. "Let's see."

With that, she set off, her long, full skirt billowing and hair flying like a young palomino's as she set off toward the trees. Gavin followed her but knew he couldn't make it. *Damn.* Would it never get better, he wondered, then laughed as Greta looked back triumphantly. He threw up his arms in a gesture of defeat and limped to where she'd stopped, flushed and breathless, conscious again of stirrings in his body that were becoming difficult to deny.

"There. You see? You're not well yet. You have to take it easy, and I have to make sure that you do. Why, you shouldn't even be walking around like this!"

"Right again," he agreed, throwing himself down in the soft bed of grass and closing his eyes. "Ah, this is wonderful. Sun, blue sky and no guns, no rats, no damp, no death. Just the scent of life." He inhaled deeply, aware of her next to him, her knees clasped up to her chin thoughtfully.

"It's magical here, isn't it? What happened to Franz, Mama and Papa seems unreal," she whispered.

"Don't." He leaned on his elbow and took her hand. "I know this will sound cruel, Greta, but you have to stop thinking about it."

"What a stupid thing to say," she cried, snatching her hand away. "How can I think of anything else? I loved them. They're my family."

"I know. But you have to survive."

"What for? There's nothing left. They're all gone. Dead. Murdered." She pulled a wildflower raggedly from its roots. "What point is there to a life without those I loved?"

"Do you think that is what they would want?" Gavin retorted. "Is that what Franz died for? For you to sit here, blubbering and feeling sorry for yourself?"

"How *dare* you? What do you know about it? You haven't lost your family. Perhaps, if it wasn't for you, Franz might be alive."

"Perhaps. But I did what I had to do. An officer's first duty when taken prisoner is to try and escape from the enemy. Franz chose to join me. I never asked him to." He rolled over again and watched her. He'd seen this state of mind. He knew how it could end up. "You can't give up, Greta," he said in a softer tone. "I won't let you. I promise I'll help you get through this, as best we can."

"You?" She looked down at him disdainfully, pulling the petals from the wilted bud. "You'll be off once you're well. Don't you want to go back to the war?" she challenged.

"Of course. At some point I'll have to get back, but I can't go like this." He tapped his leg. "And I won't leave you on your own. I owe that to Franz. We both do." He reached up and took her fingers in his. She hesitated, then allowed him to turn her hand about.

"Do you play the piano?"

"Yes." She sniffed. "How did you know?"

"Your hands remind me of someone I know who plays the piano, that's all," he said wistfully, remembering Flora playing at Strathaird, or on summer evenings in Limoges. It all seemed so long ago and so painfully nostalgic. "Will you play for me?"

She looked away. "Perhaps. Let's go back. You must be tired and I need to milk the cow." She pulled her hand away and got up, rubbing the grass from the back of her skirt.

"Cow?" Gavin exclaimed, following suit. "Where on earth did you find a cow?"

"It was standing in front of the house the morning after we arrived. I was frightened someone might reclaim it and find us, but they haven't, so I've adopted her. I've called her Gretchen."

"Then Gretchen it is. I'll help you milk her. Maybe we can make butter."

"Do you know how?" Greta looked at him doubtfully.

"Well, not exactly." He grinned. "But I've seen Moira, our cook in Skye, do it dozens of times. Shouldn't be too difficult," he added nonchalantly, not about to be defeated. "Come on," he stretched out his hand, determined to keep the smile on her face, "the only way we'll know is if we try."

"You're being silly," she demurred, then took his out-stretched hand. Suddenly the destruction of the war seemed far away and the warm summer morning was well on its way as they walked slowly back toward the Schloss, both conscious of the new intimacy that reigned between them.

The days passed and they established a comfortable cama-raderie. Summer ebbed gently into autumn and the leaves turned from green to red and gold, a beautiful mosaic among the dark pines. As Gavin's leg improved, they took longer walks, although they never went too far, in case they should be seen by a chance wanderer.

After some unsuccessful experiments, they finally succeeded in making butter, and Gavin was amazed when Greta took him down into the huge, dark cellars of the pavilion, where Baron von Ritter had stocked enough food for an army. There were sausages and hams hanging on large iron hooks from the heavy oak beams; huge, airtight canisters filled with coarse brown flour, sugar, condiments and coffee; heavy stone jars of pickled gherkins and onions; and shelves filled with whole cheeses. But that was not all. Greta showed him a passage that she said went under the forest.

The wine cellar had also been magnificently stocked, prob-ably before the kaiser's visit, if the dates of the bottles were anything to judge by. Gavin, having spent part of every sum-mer since early childhood at his uncle and aunt's in Limoges, with occasional trips to nearby Bordeaux, knew good wine.

October came and the nights grew cold. The leaves turned from red and gold to bronze, and each evening they lit the huge fireplace in the study, the smallest room in the house and the easiest to heat. It was here and in the kitchen that Greta and he spent most of their time, talking about their lives, about

Skye and Edinburgh, the MacLeod coal business, the summers in France where Gavin had learned how porcelain was made.

Greta listened, enthralled, for Gavin was a good storyteller, adding creative license when he felt it was required, in an effort to make her laugh and forget some of her sadness. Sometimes she would play the piano—which was surprisingly well tuned, for having spent so long silent—and Gavin thought of Flora.

Then one day he woke up and the forest had transformed into a magical, snow-covered fairyland that glistened in the morning sunlight. It made him realize just how long he'd been there and, as at the hospital, he was overwhelmed with guilt for allowing himself to fall into the comfortable rhythm with Greta, and making no attempt to get back to the front. Looking out the window, he realized that wouldn't be possible now until spring. His leg still hurt and the limp remained, and in the back of his mind he wondered if it would ever heal. But he shunned that idea, convinced, with the invincibility of youth, that everything resolved itself at some point.

He got up and went to the window, feeling the cold, dry air mix with warm sun on his skin. Below, a trail of tiny hoofprints in the virgin snow told him deer were about. All at once he thought of Flora, ashamed that, of late, her image was somewhat hazy. He loved her, of course, but his desire and fondness for Greta was intensifying, particularly since two nights ago, when he'd heard her weeping in her room. He'd entered and sat next to her in the dark, stroking her hair. Then—he wasn't quite sure how—she was in his arms, and their lips had met, hers closed until gently pried open, her surprise and innocent response forcing him to draw back. But he'd stayed, holding her in his arms, and there had been little sleep for him that night.

He dressed, knowing Greta would be waiting in the kitchen for them to have breakfast. They'd become like a couple, spending their days and much of their nights together. Gavin wondered with a shudder just how long he could stand the longing he felt when she laid her head against his chest, her eyes filled with love and hope. He had to keep strict tabs on himself, sure that she was unaware—as were most young girls—of the inevitable consequences of her actions. He loved her too, in his own way, but most of all he wanted her, and being so close day and night was becoming torture.

Later that day it snowed again and they sat in the study, Gavin trying to concentrate on his book, a treatise on the Franco-Prussian War, while Greta worked on a half-finished tapestry she'd found in an upstairs cupboard, oblivious of what her presence was doing to his frayed nerves. He snapped the book shut. "Damn the snow. We can't even get out for a walk."

"I like it. It's so cozy being inside, watching it fall. Especially with you," she murmured, blushing.

"I wish you'd stop that." He got up and poked the fire. "I'll be off as soon as the weather permits. My leg will be better by then. There's nothing to stop me from trying to get back to my unit. I've stayed far too long as it is."

"But I thought you were happy here," she whispered, the tapestry abandoned, eyes brimming with hurt surprise.

"How can I be happy, Greta, when I should be doing my duty for my country, not lounging here doing nothing." He poked the fire harder and a log fell sideways, sending sparks up the chimney. "I can't spend the rest of my life rotting here. You know that."

"Have I done something wrong?" she asked, troubled.

"Of course not," he replied testily, hating himself for causing her consternation and bewilderment but unable to help it.

"Then what is it, Gavin, dear?" she asked, getting up. "Tell me. Something's wrong. I can feel there's something you don't want to tell me."

"It's nothing. Nothing you'd understand," he muttered, placing the poker back on its stand next to the fire.

"Why? Perhaps if you explained, I might." She stood next to him, waiting for him to encircle her in his arms before raising her lips to his.

He pulled away and crossed over to the window. "You don't know what you're talking about," he said weakly. "You're so innocent. A baby. You—you have no idea what it is like for a man to be close to you, day and night, and not—it doesn't matter. The least said the better. I'll get some wood in before dark.''

''No.'' She stopped him, eyes glinting. ''You are going to tell me exactly what it is I'm doing wrong. I won't let you fob me off with excuses. I thought we were happy together. Almost as if we were married,'' she added, blushing again.

''But married people don't just—oh, forget it, Greta. You'll understand one day.''

''No. I want to understand now, Gavin—there may never be a 'one day.' I know married people sleep together in the same bed. Is it something to do with that?''

He looked down at her, ashamed of himself, and reached for her hand. ''They do more than just sleep together, my darling.''

''I had sort of gathered that. Could we do that other thing?'' She came close, face flushed and eyes alight. ''Would it make you happy?''

''No.'' He shook his head firmly. ''It wouldn't be right. We're not married, and well—you could end up having a baby.''

''Can you at least explain it to me, Gavin? Then I could decide, couldn't I?''

''For Christ's sake, Greta,'' he exclaimed, embarrassed.

''Well, it can't be that awful. After all, most women must do it, don't they? I want to be yours, darling, all yours... whatever that means.''

''You don't know what you're talking about. I would be betraying my loyalty to Franz.''

''Nothing's wrong anymore, Gavin,'' she said, drawing nearer as evening closed in and shadows bounced off the faded brocade walls. ''That's all the past now. We don't know what will happen tomorrow or the day after, when the war will end, or...or anything. I want to feel married to you, even if we're not. And maybe someday we can be.''

''No!'' he exclaimed, Flora's face flashing before him. ''I can't do that.''

''Why not? Don't you love me?''

''Of course I love you, Greta, but—oh, it's too difficult to explain," he said, pulling her close and casting Flora from his mind as his hand slipped to the small of her back and he pressed her body gently against his. She stiffened. "Do you understand, darling?" he whispered. "Are you sure you want to know, my Greta? Are you certain?" His senses dimmed as once more he made her feel his erection, barely hearing her whispered assent before leading her toward the large daybed.

One by one he undid the tiny buttons of her high-necked blouse, swallowed hard at her quick intake of breath when his hands reached her breast. Still he continued, unhurried, shedding each garment until she stood before him, her smooth, white skin gleaming in the shadows, her hair a burnished mane highlighted by the glow of the flames. Her eyes were misty now, innocent fear replaced by primeval female desire as she reached up, swept away the golden strands that had fallen over her breasts and stepped away from him.

"My God, you're beautiful. The most beautiful woman on earth," he whispered, awed yet somewhat hesitant. This was not one of the French whores at Paris Plage whom he'd paid to experiment with, a brief sexual fling like Annelise. He was about to make Greta a woman, and the knowledge was both frightening and exhilarating.

"Gavin," she whispered, cheeks ablaze, her voice husky with desire. "I want to see you as you are seeing me." It was as though the power of womanhood had suddenly been revealed to her, paralyzing him. Then she arched unconsciously and the need to feel her skin on his, to possess her entirely, overruled his fear. She watched, face flushed, as he undressed, diverting her eyes when he took off his underwear.

Eyes locked, they caressed one another, their bodies lit by the glow of the fire and a flame within, pure yet so intense it burned both flesh and soul. Then she was in his arms, his hands roaming down her back to the curve of her buttocks, delighting in the delicate texture of her skin, before laying her gently among the blue and gold brocade cushions of the daybed.

Her eyes closed as he trailed his fingers languorously, determined to savor the enchantment for as long as he was able. But determination grew thin when he reached the taut curve of her breasts and her eyes opened, turning from misty green to emerald as she gasped, her nipples hardening deliciously to his touch. And Gavin knew the sudden thrill of original male triumph. He was the first. To touch, to feel, to love her.

He lowered his lips to her breast, her soft moans empowering, instinct guiding him as he reached the soft golden mound between her thighs, feeling her body tense as he parted her. For a moment he was afraid, but her small cry of ecstasy had his thumb caressing and his fingers exploring until the need to possess her became unendurable and gently he parted her thighs, knowing he could wait no longer.

"I'll try not to hurt you, my darling," he whispered as her eyes flew open and he gazed down at her through the glimmering shadows, lips parted, her face framed by a sea of gold-flecked strands splayed across the pillow. Then he could wait no longer, and thrust relentlessly, her visceral cry bringing him to a thundering climax.

Later he held her, soothing her in his arms, Greta's head tucked into the crook of his broad shoulder and her hair falling like a silken mantle over his chest.

Gavin woke shivering at dawn, realizing that Greta must be frozen. He rose, careful not to wake her, his body reacting immediately when she stretched like a kitten then curled among the cushions, a magical fairy princess wrapped in her golden mane.

He moved to the fire and placed a log on the dying embers. Soon one flame caught, then another, and as daylight crept stealthily through the window, he looked for something to cover her with.

It was then he saw the bloodstains on her thighs and belly. For a moment he reproached himself for acting like a brute. Then, as she gave a contented sigh in her sleep, he smiled despite his misgivings and covered her tenderly with a blanket that lay on the chair, realizing he'd better be ready to explain what had happened, for she evidently had very little clue about the facts of life.

He felt very mature and manly as he walked upstairs to the

bathroom. Then he went to his room and put on an old velvet dressing gown forgotten by one of the kaiser's entourage and came down again, armed with a damp towel and her long silk nightgown. She was still fast asleep, so he laid the things near her and went to the kitchen to make coffee, hoping she wouldn't be upset when she woke. They were using the coffee sparingly, but today was special, so he added an extra spoonful before stoking the stove and putting the water on to boil, totally relaxed for the first time in ages.

Then, as the kettle began to simmer, he pricked up his ears, certain he'd heard an engine. It was far away, but in this silence you could make anything out. He took the kettle off the stove and rushed to the study.

"Greta, darling, wake up." He shook her shoulder gently.

"Gavin," she whispered, a lazy, satisfied smile curving her lips.

"Darling, wake up. I think I heard a car. It's probably nothing, but all the same we'd better be prepared."

She sat up instantly, pulling the blanket to her chin, then, glancing instinctively toward the window, she burst into laughter. "That's impossible. It's still snowing, look."

Gavin smiled. She was right. There were at least three feet of snow outside. He sighed with relief, realizing it would be impossible for any vehicle to reach Schloss Annenberg under these weather conditions. It must have been his imagination. Perhaps the war was getting nearer. Who could tell? They hadn't heard any news of the outside world for so long.

"Maybe the war is getting closer and it was anti-aircraft guns," he said with a shrug, sitting next to her, stroking her hair. "My God, you're lovely."

"I feel lovely," she said, blushing deliciously before sinking back among the cushions. Then all at once she winced, a dull flush darkening her cheeks, and he remembered.

"You—you may want this," he said, picking up the damp towel hesitantly and handing it to her, embarrassed. "I brought your nightgown, too."

"Oh!" Her cheeks crimson, her gaze remained riveted on the towel.

"Greta, darling, don't worry. It's normal. When I—when we—well, you've bled a little, that's all, but it's all right," he finished in a rush, reaching for her hand. "Remember, it's as if we were married now. We mustn't be ashamed with one another." She nodded, hair shrouding her face. "I'll go and finish making breakfast. You join me in the kitchen when you're ready." He leaned forward and kissed her, ready to leave her in privacy. But when his mouth touched hers, her lips parted. Coffee was forgotten as they came together in a frenzied rush, the blanket and dressing gown thrown aside as they cleaved to one another, wanting nothing more than to prolong the enchantment.

He didn't wait this time; he took her. And soon she was arching, nails sinking into his shoulders, fanning the blaze of their unleashed passion till it burst into flames and he let out a cry.

This time it was his head that sank onto Greta's breast, tired and satiated. Somewhere in the back of his mind he remembered Flora. But Greta's fingers were massaging his neck, her nails coursing through his hair, driving him into a delicious stupor where all he could do was smile, sigh and mutter softly while his unshaved chin grazed her breasts and he fell fast asleep.

7

Etaples, France, 1918

The German offensive had intensified to such a degree during the past weeks that they could not help wondering how much longer the Allied forces would resist the massive drive from the east. Although no one ever expressed their doubts out loud, each day new villages and towns fell and more and more casualties poured in.

In one of the rare moments of quiet Flora was able to grab between shifts, she wrote to Angus, shipped home three months earlier.

> It never stops. Day and night the wounded are pouring in and there is barely room to house them. The floors are covered with stretchers and they are treated there, for the beds are full. The operating theaters never stop and they arrive in everything from ambulances to cattle trucks. Bapaume, Beaumont Hamel and Péronne have all fallen and they are saying that the Germans are already in the suburbs of Amiens. Now there is very little left between us and the front lines... Angus dear, if I should not return...remember him for me, won't you? I promise that if that should be the case, both he and I will be watching over you...

But the frantic activity, dealing with destroyed limbs, removing the stench-filled basins of bloodied gauze and cotton, and treating wounds, allowed her no time to think of Gavin as she prepared surgical instruments and rolled bandages in the hectic dispensary. Not even Arras or the battles of 1917 could compare to the current threat, as the enemy inched toward them, a relentless monster avidly seeking its prey.

Letters were few and far between, and one morning, when she was handed an envelope addressed to her in Angus's neat hand, all she could do was stuff it into her pocket while she rushed through the chaotic ward to aid an agonizing patient whose blood had congealed, gluing his torn limbs to the hard canvas of the stretcher. She tried to remove it as gently as possible but finally had to cut the canvas away. The soldier's cry of pain resounded against the ceaseless clatter of trucks, ambulances, ammunition wagons and trains filled with reinforcements, making their way to the front.

When she'd cleared the ward as best she could, she told the other nurse that she was taking quarter of an hour off before the next convoy arrived. Going to the kitchen, she grabbed a cup of strong tea and sat down, exhausted, at the makeshift table, between a harried doctor and the weary chaplain, to read her letter. Taking a sip, she skimmed the lines. All at once, her eyes filled with horror-stricken tears and her hands trembled.

"Are you all right?" the chaplain asked solicitously, laying a hand on her sleeve. "Can I help you, my dear?"

Flora put down the letter and wiped her eyes. "My Uncle Hamish died of a sudden heart attack. He was like a father to me," she whispered.

"I'm so sorry," he replied quietly, pressing her hand. "You look exhausted. Perhaps you should try and rest."

"What? With this mess going on around us?" She glanced bitterly toward the corridor, where another trail of stretchers shuffled by, drenched in blood. The men didn't even see the front-line stations anymore, but were brought straight here from the shell-blown trenches.

"Still," the chaplain insisted, "I think you should take a break. If I remember rightly, you lost your fiancé as well."

She nodded wearily. It all seemed unreal. Gavin gone, abandoned forever in the trenches. Uncle Hamish, dead of shock and unhappiness. Was there nothing this endless war would leave intact?

Taking the kind chaplain's advice, she wandered aimlessly outside, seeking some solace in the fresh air, a contrast to the acrid stench of the ward. She walked over to a clump of trees and sat down, watching a lumbering horse-pulled cart bringing more injured soldiers.

She turned away, heart overflowing with sadness for Gavin and Uncle Hamish, for Angus and Tante Constance, for the life that had been theirs and that would be no more. Perhaps Angus was right after all. Perhaps the only way to survive was by creating an invincible barrier, pieced together out of painful but loving memories against which, united, they could build a future.

She gazed across the fields, her mind far away. If the war ever ended, she would go home and marry Angus. At least helping him through the ordeal of assuming a role designed for his brother, for which he had neither the nature nor the inclination, would give her life a purpose. She watched as the sun set behind the dark clouds, an ominous stretch of orange-streaked lead that seemed to foreshadow dark weeks ahead where, for the first time, the unmentioned possibility of defeat lurked.

Several days later, as she was sluicing the bedpans, Flora heard two V.A.D.s, Ana and Heather, calling her excitedly.

"Flora, come and see. They're finally here."

"Who?" she asked curiously, washing her chilblained hands.

"The Americans. They're here. Come and see them," Ana urged, and Flora followed her hastily to watch the long lines of tall, well-built, clean-cut young men marching swiftly along the road. It made her realize how tired and disheveled they must seem, after almost four long years without respite. But the sight infused her with both hope and excitement, tempered by sorrow. Gavin and the others had marched off the same way, full of strength and will… She wondered sadly how many of these young men would return, and how it must feel to come so far and fight for what must seem so alien to them. She commented on this to Ana.

"Just be happy they're here," Ana replied with the first grin Flora had seen in many months. "Now we stand a real chance of clobbering those bastards once and for all."

Flora smiled and watched the First United States Army march into Etaples, filled with deep respect and gratitude toward these dignified, purposeful young men willing to endanger their lives in the name of justice, a sentiment that she was determined to remember always.

As she made her way back to the ward, she sent up an inner prayer of thanks for the hope these soldiers brought with them.

8

Pontalier, Switzerland, 1918

If the Americans were here, he was jolly well going to find them, Gavin decided, standing on the platform of the tiny station at Pontalier, a Swiss border town north of Lake Geneva. His false identity papers, which had been provided by a priest named Frère Siméon, identified him as Michel Rouget. He grimaced, not liking the idea of being named after a fish, but he knew he could pass perfectly as a young Frenchman.

It was barely six o'clock, and the station was empty, for the passengers departing to Nancy on the 6:40 had not yet arrived. He eyed the stationmaster, his crisp, blue uniform and brisk gait as pompous as his curled mustache, crossing the tracks in the chilly, damp mist, then peered through the window and shabby net curtains of the *Buffet de la Gare, 2ième classe*. The door swung open and a whiff of coffee and fresh croissants made his mouth water, bringing back poignant memories of Greta, who was never far from his mind.

He fingered the meager change in his pocket, wondering whether to invest in breakfast or wait till later. But there was no sign of the train, so he rose and went inside where a sleepy young waitress stood behind the counter, flicking a feather duster halfheartedly over a tightly packed row of bottles. She cheered at the sight of a young customer and laid down the feather duster, smiling.

"Is that real coffee?" Gavin asked.

"Yes. But you'd better order now, before the morning crowd comes in. After six o'clock it's usually all gone. What'll it be?"

"A café au lait and a croissant," he replied, remembering the many coffees that Eugène, Angus and he had so often enjoyed in Ambazac, after an early-morning fishing expedition. It too reminded him of Greta and his hasty departure. He gazed down at the hard-boiled eggs, his mind far away as he remembered the sound of the approaching car, the two of them peering, unbelieving, from behind the heavy damask curtains; Greta's terrified look as the vehicle finally entered the courtyard, coming to a slow stop in front of the pavilion.

"It's an army car," she said, voice trembling. "Oh my God. You have to flee, Gavin. You must go to the cellar immediately. God knows what will happen if they find you here."

"That's absurd. I can't leave you. I won't."

"Wait," she whispered, clutching his sleeve as the car door opened. "That's General Meinz-Reutenbach, one of my father's best friends. He tried to save poor Franz." She turned, lips white and eyes pleading. "Darling, you must go. It's safe for me, but not for you. If they find you here, they will be obliged to take us both prisoner. I would be hiding an enemy— they wouldn't have a choice. Please," she begged, seeing the other officers exiting the vehicle, stopping to admire the facade before they approached the front door. "Go." She pushed him into the hall toward the cellar door, desperate.

"How can I leave you alone? What if you are wrong? What if—"

"Just go, Gavin, I implore you. You must," she sobbed, her face ashen. "Take some money from the safe, as we planned, and go," she said in a tremulous whisper, grabbing a jacket from the newel post and thrusting it at him. Gavin lingered reluctantly, part of him telling him to stay and defend her, whatever the consequences, the other knowing she was right, and that by staying he was placing them both in danger.

"But I can't abandon you, for Christ's sake," he insisted as she pushed him relentlessly toward the top of the cellar stairs.

The doorbell clanged through the hall.

"Go," she whispered, eyes wild. "I beg of you. Do it for me, darling."

"I'll wait in the cellar."

"No." She shook her head desperately.

"Greta, I won't leave you to face this alone. I—"

"For goodness' sake, go, or you'll get us both killed." She shoved him down the stairs, but he held her.

"I love you, Greta. Remember. I'll be back, I promise." He gave her a last tight hug. "Where will I find you?"

"My aunt's—Louisa von Ritter in Lausanne." She touched his cheek as the doorbell rang a second time, then tore brusquely from his hold, closing the cellar door and locking it firmly behind her. He stood, powerless, his ear glued to it in helpless frustration, hearing the voices. Calm, friendly voices. There was obvious relief in the officer's tone. His heart beat fast as he debated what to do.

After what seemed like ages, he heard footsteps, the distant sound of shutters being closed and doors being shut. They're closing the house, he realized, trembling. They're taking her away. He raised his hand, about to bang the door down, but knew it was useless. The echo of the front door closing and the far-off rumble of the car's departure left him sinking to his knees on the cellar stairs, besieged by guilt and frustration, praying she would be all right.

It was impossible to absorb that, in a few short minutes, their magical world had fallen apart, disappeared, whisked from beneath them like a tablecloth sending china flying in every direction. It seemed unbelievable that less than two hours earlier she had been lying comfortably in his arms, wondering whether or not to bake today. Now cold reality and doubt seeped through the damp stone steps. Perhaps he should have stood firm and taken her with him. They could have not answered the door, pretended no one was there, escaped together into the forest. He buried his face in his hands. Why had he allowed her to persuade him?

Because instinctively he knew she'd be safer without him. Slowly he drew his head up and rose, leaning against the wall, pulling himself together little by little. It was better for her this way. It was the right thing. He could manage on his own, but taking her with him would have made her a criminal. He reached up and tried the door one last time, knowing full well that it was locked and there was little choice left but to follow Greta's instructions.

He felt his way numbly down the steps, lighting the small gas lamp at the bottom, his eyes seeking the safe tucked between two casks to his right. Should he take the money? Yet what choice did he have? He braced himself and, crossing the cellar, opened it as Greta had instructed him. Stuffing his pockets with French francs, German marks and British pounds, he then searched for a bag to carry some food with him. He found a sack of flour and emptied it in a corner. After giving it a good shake, he filled it with sausages, dried meat, a bottle of red wine and some cheese. At least that would keep him going for a while.

Reluctantly he picked up the loden shooting jacket Greta had thrown at him and put out the lamp, afraid it might set fire to the place. Reaching for the secret lock on the panel in the wall, he waited, his pulse racing anxiously. What if it didn't open? He would be trapped alive in this dark, dank dungeon of a place... But it sprang open promptly and he delved into the blinding darkness.

Banging his head hard on the low ceiling, he saw stars and swore. After a while his eyes became accustomed to the dark. Thanks to Greta's tender care, his thigh and hip were much better. Thank God, for the narrow passage was so cramped there were places he could barely crawl. But he ignored the musty, festering smell, the fleeting shadows and scuttle of vermin, determined to reach his goal.

"Voilà!" The waitress's singsong voice brought him back to the present with a bang, and he blinked for a moment at the croissant and large, chipped cup of milky-brown coffee on the counter. Then he smiled and thanked her before dipping the tip of the flaky crescent pastry carefully into the beverage, relishing the moment.

"Are you from near here?" she asked coquettishly.

"No. I'm from Limoges. Ever been there?" He grinned, sinking his teeth into the soft, buttery texture, willing it to last, not knowing when he'd see another. The change in his pocket had dwindled to a few coins, just enough to get him to Nancy, where he hoped to meet up with a British or American convoy and rejoin his regiment.

"I've never been far away at all," the girl answered wistfully. "Why aren't you at the war?"

"I was wounded at Chemin des Dames," he lied. "Most of us were. I'm just getting back on my feet. I'm off to join my regiment."

"I heard the Germans are trying to get to Paris," she said in a sober voice. "They have a terrible cannon that shoots from miles." She shuddered, apparently glad to be many miles away.

"Well, now that the Americans are here, that should help."

"Oh, *oui! Les Américains.* Aren't they wonderful? I met one. He was so handsome." She giggled and looked at him from under her lashes. "But he didn't speak any French, so I couldn't talk to him. Do you think the Allies will win the war?"

He was saved from answering by the distant chuffing of the train entering the station. "Here." He shoved some change in her direction. "It was nice meeting you. *Au revoir.*"

"Au revoir, et bonne chance." She sent him a wistful wave,

wishing him good luck as he headed for the platform where the train, packed with soldiers heading north to the battlefields, wheezed to a shuddering stop. Not many passengers alighted, and before long the stationmaster announced *tous les passagers à bord.*

It took some time to find a seat, but finally Gavin squeezed in between a fat woman in a threadbare green coat that reeked of garlic, and a sniveling toddler who proceeded to wipe his nose on Gavin's trouser leg. He glanced through the foggy window as the train heaved out of the station, then leaned back, his thoughts picking up where he'd left off before the croissant. Soon the monotonous rattling of the carriage sent him into a doze and his memories drifted back, into the thick of the forest.

Panting, Gavin emerged from the tunnel and sat against a tree trunk, exhausted, his hip nagging. He wiped away the grime and spiderwebs before squinting at the few thin slivers of sunlight piercing the heavy, dark fir trees. Realizing the sun was his only compass, he knew his best bet was to head south and try to reach Switzerland, which Greta had said was less than one hundred kilometers away.

They'd had no reports of the war during their blissful interlude at Schloss Annenberg, as though nothing existed but their own idyllic world. But as he began to trudge through the forest, reality loomed, stark and menacing. He was an escaped prisoner of war on enemy territory, alone in the vast ominous silence of the forest, with only a pocketful of foreign currency and odd glimpses of setting sun for company.

Night descended, damp and chilly, and he searched for a dry spot, glad of the heavy loden jacket. Alert despite his fatigue, he listened intently to the noises of the forest, the scuttling and scurrying, the distant howl of wolves and the eerie echoes, wishing for the sound of Greta humming in the kitchen, the crackle of logs in the huge fireplace, all that they'd shared over the past months.

Finally exhaustion won and he slept, waking early to the twittering chatter of birds, scampering rabbits and deer grazing peacefully in a clearing close by.

He walked on for several days, checking the sun every so often, careful to stick to the depths of the forest. Progress was difficult, and after a few days his food dwindled to a last nibble of hard sausage. Hunger twisted his gut until he thought he would die if he didn't eat. It was then he remembered Miles's knife, which he kept as the stark reminder of a mistake he would carry with him always. He unsheathed it, averting his gaze from the lethal blade, realizing he had little choice but to use it. Either he hunted for rabbit or deer, or he'd starve to death.

After several hours of stalking warily, he cornered an unsuspecting rabbit. Soon the smell of roasting meat sizzling over a small campfire filled the air around him.

As the days passed, the landscape changed; the trees became sparser, until open country and vineyards stretched before him. Trying to find his bearings, he was careful to stay concealed from the narrow road that wound among the orderly rows of vines standing like toy soldiers under a clear blue sky.

Three days without food and water had left him so weak he could barely stand. Still he ventured out into the open, driven by hunger and the knowledge that to survive he must move forward despite the risk. Praying the border was nearby, he crouched low among the vines, staying clear of a distant village. Then, unable to take a step farther, he collapsed onto the dank earth and slept.

When he woke, Gavin knew at once that he was not alone. He held his breath, lest the person realize he was awake. Then, to his amazement, he heard an exchange in French.

"Frère Siméon, do you think we should take him back with us?" a ponderous voice with a rolling Provençal accent asked.

He was answered in clipped, cultivated, if somewhat irritated, Parisian tones. "Of course we must take him, Frère Benedict. We can hardly leave him here."

"Eh, non," the other voice agreed.

Gavin risked squinting upward. His gaze met with a brown habit stretched to its limit over a large girth.

"Allons, come along, *mon frère,"* the Parisian voice urged. "We haven't got all day. You take his feet and I'll get his shoulders."

Gavin felt Angus's cross in his pocket and, with a quick prayer, made a snap decision. If he hadn't been so afraid, he would have laughed at the sight of Frère Benedict's bulbous blue eyes popping out of his face, when all at once Gavin sat up.

"Ah! I see you aren't injured after all, *mon jeune ami,"* said the tall, thin friar whom he presumed was Frère Siméon.

"Non, mon Père. I was injured but I am better now."

"He speaks French!" Frère Benedict exclaimed, leaning forward, his eyes wider than ever.

"So I gather," Frère Siméon replied patiently. "What are you doing here?"

"Where am I? In France?"

"Unfortunately not. You are not far from the Bodensee, near the Swiss border, but still very much on German territory. Thus I recommend we do not linger. If you are indeed French, we cannot take the risk that you are found."

"Thank you," Gavin replied gratefully. "I am a British soldier. I escaped from a prisoner-of-war camp some time ago." He began rising painfully.

Frère Siméon looked around quickly. "If we should encounter anyone, you must pretend to be drunk. Here, lean on me as though you are having difficulty walking."

Gavin was so tired and weak he could barely stand. His wound had begun to ache once more and walking was difficult. Slowly they made their way through the vineyard toward a gracious manor house that stood on a slight rise, surrounded by vines. Its ancient walls were a soft vanilla yellow, and under the gabled slate roof the windows were arched and numerous. Hidden to the left stood a beautiful baroque chapel.

"Is this a monastery?" he asked.

"No. It is the estate of Baron von Lorsheid, a good Catholic, who suggested we move here when our monastery came under fire. There are several French and Italian monks among us. The locals do not bother us much. They are mostly devout, God-fearing folk."

"And the war?" Gavin asked, leaning perilously on Frère Siméon's shoulder. "What is happening?"

"Things are very bad. There is very little food and much talk of defeat among the Germans. I don't think it can last much longer. There are too many dead, too many hungry, and no desire to fight. All these poor souls want is their life back." He shook his head. "I've heard rumors that the Americans are repelling the enemy with the British and the French. Be careful." Frère Siméon held Gavin's arm tightly as he stumbled, dizzy. By the time they reached the heavy oak door of the manor, he was ready to collapse.

"Come inside, *mon ami,* but do not speak. And, Frère Benedict, do not mention that— What is your name?"

"Gavin, Gavin MacLeod."

"That is no good." Frère Siméon frowned. "Too British. We shall name you Johannes. Frère Benedict—" he turned and looked pointedly at the other monk "—this is Johannes. Will you remember that?"

"But he just said—"

"The good Lord has asked us to forget what he just said and has instructed us to call him by the name of Johannes," he said pointedly.

Frère Benedict scratched the balding patch on the crown of his head, eyelids blinking rapidly. Then he nodded and shrugged. "*Eh, bon!* If it is the Lord's wish…"

"It is," Frère Siméon replied emphatically.

Reaching a staircase Frère Siméon turned once more. "Brother, please find him a habit. One that will fit," he added, looking Gavin over with a smile. "You must be very tired and hungry."

Three monks walked toward them as they reached the gallery, and Gavin stiffened warily. But Frère Siméon merely smiled and nodded. "There is nothing to be feared from our own brethren, but we must keep you hidden from the village folk. The risk of discovery is too great. For us all," he added dryly. Gavin shivered, thinking of Franz and Greta, and the risks they had taken for his sake.

The sudden wheezing and jolting of the train as it pulled into the station at Nancy woke him, and the dreams disappeared abruptly as he joined the bustle. Leaning over, the woman seated beside him told him that Nancy was a town of *anarchistes* and *révolutionnaires*.

After some questioning, he was told the most likely spot to find an army lorry heading north was the Place Stanislas. Four hours later he was squeezed in the back of a canvas-covered truck with twenty-five French soldiers on their way to join the forces near the Sambre. There, the Americans and British armies were repelling the Germans. From the soldiers' enthusiasm, Gavin ascertained that they considered the war would soon be over. They laughed, told raucous jokes, shared their black-tobacco cigarettes with him and passed round a bottle of cognac.

He tried to get information on the British troop movements up near Arras, but no one knew much about what the British were up to. It was *les Américains* they were interested in, for apparently the Germans were terrified of them. One soldier gave a dramatic description of American G.I.s bursting out of nowhere in hordes, with such enthusiasm that the mere sight of them sent the Germans into flight. There was boisterous laughter, and the bottle of cognac made the rounds again. All the while, Gavin racked his brains for the best way to get back to his battalion.

The excitement was contagious. Perhaps Angus would be there and all would be resolved. Flora and the family would finally know he was all right. The thought of Flora made him somewhat ashamed. If the truth be told, he'd barely remembered her since the months with Greta. For the first time, he wondered what he was going to do. He had asked Flora to marry him, yet he had promised Greta that he would return for her.

Conflicted, his mind was kept busy with the dilemma until the truck chuffed up a hill and came to an abrupt halt. There were exclamations, groans and expletives from the men. Gavin leaned out of the back to see what was going on. Then he heard English voices. Without a second thought he clambered over the men and jumped off the truck, heading hastily toward a group of three officers, realizing at once they were American. One turned and he grabbed the chance to speak to him.

"Excuse me, are you heading to the front?"

"Sure are," the man replied, eyeing him curiously.

"Can I get a lift from you? I'm trying to rejoin my regiment. I'm Captain Gavin MacLeod of the Fifty-first Highlanders. I was taken prisoner and escaped." He straightened his shoulders.

"A lift?" The man raised an eyebrow and scrutinized Gavin's peasant clothes and unshaven chin.

"He means a ride," his fellow officer put in with a grin. "What's your name?"

"Captain MacLeod of the Fifty-first Highlanders." Gavin saluted smartly, hoping they'd believe him.

"Sounds good enough to me. Jump in the truck. Say, I don't suppose you understand this gibberish?" He nodded toward a flustered French lieutenant.

"As a matter of fact, I do."

"Lord be praised. Gimme a hand over here, will you?"

To everyone's relief, Gavin began translating the conversation. The Americans were suitably impressed.

"Boy, you're good. How did you learn Frog?" a gum-chewing soldier asked.

"My mother's French."

"Great. I'm Colonel Bill Donovan, First American Army, New York Sixty-ninth Regiment. We're heading to St. Mihiel. That's where the heat's on right now. The Frogs need help." He gave Gavin a speculative look. "We could use a guy like you around. I don't suppose you'd consider joining our unit for a while before returning to your own?"

"I'd be delighted," he replied without the slightest hesitation. They were headed in the right direction and that was all that mattered.

Jumping in the new American truck, they began the journey north. Soon Gavin was learning all that had occurred over the past months: the big German offensive, Ludendorff's penetration of France and how Big Bertha—a gun with a range of seventy-five miles—was *terrifying the shit* out of Paris. In June the marines had denied the Germans access to the road to Rheims which, had it been captured, would have doubled their railway capacity. The Americans laughed and joked, telling him the already legendary story of what the marines had said when the Frogs wanted them to retreat: *Retreat? Hell no, we just got here.* Thanks to them, the Germans were having a hard time feeding their troops.

"Can't fight on an empty belly," Donovan remarked, reminding Gavin of his own hunger.

"They're starving to death back in Germany," he told them, recounting his exploits since he escaped from the hospital. He left out the part about Greta but mentioned the monks who had helped him get to Switzerland. "The German people and army are exhausted. Hindenburg and Ludendorff are no longer the national heroes they once were. All they want is a peace treaty. They can't survive much longer."

The First American Army was deployed just south of Verdun, facing the waterlogged territory of the St. Mihiel salient that had been held by the enemy since 1914. After a long ride, they reached the base and Gavin tasted his first hamburger—a mouthwatering experience. As he munched, Donovan called in a private.

"Get this man a uniform," he instructed. "A captain's uniform," he added with a wink.

Gavin grinned, gripped by the dynamic American energy and the natural confidence the troops exuded, so different from the fatigued British and French armies that were stretched to the limit of endurance. He felt energized and alive, and after more French fries, ready to fight.

Later, donning the uniform they had found him, he glanced at the name on the jacket. Captain Dexter Ward, New York Sixty-ninth. He experienced a moment of hesitation, then put it on. For an instant he wondered how Ward had died, and felt strange about stepping into a dead man's shoes. He fingered the dog tags forgotten in the pocket, wondering if he should hand them over. Then he cocked an eye at himself in the small shaving mirror, holding it back far enough to get a good look. He wondered if he should add an American twang to complete the image. It wouldn't be too hard, accustomed as he was to chopping and changing languages with ease. All at once he slipped the dog tags on his wrist, then saluted smartly. If he was going to borrow Captain Ward's identity, he'd better do it right.

The overwhelming need to return to his unit had diminished against the enthusiasm and excitement surrounding him; the thought of rejoining the worn-out British army and perhaps having to face the problem of Flora was simply less enticing than where he was. He felt a sudden pang of guilt as he took a last look in the mirror. Then, with a shrug, he turned on his heel. He'd get back eventually and solve his problems. Just later, rather than sooner.

* * *

The first all-American offensive began mid-September. In the first day of fighting, from behind a barrage of guns, they caught the Germans by complete surprise, capturing over thirteen thousand prisoners and four hundred guns.

Gavin was posted as liaison. His months in Germany had allowed him to pick up some of the language and, in addition to his knowledge of French, he quickly became an essential part of Donovan's team. Translating and resolving misunderstandings, he was fascinated by how different the two cultures were and the essential diplomacy involved. He did not feel it necessary, however, to inform his American counterparts that, although the French acknowledged their *moral superbe*, they pettily attributed their success to German weakness rather than American efficiency.

When they learned of the Wilson peace proposals, which demanded unconditional surrender, the atmosphere became one of anticipation. Gavin loved the American spirit and was instantly at home with their frank, easygoing style, their courage and matter-of-fact manner. Each time an opportunity arose for him to return to his own sector, an excuse came up and he left it for the next time, certain there would always be another opportunity.

October brought the news they had longed to hear for so many years; the Germans had called for an armistice and desired a peace settlement. On November 11, the guns were finally silenced.

By the time Gavin's troop reached Rheims, he and the other men were simply living in the present, and joined the frenzied reveling of the battered city, exulting in a riotous explosion of overjoyed relief. Girls flung themselves around the Americans' necks, champagne corks flew and golden froth gushed over the pavements, bathing them in the sparkling wine. Rheims had opened her cellars and her heart, and the air was alive with joy and excitement. Bottles were shoved into their hands as the liberators drove, victorious, through the streets of the tattered city.

Soon it became impossible to drive and Gavin found himself on the sidewalk, a bottle in one hand and a pretty brunette clinging to him, her mouth avidly seeking his. He had no problem obliging. But when he raised his head and searched the milling crowd, he realized the others had been swept into the throng. The girl was dragging his hand relentlessly, thrilled he spoke French. He took a last look at the swarm then shrugged, realizing it would be like looking for a needle in a haystack. He'd meet up with Donovan and the others later, when the excitement died down. Right now the feel of the girl's body and her pliable lips were tantamount to delirium.

Throwing an arm protectively over her shoulders, he followed her into a side street, where she stopped just long enough to kiss him and press her body closer before pulling him into the shattered remains of a rooming house. His mind went blank as her body melded to his, tasting champagne and the intoxication of victory, the need to plunder all that mattered now.

As he took another swig from the bottle and followed her up the creaking stairway to the second floor, he could already picture her moving below him, barely seeing the shabby room with the paint peeling off the splintered walls as he began pulling off his jacket. Vague thoughts of Greta and Flora gave him a moment's guilt that dwindled rapidly as the girl shooed a large tabby cat from the bed and twirled invitingly, her eyes twinkling mischievously under a mop of chestnut curls.

She unbuttoned her blouse, the material sliding off her slowly, until at last it fell to the floor. Greta and Flora were forgotten as he watched her nipples harden. He reached for her, hungry for the touch of her skin, the feel of something soft and female, the softness of her body a panacea to the death and destruction of the past months. Her hand reached for him and he pulled her toward the bed as she undressed him eagerly, her fingers running provocatively down his chest, forgetting everything but the overwhelming desire to claim the victor's prize, to plunge deep within her and obliterate reality.

It was dark when he awoke, but the sound of celebrating continued in the streets below. He glanced at the naked girl breathing softly at his side and realized he didn't know her name. Nor did he want to. He got up quickly and dressed, anxious to get away, to find the others and get on with his plan to send a cablegram home to his parents. It would have to wait until tomorrow, he realized, pulling on his shirt and glancing through the shattered window at the street below, where a young couple stood kissing in the glow of a remaining street lamp.

He turned and looked at the girl, still fast asleep, wondering if he should leave her money. She might be insulted. On the other hand, perhaps it was expected. In the end, he found an empty jam jar and stuffed some bills and a note inside, that read *Thanks for a wonderful night. Please buy something to remember it by.* Running down the rickety stairs, he avoided the weary gray-haired concierge who mumbled crossly as she swept the remnants of the previous night from the dingy hall.

As soon as he stepped into the street, he realized the city was still celebrating, drunk with relief. He stared at the crowds and wondered how he was going to find the others. He made his way down the Rue Gambetta, through the bombed buildings and debris, and headed for the Boulingrin, a restaurant he had heard Colonel Donovan say had the best French fries in town.

Arriving at the bistro, he peered through a throng of Allied uniforms and girls in their Sunday best, hanging at their heros' necks. Determinedly, he made his way slowly but persistently to the counter, where he managed to squeeze into an empty spot. He was immediately handed a glass of champagne. He smiled his thanks to the bartender and turned, hoping to begin a conversation with the two British officers standing next to him.

But before he could speak, someone grabbed his arm. Once she had his attention, a pretty redhead with a provocative smile and ruby lips reached up and kissed him full on the mouth.

"Oy, you're with me," an outraged cockney voice exclaimed.

"*Non!*" the young woman exclaimed with a provocative pout. "*Moi,* I like *Américains.*" As she gazed up at Gavin and slipped her arms around his neck, the man's face reddened angrily.

"Oh ye do, do ye? Let's see how ye like this." Gavin tried to disengage himself from the girl's grasp, but the more he tried the more tightly she clung. As the full force of the man's fist crashed into the right side of his face, Gavin reeled back, flying against the counter with the girl squealing on top of him. He picked himself up painfully, his right eye closing fast. Through the other he saw four marines rising, balling their fists, while two British Tommy's prepared to back their mate. Then all hell broke loose.

One marine swung at the officer beside him, and after that it was mayhem. Chairs flew, bottles crashed, girls screamed and waiters yelled. The last thing he saw before being knocked out cold was the barman, swearing rapidly and smashing an empty champagne bottle over the head of a drunk marine.

9

Isle of Skye, Scotland, 1918

It seemed strange to be married in November, Flora reflected, looking out across the sea from her perch on the window seat where she sat curled up among the old chintz cushions. Tomorrow she and Angus would be married. It was the right thing. The only thing she could do for him, now that Gavin and Uncle Hamish were gone, for he'd never manage on his own, and Gavin would have expected it of her.

Still, it seemed unreal. But then, everything seemed unreal, even Gavin's death. She was still not able to register that he would never again walk into a room, his eyes glinting in that unique way, inviting her on some impossible adventure. She turned and stared at the door as though he might suddenly materialize. She didn't feel his death—she never had. Of course, hoping he might be alive was wishful thinking. She knew that. But still... Even the memorial service and the engraving on the family tombstone, next to Uncle Hamish's name, hadn't made it sink in.

And tomorrow she was to become Angus's wife. She tried to suppress her sadness. Being his companion, helping him with the estate and doing her duty by him were one thing. But the other... She clasped her arms tight, pulling her heather-colored cardigan tight as a shudder went through her. How was she going to react when he... She closed her eyes and tried desperately not to think about tomorrow night or the grief of being anyone but Gavin's.

She sighed and turned again toward the churning gray waters that smashed against the rocks below. The lump in her throat, which surfaced so often of late, returned. The last thing she wanted was to hurt Angus's feelings. On returning from France, after learning of Uncle Hamish's sudden death, she had agreed to be married as soon as possible, and she was determined not to spoil it for him.

It was dark and misty outside. In the distance, a small fishing vessel bobbed on the horizon, heading into port. Flora listened to the rush of the wind and the gulls squawking overhead. She heard Millie barking in the distance as she gazed across the leaden November waters, feeling as if part of her had remained in the Somme with Gavin, leaving her distant, as though in another world.

It was hard to show enthusiasm for the lovely trousseau that Tante Constance had lovingly chosen, all the while lamenting that it could not be bought in Paris. She hated standing for hours while dressmakers pinned her wedding dress and fussed. Angus had presented her with a beautiful ring that had belonged to his great-grandmother and which Tante had suggested for their engagement. When he had slipped it onto her finger, she had shuddered, forcing back the tears in an attempt to show a happy front. She was determined not to think of what might have been, but that was proving impossible. Each folded sheet, each delicately embroidered pillowcase where the wrong initials entwined were an agonizing reminder of the nights she would never spend in Gavin's arms.

She watched the boat disappear from view with a sigh. Tante would have a list of last-minute things to go over before the formal dinner tonight. Oncle Eustace, Tante Hortense, Cousin Eugène, René and little Geneviève, who was to be a bridesmaid, had arrived earlier in the day and were resting in their apartments on the second floor.

The wedding was to be a small affair, for which she was thankful. She couldn't have handled a huge ceremony, the pomp of a cathedral. The tiny chapel erected at Strathaird four centuries ago was beautiful, and would make the event bearable, even though the place was permeated with memories of Gavin. She smiled and a tear rolled down her cheek as she remembered eating apples with him under the altar, his foot nudging hers as he tried to make her giggle during Mass.

She wiped her face and wandered reluctantly down the wide oak staircase, wondering if she was right to be marrying one man while mourning another. Should she call the whole thing off while there was still time, she wondered, stopping on the landing and gazing up at a portrait of Struan MacLeod, Gavin's great-grandfather. Those same twinkling eyes met hers and she swayed in sudden panic, as though he were there before her.

"Are you all right?"

"Oh! Goodness!"

Eugène, tall and slim, stood solicitously next to her in his black priest's robes. "You gave me a fright," she exclaimed, trying to smile.

"*Je m'excuse,* Flora. You seemed so...sad. Is there anything I can do?"

She thought, then smiled. "Will you take my confession?"

"I'm afraid I can't. I'm not fully ordained yet. But if you wish, we can talk and I will give my vow of secrecy."

"I would like that. Perhaps we could go for a walk after tea, or up to the old drawing room."

He nodded, with the understanding smile that made him appear so much older than his years. "Your dreamery. I remember."

She nodded, blushing. "It's a place I feel comfortable. Do you mind?"

"Not at all, *chère cousine.* Shall we join the others for tea? Afterward we can slip away and have our chat."

"Thank you, Eugène." She took his hand and their eyes met. "You're going to be a wonderful priest. You truly care about others."

"I will try my best," he said, seeming suddenly younger

again. "That is all we can do, dear Flora, our best. God knows that, I am certain."

She nodded silently, and together they descended the stairs, then crossed the great hall to Tante's salon, where voices and the tinkle of fine porcelain could be heard.

Part Two

1918–1932

That no cause, indeed, of this killing art thou? Who shall be the witness-bearer?

—Robert Browning
The Agamemnon of Aeschylus

10

∽∽∽ ❦ ∽∽∽

The *Mauritania,* 1918

"Hey, Doc, our boy's wakin' up. And he ain't ramblin' on like he was."

"What? You mean he's not delusional any longer?"

"I dunno," the other voice responded doubtfully. "At least he's quiet."

Somewhere in the distance, Gavin heard the conversation and slowly opened his eyes.

"Hey, buddy, good to see you lookin' better. Feelin' okay?"

"Uh, yes. I—" Gavin blinked and looked about, realizing he was in a bunkbed. He frowned, trying to remember but unable to think clearly. "Where am I?" he asked the young American orderly standing next to him in a white coat.

"On the boat. We're goin' home. Before you know it, you'll be back in Oklahoma City."

"Oklahoma City?" Gavin sat up with a start and banged his head on the upper bunk. "Damn," he exclaimed, rubbing the bump that began to form immediately.

"Easy does it, boy. Take it slowly. You ain't been too good these past few days. But, in a way, you're lucky. If you hadn't ended up where you did, you might have been shipped to England. You would have waited another couple of months before gettin' home."

"But there must be a mistake. You see, I'm Captain Gavin MacLeod of the Fifty-first Scottish—"

"Yeah, yeah, we know, bud. Just take it easy." The man turned and Gavin heard him murmur in a low voice to the doctor. "Looks like he still doesn't remember who he is. Better give him a shot."

"There's nothing wrong with me at all," Gavin protested. "Where the hell am I?"

"Now, don't worry." The orderly gave him a soothing pat on the shoulder. "Everything'll be just dandy. You've had a nasty injury and you've been raving. All we want is for you to remember who you are."

"I know damn well who I am. This is ridiculous." Realization began to dawn on Gavin. "I was given an American uniform, that's all."

"Right. An' I'm Yankee Doodle. Look, buddy. Your dog tags confirm it—you're Dexter Ward from Oklahoma City, no two ways about it. You've had concussion and you're delusional. It'll do that to you sometimes. Bottom line is, we'll be dockin' in New York in eight days, then you'll be able to make your way back home. I'll bet there's a cute little girl waiting for you back home. C'mon, Captain, there's no reason to get agitated."

"But—" Before he could continue, Gavin felt a needle being jabbed into his upper arm. Suddenly hazy, he couldn't seem to explain to them the mix-up.

The next time he woke was at dawn. The other bunks were filled with sleeping bodies. Rising quietly, he slipped on his uniform—or rather, Captain Ward's uniform—then made his way out of the cabin and up the steps, listening to the smooth purr of the powerful engines. He realized he truly was aboard a big ship and that it was not a nightmare after all. He was sailing to America. He glanced out a porthole but there was no sign of land, only inky water blending with dark gray sky for as far as he could see. He climbed up on deck, hit by a sudden rush of wind as he advanced toward the railing. Leaning on the polished teak, Gavin stared past the lifeboats at the wake that skimmed the dark waters in a frothy rush alongside the ship.

He gazed at the ocean, his heartbeat rapid. What was he going to do? He needed to get home; instead, he was being taken farther and farther away from his destination. The sea offered him few answers, and after a while he decided to investigate further, suddenly curious about the layout of the ship. Somehow despite himself, he couldn't help a rush of excitement at the thought of going to the United States. He recalled Bill Donovan and the other men he'd met, how at ease he'd felt in their company. As he strode around the empty deck, Gavin wondered whether fate had sent him in this new direction for a purpose. Whatever the reasons, he resolved, there was little he could do to change his situation. He unfolded a deck chair and stretched his long legs, wishing he had a smoke. Minutes later, the door opened and he hailed the man coming on deck.

"Say, do you have a cigarette?"

"Sure." The man offered him his pack. "Need a light?"

"Sure," Gavin replied, immediately falling back into the soft American lilt he had acquired during his time with the New York Sixty-ninth Regiment. There seemed little use telling his true story, as nothing could be done and it seemed no one believed him. Instead, Gavin decided in his spontaneous way, he would simply enjoy the adventure.

"Boy, am I glad to be getting home. Didn't think I was gonna make it out of that hellhole alive," the young man remarked with an engaging smile. "Mind if I sit?"

"Go right ahead," Gavin replied, welcoming the company and liking the tall, blond, green-eyed American on sight.

"Thanks. I'm Johnny Harcourt." He stretched out a hand.

Gavin hesitated a split second before responding. "Dexter Ward. New York Sixty-ninth."

"Good to meet you. What are you planning to do when we dock?"

"I haven't decided yet," Gavin answered frankly.

"Where're you from?"

"Oklahoma."

"Oklahoma? You sound more like a New Englander—
maybe Boston."

"My mother was from Boston," he answered hastily, deciding to kill her off. Perhaps it would be easier if he didn't have
a family to return to in Oklahoma; then he could justify staying
in New York. "Where are you from?" The chap had the same
clean-cut, frank look about him that he'd noticed in several of
the Americans he'd met.

"New York City, born and raised. Best place in the world,
except Paris."

"You like Paris?"

"I love Paris. When there's not a war on, that is. I used to
go over quite a bit. My father has a porcelain business in
France."

"Really?" Gavin felt a twinge of surprise. Then, all at once,
something jangled in his memory. His uncle Eustace had mentioned the Harcourt factories and their business relationship
with both la Vallière and the Haviland family, the enterprising
Americans whose dinner services graced the tables of royal
houses and the White House. It was all vague and hazy, but
the connection made sense. "Where is the porcelain made?"
he asked casually.

"Place called Limoges in southwestern France. Boring as
hell. France to me is Paris. What women." Johnny leaned back,
stretched out his legs and took a long drag from his cigarette.
"And the city itself. There's something special about it—the
avenues, Faubourg Saint-Honoré, Montmartre, you name it."
He sighed dreamily. "Do you sail?"

"Yes."

"Where, Cape Cod?"

"Uh-huh." Gavin wished he knew where the hell he was
talking about. Miss Linton and her geography classes sprang
to mind. He pushed aside thoughts of Flora, Strathaird, Greta,
his family, and the whole damn mess.

"What business are your folks in? Guess there's a lot of
wheat and farming around Oklahoma?"

"Uh, yes. A lot. In fact, that's precisely what my folks are
into," he replied blandly, more interested in the subject of

chinaware, which had always fascinated him. As a child he had spent hours investigating the huge kilns, watching as the delicate designs were painted on the unfinished wares before entering the huge ovens for a second firing. "Do you speak French?"

"Me?" Johnny laughed, showing a row of even, white teeth. "Nah. I've no talent for languages. My dad's been back and forth quite a bit and he makes himself understood, but not me. I'm no good at any of that."

"It must be a fascinating business, though. My—" He was about to say, "My uncle probably knows your father," but stopped himself in time. Poor Dexter Ward's uncle was probably threshing wheat in Oklahoma, grieving the absence of his nephew.

"Fascinating? Do you really think so?" Johnny cocked his head and grimaced. "I never thought too much about it. I prefer to sail and play polo, myself. Do you play?" His eyes lit up hopefully.

"I have."

"Great. Maybe we can play before you go back to Oklahoma."

Gavin made a sudden decision. After all, Johnny seemed a damned nice chap, and he was the only human being he knew in America. Perhaps Johnny's father even knew his uncle. "I'm not returning to Oklahoma."

"You're not?"

"My parents died shortly before the war. I'm an only child, so there's not much to go back to. We had a few losses before the war." He shrugged, feeling like a dismal liar.

"I'm sorry." Johnny looked truly concerned. "So what are you gonna do?"

"I'm not sure. Stick around New York, look for a job, I suppose."

"Well, why don't you be my guest? It'd be a pleasure to have you, Dexter." Johnny gave him a wide-open smile that lit up his whole face, and Gavin felt doubly deceitful, taken aback by this spontaneous demonstration of hospitality. Accepting it under false pretenses seemed patently wrong.

"That's very kind. Thanks for the offer."

"A pleasure. Come on. Let's take a look at the old girl. The *Mauritania,* holder of the blue ribbon. Wouldn't mind cruisin' on her, once she's refitted and running again."

"The *Mauritania?*" Gavin exclaimed. "I went to see her launched in 1907, with my father and...."

"You went from Oklahoma to Scotland to see the *Mauritania?*" Johnny glanced at him, obviously impressed, while Gavin bit his reckless tongue. Adopting another identity and leaving the past behind wasn't going to be as easy as he'd thought, he realized, finagling his way out of his blunder.

They rose and wandered about the deck, stepping aside for a group of runners led by a severe-looking sergeant, and avoided a heated baseball discussion brewing on the quarter-deck. Johnny chatted enthusiastically, and after breakfast, under a cloudy, chilly sky, they headed to the sports deck and played badminton, which later progressed to cards. Gavin quickly realized that under Johnny's innocent exterior lay a shrewd poker player. He played warily himself, careful not to show his own skills, and not getting in too deep.

The trip sped by fast after that. Johnny knew every amusing character on board, every poker player, and seemed to have an unlimited stock of whiskey and brandy.

On the morning they were to dock, Gavin rose at dawn, too excited to sleep. As he walked out onto the deck, he realized he was not alone. Thousands stood, braced against the icy wind, peering impatiently through the dense fog for their first glimpse of home.

His thoughts were also of home, and what he had to do as soon as he landed in this foreign land. Nevertheless, he was excited, anxious for his first glimpse of the country he'd been inadvertently steered to and which seemed extraordinarily enticing.

All at once the ship went silent, except for the steady rumble of the engines. His eyes narrowed, following those of the others, all glued to a thin strip of land emerging through the foggy December dawn.

Then the spell broke as a single voice traveled, loud and clear, and he listened, gripped by a curious thrill.

O beautiful for spacious skies,
For amber waves of grain,
For purple mountain majesties
Above the fruited plain!

The voice reached across the ship, pure and haunting, as Long Island emerged and the land of the free opened her arms, welcoming home her victors. Eyes damp and voices raw, they joined in the resounding chorus:

America, America!
God shed His grace on thee,
And crown thy good
With brotherhood
From sea to shining sea.

Every man stood to attention as the fog began to lift from the somber waters. Someone shouted, ''We're home!'' and backslapping and laughter followed. Soon the day had cleared enough for him to distinguish the Statue of Liberty, standing proudly on the Manhattan skyline, as they sailed into New York harbor, to the awaiting cheers of an anxious, excited crowd awaiting the homecoming of their loved ones.

''Dad'll be there.'' Johnny squeezed next to him at the railing and searched the quay below. ''Maybe Alix, my sister, will be there too. Come on, you're coming home with me.''

Gavin hesitated, torn between his conscience and what he would do if he didn't accept the offer. ''Are you sure your family will want me? After all, you're just home from the war. They'll—''

''Shut up and let's make sure we're among the first to make it ashore,'' Johnny said with a grin.

They pushed their way through the tight group of soldiers being organized in lines for the docking. As they descended the gangway, Johnny gave a shout. ''There they are,'' he exclaimed, pointing to a tall, gray-haired man, dressed in a fine black coat and a cane, standing next to a young girl who was fashionably attired in a plum-colored cape with a large fur collar. Johnny waved vigorously as they pressed through the crowd.

Gavin stood back while Alix threw herself into her brother's warm embrace. Johnny's father waited proudly, wiping a tear from his eye before gripping his son's hand warmly. Then Johnny spoke to him and Gavin saw their eyes move in his direction. Feeling like a complete fraud, he shook the older man's hand and received a warm welcome.

"Mother's waiting for you at the house, Johnny—you know how she hates crowds," Mr. Harcourt said, shepherding them to a shining black Packard where a chauffeur stood nearby.

As they left the port, Gavin could only stare at New York, all worries and quandaries forgotten, entranced by the high buildings, the streets abuzz with vendors, paperboys, cars and pushcarts. As the city unfolded before his eyes, Gavin forgot his plan to send a telegram home in his awe at New York. He gazed up, fascinated, at the skyscrapers.

Soon they arrived at the Harcourts house in Sutton Place. Tilly Harcourt, an exquisitely-attired, wilting, blond beauty in her late thirties, awaited her son at the top of the steps. She extended her arms in a languid gesture of welcome. Gavin was surprised to see how much younger than her husband she seemed. He watched as she deposited two scented kisses on her son's cheeks and murmured her utter relief at his homecoming.

Careful not to crush her silk dress, she turned with a charming smile to Gavin. All at once, her emerald eyes sparkled and he hesitated, taken aback by their sudden radiance. She extended a fine white hand. Taking it, he felt the electricity. Looking hastily away, he met Alix's speculative brown gaze. During the drive home, he'd sensed that there was something strange about the girl. Maybe she was just shy, he concluded, hearing her mother scolding her and seeing her immediately lower her head in embarrassment. It must be hard, he reflected, to live in the shadow of a mother as beautiful and elegant as Tilly Harcourt. The group moved into the exquisite black-and-white marble hall, filled with rich furnishings, flower arrangements and antiques.

The butler instructed the maids on where to take the bags, but Tilly insisted on showing him his room herself. He felt slightly overwhelmed by the mass of blue and gold silk, and stood, cap in hand, admiring.

"Elsie de Wolf just finished redecorating last week," she purred excitedly. "You'll be the first guest to stay in it. Isn't that fun?" She twirled around, her laughter young and lovely. "I wish Johnny would let me re-do that dowdy old room of his, but of course he's just like his father and won't let me touch a thing." She glanced around the sumptuous room, once again the perfect hostess, her fingertips flitting to the string of pearls at her throat. "I do hope you'll be comfortable." She laid a feather touch on his arm and their eyes met. "I'm so glad you came."

"It's most kind of you to have me," he responded stiffly, horrified at the reaction caused by her fingers on his sleeve and the whiff of exotic perfume that radiated from her. Then he caught sight of Alix, watching from the landing, and drew his arm away abruptly. "I suppose I'd better get cleaned up."

"Of course." She patted his hand in a motherly fashion and he wondered if he'd imagined the sensual vision of moments earlier. "We'll be waiting in what the British call the drawing-room. You boys come on down when you're ready." She turned away. Seeing Alix, Tilly called to her. "Oh, Alix, dear, you can make yourself useful and show Dexter the way. I hope you'll be comfortable."

"Thanks."

Finally, the door closed. Gavin sat down gingerly on the luxurious bed, afraid of damaging the impeccable bedspread, and dropped his dark head into his hands. What was he going to do? If he analyzed his life, it was a mess. He was in these people's home under false pretenses, reacting in a most inappropriate way to his friend's mother, and had not even contacted his family, who believed him missing in action... The telegram. He must get to a telegraph office as soon as possible. Perhaps after lunch he could get Johnny to take him.

He dragged a hand through his thick black hair and rose to investigate the rest of the suite, impressed despite his worries. There was a small sitting room and a bathroom with a huge white marble tub and washbasin. He touched the polished bronze taps and looked at himself in the mirror, surprised at the subtle changes in his physique. The man staring back at him was not the young boy who'd gazed into the old, speckled cheval looking glass at Strathaird. His expression seemed so different, harder, difficult to define, his eyes older. He shrugged, then washed and changed into an extra uniform that had been rummaged from somewhere on the ship and were the only clothes he possessed. That was another problem—money was short. He only had the small amount handed to him, along with his ticket for Oklahoma City, by the army on leaving the ship.

Twenty minutes later Gavin accompanied Alix down the gilded staircase, taking a closer look at the thin, brown-eyed girl of seventeen, her mouse-colored hair scraped back into an unfashionable bun. She made no attempt at conversation as they descended.

In the drawing room, a large, high-ceilinged room decorated in flowered chintzes and splattered with valuable antiques, John Harcourt Sr. was popping a bottle of champagne. Tilly reclined gracefully among the plump pastel cushions of a small sofa, beneath an exquisite watercolor. Hastily, Gavin withdrew his eyes from the enchanting vision she made and joined Johnny and his father. Soon they were toasting Johnny's return, and welcoming him into their midst. He cringed inwardly as he raised his glass, wishing now that he'd told the truth, his conscience growing heavier by the minute.

"Johnny was telling me your folks have passed away," John Sr. said, his eyes sympathetic.

"Yes, sir."

"You don't sound midwestern. But then, Johnny told me

your mother's folks are from Boston and that you were brought up in England. That explains it."

Gavin gulped down more champagne and nodded.

"What was your mother's maiden name?"

"Harriman," he said, clearing his throat and throwing out the first name that came to mind, realizing he was getting in deeper and deeper. He didn't like it. It made him feel dishonest.

"Harriman." John paused thoughtfully, his eyes narrowing. "I used to know a Maxwell Harriman from Boston. Any relation to your mother?"

"I believe I've heard the name mentioned. My mother lost contact with her family after her marriage," he added quickly, putting an end to any more inquiries.

"A shame. But that's life, I suppose. No need for you to hasten home to Oklahoma, m'boy. You can spend Christmas with us."

"That's most kind, but I would hate to impose. I'm sure you want to enjoy your son's return."

"No, no, m'boy." John patted Gavin's shoulder in a fatherly manner. "Any friend of my son's is a friend of mine. We'll be only too glad to have you stay, won't we, Tilly?" He turned to his wife.

"Why, of course you must stay, Dexter," she murmured, smiling, then turned away. She continued her conversation with Johnny, who was seated next to her on the plump sofa, patiently answering her questions, while Gavin tried to overhear.

"Such terrible conditions, darling. I almost fainted when I got your letter telling us there were actually *rats* in that dreadful trench. So unhygienic, darling." She gave a dramatic shudder. Johnny looked up and caught Gavin's eye.

"Will you excuse me, Mother? I should attend to our guest."

"Of course, darling. Alix, dearest, get me some more champagne, will you?" She handed the girl her glass, her eyes never leaving Johnny.

"I hope you will stay for a while," Johnny said, drawing Gavin away from his father, who was pouring champagne into the flute Alix held. "I get pretty bored around here on my own. We could have a lot of fun. We'll go to the Hamptons for sailing, polo, golf. Parties, too. Now that the war's over and Christmas is around the corner, it'll be a blast.''

"Perhaps I will. By the way, I need to send a telegram. Do you know where the nearest telegraph office is?''

"Oh, don't worry about that. Just write it out and Robert—that's our butler—will see that it's taken care of.''

"Right.'' Gavin sighed inwardly. So much for that. There were no end to the difficulties. He would have to wait till tomorrow to try and find the office himself, for he couldn't possibly send a telegram to Scotland without raising suspicion. There was little use worrying about it now, so he joined the rest for lunch, determined to put the telegram out of his mind until the next day, when he'd find an excuse to leave the house.

11

Isle of Skye, Scotland, 1918

Flora climbed the stairs with all the trepidation of a bride and the grief of a widow, and walked toward the room, lovingly prepared by Tante Constance and the maids, as though to the scaffold. Angus would see to the last of the guests and then he would come. She entered the candlelit room and swallowed at the sight of the delicate lace nightgown, specially ordered from Bruges by Tante Hortense, lying on the satin bedspread, unable to suppress the tears she'd been holding back all day.

It should have been the happiest day of her life, but she had never felt so miserable, her mind beset by Gavin, her love and longing crushed under the weight of her marriage vows. Had she done right to marry Angus? Doubts assailed her as she slowly unbuttoned her wedding dress and slipped out of it. Hanging it on a satin hanger on the Chinese screen, she turned toward the bed where, in a little while, she would become another man's wife. She slid off the lace garter, suspenders and silk stockings and slipped on the nightgown, shivering. The soft touch of silk caressing her skin was only a reminder of how much she wished Gavin could be the one to remove it. Oh, if only tonight could have been theirs, and not this dreadful nightmare.

Again she swallowed, trying desperately to appease her inner conflict, when all at once something fell behind her. She spun round and gasped in horror. The wedding dress lay strewn on the carpet, and her heart missed a beat, Highland enough to recognize the bad omen. Seconds later she chided herself for her foolishness and picked it up, realizing she hadn't hung it up properly or even secured the buttons at the back. Of course the dress had fallen. Then she sat at the skirted dressing table, brushing her long chestnut hair with the silver brush as the minutes dragged.

She dreaded the footsteps she knew would soon come, her conscience guilty, feeling as though she were betraying Gavin. Yet, wasn't she fulfilling his last wish? And wasn't she doing right by helping Angus face the difficult turn his life had taken since his father's and Gavin's deaths?

A knock at the door made her jump and she braced herself, determined not to let her unhappiness show. It would not be fair to Angus. He had seemed so happy today, happier than she had seen him in many months.

"Come in," she called softly. The brush in her hand wavered as the door opened and Angus slumped in the doorway, whiskey spilling from the tumbler he clutched. He stumbled forward and Flora rose, all fear forgotten as she hastened toward him.

"Sorry, Flo, terribly sorry," he slurred as she led him gently to the bed, grabbing the tumbler just in time as he collapsed onto the satin eiderdown. "Wonderful wedding, Flo. Just wish Gavin had been there. Should've been there...should've been him, not me. Not fair. Should've..." The rest of the sentence died as his eyes closed and he fell fast asleep.

Flora shook her head, filled with sudden relief, and covered him tenderly with a blanket before blowing out the candles and slipping under the covers. Angus's heavy breathing and the sporadic whiffs of alcohol made her bury her face into the pillow, ashamed at her own relief. A wife should want her husband to make love to her. But what if that wife were in love with another man, who left no room for anybody or anything else? For whether Gavin was dead or alive made very little difference; he filled her existence just the same.

After a while she managed to unwind her overwrought senses, realizing she would need to be rested to deal with Angus's inevitable embarrassment in the morning.

12

New York, U.S.A., 1918

Weeks passed but still the telegram hadn't been sent. Between fittings at Johnny's tailor, at John Sr.'s insistence, attending one Christmas party after the next and being swooped into New York's giddy aftermath of war, he had little time for anything.

But reality had to be faced. He would probably have to tell Flora the truth about Greta, he realized gloomily, standing for a moment on the Harcourts' stairs, hating the uncomfortable feelings that jostled inside whenever the subject surfaced. Why couldn't life be simple? Perhaps if the damn war hadn't fallen upon them, he wouldn't have committed himself to Flora so hastily—not that he didn't love her. He supposed he did, but now there was Greta. And, for that matter, he hadn't asked for *her* to come into his life either, had he? It had just happened, and although he knew he had loved her too, each day she was fading into a hazy memory, against a life filled with novelty and excitement.

He descended the stairs, his heart heavy yet full of good intentions. He must leave the house immediately after breakfast and get on with what was necessary, whatever the consequences. It was bad enough accepting the Harcourts' hospitality under false pretenses; John Sr. had insisted on giving him a

loan—for he had refused to accept the gift of any money—
which he would pay back as soon as he got home.

He crossed the hall and headed toward the breakfast parlor,
torn between his duty and the fascinating life unfurling around
him, the city, the people and the intense interest he felt in John
Sr.'s business. He wished porcelain and not the MacLeod coal
empire was his destiny. A dull, grimy destiny, he realized somberly, remembering the shafts, the faces covered in grime, the
deep coughing and a grimness that always made him feel
guilty. He'd hated going down into the pits with his father. He
needed to be aboveground, in a colorful, fancy-free, creative
world, not among humdrum drudgery. Just thinking about it
made him feel claustrophobic.

As he reached the parlor, he thought longingly of the long
conversations he'd had with John Sr. His pertinent questions
regarding the porcelain business had thrilled the older man, and
made Gavin wish that Oncle Eustace were the one with the
coal factory and his father were at the helm in Limoges. The
mere thought of seeking new markets, designing new patterns
and developing new techniques gave him an adrenaline rush.

"I wish my Johnny was as interested in the porcelain business as you," John Sr. had remarked, with a heavy sigh.
"You'll have to come and see the warehouses. Of course, the
factory in France is the real kicker. Things have been tough
with the war. We started making some cheaper chinaware to
get by. Hopefully business will pick up now. I'll need Johnny
in the company. I just hope he realizes it. You might want to
have a word with him, Dex?"

Gavin had agreed, although he was doubtful it would do any
good. Johnny was a delightful companion, but there was little
use talking to him about anything beyond sports, automobiles,
parties and girls. Lots of girls. He smiled wryly as he opened
the parlor door; there were plenty of those for the returning
conquerors.

Tilly sat at the table dressed in a lilac silk robe, graceful
layers of lace falling around her delicate shoulders as she nib-
bled a morsel of wafer-thin toast and browsed through the paper.

"Hello, Dex, dear." She smiled her ethereal smile and laid the paper down. "Did you sleep well?"

"Very well, thanks." He sat to her right, careful to keep his eyes focused on the napkin he was unfolding and not on her. "We were at a party at the Van Burens'."

"Of course. Isn't Lucy gorgeous? She's getting married this spring to a French count. Such a charming, refined man. I suppose her father's money will help restore all those old châteaus." She made an expressive moue.

The funny thing was, Gavin realized as he reached for the jam, was that Tilly never sounded silly, mean or pretentious or... He didn't know how to describe her. She bubbled in an understated way—like good champagne. Her sweetness was real, her charm natural, yet, if he considered her closely she was superficial and stupid, too. It was the strangest combination, a fascinating one that he wasn't sure how to deal with.

"Catching up on world events?" he asked.

"Oh, that," she exclaimed, her tinkling laugh making the toast catch in his throat. "I just read the social columns. John gets me the *Times* all the way from London so that I can read about who's doing what. One has to have *something* to talk about at parties, after all."

"Of course."

"I love the engagements, reading about the parties and the wedding announcements." She picked up the paper and handed it to him. "You've been in Europe so long, perhaps there's news of people you know." Then she folded her napkin neatly and rose. "I'm sorry to leave you, but I simply *have* to run. A meeting for the New Year's charity ball." She sighed and he laughed, enchanted.

Gavin watched her leave, then flipped through the *London Times* and tucked into the scrambled eggs and toast, hungrier than he'd thought. His eye fell on the wedding announcements and he glanced casually down the page, wondering if any of the chaps in his old platoon were getting married. Since the war, there seemed to be a rush of weddings.

Then all at once the fork clattered onto his plate, the words swimming before his eyes.

Skye, Scotland. On the 28th of November, Lord Angus MacLeod of Strathaird and Miss Flora Finlay were pleased to announce their marriage. The ceremony was held at Strathaird Castle, on the Isle of Skye. Lord MacLeod became heir to the family title when his elder brother, Gavin, was killed in action in 1917. He is the ninth Lord, following the death of his father, Lord Hamish MacLeod, in August of this year.

The room spun and Gavin steadied himself. It couldn't be right. This was impossible. His father dead? He closed his eyes, overcome with shock and grief as the dreadful news sank in. And Angus, his twin, had betrayed him, inheriting his title and stealing Flora from him. Rage gripped him and he crumpled the paper in his right fist, hand trembling as he destroyed it. Then Tilly's voice penetrated the haze. Remembering where he was, he felt cold sweat bursting over him.

"Are you all right? I forgot my hankie and came back down. You look terrible, Dex, dear. Are you feeling sick?" Tilly stood beside his chair, resting her fingers gently on his wrist, her green eyes glistening with concern.

"I'm fine. Just a little dizzy. Perhaps I've been overdoing it lately," he blurted in a desperate effort to pull himself together and control the inner chaos.

"Oh, you poor boy!" she exclaimed, passing a napkin over his forehead as he tried to breathe, to think, to function. "Robert, Mr. Dexter seems unwell. I think he should lie down. Help him into the study, will you, please?"

"Of course, madam." The butler helped Gavin rise. His legs were weak and he was thankful for the steadying arm.

"So sorry to be a nuisance," he murmured.

"Oh! Don't be silly, poor dear. We'll have you settled on the sofa in two seconds and Robert will get you a brandy. John always says that helps."

They installed him on the leather chesterfield and Robert poured a large brandy from the decanter, standing by solicitously while Gavin threw it back in one gulp. Tilly hovered, a pretty butterfly, making soothing sounds. But all he wanted was to be alone. He needed to think, to register the enormity of it all and somehow come to grips with this new reality and the mixed emotions it raised. All the misgivings about Angus that he had so resolutely banished in shame hurtled to the fore, leaving him weak with anger.

"Maybe you should rest a little," Tilly murmured. "Robert, come away. We'll give him some peace for a while."

As soon as the door closed behind them, Gavin gave vent to his pent-up feelings, never doubting the truth of what he'd read. The bastard. The bloody bastard. How *dare* he? And his father, his poor father, dead—perhaps from grief. He rose, furiously pacing the carpeted floor of John Sr.'s study, clenching and unclenching his fists, torn between the desire to rush home immediately and anger over what would greet him there if he did.

After twenty minutes, he leaned against the mantelpiece, exhausted in mind and body. If he went back now he'd kill Angus, tear him apart and reclaim his inheritance. But what of his mother? What of Flora? He raised his head and stared at the leather-bound collection of books lining the walls. It might be worse for her to know the truth than believe him dead.

Slowly, more calm, he began weighing his options. An hour ago he had been caught between his loyalty to Flora and Greta. That wasn't an issue anymore, he realized, clenching his fist once again. She was married. Married to his brother. He felt strangely unnerved. While Greta and Flora had posed a problem, it was one he had been in control of. Now it was out of his hands. There was no choice. He was free to find Greta without Flora to worry about. But the thought brought him no solace. The image of Flora in his twin's arms brought on the blinding rage once more, followed closely by a sudden longing for Strathaird, the scent of the North Sea on a cold autumn day and the glow of the heather in spring.

He forced himself to stop, to think instead of the present. He had virtually no money, and had to decide what action to take.

His gaze wandered longingly through the window. Even as his heart longed for Scotland, he loved New York, the fast pace and the American spirit. It suited him entirely. At home he'd felt stifled, anxious to break the mold. The war had given him that chance, but if he returned now he would have to take over the family business. Here he could make his own way. He stared into space, nursing an idea that had been lurking but that he hadn't dare admit. What if he didn't go back? What if he stayed and became Dexter Ward? It was utterly crazy but entirely possible. Everyone believed him dead. Nobody knew Dexter Ward, except Dexter's family back in Oklahoma. Anyway, there could be a number of Dexter Wards throughout the United States. He didn't have a monopoly on the name. But if he stayed, he would need to get a job, make some money…

Tilly reentered the room, bringing him back to reality. She had changed into a soft woolen dress that accentuated her perfect figure and the color of her eyes. A sparkling diamond pin shimmered above her breast. Gavin observed these things abstractedly, still reeling, shocked to realize his mind was almost made up.

"Oh good! You're better," she exclaimed, relieved. "I was worried about you. You were so pale." She passed her hand over his forehead again, her touch making every sense tingle. He moved abruptly out of her reach.

"I'm fine. I guess I just needed to take a break."

"Well, of course, dear. That dreadful war must have been so *awfully* tiring. Maybe you and Johnny should go to Long Island for a few days. I'll have the house opened up and you can relax there for a while. Or Palm Beach!" She clapped her hands like an excited child. "That's it! I'll tell John we want to go next week, straight after New Year's, and I'll have them get everything ready. Oh, what fun that will be." Her eyes glistened and Gavin watched her, fascinated despite his worries.

It was John Sr.'s offer of a job that clinched Gavin's decision—at least, for the moment. Later, once he'd made enough money, he would decide what measures to take. Perhaps he would try to find Greta. As for Angus, when the time came, he was sure he would know what to do about his brother. He would bide his time and the opportunity for revenge would present itself. He felt uncannily certain of it. Flora flashed before him once more, tender and gentle, and again the thought of his brother's treacherous hands touching her revived his anger, just as the thought of his mother tore at his heart. The idea of not seeing her again was devastating. But surely it was better for her to believe him dead than learn of Angus's treachery? Wouldn't that break any mother's heart?

When the thoughts became too torturous to handle he spent riotous evenings going to parties with Johnny. Time went by, and little by little Dex's identity emerged and Gavin was laid to rest. He would resurrect him when the time was right.

Lying, like so many things, became easier with practice. Not that he thought of it as lying, exactly. It was more like an actor impersonating a character to perfection. He didn't feel so bad about the Harcourts, now that Dexter Ward had become real. His smooth American accent became natural. Johnny's debonair crowd was not difficult to adapt to and he responded easily when they addressed him as Dex, amazed—almost frightened—by how simple it was to make the transition.

After returning from Palm Beach, John Sr. had taken him to visit the offices of Harcourt's. He was impressed by the volume of business the company did. Their only competitors were the Havilands, but, as John Sr. pointed out, they tended toward a more upscale market, and the two families had always managed to work alongside one another without stepping on the other's toes.

John Sr.'s one regret was his son's total lack of interest in the family business, and it was not surprising that he should find Dex's sincere interest a godsend.

"Learn the business, son. I'll be happy to see you do well. You talked of college?"

"Yes." Gavin hesitated. "I'd like to go to Columbia."

"Good choice, particularly if you had engineering in mind."

Gavin almost blurted out that his father had been a mining engineer, but remembered just in time.

By spring he and Johnny had moved into a bachelor apartment in the heart of New York City, and before he knew it he was enrolled in college and working at Harcourt's. The present and the future were so filled with opportunity and excitement that the past became gradually relegated to memory. By 1925, when he graduated, Dexter Ward was on the verge of a big leap into the future.

In the years that followed college, Dex focused solely on learning Harcourt's business from the ground up, absorbing all that he could of John Sr.'s experience and advice. Along the way, he invested his earnings wisely, displaying a natural business acumen, and always keeping in mind the uncertain plans he held for his future. Whether he returned to Scotland, looked for Greta or continued to build a life as Dexter Ward, he would need a substantial cash flow.

When the stock market crashed in October 1929, Dex found himself in a far better position than most. Harcourt's suffered during the Depression that followed, but John Sr. was a believer in brick and mortar—*the solid stuff,* as he called it—and thus he had escaped the fate of many of their friends and acquaintances. Tilly lamented daily on *how awful it was the poor so and so's weren't able to go to Cannes this year, and how poor Joe had jumped out the window, leaving his widow and daughter destitute.*

Tilly was good to her friends. Their misfortunes had given her a sense of purpose, albeit temporary. She still flitted from luncheons to cocktail parties, accompanied less and less by John Sr. who had developed a heart problem. He depended more and more on Dexter, now a chemical engineer and business graduate, although he still lived with the hope that Johnny would one day see the error of his ways and return to the company.

Dex was well aware that, far from rejoining Harcourt's, Johnny was distancing himself daily from anything that demanded more effort than swinging a polo stick, or donning the suitable attire for the evening's activities, ending his evenings astride the latest model willing to spread her legs, in the hopes of becoming Mrs. Harcourt Junior. That was a fate he had escaped so far, thanks to Dex's talent for extricating him from unfortunate circumstances.

Unlike Johnny, Dex never got seriously involved with anyone. Sometimes he wondered at himself. It wasn't that he didn't seek involvement with women, but none of them seemed to be quite what he wanted. And each time he felt drawn to someone, an afternoon in Tilly's sophisticated, charming company was enough to temper his interest. It troubled him deeply that his friend's mother, and the wife of a man he admired like a father, could hold such an attraction for him. He began avoiding Sutton Place, making excuses until John Sr. brought up the subject and Dex realized to his chagrin that the older man was hurt. After that, he schooled himself and came regularly, but his obsession for Tilly was increasingly difficult to surmount. He dreamed of her day and night, his mind tortured by her image, her scent, her shimmering gaze. Flora had been the love of innocence, Greta the discovery, but Tilly...Tilly was an intoxicating, compulsive habit he couldn't rid himself of.

13

Southampton, U.S.A., 1932

In the summer of 1932, New York was hot and muggy and John Sr. had traveled to Switzerland to avoid the discomfort. One afternoon, desperate to escape the stifling heat of the office, Dex decided to drive to the house in Southampton. As he turned into the driveway, bordered by manicured hedges, magnolias and roses, he wondered uneasily what had brought him here.

One glance at Tilly, lying on the terrace in a white wicker chaise, with one arm dangling languorously at her side while she fanned herself with the other, told him the truth. *Leave now, before it's too late,* he told himself, turning quickly away. He was about to slip out as quietly as he'd come when she spoke and he stopped in his tracks, spellbound by the smooth lilt of her voice.

"Dex, darling, what a wonderful surprise!" Her eyes sparkled, as green and intense as ever. The fourteen years that had passed since their first meeting had enhanced rather than diminished her sensuous beauty.

Dex smiled and murmured politely before removing his blazer. He opened a bottle of champagne, handed Tilly a glass then sat on the parapet and leaned against a Roman column, his white-clad legs stretched out before him, ankles casually crossed. He watched the sun as it set, wishing he hadn't come. What was the point of going through this torture? He had no right. Sometimes he wondered if she knew how he felt. There was an expression in her eyes, a longing…but only sometimes. Perhaps it was only his imagination. He hoped it was. The whole thing was utterly wrong. He should find himself a girl-friend, or go back to Europe and find Greta, perhaps get married.

"I wasn't expecting anyone for dinner, so I gave Sarah the evening off. The other servants are still in New York. I really should have hired a full staff, but with John being away and one thing or another…"

"Don't worry, Mrs. Harcourt, I'll fix us something."

"Will you really? What fun! I'm *so* thrilled you came." Her laugh, as innocent as a child's and as provocative as a siren's, filled the air. They chatted of this and that, with Dex finding it increasingly difficult to simulate indifference. But he knew he must, certain Tilly would be shocked if she had the slightest suspicion of what he felt for her. He watched as the sun dropped over the horizon and evening settled, bringing with it a fresh, gentle breeze, and wondered if he could make an excuse and leave.

"Oh, isn't this delightful." Tilly stretched like a satisfied cat, her white, sleeveless chiffon dress flowing with every movement.

"I'll fix something for dinner," he said abruptly, needing to take his eyes off her, ashamed when they strayed yearningly to her breasts, which seemed as taut and tempting as fourteen years ago. But years ago he had possessed some sense of loyalty for his friend, and for the man who'd made him what he was today, he realized savagely, hating himself.

"I'll come and help you, Dex, dearest. You'll never find a thing on your own." She rose and took his hand lightly in hers. "Think what fun it will be to make a meal together. We could eat in the kitchen like the servants."

She linked her arm in his and they entered through the tall French doors, Tilly's heels echoing on the polished parquet. Dex's heart beat fast as her skin grazed his.

"Let's put on the Victrola!" she exclaimed, stopping excitedly. "I brought some new records from New York." Disengaging herself, she ran to the Victrola that sat on the grand piano and wound it up, placing the needle on the record. "Let's dance, Dex!" She beckoned to him, reaching her sinuous white arms toward him. "I've missed dancing since poor John became ill."

"Ti...Mrs. Harcourt, I don't think it would be suitable."

"Oh, rubbish. Come on." She began gliding about the floor, chiffon floating in the evening light as shadows shifted, playing tricks against the wall, making her movements as entrancing as a witch's spell. Slowly he moved toward her, drawn like a magnet by a force too strong to resist. An electric shock coursed through him, dazed when she glided up to him, the feel of her body swaying in his arms the embodiment of an impossible dream.

As her eyes locked with his he trembled, realizing instantly she wanted him, too. Fighting an inner battle, he tried to draw away but her scent, the fragility of her tiny body against his hard, muscled frame, so light he was scared of breaking her, made it impossible. Still he made a last, halfhearted attempt to move away.

"Mrs. Harcourt...we shouldn't—"

"Dex, darling, don't you think I know? Don't you think I've suffered the same longing you have, all these years?" she whispered, eyes brimming with tears as the music slowed. "I've tried so hard not to think of you, to banish you from my mind. And every time I thought I'd succeeded, I'd see you again and it would all come back in a terrible rush. I've tried to tell myself it's wrong. You're so young, and I'm married to dear John, and so much older than you. But I can't help it." A tear dropped from her lashes and he wiped it tenderly away.

"Oh, Tilly. My darling, precious Tilly." She closed her eyes as he drew her into his arms. "I'm the one to blame, not you. I should have gone, left as soon as I realized what my feelings for you were. I can still leave now."

"Dex, darling, it's too late. We both know it's too late. Even if you left me, it wouldn't make any difference in how we feel.

I've burned, longed for you night and day for so long. I couldn't bear it if you left me now," she whispered, sighing into his shoulder. "I think I'd die."

"But Tilly, there's Johnny and Alix and your husband and…" He pulled away in a last, frantic effort not to concede.

"I know," she sighed, her shoulders drooping sadly. "I know it's considered very wrong. But is it? Can you help what you feel, darling? Because I can't."

"No," he responded truthfully. "I can't." He pulled her close once more, delighting in her. "And I hate myself for it."

"Shh…" She raised a finger tenderly to his lips and they danced on and on to music that had long since died. As evening faded into night, his lips finally sought hers, their bodies entwined, swaying to nothing more than the scratching of the needle.

Then, hand in hand, her head barely reaching his powerful shoulder, they headed toward the huge staircase. He reached down, lifted her into his arms, and she nestled against his chest as he carried her to his bedroom. The white voile curtains swayed gently in a soft breeze, the room lit by the mystical hue of dazzling stars, and the crescent moon shining high above.

He lowered her gently to the bed, hesitating, wishing he could draw back but knowing he'd gone too far, her eyes two brilliant jewels entreating him to seek further. His fingers brushed her soft white shoulders, then his lips followed, as his passion finally let loose. It would be one perfect night. Then he would leave the Harcourts behind.

The dress fell from her like the unveiling of a statue. Underneath she wore nothing.

"Tilly, my beautiful Tilly," he whispered, gazing at her in awe, yet still restrained by a fragment of guilt. "I'm making you betray your husband. I—"

"No." She shook her head. "I am not. This is different. I have never been unfaithful, Dex. What's happening between us is not an idle fling. We both know that we've longed for one another, unable to stop. It's meant to be. Just once, darling, once after all these years."

So Dex obliterated all else but the feel of her skin, the scent of her hair, as she leaned forward, unbuttoning his shirt. Slowly, gently, they indulged one another, seeking out secrets dreamed of for so long, knowing each would take part of the other away with them at the break of dawn. His hands roamed possessively, committing each curve to memory, while hers traveled playfully, hungrily, driving him to distraction, tantalizing until he could bear it no more. Then her legs circled his waist and he thrust deep within her, loving her, appeasing his longing, promising himself it would never happen again. Each sensation was an exquisite purging of body and soul, his guilt forgotten as his hands met around her slender waist, their rhythm one until she cried out and he finally gave way.

He lay awake all night listening to the soft, sweet rhythm of her breathing as she slept curled next to him, torn between crippling guilt and satisfaction. At dawn he woke her, caressing her softly, loath to have the moment end but knowing it was time. Sarah would return to work soon and their secret had to be kept, for everyone's sake. He sighed, hesitating for one last minute.

"Tilly. Tilly, wake up, darling."

"Mmm."

"Sarah will be here soon to make your breakfast," he whispered, holding her tenderly in his arms as she woke up, wanting desperately to keep her close always.

Her eyes filled with love and sorrow as she gazed at him. Slowly she took his face in her hands and kissed his mouth tenderly.

"Goodbye, my darling. I shall always love you. And I know that, somewhere inside, you'll always love me."

She rose silently from the bed. There was nothing to do but watch numbly as she slipped on the white chiffon garment, ghostlike and ethereal now in the dawn light.

"Goodbye, Dex," she whispered. "I'll never forget you. As long as I live."

"Go, Tilly," he whispered, his voice raw. "Go now, before I ask you to stay."

She hesitated, but he closed his eyes. When he opened them again she was gone.

It took him several weeks to be able to face John Sr. again without dying inside, knowing he would never overcome the shame and guilt he felt. Still, he could not deny the sweet knowledge of her touch and the scent of her, haunting his dreams and his days.

He knew he must find a place of his own, far enough away to give him an excuse to go less often to Sutton Place, for being near her was torture. He roamed New England every weekend until he found the ideal spot, an estate near Old Lyme, in Connecticut.

Harcourt's had grown tremendously under Dex's capable administration. He had worked hard before, but now he pushed himself to the limit, as though he could in some way compensate for his sin. His weekly visits with John Sr. were hell; each kind glance, each word of praise was a spear. Never before had he felt revulsion toward himself, not even when Annelise had died. That was, after all, not entirely his fault. But this...

Up until now he'd avoided John Sr.'s suggestion of visiting France, afraid of confronting the past and unsure of what future he one day would have to face. But when John Sr. raised the notion again, he welcomed the chance to escape. Perhaps now that he was wealthy and had a secure position, it was time to seek out Greta. The past seemed so long ago, yet Dex felt sure it was the right thing to do. At least he might redeem part of his soul. He began preparing for the trip, anxious to leave as soon as possible.

14

Lausanne, Switzerland, 1932

The moment the ship sailed, he felt better, and as he watched the New York harbor fade into the distance, he set his mind toward the future. His final destination was Limoges, a town he knew well from childhood. Perhaps he would meet his own relations; doing so under a false identity was not going to be easy. But the excitement of shaping Harcourt's destiny and being given free rein to implement his innovative ideas was foremost. That, he reminded himself, and seeking out Greta, of course.

He had decided that after arriving in Cherbourg he would head directly to Lausanne and seek out Greta's aunt, Baroness Louisa von Ritter, whose address he had managed to locate.

He arrived in Lausanne on a pleasant autumn afternoon and drew back the net curtains of the windows of his hotel suite at the Beau Rivage Palace to gaze down at the passersby, wandering along the boardwalk. The lake lay tranquil and the golden hue of the trees reminded him of that autumn long ago when he and Greta had loved one another. It was only right and fair that he seek her out, discover if she still wanted him to marry her and give her his name. For what *that* was worth, he acknowledged with a wry smile, watching children and couples in red and white pedal boats meandering between the swans and ducks that lingered in hope of a stray crust.

He decided to phone the baroness right away, realizing Greta should not be kept in suspense any longer after all these years. What would her reaction be, he wondered, waiting for the operator to put through the call. Happiness? Anger at him for having waited so long?

The baroness spoke perfect English, and sounded very formal. Dexter was invited for tea the next day, at which point she said, she would furnish him with more information concerning her niece. Somehow, he didn't think that sounded very promising. Wouldn't Greta want to see him at once? After all, he had written to the baroness from New York, under the name of Gavin MacLeod. Surely she must have told Greta?

At precisely four o'clock the next day, the driver entered the ivy-robed portals of the stately villa on the Avenue Denantou. A portly butler opened the front door and he was shown into a stiff, formal salon that reminded him of his mother, giving him a moment's sadness. The furniture was Louis XV, both authentic and uncomfortable, and he stood instead, uneasily waiting for the baroness to appear. He did not have to wait long before a large, statuesque lady dressed in black silk entered the room. She was not smiling and barely stretched out her hand, asking him to sit, with a cold glance at the chair next to him.

"Baroness, I realize this is a somewhat awkward situation. Many years have passed and—"

"Not only have many years elapsed—which in itself makes your visit *most* inappropriate—but there are also certain facts of which I think you should be aware. I might as well tell you, before we go any further, that my niece is happily married and living in Germany. It would be very wrong of you to seek her out, Mr. MacLeod. She has built a life for herself since you disappeared into the woods and has suffered enough for one lifetime already."

"Married?" Dexter gaped at her, unbelieving, realizing what an idiot he was. The possibility that Greta might have married and had a family had never crossed his mind. He simply remembered her as she was, the sweet young girl whom he had made into a woman. He cleared his throat, feeling like a complete fool.

"Does she have a family?" he asked in an attempt to appear natural.

"A son. Which makes you see how impossible it would be for Greta to have contact with you, without completely upsetting her present life. Her husband, Rainer Sharenberg, is a successful businessman. They live in Berlin. I do not believe he would appreciate his wife's old lover appearing out of nowhere," she finished witheringly.

"I see. I wonder, have you told Greta that I am here?"

"No, I have not. Neither do I plan to. Greta is happy as she is. You upset her life enough the last time. Leave her alone, Herr MacLeod, and all will be for the better."

"Very well, Madame." He rose, flushed. "You must excuse me if I don't join you for tea. I believe we have covered the matter thoroughly. Thank you for receiving me. I shall not importune you—or your niece—ever again. Good day."

He departed with a formal bow and returned to the hotel in a fury, trying to piece together his tattered pride. What a fool he was to not have thought of this. It should have been obvious, after all these years. But somehow, the thought of Greta married to a German, after all that had happened to Franz and her parents, shocked him. And she'd given him a son, no less. The thought made him writhe in anger.

The next day Dexter got on the train and headed to Limoges, determined to spend the next several weeks of his trip throwing his energy into plans for the factory, his mind absorbed by the work that awaited him. No one knew he spoke fluent French and neither did he intend to tell them. He would "pick it up" surprisingly quickly, but not too well. It was better that they think he couldn't understand half of what they were saying. The factory was running a loss and had been for a while, since John Sr.'s health had begun to deteriorate. Thankfully the director had kept an eye on things and appeared to be an honest, hard-working man.

It was strange, driving through the town he had known so well, and impossible not to feel the tug of the past, the regrets and reminders that were never forgotten but kept dormant. Here, that was impossible and they surfaced in a rush, like water breaking through a dam. The first few days were spent in an agonizing string of remembrances. It was hard not to be able to drive to Ambazac and visit his aunt and uncle, or see his cousins, Eugène and René and little Geneviève. For the first time since becoming Dexter Ward, he questioned his decision.

But work and logic made him pull himself together and get on with the matters at hand, leaving no time to think. Consumed by Harcourt's, he gave no more consideration to the identity and family he once belonged to. Instead, he worked constantly, filling his time until the day he was to return to the United States.

15

New York, U.S.A., 1932

When he returned to New York, Dex learned from Johnny that John Sr. had been particularly unwell the last few weeks. He worried about the man who was both his surrogate father and the husband of a woman with whom he was obsessed. Arriving at Sutton Place, he rang the bell and waited for Robert to open up.

"Ah! Mr. Dexter. Mr. Harcourt's in the library, sir," he said softly, showing Dex in. "He hasn't had too good a day, sir."

"I'm sorry." Dex hesitated, concerned by John Harcourt's deterioration over the last year. It was as if the older man had suddenly given up on life. His usual passion for business had waned, and more and more decisions that would normally have been his had become Dex's. It was worrying—as was the future, he realized as Robert knocked gently on the heavy door of the library, then pushed it open. Standing aside, he held the door for Dex to enter the room.

"Ah! Dex, m'boy. Good to see you."

"Good to see you, too, sir." Dex moved toward the deep leather chair, swallowing the self-loathing he was unable to suppress when he carefully took the frail outstretched fingers into his strong young grip.

"Get yourself a drink, m'boy, and give me all the news.

How was France, and how is Johnny? I believe you dined together last night.''

"He's fine, I believe. His polo club won again.''

"I see.'' There was a moment of silence while Dex poured himself a malt whiskey before sitting down. "Tell me, Dex, do you think Johnny will ever take an interest in anything other than polo, women and fast cars? I thought at first that it was part of growing up, sowing his wild oats, so to speak. But I don't believe that anymore. It has been hard—*is* hard—to face the truth.''

Dex shifted uneasily in his chair.

"Perhaps he could be brought into sales,'' he murmured doubtfully.

"Dexter, it is not sales we are talking about. You know as well as I do that the company is perfectly strong without Johnny—mostly thanks to you. I'm entirely aware of all the hard work and good decisions you've made over the past few years. You've surprised me. I always believed you were capable, but it is only recently that I've understood how truly committed to Harcourt's you really are.''

"T-thank you, sir,'' Dex stammered, taking a sip of whiskey and waiting for the other man to proceed, but a knock on the door interrupted them.

"Yes?'' John Sr. turned a questioning eye toward Robert.

"It's from the polo club, sir.'' The butler glanced at Dex, his expression worried.

"The polo club? What on earth do they want?'' John Sr. exclaimed, irritated at the disturbance.

"I couldn't say, sir. Perhaps Mr. Dexter could talk to them?''

"Yes, yes. Dex, you go and see what they want. Damn menace, these people. Haven't anything to do all day and think everyone else is the same,'' he mumbled as Dex rose and headed for the door, gripped by sudden foreboding.

"What is it, Robert?'' he asked as soon as they were out of earshot.

"There has been an accident, sir,'' he whispered, face creased with anxiety as he handed Dex the phone.

It was only as he picked up the receiver that he saw Alix standing in the shadows, watching. Her tall slim frame was almost hidden from view, her dress a muted shade of mauve that, like her, melted into the surroundings.

"Dexter Ward speaking. Mr. Harcourt isn't available, I'm afraid. I'm a friend of the family's. Can I be of any help?"

The voice on the other end hesitated. "There's been a bad accident, sir."

"I'm aware of that," he replied, eyeing Alix warily, worried his expression would reveal too much.

"It's fatal, I'm afraid, sir. Mr. Harcourt's neck was broken in the fall."

"I see. I—uh...thank you." He hung up, chilled and dizzy. It wasn't possible. Johnny—happy-go-lucky, wild Johnny—was dead. He closed his eyes for a moment, the last fourteen years playing out before him. He reached for the back of the chair and took a deep breath.

"What is it, Dex?" He spun around to face Alix. In his anguish, he'd forgotten her presence. "What's happened to Johnny?" she asked, her brown eyes like a cocker spaniel's, too big for her small face, demanding the truth.

"He's had an accident," he whispered, his voice hoarse. Then he cleared his throat, determined to pull himself together. "He's been hurt."

"How badly? Have they taken him to the hospital?"

"I—" He realized suddenly he had no idea where Johnny was. The hospital? The funeral parlor?

"He's dead, isn't he?" she said quietly, eyes boring into his.

He reached for her hand, as much for his own sake as hers, and nodded. They stood silent, both unable to assimilate the truth. Alix and he had never been close—she wasn't close to anyone—but now tragedy bonded them. Dex glanced at Robert, whose eyes glistened with unshed tears.

"I'd better tell your father," he said, squeezing her hand. She nodded. "Will you speak to your mother, Alix?"

She drew her hand away, paling visibly, her eyes filled with fear.

"No. I can't. I won't."

Dex touched her shoulder gently. "Don't worry, dear. I'll deal with everything, Alix. Don't worry. But your father and mother will need you. You're going to have to be strong."

"Will they?" she asked, her voice barely a whisper. But he'd turned and was walking slowly toward the library door, each step a burden. He turned and signaled to Robert before entering. "Call Dr. Burns, Robert, and Reverend Parsons. I think they should come as soon as possible." Then he took a deep breath and opened the door.

"I suppose Johnny forgot to send in his subscription," John Sr. said with a low chuckle. "Now, where were we? Ah, yes, Johnny. Well, I suppose there's no use pretending, is there?" He shrugged.

Dex remained standing, not knowing how to break the news.

As though realizing something wasn't right, the older man's forehead creased. "Is everything okay, Dex?"

"I'm afraid not, sir. There—there's been an accident."

"What accident?" He stiffened, his thin form rigid, his face pale. "Is it Johnny?"

Dex's throat tightened. He nodded slowly, unable to pronounce the words, and watched horrified, as John Harcourt Sr. withered before his eyes. *He knows,* he thought. *He knows instinctively that he's lost his son.* A sudden image of his own father and mother and the grief they must have suffered flashed before him and he closed his eyes.

"What happened?"

"He fell, sir. He broke his neck." There was no use lying.

"I always knew that damn game would kill him. That, or the drink or the cars." His hand trembled, gripping the arm of the chair. "But he was my boy. My only son. I love him, Dex. God, how I love him. How couldn't you love him? He's the image of his mother, the same beautiful smile, those same laughing eyes, that same charming giddiness." His voice broke as he leaned back, his eyes closed.

Dex sensed Alix's presence behind him and turned.

"Stay with him, Alix. I'll see to your mother."

She nodded and approached her father hesitantly, moving silently, a phantom that flitted through the great house, unseen, like furnishings that nobody really saw or bothered much about.

Dex mounted the stairs heavily, heart broken, the thought of facing Tilly almost too much to bear. He felt suddenly old, responsible and tired. Perhaps he could have done more to stop Johnny from leading the wild existence that had finally led to his death. But Johnny had had a stubborn streak, concealed in an easy charm, that had always made one give up.

He walked along the thickly carpeted corridor and stopped in front of Tilly's bedroom door. Downstairs the doorbell clanged. He was thankful that either the doctor or Reverend Parsons had arrived. Perhaps he should let one of them tell Tilly? But he knew he owed it to her and, bracing himself, he knocked.

"Come in," her soft, elegant voice replied.

He entered and stood in the doorway, watching her. She was seated at her writing desk, her long, cream, silk peignoir flowing gracefully to the floor.

"D-Dexter! I—I didn't know you were back from France." The pen fell to the floor, splattering ink onto the fine Isfahan rug. "Is something wrong?" she asked, looking straight into his eyes.

"There's something I need to tell you, Mrs. Harcourt."

"What is it, Dex?" She reached for the pearls at her throat, panic reaching her eyes.

He moved across the room and took her arm gently.

"Mrs. Harcourt, I…"

"Oh, for Christ's sake, Dex, what on earth is it?" she cried.

"I'm afraid there's been an accident," he whispered thinly. "It's Johnny."

"Johnny?" She looked at him blankly.

"Yes. At the polo club."

"Oh my God! Why didn't you tell me immediately? We'll go straight to the hospital. My poor baby. Does John know? You'd better tell him, he'll want to come, too. Oh, and ask for the car, will you, Dex? I'll be down in five minutes. I suppose they've taken him to St. Michael's," she continued, shaking her head, not allowing him to speak. "I knew something like this would happen, with those stupid horses. Thank God he's strong and resistant. A few broken ribs won't be all that hard to heal.'' She rushed to her dressing room, babbling, before he could interrupt her. Perhaps this way was better. Maybe the news, broken slowly, would be easier to assimilate. He turned, surprised to see Alix standing in the doorway, silent and dark, her eyes filled with grief. All at once he went to her and pulled her close, but she stood stiff and unbending within his arms.

"I'm sorry, Alix. So very sorry,'' he whispered into her hair.

"Are you?''

He drew back, shocked. "What do you mean?''

"Are you really sorry? Won't this make things easier for you?''

"What are you talking about?''

"Don't you think I've seen what you've been up to over the past few years? Climbing your way up in the company, getting Daddy to place all his confidence in you. Now there's no competition any longer.'' She threw him a look filled with bitterness.

"Alix, you're in shock. I won't take what you've said seriously. It's absurd and you know it. I loved Johnny as much as any of you.''

Tilly came back into the room, carrying a sable jacket and fixing a hat on her pretty, crimped hair. "Come along, we'd better be quick. My poor, *poor* baby. He must be suffering, all by himself in that dreadful hospital.''

"Mother, stop it.'' Alix faced her, face stony. "He's gone, Mother. He's dead. I'm afraid all you have now is me.''

"Alix, don't—'' Dex grabbed her arm helplessly. "Stop it.''

"Well? It's true. You know it's true.'' She wrenched her arm from his grip and clenched her fists. "Johnny's dead, Mother. Dead. He broke his neck. Now all you have left is me, and that's as good as nothing, isn't it? *Isn't it?*'' she insisted, tears pouring down her cheeks, her voice rising before she fled from the room.

Tilly blanched and the sable slid to the floor. She was trembling. Dex hesitated, then moved toward her, unable to bear the sight of her suffering. But she shook her head and began talking as though to herself. Then she laughed, a shrill, tinkling, hysterical laugh, her eyes bright and uncomprehending.

"She's just jealous, poor child. You have to excuse her, Dex. I suppose she hates him for being everything she's not. Johnny…well, Johnny just has it all, doesn't he?"

"Til…Mrs. Harcourt. I think we should go downstairs," he said, picking up her jacket and taking her arm gently, leading her past the canopied silk bed to the door.

"I don't understand how Alix can behave in that appalling manner when her brother is lying in the hospital with broken ribs. I'll have to talk to John about it. She's too old to behave like this." The stream of words continued as they descended the marble staircase to the hall. Turning toward the library, he saw John Harcourt, erect and silent, looking ten years older than he had an hour before.

They reached the bottom of the wide stairway. John walked across the black-and-white marble foyer, his steps echoing in the sudden quiet of the hall. Tilly had gone silent at the sight of her husband's face, and Dex's heart bled for them. God, how they would all miss him.

Tilly stood motionless as her husband reached for her arm. "We must go, my dear. The car is ready."

"Alix is being cruel and rude, John. I don't know how she can still make up fibs at her age. It's appalling. I can't help it if we haven't been able to find her a husband. It's that surly nature of hers. If she'd only try and be more pleasant, and less disagreeable about her brother. Johnny can't help being what he is. He—"

"He's gone, my love." John spoke softly, holding her arm firmly and reaching beyond the faint delirium in her eyes. "I'm afraid our Johnny is dead. He's not coming back, Tilly. Alix wasn't lying."

For an instant she blinked, as though seeing him for the first time, then shook her head vehemently. "No. *No!* I won't have it. They can't do that. It's not true. I can't, I won't—" She grabbed John's arms and shook him hysterically, "Tell me it's not true, tell me—"

"Tilly, darling, you're going to have to be brave." His face was strained and gray. "Get Dr. Burns, Robert," he said in an undertone as Tilly shook and wept.

Then, suddenly, she turned and threw herself into Dex's arms, wailing. "Tell me it's not true," she sobbed. "Tell me it's not true—"

Dex stood motionless, unable to hold her as he wanted to. He glanced helplessly at John Sr., leaning on the bronze newel post with his eyes fixed on the portrait of his grandfather hanging at the top of the stairs, his expression distant. He knows, Dex realized, shocked. He's known all along. How can I face him now, Dex despaired, when he needs me most? Blindly he led Tilly into the library where Dr. Burns, an elderly, portly man, sat her in the wing chair near the fire. Dex poured her a stiff brandy and handed it to the doctor, who forced her to drink it. Then, before she could protest, he gave her a shot.

"I'll stay with her," he said to Dex. "You go with John. I'll see to things here."

"Don't forget Alix, Doctor. She's upstairs and she's taking it very badly. She needs as much help as anyone."

"Of course. As soon as I've settled Tilly, I'll go to her, poor child."

"Tell her I'll be back," he said, feeling guilty for all the years he'd never bothered about Alix. She had simply been there, a permanent fixture in all of their existences. Now the shadow had emerged, filled with pent-up emotions and bursting forth at the worst possible moment.

Together Dex and John Sr. got into the Packard and were driven by the chauffeur to the morgue, where they identified the handsome body of John Harcourt III. Together they gazed down at the peaceful face; it held the expression he wore when he was about to spend a particularly pleasant evening out. Perhaps he was truly at peace, Dex thought, suddenly glad that he had seen him. The fact that there was no bitterness, no pain or sadness in his visage was a relief. Maybe this was how Johnny was meant to go—in the midst of it all.

As he stood in the cold room beside the trolley, Dex knew Johnny would have preferred it this way. He sighed inwardly and glanced at John Sr., watching in agony as tears poured silently down his wrinkled cheeks. There was nothing to say. The man had lost what was most precious to him. In one way Johnny was a disappointment, yet he had such personality you couldn't help but love him and let him get away with anything.

After a while, John Sr. pulled out a large white handkerchief and wiped his eyes. Dex's were wet, too. There was deep pain for the friend he had lost, but also for the wrong he'd committed against his mentor.

They left the morgue in silence. At Sutton Place, Tilly had been sedated, and Dr. Burns suggested she be transferred immediately to an upstate clinic. After speaking with the doctor, John Sr. went to the library, and Robert closed the door reverently behind him.

"Keep an eye on him, Dex, will you?" the doctor, an old family friend, said, his expression worried.

"Of course. Where's Alix?" Dex was concerned for her.

"She's in Johnny's room. I couldn't get her to budge. Perhaps you might do better."

He nodded. "Did you leave anything for her to take?" he asked matter-of-factly.

The doctor handed him a small vial. "Ten drops in half a glass of water. If you can't get her to take that, slip it in a glass of liquor. Do what's necessary to get it down. And take care of yourself, too, Dex. I know this has hit you as hard as any of them."

He accepted the medicine and nodded. After seeing Dr. Burns out, he headed heavily up the stairs and down the corridor toward Johnny's room. He knocked but there was no answer.

Silently he pushed open the door. It was almost dark. Alix sat curled in an armchair in the shadows, beneath the photographs, trophies and polo sticks covering the dark plaid walls and mahogany shelves.

She made no movement as he entered. Perhaps he should have brought a brandy with him. He could use one himself, he realized, sitting at the end of the bed, suddenly exhausted. He didn't feel like turning the light on, and for a while he sat in silence, eyes closed, thinking about that day on the *Mauritania* when he and Johnny had first met. It seemed so recent, yet so many years had passed and so much had happened. He'd become a different person. Literally.

How much of Gavin MacLeod was left, he wondered suddenly. Enough to follow exactly what was going on in Scotland, he acknowledged. Enough to make him still want revenge against the brother who had betrayed him. Someday.

Alix's voice interrupted his thoughts.

"I loved him, you know."

"I know."

"It's just that—they never cared. They never even realized I existed. But then, who would with him around? Johnny was a light, a beacon that shone. I'm just a disappointment. Girls are meant to be like Johnny. Sparkling, pretty little fools, who wear pretty dresses, laugh and make conversation—all the things that Johnny knew how to do. I read books. Ladies shouldn't read books—except those that are in fashion, of course." There was a bitterness in her tone that he'd never realized existed.

"I'm sorry, Alix. Sorry I never recognized what was going on. I guess we've all been too self-absorbed. But you're right. It's been damn unfair on you."

"Who says life is fair? Is it fair that Mother and Father should lose Johnny? If it had been me, after a few weeks nobody really would have noticed. They would have been sorry, of course, but it wouldn't have wrecked their lives. After Johnny, nothing will ever be the same."

"Don't say that. It's not true."

"It is and you know it." She got up and switched on the lamp. The room came into focus: Johnny's tweed jacket thrown carelessly over the leather chair, some invitations scattered on the desk. She picked one up and bit her lip. "He was invited everywhere. The only reason I ever get an invitation is because people are being polite to Father and Mother. They don't want to have me. I'm a bore. I don't feel right and I hate every minute of social events."

"Why do you go?"

"To save myself from having to listen to Mother harping on

about how I'll never find a husband. I don't *want* a husband. She can't understand.''

"I thought all girls dreamed of getting married and having a family.''

"Did you?'' She glanced at him, her expression unfathomable, pain glistening in her huge brown eyes.

All at once he became aware of what an intelligent face she had. She wasn't beautiful in the classical sense, but there was something else present, a sensibility he had never perceived.

"Alix, stop beating yourself up. I loved Johnny as much as anyone, but you know, when I saw him at the morgue…he looked happy. At peace. Almost like he was going out for a great evening. Maybe this is how he would have wanted to go. I couldn't see him fading into old age. He went out as he lived, with panache. His way.''

She nodded thoughtfully. "He was wonderful, wasn't he? Nobody will ever be as wonderful again. He loved me, you know. He really did. He cared. He—''

"Of course he cared, Alix. And I care, too.'' He reached over and took her hand in his. "I swear I won't let you down. I'm sorry I haven't been a better friend to you.''

"What do you think Father will do about Harcourt's now?'' she asked, eyeing him.

"I have no idea. I haven't had time to think. Neither has he. I'll take care of things for the next few weeks, then we'll see.''

"What about Mother?'' Her face closed as she said the words.

"Dr. Burns is making arrangements for her to be transferred to a clinic.''

"I see.'' She hesitated. "I want to see him, Dex.''

He nodded. "I'll take you there tomorrow. But now let's get a drink. It's what he would have wanted us to do.''

All at once she smiled. Dex realized he'd never seen Alix smile. She had a sweet, sensitive smile, and he felt guilty once more that they hadn't paid enough attention to her. They were all to blame, including him.

During the next week the house felt like a mausoleum. Tilly had been sent to the clinic, where she remained under sedation, and John Sr. remained closeted in the library, leaving it only to sleep. He barely ate. Alix took silent charge of the house and Dex moved back to be of what use he could. He spent the better part of his days at Harcourt's, doing his best to run things, but there were certain decisions that only John Sr. could make final.

On Tuesday, exactly one week after Johnny's funeral, Robert spoke to him as he entered the hall.

"Mr. Dexter, sir. Mr. Harcourt would like to see you in the library at your convenience."

"Of course. Thank you, Robert." He handed the butler his coat and hat and moved across the hall to the library, knocking softly. He heard a muffled answer and entered, shocked to see a diminished John Sr. huddled in the leather chair next to the fire. Never, in all the years Dex had known him, had he ever seen him like this.

He stood, stricken as though he had seen his own father crumble. He shuddered. Had Hamish MacLeod had a similar reaction when he'd learned of his son's death? Perhaps not. After all, it was war. Others were losing their sons, too, and he would not have been alone in his pain. A whole nation had borne it with him. And there was Angus to take over, he thought bitterly.

John Sr. smiled, the tired, sad smile of a man who had lost all his impetus. Dex swallowed, hating seeing him look so beaten. The suit that a week ago had fitted him to perfection hung limply over his withered frame.

"Sit down, m'boy. Or rather, get us both a drink first."

"Yes, sir." Dex moved to the butler's table that held the decanters, then handed him a snifter before seating himself in a deep leather chair.

"Tilly's doing a little better." John Sr. sipped the brandy and Dex murmured that he was pleased, noting a slight tremor in the older man as he raised his glass, sipped, then went into a reverie.

What was there to say? They were all bereft, and the only thing keeping him going was work. The house was a tomb, with Johnny's presence everywhere. Without him, the Harcourts would never be quite the same.

"I want you to take over the company."

Dex sat up, shocked. He had been gazing at the fire, thinking of his arrival in New York and all he owed Johnny and the Harcourts.

"But that's impossible, sir. I'm not a member of the family. I love working for you but..."

"You're as good as a member of the family. The son I would have wanted. I loved Johnny more than—" His voice cracked. "Spoiled him more than I should have. I don't know. But he never would have taken over. We both know that, Dex. You're the man Harcourt's needs. I'm willing to give you a forty percent interest, and you'll get the rest when I'm gone, except for Alix's twenty percent. I've set up a trust for Tilly and Alix that will take care of their great-grandchildren, but still, I feel I should give her part of the company."

"Why not give her more?" he suggested, desperate. The burden of accepting this, on top of his existing guilt, was too overwhelming to conceive. "Why not bring Alix on board? She's bright and intelligent. Perhaps she could help."

"No. I don't believe in women running things. And I don't want her travelling to France—I don't like what's happening in Europe. This Hitler chap in Germany..." He shook his head. "You know yourself what the war brought. I never believed in the Versailles Treaty. You don't treat an enemy like that—not a people like the Germans. But that's beside the point. I want your cooperation in this matter, Dexter. I'm asking you to make a decision that will change your life. I'm counting on you. You see, I've been thinking this over for some time. Johnny's death has merely brought it to a head."

"Sir, you're upset right now, but shortly you'll be back at the helm. I'm certain of it."

"No." He shook his head sadly. "I'm afraid I've only got a few more months myself. I had some tests run a couple of months ago, Dexter, and the results were definitive. I made Burns tell me the truth."

"I'm sorry, sir," Dex responded quietly, shaken to the core

by this latest blow. A world without John Sr. and Johnny would be very lonely. He sat, torn by a destiny that forced him onward in his role as Dexter Ward, yet tugged him back to his origins, bringing him closer to his family.

"What will Alix do?" he persisted.

"She'll have to stay here and take care of her mother. Tilly will be out soon. Once I'm gone, I don't know how she'll manage. She'll need Alix to be here for her. Little by little Tilly will get her life back together. She has a lot of friends." He drifted off again, gazing into the flames as though seeing the world after his demise.

Dex was shaken. He knew a decision—an immediate one— was expected of him. There was no choice, he realized, no means of refusing. Perhaps in some way he could atone for all his lies. Running Harcourt's would mean a return to Limoges, not briefly like last time, but on a much more permanent basis. He would be expected to socialize, perhaps meet the family he once knew and loved, as strangers. But all that seemed irrelevant next to what he owed the man before him.

"Well?" John Sr. looked him straight in the eye. "Can I count on you, Dex?"

He swallowed. "Yes, sir. But you don't need to leave me the shares. I'll buy in."

"Oh?" A flicker of interest sparked in his watery gray eyes.

"I—well, Johnny and I did some business on the side over the years. I have some money put away—" He blushed, embarrassed despite himself, then relaxed when he saw John Sr. smile for the first time since Johnny's death.

"Well, well. So he did have a spark of common sense after all. I will not ask what you were both up to, I still have an imagination. As for the shares, I want you to have them. Without them you won't have the clout necessary to impose your decisions. A board is all fine and dandy to take advice from, always listen to it and take on good advisers. Derringer is one of them—I'll put him on the board. But make sure you have the last word. It takes one general to lead an army, not ten. And you're a leader, Dexter, make no mistake about it. If I didn't think that, I wouldn't be handing Harcourt's over to you.

I've studied you over the years, and I've liked everything I've seen.''

"Thank you, sir," he murmured, consumed once more by guilt and remorse.

Just then the door opened and Alix slipped quietly into the room with a tray.

"Your medicine, Father," she said, placing the tray onto a small table and handing him a glass of water with the pills. As he took them with a murmur of thanks, she gave Dex a surreptitious glance and he wondered just how long she'd been listening. There was something odd in her look.

"Perhaps I should leave you to rest, sir," he said, rising.

"Very well, m'boy. We'll talk in the morning. Come and see me before you leave. There are a number of things I need to go over with you. The board meeting is next week."

Together Dex and Alix slipped from the library. Once in the hall she turned and faced him.

"I'd like a word with you," she said.

"Of course." They crossed the hall and he held the door for her to pass through, into the bright room that Elsie de Wolf had finished redecorating a month before. Alix sat on a large ottoman and fiddled with the tassels, while Dex remained standing. He lit a cigarette, and then remembered to offer her one, surprised when she accepted.

"I didn't know you smoked," he said, passing her a light.

"There are a number of things you don't know about me, Dex. In fact, none of you know much about me at all. I heard some of your conversation with Father."

"Snooping behind doors, Alix? That's not a very nice habit, you know." He tipped his ash into the Tiffany ashtray on the mantelpiece, catching her eye.

"It's the only way to keep abreast of anything in this house. If you're me, that is." Her smile had a cynical twist. "So, you're going to head Harcourt's after all. You've finally got where you've always wanted, haven't you? And I'll have nothing."

"Alix, you must have heard your father. He's left you and

your mother very well provided for. You'll have no difficulties maintaining your lifestyle and caring for your mother.''

"But there's one problem. I won't do it. I won't stay here and care for Mother. And the only way I can escape the fate they've chosen for me is through you, Dexter.''

"What do you mean, Alix? I already asked your father about allowing you to take over some of the business, but he refuses,'' Dex said, confused.

"Not the business, Dex. I know he'd never allow me—a woman—to take control. No. I want you to marry me.''

"*Marry* you? Are you mad, Alix?'' Dex exclaimed. "Why on earth would you want to marry me? I don't even know if you like me. Alix, what's gotten into you?''

She stared at him from across the room, the shadows etching her outline. Suddenly he realized she meant what she was saying.

"I am not staying here with Mother. I refuse. I've had enough. Dex, I want to go to Paris. I want to meet all those people I read about, women who think, who live as they want. There are a whole group of them over there—Gertrude Stein, Alice B. Toklas. Sylvia Beach even has a bookshop—Shakespeare and Co. They all hang out in cafés, on boulevards, talking about things that matter.''

"Why don't you tell your parents you want to take a trip, then?'' he asked uncomfortably, already knowing the answer.

"You have to be joking! Little, pathetic, incapable Alix, go to Europe by herself? Oh my. What would the whole of New York think! No. The only way I can go is if I marry you and this whole thing takes on an aura of respectability.''

"What you're saying is you want a marriage in name only.''

"Yes. I don't want to sleep with you, if that's what you mean. I won't impose *that* penance on you.''

"What if I wanted to sleep with you?'' he asked perversely.

She hesitated, taken aback, then shook her head, and her eyes filled with tears. "You wouldn't. Who would?'' she asked simply.

"You underestimate yourself. You've never been given a chance. Sit down.'' He crossed the room and pulled her over to the sofa, feeling sorry for her. "Let's see what we can work out. How about I talk to your parents and get them to let you go? I can be your guardian, so to speak."

"No." She shook her head stubbornly, eyes bright, biting her lip. "I won't change my mind, Dex. I can't go on. I hate it here, living in Mother's shadow, never being my own person. Please." She swallowed, her tone changing to a plea.

Dexter realized she was speaking the truth. John Sr. and Tilly would never allow her to go. She was just a woman. An unattractive woman, in their eyes, too old to be married off, and whose only purpose was to make herself useful. He thought of his own life. All at once Greta and Flora flashed before him. All that was passed now. He thought of the responsibilities he had now, the debts he owed to Johnny. Perhaps caring for Alix would be a way of honoring his friend. He looked down at her wide brown eyes filled with fear, bitterness and expectation.

"What would we do if I agreed?"

"We'd get married here and go to Paris. I'd stay there and you can go to Limoges. I promise I wouldn't expect you to take me around or be faithful or any of that. Just the occasional cocktail party at the embassy, that sort of thing, so the right reports come home. Oh please, Dex. It's my only chance, and I swear, if you don't agree, I'll do something desperate. I don't care who I hurt anymore. They've never cared about me. Why should I care about them?"

"Because they're your family and they love you."

"They don't. They bear with me. You know I'm just a disappointment. If I'd looked like Mother, if I had charm...but I don't. I like books, I want to meet James Joyce and Hemingway, not a bunch of silly socialites for lunch."

Dex was amused despite himself. He had never encountered this hidden side of Alix's nature and was intrigued. "You really are an interesting person, Alix." Then he smiled at her. "Perhaps we'll have time to catch up on our way to Europe."

She jumped up, her mouth open. "You mean you'll do it?"

"Hey, hold it—"

She flung herself at his neck and hugged him. He hugged her back, and for a moment they held each other close. Then he pulled her onto the sofa. "Listen, there's a condition to all this."

"What condition? Anything you want, as long as we can leave as soon as possible."

"I want a child."

"A child? I don't want a child," she exclaimed, stunned.

"It's the condition, Alix. Don't you think we owe it to Johnny? To your father? It would be the continuation of Harcourt's, a grandchild who would inherit all your father had built."

"Dex, I—" Alix looked uncomfortable.

"This is a bargain we're striking here," he said softly. "I'll meet my end. Are you willing to meet yours?"

She remained silent.

"This is more important to me than you can possibly imagine," he insisted.

She stared at him, her face pale.

"Will you accept these terms?"

She hesitated only a moment.

"Yes."

Part Three

1934–1947

Would that I could be the peacemaker in your soul, that I might turn the discord and the rivalry of your elements into oneness and melody.

—Kahlil Gibran
The Prophet

16

Paris, France, 1934

They arrived in Paris on a bubbling summer afternoon. The boulevards were packed with strolling young couples, the sunlight reflecting off the stained-glass windows of Notre Dame across a glimmering Seine. Barges floated, decked with colorful washing lines that waved in the light breeze, and *bateaux mouches* purred gently under the bridges.

It had taken so much longer to leave New York than they'd ever imagined. Tilly had managed to be strong for the wedding, but still spent long hours silently sipping champagne in Johnny's room, barely aware of John Sr.'s deteriorating health. Unexpectedly she would surface to pick up her social life where she'd left off, going out on luncheon dates from which she returned drunk, and the staff got used to carrying her up to her room, where she slept off the stupor.

Dex had assumed the chairmanship of Harcourt's and Alix had held the fort at Sutton Place. There had barely been time to think about her consistent reluctance to sleep with him. By now, her response to Dex's advances was outright refusal.

Why was she so frightened, Dex wondered, reaching Sutton Place after a particularly long day. Distracted by his confusion about their marriage, he barely noticed two vehicles parked on the curb. He'd really have to talk seriously to Alix about the matter. Perhaps she should see a doctor. Maybe she needed help. He entered the house, then stopped. There was no sign of Robert, and the maid who'd opened the door had scuttled into the shadows. Voices murmured from the study, where a beam of light filtered onto the glistening marble of the hall. He knew immediately something was wrong. Dropping his briefcase on a chair, he rushed to the half-open door of the study and stopped at the sight of Alix, her face white and drawn, leaning over her father, who sat crumpled in his armchair. Two men in raincoats and a police officer stood by uncomfortably. They turned simultaneously, relieved to see a new face.

"Mr. Harcourt, sir?"

"Ward."

"Mr. Ward." The man walked over to where Dex stood, gripped by foreboding. "Detective Thompson, sir. I'm sorry to be the bearer of bad news."

"What is it?" He looked over the man's shoulder at Alix, still unaware of his presence, disturbed by the grief in her eyes.

"I'm afraid it's Mrs. Harcourt, sir. She had an accident leaving Long Island. Just raced out into the street. Nobody knows why. Seems the car was on the other side of the road—she almost threw herself under the oncoming vehicle." He gave Dex a penetrating glance. "Any reason you can think of that she might have committed suicide?"

He shook his head blindly. The beautiful, frivolous, unique Tilly was dead. In the seconds that followed, he could hear the needle of the Victrola scratching the record, smell the scent of her perfume fleeting up from her delicate skin, the feel of her in his arms as they twirled slowly over the floor. He closed his eyes and leaned against the doorjamb, afraid of losing his balance.

"You okay?" the detective asked, concerned.

"I'm sorry. It's a shock," Dex murmured.

"She was your mother-in-law, is that correct?"

He nodded absently. She was that, and so much more. For a moment he wondered if he was to blame. Perhaps he should have sought her out after their interlude and helped her. But she'd avoided him, as he had her, by silent mutual understanding. He stood straighter, realizing he needed to take charge.

"So you're certain this wasn't suicide?"

"Out of the question," he replied firmly. He would not allow her memory to be besmirched. Dex stared past the detective, caught in his own musings. Was death his shadow? Did he carry it with him, to the women who surrounded him? There was Annelise, dead only because she'd succumbed to a moment's pleasure, and now Tilly. But perhaps he was blaming himself unduly. Maybe it was Johnny's death that had killed her and not—

"Sir, I need some information from you, if you don't mind." Detective Thompson looked uncomfortable, although he was probably used to scenes like this. Dex pulled himself together, answering the questions automatically, then excused himself and went over to Alix and her father. Slipping an arm gently around her shoulders, he felt the taut tension of her body and held her close. Looking down at John Sr., he saw blank eyes, a withered face already half-dead with pain and defeat.

Together, Dex and Alix had mourned Tilly. Then, to their utter grief, a week later John Sr. passed away gently in his sleep. Robert found him in the morning, seated in his favorite chair, a photograph of Tilly held limply in his right hand.

Alix had collapsed after her father's death and Dex knew he must get her away, out of New York. But settling the estate took time. Preparing Harcourt's for his absence, while he and Alix traveled to Europe, demanded much organization. They had been married almost two years by the time the arrangements for the estate and their plans to spend time in France were finalized. With the past behind them, Dex hoped there would be a chance for them to build a new life together.

Now, as they ambled silently along the Seine, tension thrived between them. It had since they'd boarded the ship in New York and she'd adamantly refused to consummate their marriage. But Dex was determined. Enough. It was time to begin a new life and he didn't want her slipping into her fears, her dread of her inadequacies.

But nothing he said to convince her helped, and as the days

went by she began avoiding him, leaving him hurt and angry. Hadn't he done everything he could? He'd married her in what was certainly the most opulent wedding of the season, comforted her in her grief, dealt with every practical detail he could think of, hoping to save her pain or suffering. His own pain was as intense, if not more, than hers. Losing John Sr. was like losing his father over again, and Tilly's death had destroyed another little part of himself.

Now they had a chance at a fresh start. Why couldn't she see that it was time to think of giving Harcourt's an heir that would allow John Sr.'s work to prosper throughout future generations? Didn't he realize he was a man who desired a sexual relationship with his wife? If she was aware of the occasional flings he'd had lately, she didn't show it. He'd been very discreet. The last thing he wanted was to hurt her, but after two years of marriage, his patience was at its end.

That morning, before departing from the ship, they'd had another heated discussion and Alix had begged for a little more time—enough to adjust to the new life they were beginning. How could she handle that and a baby, she'd argued, pleading.

As they passed the Pont Neuf, glancing through the book vendors' stalls and watching the street artists, he realized that perhaps she was right. Maybe they needed some time to get to know one another better. After all, their marriage had been a constant series of meetings at meals or for a drink, rushing to a show or dinner party. Perhaps in a few months things would be different and she would be more comfortable.

"Look!" Alix grinned like an excited child at a one-legged organ grinder with a brightly clad monkey perched on his left shoulder.

"Don't pet it, Al, it probably has fleas."

"Oh, Dex! Surely there's nothing wrong with it. It's so cute. Do you think he'd sell it?"

"Alix, no," he answered, laughing, the tension easing. "Not a monkey, please. I know the Ritz is flexible, but still."

"Okay. But once we find an apartment, maybe we could get a dog. Or a cat. Maybe a parrot."

Or a baby, he mused. "Parrots have parrot disease."

"I never knew you could be so difficult, so American." He watched, amused, as she threw her head back, her bobbed hair swinging in the sun, glad they'd gotten over the quarrel.

Perhaps he *had* become very American, he thought, smiling at the irony. He reached for Alix's hand, determined to keep up the goodwill and start their time in Paris on a new footing.

They wandered past the antique shops on the Quai Voltaire, then sat in a bistro and drank wine, the conversation more relaxed than he remembered it. Already Paris was exercising her influence over Alix. Before returning, tired and happy, to the Ritz, they stopped on the Rue Cambon to visit the much-discussed house of Chanel.

The following days were spent exploring, browsing through Montmartre, lunching in tiny bistros off the Boulevard Saint-Germain, at the Brasserie Lipp or across the road at Aux Deux Magots, Alix nudging him with excitement whenever she saw a famous face at a nearby table. Soon they were striking up conversations with other Americans, friendly artists and intellectuals.

"It seems unreal, doesn't it? We seem to be making friends all over the place. I thought those people tonight were delightful," Alix commented as they walked back to the hotel. Dinner at the Café Flore that night had developed into an animated conversation with the couple at the next table.

"Seemed like a nice guy," Dex remarked, pulling a visiting card from the pocket of his lightweight jacket. "Sylvain de Rothberg. Does that ring a bell, Al? I'm sure I've heard the name before."

Alix snatched the card from Dex's hand. "Was that *really* him?"

"Him?" Dex frowned, puzzled at her sudden excitement.

"Of course you've heard of him, Dex. He's the most famous jeweler in town. Trust you not to know that!" She laughed and grabbed his hand as they crossed the Place Vendôme. "Sylvain de Rothberg is every woman's dream. He fashions the most beautiful jewels in all creation, and everyone—I mean *every-*

one, even the queen of England—has a piece of his. Except me," she added with a moue.

"We can remedy that," he said, laughing, struck again by the change in her. There was a lightheartedness he'd never known existed, a sparkle that he was determined should remain. Tomorrow he would go to Sylvain de Rothberg's store and buy her something to mark this new beginning.

The next day Dex headed to the Faubourg Saint-Honoré, walked down the Rue de la Paix and searched for the address printed on the card. Finding it, he wandered curiously through the arched alley, agreeably surprised. Rothberg's was discreet; the only indication was the small, engraved gold lettering on the door, and one eye-catching necklace exhibited on a velvet stand in the window. He gazed at it, impressed by the perfection of the stones, the cut of the diamonds and the unusual design. It was modern, yet classic, and could be worn just as well by a very young woman as by a matron. He stepped back and eyed it critically, wondering if the piece would suit Alix.

"Good morning."

He looked up to see Sylvain de Rothberg observing him. He smiled. Rothberg was medium-size, dressed in a well-cut, light gray suit and fine silk tie that suited his dark hair and eyes. He was handsome in a dark, brooding, dramatic way, and Dex was willing to bet that women flocked here as much for the jeweler as the jewelry.

"Good morning." He smiled and the two men shook hands. "No sooner did I mention your name to my wife than she had me rushing over here. I hope it won't make too deep a hole in my pocket."

"It will. I'm disgustingly expensive, but worth every penny. I only work with the best materials, the finest stones and the most skilled craftsmen." He raised his hands and laughed. *"C'est la vie,* my friend."

"Okay, I'm willing. Show me some more. I can't leave here without something for Alix."

"With pleasure. Come inside and I'll show you." Sylvain pushed open the door. A slim woman in a black dress and perfect pearls ushered them in. "Is Alix the lady who you were with last night, *chez* Lipp?"

"Yes."

"Then I think I have the perfect thing for her. Louise," he murmured, turning to the shop clerk, "bring me the ruby and diamond leaf."

"*Tout de suite,* Monsieur de Rothberg."

"It's a piece I've been working on for a while. It is refined, yet vibrant, like your wife."

"How do you know Alix is like that?" Dex asked, surprised.

"I don't." Sylvain shrugged. "I am—how do you say in English? Taking a guess?"

"Well, you're right. She's full of surprises. Paris has done her good. She had a hard time back in the States. Lost her brother and her parents in a short space of time. I'm hoping she'll find herself here."

"That's what Paris is all about." Sylvain smiled elusively, accepted a velvet tray from Louise and laid it carefully on the highly polished table. "*Voilà.* The leaf. It is closed, long and refined, yet when we turn it, change the angle slightly, the light catches and it opens, just enough to reveal the glimmer of diamonds inside." He lifted the brooch, tilted it, and a cluster of perfect diamonds twinkled among the rubies.

"Amazing. It's perfect. I suppose I should see what else you've got, but I already know that's the one. It's perfect for Alix. Full of hidden secrets."

"Come and have a look around." Sylvain gestured to the glass cases.

Dex followed him around the store, entranced. The designs were utterly unique. Two perfect emerald earrings, and a perfectly proportioned sapphire and gold ring set in a square of encrusted diamonds took his breath away. "You're an amazing artist. Do you only design jewelry?"

"Mostly, though I've tried my hand at textiles. A friend of mine in the fashion business asked me to design some fabric for her. It was *amusant.*"

"What about designing for porcelain? Have you ever thought of that?"

"Never. It's a complicated business, I understand. Very time-consuming. Why do you ask?"

"Oh, just a question," Dex replied casually, already determined that de Rothberg would one day design for Harcourt's. "Have the brooch wrapped and delivered to the Ritz. Would you like to join me for some lunch?"

"Why not? It would be bad manners to refuse a new customer, especially one who has started out so well."

"Quite so." Dex grinned. You don't know what you're getting into, he thought, relishing the idea of a dinner service designed with emblems of precious stones, the colors and techniques swimming before his eyes. *Before the year's over I'll have you in Limoges and a new collection with your signature on it, buddy,* Dex vowed to himself, nodding to the shop clerk as they departed.

They walked to the Place de l'Opéra toward the Café de Paris, navigating between round tables squeezed close together, the waiters' trays held high to avoid collision.

Sitting inside, they ordered champagne and pâté.

"What do you think of all that's going on in Germany?" Dex asked, turning the conversation to the concerns that were becoming more evident each day.

"It's worrisome. My family is Jewish, and we have a number of relations who have left. But I don't think it will develop into anything. Hitler is nothing but a phase. It will pass. Germany is a civilized, advanced country, after all. Anyway, to your stay in France." Sylvain lifted his glass, apparently wanting to change the subject. "Do you plan on a long visit?"

Dex returned the toast, and conversation drifted onto other, more trivial matters. But it bothered him to think of all that was occurring nearby, while they played in a perfect world of wandering tourists clutching Baedeker guidebooks; old ladies marching purposefully home from market, their shopping bags filled with fresh vegetables; bejeweled women walking diamond-collared poodles, and handsome young men flirting outrageously with pretty young girls in flowered summer dresses. It seemed impossible that a dictator had risen to power, and that tensions were rising throughout Europe as they sat dawdling over champagne. He glanced at the young men on the street, feeling suddenly old. He was only thirty-four, yet the sight of their invincible self-confidence made him wince like an old man. Surely this generation would grow old, not meet death in the mud, blood and misery he had known?

That evening he gave Alix the brooch, which she was delighted with. But when he tried to take her in his arms she slipped from them, laughing and saying she must try the brooch on. He shrugged and decided to wait. Tomorrow he was meeting with an estate agent to see property, since Alix had decided she definitely wanted to stay in Paris for the winter.

Time flew by, and although he knew that soon he'd have to face reality and journey to Limoges, he was loath to leave Paris. Sylvain de Rothberg had invited them several times to dinner and they had returned the invitations. Sylvain usually came alone.

"Maybe he's, you know, a fairy," Alix said as they watched the world go by seated at Fouquet's on the Champs-Elysées, the warm evening air lazy and pleasant.

"Mmm. I don't think so. Very much the opposite. Probably just hasn't found the right girl."

"Did you know he's Jewish?"

"Yes, he told me. Does that bother you?" Dex asked.

"No. Of course not. Why should it?"

"Oh, you know how some folks are."

"I do and I hate it. Daddy was a staunch Democrat and always defended everyone's rights. We had Jewish friends."

"I know. Don't get upset, Alix. I know as well as anybody what your parents were like." He thought nostalgically of New York and sighed. "It's crazy, everything that's happening in Germany. Do you know they've stopped Jews from teaching in universities, prohibited them from entering parks and certain public places. Hitler's mad. And the madness seems to be catching hold of many," he added grimly.

"Do you believe he can go on doing this kind of thing? Why don't people stop him?"

"Because those who oppose him disappear. They get sent

to some kind of labor camp. I don't want to believe it, Alix, but when I read the news I can't help but wonder. Who would have believed that the Nazis would take over a civilized country, or that this can all be happening a few hours away? I don't understand how people like Sylvain go on, trying to stay oblivious to all that's happening there.''

"I don't know, Dex. I've never thought about it really. Oh look! A balloon!''

He followed her finger, watching the brightly striped hot-air balloon glide smoothly through the darkening sky, enjoying Alix's excitement. He was glad to see how far she'd come out of her shell. She even looked different—more at ease, prettier. She reveled in new fashions and tried on endless outfits at Vionnet and Chanel, constantly soliciting his approval. But there was more to her than just pretty clothes and trinkets. She'd discovered the Louvre, the Tuileries Garden, the Jeu de Paume and various off-beat galleries, imparting her finds enthusiastically. Shakespeare and Co. had become a regular haunt and she'd struck up a conversation with Sylvia Beach herself, after spending hours wandering among the books, gazing in awe at the pigeonholes stuffed with envelopes addressed to F. Scott Fitzgerald and Ernest Hemingway, for whom the bookshop had become the general post office.

One day, as she was choosing books with Dex, Sylvia appeared from among the shelves.

"Hello, Mrs. Ward, I didn't see you hidden away among the classics.'' She turned to a red-haired woman standing next to her. "Arianne, this is Alix Harcourt Ward. She's just arrived from the States and plans to stay in Paris for the winter. I think we should introduce her to Gertrude, don't you?''

The other woman looked Alix over solemnly. Dex, stepping back into the shadows, watched Alix blush under the critical gaze. It was not an ordinary gaze, but more like the stare a critic would give a painting, he realized, taken aback and feeling strangely resentful.

The following day, Sylvia and Arianne de Forges introduced Alix to the writer Gertrude Stein, and she was immediately taken into the fold. As the days went by, Dex saw less and less of Alix. She left the apartment-hunting to him, thrilled to have been so readily accepted. Instantly, she was more at home at Gertrude and Alice Toklas's apartment than she had been all her life in Sutton Place.

Dex was not so quick to accept her new friends wholeheartedly but said nothing, happy to see her blossom and loath to burst her bubble. But Arianne's possessiveness left him ill at ease. It disturbed him more than he liked to admit. It was one thing for Alix to have a close girlfriend, but the impression he had of Arianne was more like a challenge. Shrugging off the thought he concentrated his energy on finding a suitable apartment and quickly closed on a delightful property on the Avenue Foch.

Alix grimaced at some of the furnishings, but agreed they could be changed. She was enough of her father's daughter to recognize a good deal.

As she drifted more and more into her own world, so did Dex. Sylvain became a regular companion, and Dex was introduced to a select group of the jewelry designer's friends—writers and artists, bankers and businesspeople. There were the evenings at the embassy where they were welcomed by the American ambassador, dinners with friends from New York at Maxim's, lunches at the Pré Catalan. It was at Aux Deux Magots, sharing a bottle of wine with Sylvain, Picasso and some of the writers and other artists that frequented the bistro, that he truly enjoyed.

But as summer blossomed so did the need for him to return to the helm at Harcourt's.

Now that Alix was settled, Dex knew that he must face Limoges and the past. He spent his last few days in Paris roaming the art galleries and studios with Sylvain, determined to acquire as much knowledge as quickly as possible. He was intrigued by Picasso and went regularly to the artist's studio, lounging among palettes and canvases, drinking strong Spanish wine while beautiful women swarmed around the bald, bronzed Spaniard, as empowering and enthralling in person as the art he produced. The suite at the Ritz now had several paintings propped against the wall that Dex had not intended, at first, to buy but knew he couldn't live without.

Finally he left the capital, driving south and stopping in sleepy villages, eating at the local *auberge* and reveling in the pleasure of ordering the *menu du jour* and local wine. Speaking French gave him a renewed sense of freedom which, although only temporary, was refreshing.

But as he drove through the long, silent stretches of road bordered by fields and poplars, there was time to think. The farther south he drove, the more nostalgic his memories became, until he finally faced the question that had been nagging him ever since his arrival. Just how much of Gavin MacLeod remained?

What would it feel like meeting his mother's family, the la Vallières, under false pretenses? During his brief visit to the factory in Limoges, when he was still reeling under the impact of his meeting with Greta's aunt in Lausanne, he'd barely had time to deal with business before returning to the States.

But now that he was here to stay, at least for a while, he would be expected to socialize. He sighed, thinking of what it would feel like, meeting his mother's family as he inevitably would.

Glancing up, he stepped hard on the brakes, barely able to avoid colliding with a tractor that was ponderously crossing the road. The incident left him shaken, and he stopped in the next village, drank two strong coffees and a cognac to steady his jittery nerves. The near accident made him realize he needed to shrug off the mood that had enveloped him ever since leaving the capital. He had to come to grips with the fact that there was no room for the past. He had taken the final step into his new life when he'd married Alix, and it was too late to look back.

He nodded to the florid owner of the café, swallowed the last of the cognac and slipped some change on the counter. But the feelings kept surfacing, and as he passed the spots where he'd played as a child, the memories and anger he tried so hard to keep at bay emerged once more, leaving him vulnerable and raw. Each field of grazing cattle, each sunflower tilted yearningly toward the sky was a poignant reminder of his brother—not the treacherous man who'd left him to die, but the companion of his youth, whom he'd loved and trusted.

It was late afternoon when Dex finally drove into the town center, headed past the cathedral and up the hill to La Renardière, the Harcourt residence that overlooked the city.

He reached the wrought-iron gates, with J and H entwined in bronze, and gazed through the grille at the eccentric castle, built by John Sr. in 1903. Dex smiled. It was the extraordinary fantasy of an extraordinary man, with a square tower to the right, a round one to the left, an ornate exterior, thirty-four bedrooms and several telephones that linked him straight to the factory. There was no room for the past in this new life, he realized again, no room for weakness. Any emotions must be safely put back where they belonged, for here there was room for one man only, and that man was Dexter Ward.

17

Limoges, France, 1934

Several weeks passed. Summer eased into autumn and Dex threw every ounce of energy and effort into improving the factory, streamlining production and bringing down costs, pushing all else to the back of his mind as he concentrated on the performance of the furnaces. It was the furnaces that gave him the idea of buying MacLeod coal.

Dex recalled that MacLeod's had been selling coal to his uncle's company and to Haviland's for years. It was of fine quality and gave extra burning time. Why shouldn't he buy Harcourt's from them, too? He debated the matter, opened his desk drawer and took out a thick report he'd received from the detective he'd hired in London. Angus was slowly destroying MacLeod's, that much was clear. At the rate he was going, there would soon be little left of his father's heritage. Dex's lips tightened and the vein in his temple throbbed as the anger that seethed each time he thought of his brother took hold. He had no desire to assist Angus, but the thought of his father's life work being desecrated devastated him.

A bitter smile hovered about his mouth as he sat swinging in the old leather chair that had been John Sr.'s, his eyes wandering abstractedly to the high wooden shelves filled with porcelain samples, some ready for a second firing, some approved, others rejected. Pondering the question of MacLeod's, he flipped through the report and his eyes narrowed. There was a lot of debt. And debt could be acquired—at a price.

He rose and leaned his hands on the large table among the unfinished sketches. Perhaps, if he was patient and bided his time, the moment would come when he could confront Angus face-to-face. And when that moment came, he would be prepared. He gave a low laugh that resonated. Let Angus get deeper in debt. Let him meet Dexter Ward. The thought sent a chill, then a thrill, up his spine. Then he bared his teeth. Let Angus step into the lion's den. And then, when there was no way out, he would move in for the kill, slowly. But enough of that for now, he thought.

Slipping the report back in the drawer, he locked it and wondered whether to give Alix a call before he took lunch. She seemed perfectly content in her new life, so he'd stayed in Limoges and got on with his work. He'd have to make a trip to New York soon, but for the moment things were under control.

During the first weeks in Limoges he'd kept a low profile, but now invitations swamped his desk and there was nothing to do but bite the bullet and accept. He picked up a thick ivory card, immediately recognizing the la Vallière crest, and eyed it with mixed feelings. The thought of attending his aunt's house as a stranger left him depressed, and he threw the invitation down, grabbed his tweed jacket and left the office before lunch. Getting into the wine-colored Delahaye he'd had shipped from the States, he drove aimlessly south.

The past few days had brought cooler weather. A cold east wind blowing in from Bordeaux was stripping the branches of leaves, making him more nostalgic than usual, and all of a sudden he felt tired and more bereft than he would ever have believed possible. It had all seemed so simple, back in 1918 when he'd impulsively chosen this life, but as he gazed blindly at the fields turning from green to brown, he had real doubts.

He gave himself a mental shake, shocked by his own negativity. Perhaps he needed a break. A trip to Paris and a few dinners with Sylvain would blow away the blues. Maybe Alix had come to accept herself and the new life she was leading and they could begin a family of their own. The thought of an heir always helped.

By the time he reached Chalus he was hungry. Entering the fortressed town, he parked at the foot of the castle, where Richard the Lion-Heart had died a careless death.

He thought about the crusader as he switched off the ignition. It was strange to think that a man who'd braved such peril had ended up smitten by a roaming arrow he'd invited upon himself. Too damn sure of his luck, that was the trouble. When one was very young, Dex mused, everything seemed so easy. Then, all at once, things had begun catching up with him and he didn't like it. Getting out of the car, he slipped the keys in the pocket of his corduroy trousers and headed toward the small inn.

It was lunchtime and the auberge was busy. Locals sat, tightly squeezed, on wooden benches, tucking into *magret confit d'oie*, the goose pâté for which the Périgord was famous. The *patronne*, a trim, busy woman with an eagle eye, a ready smile and a quick word for her customers, came up to him.

"*C'est pour manger, Monsieur?*" she asked, searching for a free table to seat her guest. "*Ah! Voilà.*"

He followed her across the low-beamed room, waited while she replaced the checkered tablecloth and placed a basket of fresh bread and carafe of red wine on the table. Seating himself, he ordered the *plat du jour*, glad he'd gotten away from the stifling atmosphere of the factory. He reached for a piece of bread and poured himself a glass of red while Madame addressed the customer at the next table.

"*Tout va bien, monseigneur?*" she inquired.

A politely murmured response drew Dex's attention briefly to a tall figure in a black cassock sitting directly to his right. The priest raised his eyes. For a moment, there was a hesitation. A frown followed, then he smiled and nodded congenially.

Dex's pulse missed a beat. It couldn't be. Yet the nose, long and beaky, the chiseled cheekbones and those eyes, so typical of all the la Vallières, were unmistakable.

"*Vous allez bien, monsieur?* Are you all right?" The priest leaned forward, frowning with concern.

Cold sweat burst on his forehead. He reached, trembling, for his glass and gulped down the rest of the wine, unable to draw his eyes away.

"Are you ill, my friend?" The familiarity in the priest's grave voice sharpened the anguish, and nostalgia stabbed him like a pointed dagger until he couldn't bear it. Reaching out, he grabbed the priest's sleeve. "*Mon père,*" he whispered. "I would like you to take my confession."

"Very well, *mon fils.* But not here. Perhaps later this afternoon at the church?"

"Now. I beg of you."

"This is highly unusual." He glanced at the hand that gripped his sleeve.

Dex loosened his hold. "I beg of you, *mon père.* Call it a personal conversation, if you prefer. All I ask is that anything I reveal here today be considered with the same degree of secrecy that it would be in the confessional."

"If that is your wish and I can be of help, then by all means. Something troubles you deeply? May I?" He pulled out the chair and sat opposite. "How can I help you?"

Already regretting his impulse, Dex fought the urge to get up and flee, to run as far as he could and hide, knowing the risk he was about to take could destroy him.

"Have we met before?" the priest asked with a slight frown, as though trying to place him. "Allow me to introduce myself. I am Eugène de la Vallière."

Dex poured some wine, and took a quick sip, his mouth dry. Then, all at once, words rushed to his lips. "We have met before. The last time was during the summer of 1913. Surely you remember—you must remember—the summer of 1913. It was glorious," he whispered. "That day at Château de la Vallière, when we fished the trout and Flora almost fell into the river." It seemed like yesterday.

"I'm sorry, I don't follow you. The only people there were my cousins, Gavin, Angus and Flora. Do you know them? You couldn't possibly—"

"No, you're wrong," Gavin interrupted. "René was there, too. You, Angus, Flora, René and I. It was the biggest trout we'd ever seen. And *I* reeled it in."

"This is a joke. *Ce n'est pas possible!*" The priest sat, pale and rigid.

"I know it is hard to believe, but…I am Gavin." His voice was barely audible in the noisy room.

"Gavin MacLeod is dead. He died almost twenty years ago during the war. I do not appreciate this farce."

Gavin grabbed his arm as Eugène rose angrily.

"Wait. Please." He plunged his free hand into the inner pocket of his jacket and retrieved Angus's gold cross that he carried everywhere. "Look." He opened his palm. "You have the same one around your neck. It was given to you by your mother, Hortense de la Vallière, at birth. Constance, my mother, gave me mine." He loosened his tie and wrenched open his shirt collar, displaying the cross.

Eugène de la Vallière looked at the gold crucifixes, aghast; they were identical to the one he wore himself, each the same unique design, crafted by a jeweler in Bordeaux. Could this man truly be his cousin? He sat down with a bang.

How many masses had he said for Gavin? How many candles had he lit for his cousin's soul? *Mon Dieu,* was it really possible? He glanced across the table, wondering if this tall, square-shouldered, dark-haired man before him could be his cousin, returned from the dead? His eyes were as blue and piercing as Gavin's had been and his complexion as tanned. Taking a quick sip of wine, he tried to calm himself. Perhaps he was an impostor, perhaps…

Then Dex smiled, and all at once Eugène knew.

Shaking, he rose and folded his cousin in his arms without wiping away the tears of joy, realizing God had performed a miracle. A thousand questions fell from his lips as he listened to a tale so incredible, so utterly outrageous, that if it were anyone but Gavin speaking he would have had a hard time believing it.

"*Cela tient du miracle,*" he repeated, shaking his head.

"But that Angus intended to kill you is absurd. He returned from the war a broken man, Gavin."

"Call me Dex."

"If you insist." He smiled reluctantly. "I will never get used to calling you that, or thinking of you as an American tycoon. Strange that we have not yet been introduced in society."

"I've kept to myself. And I trust you with my secret, Eugène. If you call me by the wrong name, the cat'll be among the pigeons."

"Of course. Excuse me, I—" Eugène raised his hands in mock despair.

"Oh, but it's good to talk to you, *mon cousin*, to unburden my soul. I thought I could carry on alone, bear it till the end, but the moment I recognized you I knew I wasn't as strong as I'd believed."

"True strength is the ability to recognize one's needs and feelings, not hide them."

"Perhaps. But I made choices. At the time, they didn't seem quite as complicated as they do now. But whether I like it or not, I must abide by them."

"We all make choices," Eugène said. "Some right, some wrong. Few are those who go through life on a straight and smooth path, with no stones to step over. It is part of God's lesson, part of what we must learn during our stay on earth."

"Right now they seem like boulders," Dex murmured.

"That too will pass. All in good time. God takes care of his own."

Dex nodded doubtfully. "It seemed so easy back then to become a different person. Home seemed so far away. But here, with so many reminders, so many familiar spots, places and people..." Their eyes met.

"Would you consider returning to being Gavin MacLeod?"

"How?" Dex gave a bitter laugh. "I've built an existence as another person, Eugène. I'm married, run a business, have people who depend on that other person. Plus, the scandal would ruin Harcourt's." He shook his head firmly. "There's no looking back. I owe it to others to stick to my choice."

"That only you can decide. It is your conscience that must

do what you believe to be right. I can only guide you, be here to counsel you, if and when you need me.''

"Thank you, *mon cousin*. You cannot conceive the relief, the weight, that has been lifted from my chest.''

Eugène reached across the table and gripped his cousin's hand. "Believe me, that is what being a priest is all about.''

"I suppose it is. Eugène, what do you think prompted Angus to do what he did?''

"I cannot believe Angus had any intention of killing you. It is absurd and not in his nature. Of all people, you should know that. He suffered from shell shock and was in a terrible state, psychologically, when he returned from the war. Your death, and his feelings of guilt were overwhelming.''

"So he pretended he was sorry? That's rich! He didn't waste much time getting over it, did he?''

"He has never gotten over it.''

"No? You don't consider allowing my father to die from grief, leaving my mother bereft of a son and marrying my fiancée getting over it? Not to mention gaining the MacLeod title and holdings, which he's proceeded to dilapidate over the past twenty years.''

"He has spoken so often of his pain, his regret. His lack of action, his inability to help you, has haunted his life, *mon cousin*.''

"Bullshit! I don't believe it.'' Dex lit a Gitâne and inhaled slowly. "I saw the look in his eyes, the indifference. And I know. Here, deep inside—'' He tapped his chest. "And my poor Flora…I wonder what her life has been like?''

"Not the happiest, I'm afraid. She married Angus out of a sense of duty toward you. He is rarely home and they have no children.''

"She deserved better than either of us. I wish she could have been happy,'' Dex said, saddened to learn of his first love's fate.

"Perhaps, had you made other decisions, she might have been,'' Eugène murmured dryly.

"I know. I've thought of all that. But I can't return to the past or change it. Life is as it is now, for better or worse. As for that bastard, I keep tabs on him.'' He clenched his fist, then relaxed it once more. ''One day I'll settle the score. When the time is right.''

''Tell me,'' Eugène asked softly, ''has it never occurred to you that Angus's reaction was merely a consequence of a situation? Not a deliberate intention?''

''I tried to tell myself that. Then I read the wedding announcement, learned of my father's death and of Angus assuming the title. I felt like a bloody fool.''

''And Flora? Can you just shrug her off? Discard her like an old pair of gloves?''

''I didn't discard her,'' Dex responded resentfully. *He* was the victim, after all, not them. ''I think of her with much fondness, but as a part of the past. We were very young. Had it not been for the war, I might not even have proposed so quickly.''

Eugène gave an unsatisfied grunt. ''She still lives in that mystical world of hers. She is very much the same. But I don't think she ever got over your...er...death. I'm surprised you don't seem to care for her as you used to.''

''Of course I care,'' he exclaimed, irritated. ''But it was a long time ago. There have been other women. Lots of other women. And now I'm married and so is she.''

''Angus told us that shortly before the shell hit the trench, you had received a letter from Flora,'' Eugène said slowly. ''And that you specifically requested that he marry Flora, should anything happen to you.''

''The bastard,'' he whispered, giving the table leg a vicious kick. ''Can't you see how cleverly he's construed everything? Manipulated everyone like pawns on a bloody chessboard?''

''It is not my place to tell you what is and what isn't. All I ask is that you be rational. You were always tempestuous, Gavin—''

''Dex,'' he replied automatically.

''Whatever you want to call yourself, *n'importe*. The facts remain the same, and at some time or another will have to be faced.'' Eugène eyed him severely.

''Perhaps. What do you think of all that's happening polit-

ically, Eugène?'' he asked, abruptly changing the subject.
''Germany is on the move. If France should fall again—''

''France will never fall again,'' Eugène rejoined proudly.
''We have the Grande Armée, the Maginot line. The situation
is very different from last time.''

''You must be kidding.'' Dex laughed outright.

''We must trust in God and our nation.''

''Right. I'd rather trust myself, thank you very much. The
governments are running scared, trying to placate Hitler. And
Germany's on the warpath. I'm telling you, Eugène, I can smell
it and it stinks. Hitler will be on the march before long. First
it'll be the Sudetenland, then God only knows.''

''But Chamberlain has been negotiating. The danger appears
to have passed.''

''You can kid yourself if you want, but I'm telling you. It
may not be this year or the next, but we'll be at war sooner or
later. And, as usual, France will be the stomping ground.''

''I pray that your words are mistaken.''

''So do I.'' He stubbed out the Gitâne in the glass ashtray
with a grim twist. ''And now I am headed back to Limoges.''
He glanced up and grinned. ''Here you have him, Dexter Ward,
the man I have become for the past sixteen years.'' He rose,
anxious to leave now that he'd unburdened his soul.

''Will I see you at my mother's tomorrow evening?''

''Yes. And after today it will be bearable to return to la
Vallière. Thank you, *mon cousin.* By the way, you must remember that I speak very poor French.'' He grinned wickedly.

''What do you mean? Your French is as good as mine.''

''But nobody knows—which makes for interesting inside
knowledge. You'd be surprised at all I've learned.''

''Well, well. It seems somewhat underhanded.'' Eugène
laughed despite his reservations. His cousin had not changed
that much. ''You're swimming in very deep water, Gavin
MacLeod. Be careful not to get in above your head.''

On his way home, Eugène reflected on the extraordinary circumstances of his cousin's return. Could Angus have wanted
to kill his brother? No. That was impossible. He shifted the

gears of the old Renault that came with his job of secretary to the bishop of Limoges and headed toward Ambazac, his mind tormented.

What should he do? How could he bring the two brothers together once more and unite the family? It was a problem that continued to bother him as he walked up the front steps of the Château de la Vallière, his family home for over two centuries. Recalling the past, he remembered his cousins and Flora seated on these very steps, playing marbles, laughing, teasing him about becoming a priest.

He stopped, feeling his thin shoulders heavy with the burden that Gavin had put on him this day, and watched as the setting sun caressed the stained-glass of the tower windows where Flora used to sleep those many years ago. He sighed and straightened his tall frame. Poor Flora. How unjust it all seemed and how easily it could all have been resolved, were it not for Gavin's impetuous nature.

He trod up the rest of the steps with a heart filled with both joy that his cousin was alive and annoyance with him, for being obtuse and blind, and prayed for Gavin's enlightenment.

18

Edinburgh, Scotland, 1934

"I'm afraid we'll have to rid ourselves of more stock, Lord MacLeod." Mr. MacDougal, a bespectacled lawyer, raised his eyes disapprovingly from the stack of papers lying before him on the desk and eyed the disheveled man sitting before him. Not so young and aging badly, he observed. It was a damn shame his brother had been killed in the war. Gavin MacLeod was made of a different cloth. But this Lord MacLeod had no fiber, no backbone whatsoever, and if his present habits continued, there would be little left of the MacLeod holdings. Not to mention Strathaird Castle, mortgaged to the hilt. Between the gambling, drinking and mounting debts, it would be virtually impossible for the whole lot not to go down the drain.

After old Lady MacLeod's death, things had become steadily worse. The present Lady MacLeod seemed to have little influence or interest in her husband's affairs. At first he'd believed she might keep him on the right track, but that was before the visits to London and Monte Carlo began.

"The only opportunity I see is the interest that American company, Harcourt's, has shown in our coal. It burns better, making the firing process more economical and thus—"

"Spare me, MacDougal. We know all that. La Vallière

and Haviland's have been buying our coal for years, for Christ's sake!''

"I was merely reiterating what your cousin, Father de la Vallière, mentioned," MacDougal replied with a sniff.

"Well, Eugène's usually right, isn't he?''

"I believe your cousin is as concerned as we all are about the present…er…state of affairs," he said primly, noticing that at least Lord MacLeod had the grace to look uncomfortable. The blush gave him hope and he pushed his point home. "It is on the Haviland's recommendation that Mr. Ward is seeking to acquire our coal. If he is pleased with it, perhaps—''

"What's the name of the damn company?''

"Harcourt's, my lord. Surely you remember? It is run and owned now by a Mr. Dexter Ward, the deceased John Harcourt's son-in-law. He does a very good job. According to the reports I have received, they supply a large part of the lower echelon of the American porcelain market, and leave the higher echelon to Haviland's. He also does special orders—rather off-the-beaten-track work, shall we say, artistic, unconventional—''

"Yes, yes…" Angus raised a weary hand. "Is it really necessary to get involved with all this?''

"My lord," MacDougal explained patiently, "we *need* the orders. I know we have the reputation of having an exceptional product—which indeed we do—but we have competitors who would be only too glad to do business with Mr. Ward. I think we should consider ourselves blessed that he wants to deal with us.''

"Oh, very well, if you insist. Are we finished? Can I get you a drink, MacDougal? Whiskey?" he added hopefully.

"No, thank you, my lord. I think I'll be making my way home now. I'm most relieved that you've decided to work with Harcourt's. I believe a fruitful relationship with Mr. Ward could prove to be of the utmost importance for the survival of the collieries.''

"Mmm. Yes. Well, good day to you, MacDougal." Angus thrust a hand out, then showed the lawyer to the door.

MacDougal departed, relieved. The worst could be held at

bay if Harcourt's ordered. But for how long? The bank and several private loans were coming to term. Well, all he could do was his job, he reasoned as he trudged out of Buckingham Terrace, pulling his mackintosh close and putting up his black umbrella. You could lead the horse to the water, but you couldn't make it drink. At least today the horse had glanced in the water's direction.

19

Paris, France, 1934

When Dex returned to Paris, he was surprised to learn that Arianne had practically moved in permanently to the apartment in the Avenue Foch. Although he said nothing to Alix, he found her presence disturbing.

Over the past months he'd had little time to think about much except work. His desire for revenge was still latent, and often, thoughts of Angus made him enter negative spells, but he knew the time wasn't right. He sensed the right moment would come, and chose to live with it. Alix seemed happy now, and he was determined to dedicate more time to her and to beginning their family.

After an early cocktail party at the American embassy, he broached the subject of the baby. It was nearly Christmas and it had been several months since their arrival. Surely now she could not refuse to consummate a marriage that had lasted nearly three years?

He opened a bottle of champagne and sat next to her on the gilded sofa that still hadn't been changed. Alix had charged Elsie de Wolf to buy her furniture and ship it from the States.

"You're happy here, aren't you, Al?" he asked, not mentioning Arianne. Perhaps she was lonely and liked having a friend to keep her company at the apartment. Still, it annoyed him that Arianne obviously considered herself at home.

"I love Paris, Dex—as Gertrude says, America's my country but Paris is my home."

"Maybe we should consider buying a house in the country or something. I know you'd hate Limoges. Far too provincial."

"Oh, I'm fine here." She smoothed her black silk dress, a Molyneux that did wonders for her figure, he noticed. There too she'd changed. She was prettier than he'd ever imagined she could look, making the thought of consummating the marriage more and more tempting. He leaned over and dropped a kiss on her mouth, slipping an arm around her.

"I'll do whatever you want, Al, but what I really want is you." He felt her stiffen and held her closer. "It's been far too long already."

"Dex, I—" She lifted her hand, then dropped it in her lap, the pearl and diamond ring designed by Sylvain for her birthday sparkling.

"It won't be as terrible as you think, baby. In fact, you may just enjoy it."

"It's not that. It's that, well—I can't. You'll just have to accept it, Dex. I don't want to sleep with you or have a baby or any of that," she said in a rush.

"But why not, Alix? I don't understand. Do you think I'm made of stone?"

"Don't you have other women?" she asked, looking directly at him.

"I—well, I won't say I've been an angel all these years, but nothing that matters, nothing serious."

"But I don't mind, Dex." She gazed at him, her eyes wide and earnest. "It's fine with me if you sleep with other girls. It's normal."

"Is it?" He rose, annoyed. "There's nothing normal about a man not sleeping with his wife, Alix."

"But *all* the men here have mistresses. You know that."

"That's not the point. I want a home, a family, something to build our lives on. This French way of life is fine, but eventually we're going to go home to the real world."

"No, we're not. I never want to leave here." She glanced up as he paced along the fine Persian rug, her enigmatic expression sending a strange chill up his spine.

"What the hell's the matter with you? I don't know, maybe you should see a doctor." He turned to the window, exasperated, and watched the lights of the city and the passing cars twinkling below. "It's not normal that you don't want to sleep with me and that you won't give me a child. I don't understand."

He turned as the door opened and Arianne walked in without so much as an acknowledgment.

"I'm having a private conversation with my wife," he snapped, running his fingers through his thick, dark hair, graying now at the temples.

Alix turned, abruptly spilling some champagne. "You can say whatever you like in front of Arianne. I don't care. We don't have any secrets."

"How touching. But this is a somewhat delicate matter that I think would be better discussed only between us." He directed a meaningful look at her, hoping she would take his hint.

"Oh, do stop talking in riddles, Dex. Arianne knows everything there is to know." She tossed her head, challenging him.

"As you wish," he answered, annoyance turning to anger when he noted Arianne's triumphant smile. "Alix, you know that before we got married we made an agreement and you made me a promise. We've discussed it and you know exactly what I'm talking about, so don't try and slither your way out this time, because I've had enough." He saw her pale and continued.

"What agreement?" Arianne interrupted. Dex turned to tell her to mind her own damn business.

"I—you don't plan to hold me to that, do you, Dex? It's ridiculous. You can't," Alix blurted, frightened.

"Why on earth not?" he interjected, antagonism getting the better of him. "You are, after all, my wife. I don't find it in any way astonishing that I should want an heir."

Arianne gasped. "What are you saying?"

"You don't know? A secret, after all, eh? Though what it has to do with you, I fail to comprehend." He crossed his arms, satisfied at the shock he was causing. "Alix and I agreed that she would give me an heir. I'm merely asking her to keep her word."

"But this is appalling!" Arianne cried, staring at him with heightened venom. "You can't do this to her."

"Ask her to be as good as her word? Why not?" He flicked an imaginary speck of dust from his sleeve before continuing. "I believe the nonconsummation of a marriage is grounds for annulment?"

"You are an animal, a beast," Arianne hissed, then turned accusingly toward Alix, who was sniveling. "How could you agree to this? It would be rape."

"Interesting. I wasn't aware that a man having sexual intercourse with his spouse was considered rape. Particularly when she gave her consent before the wedding."

"You know exactly what I mean." Arianne stamped her foot angrily. "It is…it is—you are a pig, I will not allow it!" She went to stand next to Alix, slipping a protective arm around her shoulders.

"Well, I'll be damned if you can stop me." Dex withdrew a cigarette from a gold cigarette case and casually offered it to them.

"I will not let you harm her."

"I have no intention of harming her. But I have every intention of consummating the marriage." He took a long drag, enjoying Arianne's discomfort.

"Alix, you won't allow him to do this to you?"

"What can I do?" she whispered through her tears. "I *did* give my word."

"So what? He has nothing to prove it."

"That's not the point," she sobbed. "I gave my word of honor."

"Damn your word of honor," Arianne exclaimed, furious. "He should never have extricated such a promise from you."

"Perhaps," Dex said. "But my reasons and my marriage are no concern of yours. Alix, it's up to you. You know I would never force you. But I will be obliged to annul the marriage if you don't feel you can go through with consummating it. After all, I'm a man, damn it. I want sex with my wife, a child and a normal life.''

"You're just doing it to spite me," she said feebly.

"No, I'm not. Where you found that excuse, I don't know. And why are you so interested in all of this, Arianne? I know you and Alix are good friends, but I'm curious to know just why you take this so to heart?" He eyed her suspiciously, then stubbed out his cigarette. "I'm going out for a drink. If you decide to go ahead and keep your promise, Alix, I'll be here for a couple of days. If not...well, so be it."

"I don't want your filthy brat," she cried. "I don't want a child. You can't make me. I won't let you," she wailed, burying her face in her hands while Arianne hovered over her.

"I repeat—there is no question of forcing you. We can end our marriage in a civilized manner and go our separate ways." He glanced at his watch, realizing he was running late for his dinner with Sylvain.

Dex left them, striding down the street, enjoying the crisp late autumn, the chill of the coming winter and wisps of fog that hovered as he approached the river. He crossed the Pont Neuf and picked up his pace. Why was Alix being so difficult? What fear was it that haunted her? He'd been understanding enough, but now he was angered by her attitude. And that woman. He gritted his teeth, then realized he was late and hailed a passing cab. He was glad he'd finally had it out with Arianne. Damn the bitch.

As usual, he and Sylvain dined at his favorite table at the Brasserie Lipp, inside on the ground floor, reserved exclusively for patrons and special guests. They ordered boeuf bourguignon.

"You don't seem yourself tonight. Is something bothering you?" Sylvain inquired, watching Dex.

"I'm sorry." All at once, he decided to confide in his friend. After all, Sylvain and Alix had spent time together discussing the design of her ring and the necklace he was giving her for

Christmas. Maybe Sylvain could help him understand her better. "It's Alix."

"Oh? Is something wrong?"

"Not wrong, exactly. It's embarrassing to go into this, but maybe you can help me see more clearly."

"Please, if I can be of help…"

"Ever since we married, Alix has been reticent about, well, consummating the marriage. To put it bluntly, she refuses to sleep with me." He took a gulp of wine and continued, embarrassed. "This has been going on for three years and I'm fed up. She promised me an heir and I'm damn well holding her to her word."

"I see," Sylvain mused. "Has she said *why* she doesn't want to share her bed with you?"

"No. And that's what doesn't make sense. She oohs and aahs and slithers her way out of things, but I can't put my finger on what she's so afraid of," Dex exclaimed, glad to vent his frustration. "It's not like I would harm her in any way. And that friend she has as a permanent houseguest doesn't help," he added darkly. "I don't like the woman. There's something weird about her."

"You mean Arianne de Forges?" Sylvain's eyebrow raised slightly as he carefully selected a roll. "Perhaps that is where you should look for answers," he said gently, spreading the bread with butter.

"Why?" Dex lowered his glass and stared at him. "You can't mean what I think you mean." He closed his eyes, a vision suddenly playing out in his head. *Of course.* What a damn fool he was not to have seen it for himself. "Jesus, what an idiot they must take me for."

"It is quite common today. And if you look at the people she and Arianne hang around, well, *mon ami*, I hardly think it is surprising."

"My God, that's why she's refused me. It never occurred to me that she and Arianne could be lovers." He laid down his fork, deflated.

"A delicate situation but one that can surely be got around. Perhaps you can come to an understanding?"

"Damn understandings. It's bad enough being the last idiot to know. I suppose the whole of fucking Paris is laughing behind my back. Am I known as the cuckold with the lesbian wife? I'll kill them both." He threw his napkin on the table.

"Calm down, Dex. This is Paris, not New York. It is usual here for such things to occur. Nobody imagines that she is not sleeping with you as well," Sylvain consoled, "just as everybody assumes you are aware and have a mistress tucked away somewhere."

"I'll be damned. Pick up the check, will you? I'm going home to sort out this mess right now." He rose.

"Maybe I should come with you."

"Don't worry. I'll settle this my own way."

"Don't do anything foolish, Dex, I beg of you." Sylvain laid a restraining hand on his sleeve.

"I'm fine. Just time to clean house."

When Dex reached the apartment, the lights were dimmed and the servants nowhere to be seen. Hiding out, were they? Well, they'd get a piece of his mind tomorrow. And he'd make sure Arianne was out in the street before breakfast.

He reached the master bedroom, grimaced at the burnished bronze silk hangings that shrouded the huge canopied bed, gleaming in the soft glow of the bedside lamps. Absently he wondered why Alix still hadn't bothered to choose something more modern. As it was, it reminded him of something out of the *Arabian Nights*. He noticed the sheets had been turned down and the pillows plumped invitingly.

He slung his jacket over the gilt armchair and switched on the light in the dressing room, changing into silk pajamas and a robe. Picking up the *Paris Tribune* from the dresser, he walked back into the room and stopped in transfixed amazement. Arianne and Alix lay entwined in the center of his bed, dressed in scanty silk nightgowns.

"What the hell do you think you're doing?" he demanded, once he'd caught his breath.

"It's *très* simple." Arianne shrugged, her stare provocative under her crop of red curls. "If you want her, then you'll have to have me, too." Her French accent was pronounced, her voice husky. He noticed that her expression was softer, her pupils somewhat dilated. Alix lay silently next to her.

"Get out of my room," he growled, trying to ignore his body's reaction.

"*Non.*"

"Cut the crap, Arianne. Out. Both of you."

"You Americans can be so crude," she murmured, her voice languorous. "If you were French you would probably want to watch. You might even enjoy it."

Dex gave an involuntary gasp at the erotic vision of the flickering light from the fringed lamps playing subtle games with the creamy texture of their skin. He watched paralyzed, as Arianne's fingers trailed possessively down Alix's throat, reached the curve of her breasts, and her gaze locked with his in an unspoken challenge as she reached Alix's taut nipples, circling them slowly before untying the straps that held together the flimsy silk nightgown.

Dex closed his eyes, willing this not to happen. Opening them, he stared as Arianne pulled back the silk and unveiled Alix's small, round breasts. Then she cast him a veiled, inviting smile. He moved toward the bed, entranced, removed his robe and pajama top, and lay down next to them.

The silk had fallen to Alix's hips and he surveyed her, fascinated. He had never thought of her as beautiful. Yet she was splendid, lying motionless, like a vestal virgin being prepared for sacrifice, as Arianne gently stroked her legs and smoothed her shapely thighs, an elusive half smile hovering as she raised the silk and her fingers disappeared. Her gaze locked once more with his, excited and triumphant, as Alix writhed then let out a sharp, ecstatic cry, collapsing among the pillows.

"Now," Arianne ordered in a commanding whisper. To his amazement, she leaned over and deftly undid his pajamas, caressing him with a feather touch as he sank next to her, his eyes closing, drunk with pleasure. Then she rose and stood at the foot of the bed. Her hair flaming in the glimmering light, she resembled a pagan priestess before the altar of sacrifice, performing the ultimate ritual, as she spread Alix's legs then stepped away.

"Take her," she ordered.

Desire and weakness battled with the knowledge that what he was about to do was wrong. But Arianne's eyes mesmerized, Alix's pliant body called and the last shreds of resistance gave way.

Arianne was at the head of the bed now, clasping Alix's wrists and murmuring soft, soothing words as Dex caressed, kissed and enjoyed, swallowed into a fantasy world.

She trembled as he gently slid his fingers inside her, determined to give her pleasure, his satisfaction mounting as she sighed. Arianne tensed, their wills clashing like sharp-edged blades when Alix gasped. Two could play at this bizarre game, he realized triumphantly.

When finally she cried out, he entered her, thrust deep and purged his anger. But when he came it was bittersweet, and shame at having allowed instinct and passion to overcome better judgment made him rise quickly from the bed, determined to leave.

Then he glanced at them.

Alix now lay languorously in Arianne's arms, but his gaze was riveted on Arianne, slowly touching herself, her eyes gleaming and searching out his. Instinctively he leaned forward, drawn once more into the mythical circle.

"Come," she murmured in a husky whisper that made him groan, the invitation impossible to resist. "There are desires that only a man can satisfy," she whispered, disengaging herself from Alix, her hands suddenly kneading his shoulders, nails driving him wild as he pulled her to him. He dragged his fingers through the mass of short red curls, lips seeking her voluptuous mouth, hands gripping her taut buttocks, grazing her inner thighs, determined she would plead.

When he felt Alix stroking him, he wasn't surprised. Their eyes joined in a strange new complicity as her fingers wandered. But soon Alix lay aside and Arianne reached for him, legs entwining, his hips strong and demanding as they joined in a frenzied purging of souls.

That night they slept together in the huge canopied bed, and next morning they wandered arm in arm along a misty Seine, under bare trees, to Aux Deux Magots. There they sipped *cafés crème* and discussed politics, while Alix fed bits of croissant to the sparrows hopping on the sidewalk.

A few weeks later he learned that Alix was pregnant. The news left him with mixed feelings. He spent the winter coming and going between Paris and Limoges, lavishing gifts on Alix, worried, for she seemed frail, and grateful now for Arianne's constant presence and attention.

20

Skye, Scotland, 1934

Even now, after so many years, Flora always expected Gavin to walk through the door of the dreamery. There was no logic to it, and if anyone knew, they would think her mad. But still she dreamed. It was her solace, her way of dealing with a life devoid of love, a husband who was rarely around and had never, since that first disastrous wedding night, approached her again.

At first she'd been relieved. How could she give herself to anyone but Gavin? But as time went by, being alone with only her spirits to talk to didn't seem enough. With each year that passed she longed for a child, afraid now that she would soon be too old.

It had been five years since Tante Constance died, leaving her in an even more solitary state than before. Perhaps this Christmas she would finally get up the courage to confront Angus and tell him what she wanted.

She gulped, pulled her cardigan close and shivered at the thought, her eyes wandering to the heavy gray swell writhing below the rocks. It was going to be a cold, stormy night and she prayed that the fishermen were well tucked away in their cottages, not out battling the winds and the sleet.

It was time to go downstairs and get on with the baking.

Angus had gone to Portree and was supposed to be back by four o'clock. Already the sky was darkening and she turned on the lights of the room she loved so dearly. Little had changed here in twenty years.

She rubbed her arms, then tucked a stray wisp of soft brown hair back into her bun. She was thirty-three. Would she soon be too old to have a baby? She pulled the faded chintz curtains closed and plumped the worn cushions on the window seat before heading down the staircase to the great hall. How would she put it to Angus? They rarely talked, really. They kept up a polite, friendly exchange from a distance. But could she cross that distance now? How could she reach enough to explain how badly she wanted a baby, something of her own to love and cherish?

She walked over to the tall Christmas tree, straightened a candle and replaced a piece of fallen tinsel. The tenants would be arriving at seven for the yearly Christmas party. A few neighbors would be joining them, too. Angus usually got rather drunk. But perhaps tonight after the party, if she watched what he had to drink, she could bring up the subject.

She switched the lights on in the hall. The Yule log had been placed in the vast grate, ready to be lit, and holly decked the gallery above. A sudden vision of Gavin aiming mistletoe at her flashed through her mind and she smiled. It was odd how the memories helped rather than pained her now. It was as though part of him had remained, a part she could enjoy. It remained a mystery why he'd never appeared to her in all these years. Flora had received messages from so many and was sought after by those seeking solace, trying to get in touch with a loved one now passed to the other side. But she could not reach the one soul she longed for.

"Is the cake to be frosted, m'lady?"

The cook's sudden question made her turn and smile. "Yes, please, Moira. I'll pop along to the kitchen. I hope we have enough food for tonight."

"Och aye. Don't fret, m'lady." Moira gave a broad, ruddy smile and admired the tree. "Reminds me of the old days, it does. That wee horsey hangin' there was Master Gavin's."

"Yes. He loved it, didn't he?"

"Aye, that he did. Wouldna' let anyone else put it up. A determined wee soul, he was."

"Hmm. He used to have us all running around doing all the work while he directed." Flora laughed, remembering Gavin's dictatorial orders regarding the tree-decorating. "Even Tante Constance gave up in the end and let him have his way."

Moira's shoulders shook under the heavy Arran cardigan stretched across her wide girth, and wiped a tear from her crinkled cheek. "Aye, he was quite a one, our Gavin." For a moment she and Flora stood gazing at the tree, memories of laughter, hummed carols and roast pheasant reaching out from the past and filling the silent hall.

All at once, Flora knew she wanted that again—the children, the laughter, some joy inside these thick ancient walls that had known so much love, death, sorrow and longing. The MacLeods were calling out for an heir.

Bracing herself, she turned from the tree. "I'd better get along to the kitchen. Have they brought enough whiskey?"

"Enough for a regiment, m'lady. It'll be as fine a party as ever there was when the old laird was alive."

"I hope so. We haven't done much the past few years, but tonight I want Strathaird to come alive again. We've had too much sadness. It's time for a change, Moira." The older woman looked at her curiously. Everyone on the island respected Lady MacLeod's sight. "I think we need to brighten up the place and move forward. Living in the past isn't right. We must build the future, too."

"Aye. 'Tis time," she answered, nodding. There was no need to explain. Both women knew what she meant. "But his soul will never leave, m'lady. 'Twill always be entwined with yer own."

"I know." She leaned forward and touched the painted wooden horse, watching it swing back and forth on the branch. *Forgive me, Gavin darling, for wanting a child even though it won't be yours. I'll show it this very ornament; we'll place it on the tree together and you'll be with us.*

* * *

The party was a success and lasted well into the night. It was past eleven by the time the last straggling guests were waved on their way. Flora and Angus headed to the sitting room for a nightcap before turning in.

"Lovely party, Flo," Angus said. "I think the tenants loved it. The Colonel seemed in high fettle, didn't you think?" He poured a Drambuie for her and a whiskey for himself, before settling in an armchair next to the fire.

"Yes, I thought everyone seemed in good form. I wonder how things are doing at la Vallière. I had a letter from Tante Hortense yesterday. She says Geneviève has a stream of young men in love with her."

"Not surprising. She must be a lovely girl. Long time since we've been over, isn't it?"

"Yes, it is. Eugène is secretary to the bishop now, and René's doing nothing, as usual. You know, I wouldn't be surprised if Eugène ends up at the Vatican at the rate he's going."

"Quite likely. Always knew he had it in him. Remember when we used to tease him?"

"You didn't. Gavin did. He was very naughty. Eugène really has a vocation. I wonder what Gavin would say if he knew what a wonderful priest Eugène's become?" She sipped the Drambuie thoughtfully and curled among the cushions, gazing into the crackling flames.

Angus shifted and glanced at her, sensing a strangeness in her expression. She rarely mentioned Gavin.

"Angus..."

"Yes?" He shifted again, uncomfortable. She was trying to say something, and he hated conversations that went beyond the surface, making him remember things he'd rather not. He never failed to feel the terrible rush of guilt that for years had engulfed him. He could have saved Gavin. He should have reached out and saved him. Instead, he'd stood, frozen, desperate, unable to move as the brother he loved sank into oblivion. He couldn't remember anything after that, until Flora and the field hospital. My God, would that moment never leave? Was he destined to suffer the same agony over and over again for the rest of his life? He finished the whiskey and got up to help himself to another.

"Angus, please don't."

He held the decanter in midair, frightened by the appeal in her eyes and voice, then laid it back on the silver tray, hesitant.

"Angus, I must talk to you. It's a little difficult and I don't quite know how to begin." She was twisting her hands, her glass abandoned on the little mahogany table at her side, eyes glistening yet determined. "I know we've never mentioned it, but isn't there— Well, we've never thought of having a baby," she finished in a rush, cheeks flaming.

He trembled and wished desperately that he were anywhere but here, facing his demons, knowing he'd subjected her to a miserable life. He looked away, past the photo frames and the etchings at the closed curtains, guiltily naming the whores he spent his nights with in London and Paris, the girl who'd become his mistress for a while in Monte Carlo, whose whims he'd catered to by selling more MacLeod land. Flora knew nothing about any of them. For a time, they'd made him feel like a man instead of a failed weakling. Yet Flora's words plunged deep as a dagger. He couldn't, and knew he wouldn't, ever touch her.

"I want a baby," she was whispering, staring fixedly into the lap of her evening kilt.

He poured more whiskey automatically, took a long gulp and stared at her across the tray. He couldn't deflower Flora. She was Gavin's and always would be. The only way he'd been able to come to terms with life was by preserving her, by not touching what wasn't his. He would never sully his brother's prize possession—he, who was nothing but a coward, not man enough or worthy of stepping where Gavin's footsteps should have trodden.

"Why now?" he whispered, frightened.

"Because soon it will be too late," she said softly, her eyes pleading. "I *so* want a child, Angus, something to live for. I—" She broke off, her voice cracking. He closed his eyes, dizzy with the kaleidoscope of images he detested, the visions he woke up to each morning and managed only to assuage after several drinks.

"I can't, Flo." The words came out hoarse and tortured.

"But why? I just want a baby."

"No!" All at once he slammed the tumbler down on the tray, clenching his fists desperately. Couldn't she see? Understand? "I won't. I *can't*."

"But why, Angus? What's so dreadful about it? Am I so ugly, or so dull, or...I don't know." She shrugged and faced him. "Do I disgust you?" she asked, rising, her head held high, tears trembling on her lashes as the pain and anger seethed in her eyes. He quailed.

Everything he had always dreaded was happening. He must leave, escape, run away before he suffocated. "I can't, Flo. I'm so sorry." He gave her a last desperate glance, then rushed from the room and ran upstairs. He would sleep in his old room, away from her, and leave in the morning. *Damn.* It was Christmas; she'd expect him to stay. He didn't care. Reaching the landing, he covered his face and sobbed in tortured agony, falling to his knees in despair below his brother's portrait. *Help me, God. Please, please release me from this hellish torture,* he begged.

Flora, following Angus from the room, watched, horrified, as he prostrated himself below Gavin's picture, then collapsed. She rushed up the stairs, lifting her long skirt as she tripped on the steps.

"Angus." She crouched over him, trembling. He was ill, in more senses than one. Slowly she leaned back and looked up, sobbing, at Gavin. There was no use trying to change anything, no use at all. She hadn't the right to make him suffer.

She glanced down at Angus's pale, withered figure crumpled before her and shook her head numbly, feeling neither pity nor anger. She would let him go away again, back to whatever it was that helped him survive. There was no use in fighting destiny.

That fall, Dex arrived at the American Hospital in Paris to learn that Scott Harcourt Ward had been born three hours earlier and weighed nine pounds, three ounces. Anxiously he waited to be allowed to see Alix and the baby.

"He's beautiful, Dex," Arianne cooed as they waited in the corridor.

"Is she okay?"

"I hope so."

"Do you think she'll take to the baby?" he asked suddenly. Alix hadn't been overly enthusiastic about the pregnancy. In fact, Arianne had been more excited.

"She will. Don't worry. Everything will be fine." Arianne had somehow become the stabilizing element in his strange relationship with Alix.

A nurse appeared outside the room. "You may come in now. But not for too long, Mr. Ward. The mother and baby are tired." She smiled professionally and showed them into a room filled with roses, where Alix lay with a bundle in her arms. She smiled at Dex.

"Here he is. He's all yours."

"May I hold him?" Dex looked warily at the tiny package, wondering if it might break. He'd never held a baby before. What if he dropped it?

"Here. Like this." Arianne swooped the baby into her arms and handed him over. Dex gazed down, amazed, into his son's crumpled red face. He'd never felt anything like this.

"He's great," he whispered, unable to take his eyes away from the tiny fingers and red lips.

"You got what you wanted," Arianne murmured, then smiled, removing any sting from her words. "He will grow up to be a wonderful man."

"Like his grandfather and uncle," Dex murmured, smiling affectionately at Alix.

"Like you," she answered, her eyes meeting his as he handed her back their son. "Thanks, Dex. I'm glad it worked out this way."

21

Limoges, France, 1938

It was early spring when Sylvain finally hit the road and
headed to Limoges. He loved the sensation of freedom that the
little MG convertible afforded him—the wind in his hair, the
scent of the countryside, the cherry blossoms and sunflowers,
the mass of puffy clouds that became enchanted wisps. Life
was smiling. He had orders pouring in from every American
heiress in town, and right now Paris was swarming with them.
The Duchess of Windsor was a faithful client, his several mistresses were under control and for the past three months his
mother and sisters had stopped introducing him to suitable Jewish girls they felt would fit well into his erratic existence. No
marriage for him, thank you very much.

He thought about Dex and Alix, wondering what had
prompted that marriage in the first place. He knew Dex had
been great friends with her brother. And now, of course, there
was Harcourt's, to which he seemed totally dedicated, and their
young son. He'd never heard what happened that night Dex
had found out about Alix and Arianne, but something had obviously occurred. He smiled, shook his head and laughed aloud,
glad it had worked itself out.

As he approached Limoges, he leaned over and pulled out
the directions he'd scribbled from the glove box, steering with

his left hand as he studied them, frowning. He glanced up the street as he entered the industrial city. It had boomed over the last century, thanks to the porcelain industry created by the Haviland family. Despite the drab side that accompanied all industrial cities, Limoges had character—a beautiful gothic cathedral and Benedictine cloister and the ancient aura of Eleanor of Aquitaine and her tempestuous spouse, Henry Plantagenet.

Sylvain was terrible at following directions and after ten minutes of turning in circles he realized that he was back where he'd started. He pulled up to the curb opposite the *mairie*. It was Sunday and there were few people about. He scoured the street hopefully but it was empty. Leaning back in the MG, he was wondering how to proceed when the door of a house opened and a young woman emerged.

Jumping nimbly out of the car, he was about to accost her with a seductive smile. Then he stopped, tongue-tied, and searched for breath, stunned by her beauty. Titian hair stylishly cut fell thick and wavy, framing a face more lovely than any he'd ever beheld, her eyes two sparkling amethysts.

Realizing he was gaping, Sylvain pulled himself together and hastily produced the address.

"Excuse me. Perhaps you can help me, *mademoiselle*."

"Where are you going, *monsieur?*" She squinted at the paper and he held his breath as a ray of afternoon sun slipped between the gray buildings, transforming her hair into a burnished mane of fire.

"To the résidence La Renardière."

"Oh! You mean to the Harcourt place?"

"Exactly," he replied, pleased she knew where he was going. He was loath to leave and wished he could lengthen the conversation.

"It's easy. All you have to do is cross the bridge, then go up the big street opposite. At the top you make a right and then you'll see a road to your left. It's a little way down, behind a wrought-iron grille. You can't miss it."

"Thank you, *mademoiselle,* you are most kind. I don't suppose—can I offer you a lift?"

"No, thank you," she replied with a toss of her head and

an impish smile that left him breathless. "I'm going the other way. Say hello to Dexter. I suppose that's whom you're going to see?"

"Yes, it is." Before he could ask her name, she smiled, turned and walked smartly down the street. He watched as she turned the corner, leaving him wondering if she was real or just a figment of his vivid imagination.

Arriving at Dex's he stopped at the open gates and admired the extravagant construction that overlooked the city, pleasantly situated among well-designed gardens. He switched off the ignition, still reeling from his encounter, then walked up the steps of the unusual château and rang the bell. A dog barked, followed by the sound of a grumbling female voice. Then the door opened and a plump middle-aged woman wearing a white apron eyed him cautiously.

"*Bonjour, madame.*" Sylvain smiled politely.

"Ah! But of course," she exclaimed. "Monsieur Dexter told me you were coming. Monsieur de Rothberg, I suppose?"

"Exactly."

"*Excusez-moi.* I have been put out all day. I am Madame Giroud. It's this wretched animal Monsieur Dexter insisted on retrieving from the gutters. A mongrel, no less." She showed him in, wiping her hands on her apron. "I said to him, 'Monsieur Dexter, if you want a dog, buy a proper one, not a mutt with fleas off the street and *Dieu ne sait quoi!*' But would he listen? *Non.* Men never listen. They *pretend* to listen, then do exactly as they wish. My poor husband, God rest his soul, was exactly the same. Ah! Your bag. Where is that lazy *fenéant* Gaston?"

She pattered off in search of the unfortunate Gaston, while Sylvain looked around the hall. To the left, a double-paneled door opened on to a spacious dining room. Portraits of people he presumed must be Harcourts gazed somberly down at him.

Straight ahead he saw the salons, and to his right, through a half-open door, he spied a desk covered in papers and porcelain.

All at once the door inched farther open and Dex poked his head out, glancing warily up the stairs.

"Has she gone?" he asked.

Sylvain laughed. One of the things he most enjoyed about Dexter Ward was his sense of the ridiculous.

"I believe she plans to return with Gaston."

"Good Lord. Come in here." Dex beckoned. "This is the only place she doesn't dare bother me. Safe territory, so to speak. How are you, *mon vieux?* Did you have a good trip?"

"Yes, thank you. You know, your French is quite impressive, Dex. Particularly for an American," he added, following him into the untidy study.

"Just a few expressions I've picked up here and there. I still find it hard to follow conversations. Especially here, where they speak with an accent. A drink?"

"Thanks." Sylvain accepted the champagne and settled on the worn leather sofa. "I'm actually quite lucky to have arrived. I'm not good at directions. Mercifully, someone knew where you lived."

"Oh, good." Dex sat in the armchair opposite and raised his glass then frowned. "Someone I know?" A smile spread over his tanned face and his teeth flashed in a wicked grin as Sylvain sighed. "I'll bet you a thousand bucks it was a woman."

"As a matter of fact, it was," Sylvain conceded, embarrassed at his own transparency.

"What was she like?"

"Young." He took a sip, not knowing how to go on. What could he say? That Botticelli would have died twice seeing her? That she was the incarnation of everything he'd ever dreamed of?

"Go on," Dex prompted. "She's young, that's a good beginning. What else? Was she pretty?"

"No."

"Oh."

"She was perfect." He sipped his drink, allowing the image to linger.

"Shit."

"Excuse me?"

"Well, look at you. You—the womanizer, the man about town who never misses a date or a chance to make one—are sitting like an overgrown adolescent, gasping over some female you saw for two seconds in the street. That means one of two things. Either you've lost your mind or you've fallen head over heels in love with a stranger.''

Sylvain laughed, still embarrassed. ''She was truly the most beautiful creature I have ever beheld. She said to say hello.''

''Oh? Does she have a name?''

''I didn't have the chance to ask her. One minute she was there and the next thing I knew she'd disappeared into thin air.''

''Begin with a detailed description.''

''She was, as I mentioned, young, perhaps early twenties. Tallish.'' He made a descriptive gesture. ''Her hair was a tint only seen in the finest cinquecento paintings, her eyes deep-set, precious jewels that—''

''Spare me, I get the picture. What about measurements? Breasts, did she have any? Was she well dressed?''

Sylvain shook his head in despair. ''I'm afraid I don't know. I only had eyes for her beauty.''

Dex raised an eyebrow. ''This, coming from you? What happened to the luscious blonde I saw you with at Maxim's last week? Or the opera singer? She was a bit voluptuous, I'll admit, but still. You, falling for a country bumpkin?''

''She didn't seem at all like a country bumpkin,'' Sylvain replied, surprised that Dex's teasing annoyed him.

''It might help if you had her bust and waist size rather than her eye color. But Limoges is small. Perhaps we'll come across her. Maybe she works in the factory. Did she say Dexter or Mr. Ward?''

''Dexter.''

He shook his head, trying to fit the description to a name. ''Maybe she'll turn up.''

''Perhaps, if she is in my destiny. Who knows?'' Sylvain shrugged and raised his glass. ''To our collection. I had a talk with Suzanne Lalique the other day and have been drawing a lot since. She's done quite a bit of interesting work for Haviland. I'll show you some of the designs as soon as I retrieve my portfolio from the car. By the way, is that really the new Packard Super Eight sedan I spied outside?''

''Isn't she a beaut?'' Dex's tanned face broke into a smile and his blue eyes flashed. ''I had her shipped. She arrived only last week. Dietrich had one built for Richard Dupont. This one's the second,'' he said proudly. ''She runs like a dream. We'll take a spin when we go over to the factory.''

The next few days were spent between the factory and the house, with Sylvain describing his designs and Dex explaining the evolution of the techniques of porcelain making. All the while, Sylvain searched the faces of each woman he saw, in case it was her. He couldn't believe she'd disappeared, or that she might be only minutes away, yet still unattainable.

''David Haviland first arrived in Limoges in 1842,'' Dex was explaining, picking up a plate that was ready to enter the kiln for its first firing. ''The first firing dries the porcelain, yet leaves it sufficiently porous to absorb the glaze. The fired item is called *bisque*. After that, we dip it in a mixture of quartz and Felspar, combined with water, then return it to the oven and fire it again. It was Charles Haviland who installed the first coal kilns in 1868, once the railroad reached Limoges.''

''Fascinating,'' Sylvain murmured, following Dex through the factory. Together they decided which designs could be best adapted to porcelain. Dex liked the modern lines, the bright colors and fanciful decor Sylvain had drawn. Zebras and lions lent an African touch, surrounded by interesting borders and intricately drawn symbols. ''You know who will love this? Max von Waldenhof,'' he said thoughtfully. ''He's an old friend of Eugène de la Vallière's—the priest whom you met over lunch in town—and an importer from Germany. We should have a couple of samples ready by tomorrow. I think he'll be in Limoges.''

''I wonder what makes a man go into the Church?'' Sylvain commented.

''In Eugène's case, vocation. Ever since he was a child he talked about it. He always knew.''

''You knew him back then?'' Sylvain asked, surprised.

''No. Of course not,'' Dex amended. ''But Limoges is a

small place. Everyone knows everything about everyone else. We're invited to dine at the Château de la Vallière tomorrow night. You'll meet Max then.''

"Have you been to Germany lately?" Sylvain asked, studying a statuette carefully.

"Not after the Germans marched into the Rhineland."

"Remember we talked about it, when you first came to Paris? I didn't take Hitler seriously—I still don't, completely. But we have friends—other Jews—who have been left with virtually nothing. My uncle at the bank is assisting as best he can.''

"Are you worried that what is happening in Germany could happen here?" Dex asked, suddenly serious.

"What? The government issuing anti-Jewish racial and citizenship laws? Impossible. Jews have been an integral part of the French social structure since the Revolution.''

"I know, but still—" Dex picked up the car keys and they walked out of the office and into the courtyard "—I don't like the way things are being handled. Chamberlain's an ass and Roosevelt's turning a blind eye, refusing to get involved. He knows he wouldn't have the support of the American public if there was a war. Still, it will be interesting to hear what von Waldenhof has to report.''

"Is he a Nazi?"

"Max? Good Lord, no! He hates the sight of the bloody Nazis. Most of the Germans do.''

"Then how have they managed to get to power?"

It was a question for which Dex had no answer.

They arrived at the Château de la Vallière punctually at eight the next evening.

"Ah, Mr. Ward, what a pleasure to see you again. How is your wife? And your son?" The Comtesse, a stately woman in her late sixties, turned toward Sylvain. "Eugène tells me you have brought a friend. Do introduce him, please.''

Dex turned and saw Sylvain gazing across the room to where his cousin Geneviève was talking to Max. He nudged him.

"Excuse me," he murmured to the Comtesse and kissed her hand punctiliously.

"It's her," he whispered, once the introductions were over. "There."

"You mean Genny de la Vallière is the girl you met?"

"Is that her name?"

"No. She's called Geneviève. She's Eugène's youngest sister, the baby of the family. Let me be the one to introduce you," he said, casting Sylvain a wicked grin while gently moving him across the room by the elbow.

"Hello, Genny. Good to see you, Max." He kissed Genny's fingers, then shook the heavyset blond man's hand.

"I would like to introduce you both to my friend, Sylvain de Rothberg."

"Mademoiselle." Sylvain bowed low, and dropped a feather-light kiss on her wrist, holding it an instant longer than necessary while he feasted his eyes.

"Haven't we met?" she asked curiously. "Didn't you ask me for directions to Dexter's house the other day in Limoges?"

"I—I believe yes. I—thank you. They were excellent directions. It was most kind." He released her hand reluctantly and shook hands with Max von Waldenhof.

Two silver epergnes and the length of the table separated them throughout dinner and Sylvain listened impatiently to a long diatribe from the Comtesse until the table was cleared and the ladies finally rose. Geneviève took her mother's arm.

"Don't take forever," she hissed in a loud whisper to her brother. The butler placed the brandy on the dining table and cigars were passed round. Dex rose and seated himself next to Sylvain, while Eugène and Max continued the serious conversation they had started during dinner.

"So she's the mysterious beauty?"

"Yes."

"I have to admit, you have good taste. A lovely girl, Geneviève. And bright."

"I told you she was perfect," he answered, swirling the snifter then sniffing the brandy.

Dex rolled the cigar, snipped off the end and eyed him curiously. "You're actually serious about her, aren't you?"

"I know this sounds ridiculous, but I'd ask her to marry me this very instant if I didn't think she'd send me packing. I have nothing to offer a woman like that."

"Why do you say that?"

Sylvain shrugged. "I'm an artist. I live among my drawings, my art, my jewels and have always thought of women as an agreeable diversion. I suppose I don't have much to recommend me to a woman like her. Plus, I'm Jewish."

"Don't underestimate yourself—or Geneviève. She's a good egg. So are the la Vallières."

"*She* is perfection incarnate," he answered reverentially.

"Hey, don't push it."

"You're not a romantic, Dexter?" He raised a quizzical eyebrow at Dex.

"No, perhaps not. There used to be a time when I thought I was, but that was long ago."

"What happened?"

"War and life got in the way." He turned to Max, who sat across the table. "I want you to see the new line Sylvain and I are creating. I think you'll like it. Some of the pieces are quite exceptional. Perhaps we could meet at the factory tomorrow?"

"Certainly." Max smiled. Perhaps it was just his imagination, but Sylvain thought he caught a glimpse of unease. Dismissing the notion, his mind returned to Geneviève, wondering how long it would be until the men joined the ladies.

Soon afterward they wandered through to the salon where she presided over a silver tray adorned with fine Haviland china.

"Coffee?" she asked, smiling and handing him a cup.

"Thank you." He watched her pour, admiring the fine white hands and manicured nails, wondering if it was too soon to ask her out. René, her rather surly older brother, stood next to her.

"Hi, Genny, got some for me?" Dex nodded to René and glanced at the coffeepot. "Say, Sylvain and I are going to

Sarlat for the day on Wednesday. Would you like to come along? Perhaps Max will join us. You, too, René, if you like.''

"Why not? That sounds fun. René, why don't you come?'' She turned to her brother, who shrugged, avoiding Sylvain's eyes.

"I've got a lot to do,'' he answered. "Anyway, I hate those old musty towns. This place is bad enough.'' He walked away and Geneviève cast Dex an apologetic smile.

"He's so difficult. I don't know why he can't join in like everybody else. And now he has an awful girlfriend. She's the barmaid at Ambazac at the Café du Centre.''

"He'll get over it.'' Dex watched René taking leave of his mother. "We all do.''

"What, have barmaids?''

"That too, but I meant the stage he's going through. How old is he?''

"Too old to be behaving like this.''

Thank God for Dexter, Sylvain thought elated. He was less enthusiastic about Max joining the party, but thankful René had refused. Perhaps, finally, he would get Geneviève to himself, if only for a few moments.

Wednesday dawned fair, the air warm for May, and they opened the convertible roof before picking up Max and Geneviève at ten-thirty and heading southwest to the medieval town of Sarlat. Abandoning the car, they wandered through the town, enchanted by the blossoms blooming above high walls that mysteriously surrounded heavy, silent stone houses, keeping centuries of secrets. They walked up the twisting narrow streets, past ancient wooden doors, gothic windows and under heavily-beamed balconies.

"Can't you just imagine the troubadours standing under this?'' Genny exclaimed, excited.

"Yes,'' Sylvain said. "And you, on the balcony, holding—''

"Not a rose, please. Too clichéd.'' She grimaced.

"All right. A bouquet of plants,'' Sylvain amended. "That was common at the time. Perhaps some Genêt. That's where Henry Plantagenet derived his name.''

"I'd forgotten that. He stuck some in his hat, didn't he? Looked very jaunty, I'm told. And then what?" She twirled and looked at him, her eyes alight with laughter.

"Then a young gallant—perhaps not so young," he amended, "would stand here below and declare his love for you in verse."

"Like one of Henry's grandfathers?"

"Precisely. The first true troubadour. But I would try to not do too badly myself."

"You?" She looked quickly away up at the balcony. "I thought you were a jeweler, not a poet."

"And what is a jewel if not a poem, made to be worn by the most lovely of creatures?"

"Mmm. We've lost Max and Dex," she said, glancing away, her cheeks deliciously flushed.

"I can live with that."

"Well, I'm sure we'll find them. What do you think of Max? It must be awful being German these days, mustn't it?"

"Depending on what your views are, yes," Sylvain answered warily, watching her eyes change color to dark violet, matching the hue of the flowers on her blouse.

"I don't think Max likes the Nazis at all. Eugène says he's almost gotten into trouble for criticizing them."

"Well, I'm a Jew, so it's hard for me to be unbiased. We are *persona non grata* over there," he murmured dryly.

"Dex wants to sell him your work."

"In these times, that is an illusion. I haven't wanted to burst his dream, but no Jewish artist is allowed to be sold in Hitler's Aryan paradise."

"It's sick. Totally sick," she exclaimed angrily, stopping under a medieval archway and leaning her head back against the ancient stones. "I mean, why would anyone want to ban other people from having a normal life? It's crazy. The man's a lunatic."

"And a very dangerous one. Thank goodness we live in France. I know that it's selfish and I feel awful about those of us in Germany suffering, but I can't help everyone in the world."

"No, I suppose not. You don't think anything could happen, do you? I mean a war or anything? Dex seems to think it might."

"That's because he went through the last one." He moved toward her, placed his hands on either side of her shoulders and looked deep into her eyes. "This will pass. Nobody wants a war." He drew closer. "But I do want you, Genny, more than I've ever wanted anything in my life. I know it sounds mad, precipitate—even irresponsible—but from the minute I saw you in the street that day, I've thought of nothing else. You fill my days and nights, my heart, my soul. From now on I shall design the most wonderful jewels in all creation and they will be for you. Each and every one of them. Even the ones I sell will carry part of you with them," he whispered, so close he could sense the softness of her skin, the scent of her leaving him dizzy with longing.

"Sylvain," she murmured, her hands reaching up and circling his neck. Her fingers tentatively mussed his thick dark locks as he gently drew her into his arms and their lips met softly, tenderly. Then he pressed her close, unable to resist, and felt his passion returned until they were locked in a frenzied embrace from which neither wanted to part.

A wolf whistle close by made them fall guiltily apart, turning flushed and embarrassed to where Dex stood at the foot of the alley with a mischievous smile.

"Come on, you two. That's quite enough. What will the good Father Eugène say if he finds out I've been leading you astray, Gen?"

"Oh, shut up, Dex," she laughed, still holding Sylvain's hand as they tripped over the cobblestones to join him. "Where's Max?"

"Buying some trinket or other. You look hot, Genny," he said, his voice concerned but eyes teasing.

"Give us a break." Sylvain grinned, slipping an arm around Genny's shoulders.

"You have lipstick on your collar," Dex remarked, unwilling to give up.

"Merde." Sylvain twisted his neck, trying to see the collar

of his white sports shirt, over which he'd flung a lightweight navy sweater. "Is it obvious?"

"No, darl—I mean, it's fine." Genny went bright red and Sylvain smiled at her tenderly, the sound of the word she'd almost said filling him with joy.

Soon Max joined them, and he and Dex marched ahead, deep in conversation. Genny and Sylvain trailed behind, hand in hand, admiring the thatched-roof dwellings of the Rue Fénelon, browsing through tiny shops filled with pâtés, tablecloths, and odds and ends that made them laugh, stopping for a long tender kiss. Genny's laughter filled the cobblestone lanes and medieval alleys, and Sylvain knew he'd never felt so happy.

They lunched on the terrace of a small bistro on foie gras, salad with hot goat cheese, pitchers of red wine and crisp fresh bread. Max turned out to be good company and Sylvain relaxed. It wasn't his fault he was German, after all.

Dex watched them, his throat tight. There was something about Genny and Sylvain's romance that reminded him of him and Flora. It was the first time he'd seen two people fall madly in love, he realized, where each word was something special, each gesture a sign. Flora sprang before him, and for the first time in many years he truly missed her. He must be getting old and sentimental. He was married, a father, a successful businessman. Wasn't that enough?

"Superb, isn't it?" Dex remarked as Max handled Sylvain's plate, holding it to the light and examining each detail.

"A true work of art." He placed it on the desk in Dex's office and sat down.

"I'll do limited collections, of course." Dex gazed at the plate lovingly. "That will increase the value. Sylvain's an excellent artist. Have you seen his jewelry?"

"I have heard of it, of course, but never had that pleasure." Max took out a cigar and offered one to Dex.

"Magnificent. Quite unique." Dex expounded, enthralled by the quality of Sylvain's work. "He has a boutique in the Cour des Pages, off the Rue de la Paix. His clientele is as *recherché* as his work. The last time I popped in, Wallis Simpson was walking out. That should tell you something. But, coming back to the plates. How many will you be wanting? I'll try to have them ready with your other orders.''

''I'm not sure.'' There was a moment of hesitation. ''I should feel out the market first. Make sure this type of article would please.''

Dex frowned. ''What on earth are you talking about, Max? We discussed this in detail not long ago. You were as enthusiastic as I was about the whole idea. I don't understand.''

''I know. I— A change of heart, I suppose,'' he said with a weak smile. Dex noticed the flush about his collar and that Max was constantly inhaling his cigar.

''Is there something about the work that doesn't satisfy you?'' he asked, puzzled.

''Oh no. The work is, as I said, exquisite.''

''Then what?'' Dex leaned forward, observing Max's obvious discomfort. ''Something is wrong or you'd be the first to pick them up. I know you. We've been doing business long enough for me to be certain you never let a good opportunity slip through those crafty fingers of yours.''

Max stared out the window. ''It is not the quality of the work but the artist that is the problem.''

''I don't understand. You and Sylvain seemed to get on very well.''

''It is nothing personal, but Sylvain de Rothberg is a Jew,'' he said quietly. ''It would be impossible for me to present his work in Germany today.''

There was a long silence while Dex assimilated what had just been said. He forced himself to remain calm and not let his temper get the better of him. After all, he knew Max hated Hitler and the Nazis. Still, fury overcame him at the injustice. It was intolerable. Here was some of the most remarkable art, being rejected because of the artist's ethnic origin.

''Are you really telling me you don't want to buy Sylvain's work because he's Jewish?''

''No!'' Max exclaimed in an anguished voice. ''Not *want*, Dex, but *can't*. If I could, I would buy every piece I could lay my hands on. But by doing so I would be risking everything.

My reputation, my business. Even my family could suffer the consequences of such a rash act.''

"That's absurd." Dex shook his head in disbelief, but he knew that what Max said was probably true. His last trip to Berlin had been suffocating. Just crossing the border and seeing the glass-eyed, unblinking Gestapo officers overseeing the customs procedures was daunting enough. There was an aura of silent fear that reigned below a veneer of jolly cheer and glitter.

"You have no idea what it is like. There are times now that I am ashamed to be German.'' Max sighed heavily, no longer the gregarious aristocrat but a tired, strained man who had had enough. "It is dreadful, Dex. Some of the people have been brainwashed. They are enthralled, *begeistert*, by Hitler's new Germany. Those like myself, who see what is really happening, are too afraid to speak. Every day things are getting worse. You heard about the Nuremberg Laws that were passed in 1935? Even before that, the Nazis were boycotting Jewish businesses, excluding them from teaching at all levels. Today neighbors whisper about one another; schoolchildren are taught how to recognize pure Aryans and to report their parents if they do not conform to party rules. And so it goes. Jews are *relocated.* Do you realize how many people have lost their homes, everything they owned for generations? There is a constant fear of being interned in a *Konzentrationlage.*

"I have managed, with difficulty and a lot of cash, to help some of my friends leave the country, but it is becoming increasingly dangerous. I have already had two very *polite* visits to my home, asking if I know the whereabouts of these people. The only reason they don't send the brownshirts in to beat me up is because of my family's influence. And, of course, I am in good standing with the party.''

"By adhering to the system, Max, you're a part of it,'' Dex countered self-righteously.

"It's easy to say that sitting here with no worries,'' Max answered bitterly. "You don't have the threat of the Gestapo knocking on your door in the middle of the night to take away those you love, never to be seen again.'' He stubbed out the cigar and lowered his voice. "Don't delude yourself, Dexter.

Germany is preparing for war. I have inside information that they are working on a special tank. Look at what is happening. Hitler has annexed the Rhineland, while Europe sits by and watches. Next it will be Austria and then, God knows. Who can tell how far the man's ambitions go?''

"Why don't you leave?"

Max gave a harsh laugh. "You sound like a child. Why don't I leave? I am German. My family has lived for generations in the same place. My wife is the daughter of my parents' friends, our children are at home. I make my living there. I just hope that I am wrong and that everything will be sorted out for the best. Maybe I am overly anxious. Even if I did want to leave, it would be difficult. Special permissions are required for travel. I have a legitimate excuse for myself, because of my business, but what of my wife and my family? No, Dexter, unfortunately I have no choice."

"Are you a Nazi, Max?"

"Good God, of course not, you know that. I will have nothing to do with those pigs."

"But you said yourself you are in good standing with the party."

Max raised his hands in a gesture of despair. "I have to be. If I were not, I would have everything seized. No more job, no more work. It is too late. They have taken hold. If the Allies and others had not participated in those farcical Olympic games—if only people realized how serious things really are. But even those who do keep their thoughts to themselves. The political opponents have been interned in camps with the Jews and Gypsies...those that weren't summarily shot."

"I see." Dex rose. "What will you do if it comes to war?"

"I suppose I will have to fight."

"I can't believe we may go through it all again," Dex murmured. "Over twelve million dead in the last war. Wasn't that enough? Haven't they learned?"

"The last war is what set the scene for this one. The Treaty of Versailles stripped Germany of its military and political power. It was a humiliation to our nation that allowed a half-educated, shouting little corporal the chance to rise to where he is.''

''True. But he seems to have a substantial following nevertheless,'' Dex rejoined dryly.

Max sighed. ''Sadly, yes. We can only pray the Allies will—what is it you say in America?''

''Get their shit together.''

''That's right. And fast. In the meantime, Dexter, we are businessmen and business must continue as usual. Particularly if I am to furnish you with any interesting information.'' This last was said in a whisper.

Dex's head shot up. ''What do you mean?''

''If there is a war we could be useful to one another.''

A warm surge of admiration gripped him. ''You would be disposed to spy?'' He left the rest unsaid, eyes questioning.

Max nodded, tight-lipped. ''I know it is a terrible thing to betray one's nation. But Germany is at risk. Our way of life. This reaches much farther than our country. Hitler is a narcissist, and he is ambitious. If he can, he will overtake the world with his crazy ideology. What choice do I have but to stop him, in any small way I can? I know that sounds contradictory to what I just said about fighting for my country, but I consider them as two separate issues. One is an obligation, the other the desire to curtail the murderous intentions of these lunatics.''

''How would we operate?'' Dex asked, curious.

''Exactly as we always have. Same orders, same passing of sketches with new variations added.''

''You mean we could create a code that could be followed through the design modifications. It might work.''

''We would have to perfect it quickly, for if war should break out I may not be able to travel any longer. I don't think the risk would be too great, particularly if we begin now and set up a precedent. If and when a war happens, there will be no time to organize. We must pray that this is never needed. But may I give you a piece of advice for your friend Sylvain?''

''Yes?''

''Tell him to leave now while there is time. If there should be a war and Hitler invades France...God help him.''

"Thank you. I will tell him. Not that I think he will heed our advice," he added grimly, thinking of Sylvain's enchantment with Geneviève and the danger it could place her in.

Dex realized how vital it could be to have trustworthy sources of information coming out of Germany. Max's words had left him shaken, and he began imagining designs that could carry information to the Allies, yet be impossible for anyone to decipher.

22

New York, U.S.A., 1938

A month later, back in the States, Dex left his office and walked smartly up the steps of the Plaza, passed the Palm Court, and proceeded toward the Oak Room, which was filling up fast with the usual Manhattan lunch crowd of lawyers, bankers and businesspeople. He secured a place at the bar, the chatter and cigar smoke hanging low amidst the leather and mahogany, then ordered a whiskey and a prime-rib sandwich, happy to be back if only for a few weeks. He'd missed the rush, the buzz of the city and the American way of life.

He spread the *New York Times* open before him and began to read. Immersed in thought, he barely noticed the two men next to him until they began discussing the political situation in Europe. He listened casually as he sliced his sandwich.

"I don't see how we'll stay out of it when the time comes."

"Oh, I don't know. F.D.R. seems adamant."

"Like hell he is." The other man lowered his voice and Dex reached for the mustard to hear better. "Franklin knows as well as the next man that if the show goes on, then sooner or later so do we. Did you know Lindbergh's been test-flying an ME109 fighter in Germany?"

Dex frowned. The man speaking was familiar; stocky and in his late forties or early fifties. Dex tried to place him but drew a blank. Then their eyes met and the mustard pot came to a sudden halt.

"Excuse me, do I know you?" the man asked, curious.

"I don't believe so," Dex murmured, preparing to retreat behind the *Times*.

"I could swear I know you from somewhere. Sorry if I sound nosy but what's your name?"

"Ward."

"Ward, Ward..." the man repeated thoughtfully. "That rings a bell. Jesus! Ward." He gave a broad smile. "You don't remember me, do you? I last saw you in Rheims. November 1918. You were downing a bottle of champagne and had a pretty brunette hanging around your neck."

The room spun. "Colonel Bill Donovan," he whispered. The soldier who had given him Dexter Ward's uniform. The one man who could blow his cover. He forced himself to remain calm, smile and show enthusiasm. It was doubtful that among the many soldiers who'd crossed his path Donovan would remember details of his past.

They shook hands, clapped one another on the shoulder and shared a drink, and Donovan introduced him to his companion. They chatted for a while, but Dex finished his meal more quickly than he'd intended, keeping the conversation light. Nevertheless, Donovan's penetrating gaze boring into him was disconcerting. *He doesn't remember exactly what happened, but he knows there's something.*

He glanced at his watch, and after exchanging cards, excused himself, knowing all he could do was hope for the best. Donovan would probably tuck the card away without another thought. Still, the meeting disturbed him more than he cared to admit. When he returned to Sutton Place he decided to finish his business immediately and return to Europe as quickly as possible.

23

Limoges, France, 1938

In August Geneviève and Sylvain became engaged. The ring was a cluster of perfect diamonds shaped in the form of petals, and Geneviève was overwhelmed. Even the Comtesse admitted she had rarely seen anything as exquisite. But as summer dwindled into autumn, Eugène found it hard to appease his mother's concerns.

"He's a delightful young man, so well brought up *and* a Rothberg, but I can't help wishing he were Catholic. It would make things so much easier, don't you agree?"

"Sylvain is a fine young man," Eugène replied. "I like him. As for his faith? That is not my concern. I respect his beliefs, though they may not coincide with mine."

"How broad-minded of you," she replied dryly. "That's not what I'm talking about, Eugène. It's all this anti-Jewishness going about that worries me."

"I agree." He nodded uneasily. "Like you, I can't help but wonder what would happen if there was a war, as Dexter Ward assures me there will be," he said gravely, concerned with his sister's safety.

"That is precisely what worries me. Look at what is happening in Germany. That dreadful little man, Hitler. And all those poor Jewish people. One must hope that *something* will happen soon and that it will all blow over. Perhaps Monsieur Chamberlain will manage to convince him. He, at least, is a gentleman." She sniffed, sipping from the fine Haviland cup, part of a set presented to her by Theodore Haviland many years before.

"These are the times I wish your father was alive," she continued. "It's such a responsibility. On the other hand, Genny's twenty-five and an adult." She glanced at her son. "What do you think, Eugène? I mean, an engagement's all very well but, as we well know, Genny is prone to breaking them. First it was that Italian man with the factories in Turin, and then the Spanish grandee whose name I don't want to remember!" she exclaimed dismissively. "I wish she were a little less impetuous about things."

"*Maman*, should Genny finally pick a wedding day none of us will stand a chance, least of all poor Sylvain."

"True." She smiled. Despite her stubborn nature and her ups and downs, Geneviève had them wrapped around her little finger. "I wonder how the Rothbergs feel about the engagement?"

"Much the same way we do, I believe. They would prefer Sylvain to marry a nice Jewish girl, but they've accepted that this is the way things are. They were very charming at the engagement party."

"I'm glad we chose the Crillon," she murmured. "Still, all this love business. Marriage was a different issue in my day."

"Cupid's arrow strikes *ad lib, Maman*. If Genny wants Sylvain she'll have him, and there is little any of us can do to stop it."

"So be it." The Comtesse sighed and shook her head, her permed hair coiffed stiffly off her face, drawing his attention to a spectacular pair of diamond earrings.

"What lovely diamonds, *Maman*. May I guess?" he said, quizzing her.

"A gift from Sylvain for my birthday. I was loath to accept, but he designed them specially—"

"So of course you couldn't refuse."

"*Vraiment*, Eugène! For a priest you have a very odd way

of expressing yourself.'' She drew herself up straight in the high-backed chair.

"One is still allowed a sense of humor, *Maman,*'' he answered affectionately, leaning over to kiss her cheek as he rose to take his leave. ''They suit you extremely well. Sylvain has exquisite taste.''

"He does, doesn't he? Tell me, do you think I should ask the Baronne de Rothberg to tea when I'm next in Paris? I don't know her well, though we were on the same committee for the veterans' ball a few years ago. Perhaps I should—''

"*Maman,* if I were you, I would let things take their course and worry more about René's profligate behavior,'' he said sternly. ''He is outrageous. First it was that vulgar ballerina. Now it is the barmaid from the Café du Centre in the village. Can't he find himself someone of his own class and a proper activity? I have a hard enough time getting all my work done for the bishop and seeing my parishioners, without the extra burden of the estate to run. He is utterly irresponsible and selfish.''

"I know. I have talked to him but it seems to be of no avail. If only your father were alive, things would have been different.''

Realizing he would get nowhere on this subject, Eugène took his leave. Still, he felt it his duty to make his mother aware of his younger brother's activities. He just prayed that the rumor he'd heard the day before—that René was the father of an illegitimate baby—was unfounded.

As for Sylvain, Eugène liked him very much and would be pleased to have him as a brother-in-law. He frowned as the butler closed the front door quietly behind him, and walked down the shallow stone steps, hoping he was right in supporting their marriage, should it come about.

He shrugged and crossed the gravel toward his small black Renault. Who was he to stop them from following their hearts?

For a moment he thought of Flora, nursing a lost love she believed long gone. No, he didn't want that for his sister. Had time erased the longing and the pain? Probably not. He tempered the irritation he felt toward Gavin. Anyway, Flora was not his responsibility, but Genny was. If she wanted her Sylvain he would give them his blessing. The other considerations were worldly, and one simply had to have faith. Perhaps all their worries would prove pointless. After all, Chamberlain was negotiating with Hitler, and the fears of earlier that summer had dwindled, to everybody's relief. God would guide and provide where man could no more see. His plan would take precedence, whatever they decided. Lowering himself into the driver's seat, he said a prayer. "If it is to be, may you keep them and bless them, heavenly Father. *Votre volonté soit faite.*"

Three days later, Geneviève burst unceremoniously into his office in the *évêché*. Eugène wasn't surprised. "Sylvain and I have decided to get married *this* November," she announced with a defiant gleam.

"That's wonderful. A bit precipitate, perhaps, but I wish you all the best. He is a good man. I hope you will make one another happy."

She sat down with a thud on the tapestry chair and gaped at him. "You mean you're not against it?"

"Sorry." He laid down the fountain pen and smiled apologetically. "Why would I be against anything that will bring you happiness?"

"Well, I'll be damned!"

"Please, Genny, we are in God's house."

"Yes, of course. Sorry," she said contritely. "It's just that everyone else has been so against it. Even *Maman,* in her own way." She jumped up. "What does it matter that Sylvain's Jewish? Who cares? It's the fact that I love him that's important, and that he loves me, isn't it?"

"I agree. But not everyone sees things in the same light, and those who love you worry about you."

"You mean all that Hitler nonsense?" she said crossly.

"Not nonsense, my dear, a sad reality. One that cannot be ignored."

"I know. I didn't mean it like that. But that's in Germany. We're in France. It has nothing to do with us, Eugène."

"It has everything to do with us, and it is important that if you truly plan to take this step, you understand the risks it may carry. Should Hitler ever invade France—"

"Rubbish. That won't happen."

"What makes you so sure? At the Vatican we have had several alerts. The pope is concerned about the fate of many Jews, Gypsies and others."

"I know, dear." She came and sat on the arm of his chair, taking his long fingers in hers. "But Sylvain has nothing to do with all that. I mean, he's a Rothberg, for goodness' sakes, and as French as *baguette!*"

"You stole that one from Dexter, didn't you?"

"Yup. American as apple pie!" She grinned, then stroked his thin cheek lovingly. "You *know* I'm going to marry him, whatever any of you say, don't you, my darling brother? I can't wait any longer," she pleaded.

He nodded. "Is that why you came by yourself? I was quite expecting a formal visit from Sylvain."

"He wanted to. Still does. He's awfully stodgy about things like that."

"Genny, don't take this wrong, my love, but you must allow a man to do what he feels is right. If Sylvain wishes to ask for your hand in marriage tell him he will be welcome. I cannot think of a nicer brother-in-law."

"You're a doll." Genny kissed him once more and jumped up. "The worst part is the Baronne. If you think *Maman's* opposed, you should hear *her.*"

"I would imagine Sylvain exerts a certain influence over his mother and that she can be brought round," he said with a wry smile.

"True. And if he could get the Windsors to come to the wedding, that would clinch it, wouldn't it?" She cast him a wicked grin.

"If Sylvain can manage *that,* I truly believe all your worries will be over, *mon enfant.* And should this event become the wedding of the year, an alliance akin to Free Masonry will develop between the Baronne and the Comtesse and that may overwhelm even you."

"God help us!"

"He will."

He watched her leave, her eyes aglow with love and determination, a new confidence in her step. All at once he felt an involuntary shudder, his eyes seeking the wooden crucifix on the whitewashed wall.

"*Protéger les, mon Dieu.* May God protect them."

24

Limoges, France, 1938

On the day of the wedding, Dex reached Limoges in time to bathe, don his morning suit, grab his gloves and top hat and head for the reception. He hoped that no one among the throng of guests would notice his tardiness. He'd forgotten to buy Sylvain and Genny a wedding present, but Alix would take care of that. A pity she wasn't feeling well enough to come.

It was only as the Packard took its place among the long line of Delahayes, Hispano Suizas and Rolls-Royces that he realized what a big event this was. Since his return from the States, he'd been in Paris with Alix and Scott, and it was only now, as the guests poured into the Château de la Vallière, that it occurred to him Angus would be present. *Of course.* And Flora. The thought gave him a jolt and he glanced around wondering whether to leave, then realizing he couldn't. He was boxed in.

Perhaps they'd been invited but were unable to come. Surely Eugène would have warned him if they were to be here. Or maybe not. Eugène could be cunning. Perhaps he was hoping for some kind of melodramatic reconciliation. He swore under his breath, wishing he could turn the car around and leave, but that was impossible. As he waited impatiently, the cars moving forward at a snail's pace, he began thinking. If Angus *was* here, he would use the chance to his own advantage. All at once he sensed his brother's presence, just as he had when they were children.

Relinquishing his vehicle to a valet, Dex joined the line of guests waiting to shake hands with the bridal party, his pulse a tad fast. Angus was definitely here and Dex wondered if his brother felt something as well. What would it be like, meeting him face-to-face? All at once he was gripped by new determination. This was his chance to begin his revenge, slowly but surely, to gain his brother's trust and get him to confide in him. After a while, when Angus was up to his neck, he would offer to buy the MacLeod company's debt.

Kissing Genny smack on the lips, he offered Sylvain his heartfelt congratulations.

"Already trying to steal my bride?" Sylvain cuffed him in a friendly manner.

"No, just taking the only chance I'll ever get. Good luck, old man, you deserve it. You have a great life ahead of you." The two men shook hands warmly and Dex moved on into the hall, leaving room for the next guest in line.

He picked up a flute of champagne from a passing waiter, his mind ablaze. Finally, the moment he'd been nursing in the back of his mind for so long had dropped directly into his lap. He walked through the salons seeking his prey, hawklike in his pursuit, smiling and shaking hands as all the while he scanned the crowd. Pausing for a moment by the window, he looked out at the barren garden, the misty afternoon and the brushland beyond, brown now that winter was approaching.

Then, all at once, an electric current coursed through him. He stopped, turned. His eyes flew across the room.

When he saw her finally, his mind went blank.

Entering the salons of the Château de la Vallière on Angus's arm, Flora glanced admiringly at the fashions of Mainbocher's, Molyneux's and Worth's, her own dress dowdy next to them. *I've let myself go all these years,* she realized, eyeing the smart haircuts and well made-up faces, the sparkling jewels making her feel like the country bumpkin she was. Angus looked all right in his morning coat, but not her. She looked frumpy. For the first time in memory, she cared.

Genny was a magnificent bride, Sylvain the perfect groom, and together they formed a couple that made heads turn. *I wonder what their children will look like,* she thought fondly. Kissing her cousin, Flora was thrilled to see the sparkle in Genny's eyes, the tender way Sylvain hovered over her and the manner in which already they moved as one. She sighed, swallowing a lump in her throat, determined to enjoy the day and not allow selfish personal regrets to dampen it. Soon she was circulating among the guests, chatting, when all at once she felt a chill run through her that nearly made her drop the champagne flute she carried. Her head flew up and she looked instinctively toward the door.

But there was nothing unusual. She took a long sip, chiding herself. It was just being back at la Vallière, where she and Gavin had spent so many happy times together, that was all. She smiled and listened with waning interest to the description a local baron was giving on the progress of his gardens. This was reality and the past the past. She must realize once and for all that it would never return.

Still, it was disconcerting that after all the years of trying to make contact with his spirit that she should sense his presence in the middle of a crowded reception, Flora mused, barely hearing the baron's boring conversation and smiling politely.

After a while he addressed a lady to their right and she turned away, relieved. Something was pulling her, forcing her to look across the room. As though compelled by an inexplicable force, she turned, gave a quick gasp and swayed when she met familiar, piercing blue eyes only a few paces away. The man moved quickly, grabbing her arm before she collapsed in a heap.

"Take a deep breath," he said, leaning over her, helping her to a chair by the wall. "Slowly. You'll be fine, just breathe deeply." His warm American voice was soothing and she sat down, dazed, murmuring her thanks and apologizing. What had come over her? Was it that his eyes reminded her of Gavin's? He seemed to be everywhere today. The man was handing her a glass of red wine, urging her to take a sip, and her heart missed a beat when again their eyes met. Flora felt a sharp jolt as their fingers touched, certain he'd felt it, too. What was happening to her? She felt suddenly exposed, vulnerable, the same way she'd felt with Gavin. Feelings she thought she'd laid to rest twenty years earlier had suddenly come alive.

"Are you okay?" He was bending over her, his eyes searching as though for something he'd lost. She nodded, murmured her thanks. She could barely draw her gaze away, entranced by his smile, the tanned skin crinkling around those magnetic blue eyes that were so like Gavin's it hurt. He was the handsomest man she'd ever beheld. Maybe it was the wine, but she even imagined Gavin might have looked like him at a similar age, had he lived.

"I'm Dexter Ward," he said, straightening and offering her his hand.

"Lady MacLeod," she murmured, allowing him to hold her fingers longer than necessary and swallowing a tiny gasp when he raised them slowly to his lips. Her body melted, the feel of his skin on hers evoking a sudden, startling vision that made her flush a fiery red. There was an aura of steel and tenderness, energy and strength about him that she couldn't explain.

"I believe I've been in touch with your husband's coal company in Scotland. Is he Lord Angus MacLeod?"

"That's right." She tried to smile, to sound casual, to regain some composure, aware of how dark his eyes had gone at the mention of Angus's name.

"Are you feeling better?" he asked softly. "Would you like me to get help? Someone to take you upstairs to your room."

"No, no. Thank you. I'll be perfectly all right. The room's a little stuffy, that's all." How did he know she was staying upstairs?

"We should probably be heading to our tables." She smiled nervously, glancing through the open double doors to the round tables decked in fine organdy and roses, all the while folding and unfolding her gloves, trying to understand this turbulent reaction. She saw Angus making his way toward her through the throng of guests.

"My husband is over there." She gave Angus a little wave. He smiled, and Dexter Ward turned, his expression closed. All at once she felt as though a bomb were about to explode.

Angus reached them. As the two men introduced themselves, she fought for breath; her ears buzzed, and her heart raced. When they shook hands she held back a scream, for something akin to a red-hot poker was boring a hole in her head. She couldn't hear what they were saying so she merely sat, trying not to tremble, watching the American dwarfing her husband, everything about him so hauntingly familiar it ached. Perhaps it was the war. Perhaps he reminded her of those handsome young Americans marching into France. Maybe he'd even been among them.

They were looking at her now, Angus frowning. "Are you all right, Flo? Mr. Ward says you had a dizzy spell. Is something the matter? Oh gosh, there are the Ponsenbys, waving. I'll be back in half a tick. Don't move."

"Perhaps I *should* go upstairs," she murmured as Angus disappeared.

"I'll help you."

"No, really, don't bother."

"It's no trouble at all, Lady MacLeod."

"Thank you." She tried to rise, but realized her legs could barely carry her.

"Here. Hold my arm."

"But—"

"Just hold on or you'll fall." He guided her past the guests moving toward the dining room, his strength carrying her as she wafted over the parquet floor on his arm, barely conscious of the clinking crystal, the wisps of exotic perfume and swish of chiffon. Unconsciously she leaned against him, the taut muscles of his upper arm supporting her. She wished all at once that he would swoop her into his arms and carry her, as Gavin had done once at Midfield when they'd first become engaged.

They reached the hall, where only a few stragglers remained, and he led her to the foot of the ornately carved wooden staircase. They stood for an instant under the Aubusson hangings, then, as though he'd read her mind, he lifted her in his arms and began mounting the stairs.

"Dexter." She heard the sharp tone of Eugène's voice.

"In a minute, Eugène. Lady MacLeod is unwell. I'm taking her to her room.

"Flora?" Eugène hastened up the stairs after them, concerned. "Where is Angus? Why hasn't he taken care of you?"

"He was otherwise engaged," Dex retorted dryly. "Now, if you'll allow me, Lady MacLeod needs to rest." He dismissed Eugène with a nod before Flora could speak and climbed the rest of the stairs.

"Where's your room?"

"To the right," she whispered. "Please let me stand up now. I'll be fine. God knows what poor Eugène must have thought, seeing you carrying me upstairs like this," she murmured, flushing, feeling his arms tighten around her as he reached her door.

"I don't care what he thinks." The last was said in a murmur as he entered the room and laid her gently down on the bed and leaned over her. Passing a hand tenderly over her forehead, he smiled. "We'll meet again, Lady MacLeod. I promise." Leaning down he dropped a gentle kiss full on her mouth.

Dex left the room, his heart racing. The scent of her lavender perfume lingered as he returned to the stairs. As he'd expected, Eugène stood at the bottom, straight as a Swiss Guard. Dex made his way slowly down, regaining his composure, then straightened his buttonhole and smiled.

"She'll be fine. She was just a bit faint from the heat."

"What heat? It is not hot. Come to the study and tell me what happened," Eugène snapped.

"Flora, Angus and I were talking, and she became faint. Angus went to talk to some people and I took her to her room, that's all. Stop making a mountain out of a molehill."

"Don't toy with her. You've caused enough damage as it is. Let it go."

"Stop worrying, Eugène. The world moves on. The past is the past. I'm over it."

"I must look stupid," Eugène exclaimed, shaking his head.

"I swear," Dex said. "Look, I met her again, and Angus, and I'm here intact. Doesn't that tell you all you need to know?"

"Like hell it does!"

An iron hand clutched his arm. "You are not without responsibility here, *mon cousin.* Why didn't you tell me they'd be here?" Dex hissed coldly as they crossed the hall to the study. "I never expected them to be here. I've been so taken up with Harcourt's, I never thought about it until I arrived."

"So? What's new? You never think." Eugène closed the door firmly and faced him, grandiose in his priest's robe. "You act on impulse and think of no one but yourself. Look where it has gotten you. As you pointed out yourself, you've made choices. Abide by them."

For a moment their eyes battled.

"You could have warned me," Dex growled.

"I left you a number of messages in Paris, which you were probably too busy to answer," Eugène replied. "I have been in Rome. Communication there is not easy. Now get a grip on yourself. I won't allow you to spoil Genny's wedding or Flora's life. But of course," he added sarcastically, "you've already done that." His mouth was set in a thin, ironic line. "I suggest you have one more glass of champagne and take your leave. The sooner you're out of here, the better."

"I can't believe he's here," Dex replied, staring out of the window, ignoring the suggestion. "That we're in the same house. And Flora, my lovely Flora."

"She is a married woman, and therefore of no interest to you. Leave it alone," Eugène pleaded. "For once in your life, *think* before you act."

"I'll be damned if I'm leaving. I've as much right to be here as they have," he answered childishly.

"That's not the point. Grow up, for goodness' sake, and don't act rashly." Eugène gave an exasperated sigh.

"I've been buying his coal—sorry, *my* coal."

"I'm warning you, Ga—Dex, I will not tolerate a scandal. If anyone's head rolls, it will be yours."

"Very well. You know I wouldn't dream of spoiling the happiest day of Genny's life."

"Good. Or I'll kill you myself."

"How unchristian of you."

"Oh, shut up! You'd make the Lord himself act unchristian," Eugène muttered.

"Are you finished, *monseigneur?* I promise to be on my best behavior. Satisfied?"

"No. And I wish you'd stop that *monseigneur* nonsense."

"Don't tell me all these trips to Rome aren't going to pay off one of these days," Dex remarked, trying to calm his pulse and defuse the atmosphere.

Eugène cast him a quick glance before opening the study door. "You're certain you can manage this?" he asked with sudden concern.

"Absolutely."

"Then so be it."

Was she really awake, and had the tall, magnetic American really had the nerve to kiss her? She felt better and could hear the reception below, the orchestra striking up. Like Sleeping Beauty wakening from a twenty-year sleep, she viewed her surroundings, which suddenly seemed brighter, the champagne bubblier, the air more pungent. Flora remembered his eyes, riveted to hers, until she'd had to drag her gaze away, blushing, her body pliant and vulnerable, feeling deliciously feminine.

The house was dark, despite the party below, as she stumbled to the dressing table, her heart racing and mind full of evocative pictures that had her blushing again. In all these years, she'd never looked or thought of anyone but…Gavin. Now all she could think of was a stranger's hands caressing her body, his lips kissing her neck, her breasts, every last part of her. She closed her eyes tight, the touch of his lips on hers still tingling. It was indecent, immoral, that she would kiss a stranger while her husband was downstairs at a wedding reception. Yet instead of guilt, she felt a lightness of heart, an inner excitement akin to that of a young girl before her first grand ball.

She glanced at herself in the heavy gold mirror and frowned.

The woman staring back at her—brown hair pinned in a chignon, nice skin, large gray eyes and barely any wrinkles—seemed dowdy. But there was a light in her eyes that had gone out the day Gavin died. For the past twenty years she'd never used a mirror except to make sure her hair was brushed and her face clean. She smoothed her hands over the dull mauve dress, wished she owned lipstick, something to enhance herself before she saw him again. Perhaps she wouldn't even see him, and this strangeness was nothing but an illusion.

She turned from the mirror. What if Angus returned to London and she stayed? Perhaps she could go to Paris for a few days, once Geneviève returned from her honeymoon, and go shopping. The thought gave her a sudden thrill. She hadn't been shopping—*really* shopping—since Tante Constance had bought her trousseau. And then she'd been so miserable about Gavin, she hadn't cared a hoot what they bought. But now, something deep inside her wanted to shine.

She went back and lay down again, relinquishing herself to her dreams. What had come over her? It was unwise to tempt fate, but what happened if fate tempted you?

"I'm off to London the day after tomorrow, Flora. Ward wants to buy large amounts of coal and I need to see to it with MacDuff."

"But I thought we were going to stay for several weeks," she exclaimed. "I would like to see Geneviève and her husband after they return from their honeymoon, and Eugène and René. It's so long since we've all been together. I think Tante Hortense expects us to stay."

"I suppose you're right. Why don't you stay on, dear? Don't worry about me. I'll shack up at my club. Stay as long as you like. You need a holiday." Angus hesitated, then gave her a shamefaced smile. "Sorry, Flo, but I feel haunted here. I can't explain it. It's as though—" He shook his head. "I could do with another drink, couldn't you?"

The joy of Geneviève's wedding was tempered by the dreadful news that reached them from Germany shortly afterward. On November 9, more than seven thousand five hundred Jew-

ish businesses were destroyed and one hundred ninety-one syn-
agogues set on fire in an action known as *Kristallnacht*—the
"Night of Broken Glass." Almost one hundred Jews were savagely murdered, others seriously injured and another thirty
thousand rounded up and taken to concentration camps. The
Jewish community was assessed a fine of one billion marks, to
pay for the damage done to damaged non-Jewish property.

The horrific news left the family in shock.

"Eugène, we must get them home as soon as possible," the
Comtesse exclaimed, clutching her hankie. "I knew this wasn't
a good idea. If only your father had been here, he would have
done something."

"*Maman*, stop worrying. Sylvain and Genny are in Switzerland, not in Germany. They'll be quite safe."

"But Switzerland is so close. What if that dreadful man de-
cides to invade?"

"I don't believe that will occur, ma'am," Dex, who'd just
arrived, put in. "Whatever happens, I believe Switzerland will
remain neutral."

"Oh, it's too worrying." The Comtesse took Flora's hand
and squeezed it. "Thank goodness you're here, my love. It's
such a relief to have you in this difficult time. I put a call
through to the Baronne. She is less worried than we are. Apparently she talked to the Grand Rabin this morning and measures are being taken. But what measures? How can anyone
take measures when a monster is on the loose?"

"We must pray that this will bring it all to an end. That after
this, Hitler will realize he has gone too far," Eugène said
firmly. "*Maman*, are you lunching in Limoges? Perhaps Dexter
could give you a lift?"

Realizing Eugène was trying to divert his mother's attention,
Dex quickly seconded him. "Why don't we all have lunch in
Limoges?" he proposed. "Lady MacLeod would enjoy a visit
to Harcourt's, I'm sure. We have a new collection and I could
show her Sylvain's work."

"Lady MacLeod is going to Paris in a few days. Is that not
so, Flora?"

"Yes. I shall be helping Genny organize her new home."

"What a coincidence," Dex exclaimed. "I have to be there next week, too. My wife and I have several engagements at the embassy. I tried to get her to go back to the States after the scare in September but she refused to leave."

As they were leaving the house, Eugène held him back. "You're going too far. What you're doing is wrong, unfair to her. You don't love her, you're using her as a tool. You don't have the right to hurt her more than you already have."

"Leave me alone, Eugène. I know what I'm doing. And yes, I do love her. I always have."

"No, you don't. You're a fool, and a selfish one at that. You must not see her in Paris or pursue this scandalous nonsense. People will notice, and what will become of Flora's reputation? Or don't you care?"

"Of course I care." Dex wrenched his arm away crossly and hastened down the steps of the château, disgruntled.

Damn his conscience and damn everything. The last few days spent in Flora's company, even though they included the Comtesse, were the most wonderful ones he'd spent in the past few years. And damn Eugène for always preaching at him. It was his life, his problem, and Flora was his. And even though the thought of Angus, cuckolded and humiliated, was too sweet to be denied, it was not uppermost in his mind. He was consumed with the thought of Flora, of making love to her as he'd always dreamed of doing, of taking possession of the woman who should have been his and soon would be.

25

Paris, France, 1938

Geneviève returned from her honeymoon and Flora joined the lovebirds at their new home in the eighth arrondissement, near the Faubourg Saint-Honoré. Geneviève was ecstatic. They had motored to Switzerland, spent delicious days making love and lounging in the Boromean Islands, then had driven back via Montreux and Lausanne, spending a wonderful night in Beaunes.

"It was sublime," she told her cousin as they sat among tissue paper, unpacking wedding gifts. "Simply divine. Sylvain is a marvelous lover. I thought it was going to hurt. It did, just a little, you know what I mean. But oh, after that. I wouldn't change anything for the world." She squeezed her eyes shut tight, holding a Tiffany vase high in the air. "Isn't sex the best thing in the world, Flora? Better than ice-cream soda!"

"Genny! What a way to talk!"

"Well, it is, and why can't I say so?" Genny pouted. "I'm a married woman now. I can talk about these things. Do you have great sex with Cousin Angus?" she asked doubtfully. "I don't mean to be rude, Flo, but he doesn't look, you know, terribly—"

"Genny!"

"Oh, pooh!" She got up, straightening her skirt, and

stretched like a satisfied young leopard. "Let's have lunch at the Café de Paris and go shopping."

"What a good idea," Flora answered, relieved the conversation had taken a turn.

"I definitely think you should buy the pink Chanel suit, Flo. You look superb in it. The Worth dress is perfect, of course, but for a different occasion. And I love the way you've cut your hair."

"It feels funny, as though something's missing." Flora touched her hair, permed and short now, knowing the style became her. "As for all these clothes, I don't know when you think I'm going to wear half of them. Life at Strathaird is hardly Paris."

"You never know." Genny wagged a knowing finger. "To be forewarned is to be forearmed." She linked her arm with Flora's. "Isn't this fun?"

The chauffeur dropped them at the Place de l'Opéra, and they made their way among the tables, artists and fashionable gossips mingling under chubby cherubs that gazed down from the painted ceiling.

"Take a look to your left," Geneviève whispered from behind her hand as they sat on the velvet banquette.

Flora glanced surreptitiously, surprised to see the Duke and Duchess of Windsor seated to her left. She had seen them briefly at the wedding. What did this woman possess, she wondered, for a man to give up a kingdom?

"Do you think you should say hello, Genny?"

"No. They can't see us and I don't want to disturb them. Oh, look who's here? Hello, Dex."

"Madame la Baronne," he said.

Flora turned quickly, feeling her cheeks flush as Dexter kissed Genny's hand gallantly. "Marriage definitely suits you, my dear. And Lady MacLeod. What a pleasant surprise," he said, smiling down at her in that way that made her feel like jelly. Dex looked cool and collected, as always, dressed in an impeccable tweed suit, a cane and newspaper tucked under his arm.

"Dex, what a lovely surprise. Are you in Paris for long? Why don't you sit down?" Genny exclaimed, sliding down the banquette.

"I'd be delighted, if you're sure I won't be interrupting your lunch." He gave a small bow in Flora's direction, the obvious admiration in his eyes making her smile inwardly. He liked her new look. She could tell.

"Not at all. It'll be fun. Tell me, how are Alix and the little one?"

"Well, thank you." He sat down and laid his cane, hat and paper on the next chair, then signaled the waiter.

Flora smiled nervously, hoping she didn't seem as shaky as she felt. His gaze devoured her, as though he could see straight through her elegant Mainbocher suit and new lace underwear. She avoided Geneviève's mischievous glance.

"Let's have champagne. Since you're picking up the tab, Dex, we'll have Cristal."

"Baroness, your wishes are my desires. How are you enjoying your stay, Lady MacLeod?"

"Very well, thank you."

"We must enjoy all this while it lasts," he remarked as the waiter approached.

"What do you mean?"

"Geneviève, if you bothered to read the newspapers, you might be aware of all that's taking place in Europe."

"Oh, pooh, Dex. Don't be boring. Flora doesn't want to hear about Hitler. It's so disheartening."

"I just wish your husband could be persuaded to listen to me. I'm on my way to the Cour des Pages later this afternoon."

"Don't be a party pooper. Listen, since you're here, why don't we all go out to dinner tonight? Alix won't mind, will she?" Flora got the impression there was a hidden meaning to the question.

"Not in the least," he responded blandly. "She's very busy caring for Scott."

"Of course. Let's go to Maxim's, the Pré Catalan for lunch tomorrow and—"

"Geneviève, I would be delighted to accompany you where

and whenever you wish. But hadn't we better make sure that Lady MacLeod concurs with your plans?'' The look he sent her left no room for doubt about his intentions. He was forcing her to take a step.

"Of course it's fine, isn't it, Flora? You don't mind Dex coming along? It'll be more fun going *à quatre*. Then we can dance.''

The thought of Dexter's arms encircling her on a dance floor left her so dizzy that she murmured incoherently, glad the sommelier was pouring the champagne.

"To what shall we drink?'' Geneviève asked, raising her flute excitedly. "I know. To meeting Dex. Now we have an escort for you, Flo,'' she added with a naughty grin.

During the days that followed, Dex became a permanent fixture in their lives. Each time they met, Flora felt more entangled in a web of new emotions she was loath to admit but anxious to satisfy. Paris was glorious, despite the gathering tensions of wondering if Hitler would fight. The general feeling was that Eduard Daladier, the premier who had signed the Munich Pact, was not capable of standing up to the oncoming pressures. The leader feared the Communists as much as Hitler himself.

"You have a crush on Dex,'' Geneviève teased one morning at breakfast, after Flora had staunchly denied any such thing. "And so you should. Cousin Angus is a bore and I would imagine he's not much fun in bed.''

"Genny! You must stop these unseemly remarks. It's most unladylike. What would Tante Hortense say?''

"Exactly what you think. But that's not the point. Flo, don't tell me you're not in love, because it's written all over you. And the funny part is, I think he is, too. The way he looks at you.''

"Geneviève, stop it. He's a married man.''

"Alix doesn't give a damn. She's a lesbian. I think they have an arrangement.''

"Are you serious? But what about their son?''

"An heir for Harcourt's, I imagine. But that's neither here nor there. Darling, love doesn't necessarily knock twice. Look at what's happening around us. Everyone says there may be a war. Think how you'd feel if you never saw him again, or if he was killed.'' She stopped, suddenly hesitating. ''Is it true, Flo, that once you were in love with Angus's twin, Gavin? The one who died in the war?''

''Yes.''

''I'm sorry. I shouldn't have asked. But you see what I mean, don't you? What if it happened again? Think of that. Sometimes you have to forget about the rules and live for the moment. And anyway, who would know?''

The city buzzed with excitement, new fashions, concerts and plays, and Flora—now the proud owner of two Chanel suits, several Vionnet dresses, Schiaparelli jerseys and numerous extravagant hats that Geneviève had insisted she buy, despite her protests—felt young and free for the first time.

At Guerlain's she selected Shalimar as her perfume, excited at viewing herself as a sophisticated, fashionable woman rather than a dowdy nonentity heading toward middle age. But though she desperately tried to deny it, she knew it was for Dex's sake she wanted to shine.

''Ever since Dex arrived, you've come alive,'' Geneviève remarked one morning as they lounged in the drawing room after breakfast. ''I think it is time to get rid of Cousin Angus.'' She studied an array of chocolates, then popped one into her mouth. ''I think Cousin Angus is a pain. *Merde*,'' she exclaimed, seeing a spot of melted chocolate on her silk dressing gown.

''You shouldn't say things like that, Genny. It isn't seemly.''

''So you keep repeating,'' she remarked, eyeing the spot crossly. ''But let's face it, Flo, it's the truth. He's dull and offers no conversation. I don't know how you stand it. Tell me,'' she leaned forward, eyes glinting with mischief, ''what would you do if Dex tried to kiss you! And *please*,'' she begged, wringing her hands dramatically, ''don't say *now, Genny!* in that shocked voice, because you know as well as I do that you're dying for him to swoop you into his arms and—''

"Stop it!" Flora burst out, eyes burning. "Leave me and Dex alone."

Genny gaped at her. "I'm sorry, darling." She sprang to her feet and came over to the sofa. "I just want you to be happy, Flo. I promise I won't say another word. Here, have a chocolate."

That evening, Dexter arrived to accompany them to the opera, handsome in white tie and tails. Flora sighed. She moved differently under his gaze, conscious of her waist, her breasts, her legs encased in the beautiful silk stockings and a daring lace suspender belt Geneviève had told her was the *dernier crie*.

"I can't imagine what it would be like doing it with someone I wasn't totally crazy about," Genny commented the day after the opera sitting crosslegged on her bed and flipping through a book called the *Kama Sutra*. "Look at that." She giggled.

Flora peeked surreptitiously at the picture, wondering if it could truly be *that* complicated.

"Sylvain and I bought this in Montmartre. It's from India and tells you the art of making love. Aren't some of the positions quite impossible? But we try them anyway. For fun," she added naughtily, obviously enjoying Flora's embarrassment. "I've even had multiple orgasms," she added proudly.

"Oh," Flora replied blankly, wondering what Geneviève was referring to.

"Tell me something," Genny asked, back to her favorite subject. "Do you enjoy going to bed with Cousin Angus?"

"Geneviève!"

"There you go again," Genny sighed.

"But we've been through this already. You shouldn't be asking me personal things like that." She jumped off the bed. "What does it matter, anyway? He's my husband and that's an end to it. And if you want the truth, I don't think much about the matter."

"Liar. You've been thinking about it ever since Dex sat down at the Café de Paris. I wonder if he's a good lover?" she mused. "I'd be willing to bet he is."

"Well, perhaps you'd better find out," Flora replied tartly, ashamed at how close to home Genny's words were. In fact, it was all she thought of lately.

When Dex had traveled to Paris, he'd set out to woo Flora as he'd never wooed a woman before. The meeting at Café de Paris was a happy coincidence, which had made his life easier and opened the door to further encounters. Now, after ten days of walks in the Louvre, dinners and operas, he could wait no longer. Soon it would be Christmas, time for her to return home. He'd been careful to mask his heightened longing, but now he knew she was ready. He sensed it in the way her eyes held his, how she allowed her hand to linger, little gestures that spoke volumes.

One night, after the opera, he asked her out alone, wondering how she would react, surprised when she accepted. They dined at Monseigneur, the Russian restaurant on the Champs-Elysées, lingering over champagne and after-dinner drinks, time always too short. On the way home, he stopped the car near the Seine and they sat in silence, watching the moon gleaming on the river, intensely aware of one another.

He glanced sideways, longing for the touch of her hair, the softness of her skin, reminders of how much he'd left behind.

"Your husband hasn't returned," he said, taking out a cigarette and lighting it, watching her expressions change in the moonlight.

"He doesn't plan to."

"Oh?"

"He—he has affairs in London."

"I'll bet," he muttered under his breath.

"I'm sure he has his reasons," she murmured, looking away.

"Not good enough, my dear. You are too young and too charming, too beautiful to be on your own."

"Well, you don't seem to spend much time with your own wife," she countered, leaning against the window, wrapped in Genny's sable.

"True. My wife, like your husband, is very busy," he responded dryly.

"I'm sorry." All at once, she remembered what Genny had told her and was afraid she might have hurt his feelings.

"Don't be," he said, seeing her embarrassment. "We have our own arrangement and it suits us."

"I see," she replied, wondering about the child whom he seemed so proud of.

"No, you don't," he whispered, taking her chin in his hand and looking into her eyes through the darkness. "All that matters now is us, Flora. What we feel, what we want. I've been dreaming of kissing you again ever since Genny's wedding."

"Why don't you?" She could barely believe it was her voice, whispering through the darkness, and her eyes closed as he leaned toward her, drawing her to him.

"I think I've always loved you, Flora. I've been searching for you all my life and, now that I've found you, I don't want to let you go. Unless you want me to?" The question filled the cold night air. He could feel her hands tremble, her chest heave, and knew what he was asking went against every belief she held. But he asked, just the same. "I need to know how you feel, Flora." He grazed his lips over hers, murmuring, intoxicated by the sweetness of her breath, her closeness. "My Flo," he whispered and felt her stiffen. "Are you all right?" he said softly, drawing away enough to see her eyes gleaming in the darkness.

"Yes," she whispered. "I—you just reminded me of someone. For a moment I could've sworn—"

"I was your fiancé, the one you lost in the war?"

She nodded, looked away.

"Do you still love him?"

"I'll always love him," she murmured. "Part of me died with him. But since you came into my life, something's changed." She reached up and stroked his cheek gently. "You're like him. Rather, what he probably would have been like, if he'd grown up. I—"

"Don't apologize. I understand. We all lost something in the war, a part of ourselves." He held her close, and for a moment they cleaved to one another, until Dex pulled away. "If I go on like this, we'll be picked up for indecent behavior. That would be embarrassing.''

Flora laughed, that same youthful laugh of long ago that made his blood tingle and the longing unbearable. "Are you afraid of being unfaithful, Flora?"

"Yes." She nodded as he trailed a finger down her throat to the neckline of her dress, coming to an abrupt stop.

"Guilty?" he asked, forcing himself to remain calm.

"Guilty that I *don't* feel guilty," she said reluctantly.

The relief was overwhelming. "My darling. I promise you won't regret this. I don't know what's going to happen—only time will tell—but I swear I won't let you get hurt."

"You can't promise that, Dex. Nobody can."

"I'm going to make an outlandish proposal," he continued, pulling her close and kissing the top of her head. "If you don't agree to it, we'll leave. I'll drive you home immediately and swear that I will never come near you again." He felt her fingers trembling in his. "I want to go away with you, make love to you all day and all night, until there's not one bit of you I don't know. It is impossible to go on seeing you like this, pretending there's nothing more between us but casual friendship."

"I—I don't know what to say."

"*Yes* would be good." He turned her toward him, saw the smile hovering on her lips, and knew he'd won. "I wish we could leave tonight, Flo, at once. God, I want to—" He squeezed her close, smothering her. Dropping endless kisses on her neck until she gasped, he trailed his fingers over the thin silk of her evening gown, touching her nipple through the gauze and holding her as she moaned his name.

"Tell me you'll come with me, Flo," he insisted, his hands taunting. "Please."

"How can I refuse?" she gasped, leaning toward him, his scent rediscovering some long-lost recollection, buried in the confines of her memory.

"We'll go places together you've never dreamed of." Dex traced his lips over her cheek, slipped his hand reverently through her hair in a familiar gesture that made her shiver with a mix of fear and excitement. It felt so right, so familiar it was almost déjà vu.

"We'll leave after I come back from Berlin."

"You're going to Berlin?" she asked, suddenly afraid something dreadful might happen and he wouldn't return.

"I'm leaving in three days on business. But I'll be back by the end of the week. And then, it's up to you."

When he wasn't courting Flora, Dex worked diligently to develop a code that he hoped would be unbreakable. After several designs, he'd tried out revised sketches, sent them to Max and had them returned successfully. The signs and their meanings had become so familiar that he felt confident should the need arise, their system could be safely used.

On his last trip to Limoges, he'd taken a radio set imported from the U.S. to the factory. Entering Harcourt's late at night, he'd climbed up one of the broken chimneys and placed it on a shelf constructed out of plywood, supported between niches in the bricks. Once he was sure it was secure, he extended the antenna as far as it would go. Happily, it reached just beyond the mouth where the reception would be best. Then he'd tuned in, setting the frequencies and making sure it worked, before leaving it safely covered and hidden. Carefully he piled rubble at the foot of the furnace to avoid suspicion. No one would dream of looking inside. Perhaps it was an unnecessary precaution, but with the unease surrounding them and the coded reports coming out of Germany via Max, he felt it was justified.

Now that Flora had agreed to the trip, he was loath to go to Berlin. But he'd promised Max and knew it was vital for the success of their plan that they be seen together in public. Some of the information he'd received regarding anti-aircraft devices had already been put to good use. As soon as he was sure of the system, he'd contacted William Bullitt, the American ambassador, and told him in confidence what he was doing. The information was then discreetly relayed, via the embassy, to the State Department.

"It's a great job you're doing, Dex. Your guy's a brave man," the ambassador commended him. "Gee, the boys back home'll get a kick out of this. We depend on MI5 and the Brits for every damn piece of info they deign to give us.''

He left for Berlin the next day, and the long train journey through France and Germany gave him time to think of what lay ahead. These were precarious times, and he wished he'd met Flora again, after all these years, at an easier moment. Why was it that outside events seemed to rule their lives? Would another war come to tear them from one another? No. He would not permit it. This time he'd see to it that nothing parted them.

As the train trundled through bleak stretches of countryside and rain slashed the windows of his first-class carriage, he thought of Flora lovingly. There had been few words exchanged in the Packard; there had been no need. That same complicity that had always reigned between them had made its presence felt once more. Its familiarity took him back to Strathaird, to those glorious days of his youth, and he wished he could tell her the truth. He knew it was impossible though— for now, at any rate.

He hadn't a clue how it would all progress. But Angus had dwindled into the shadows of this newfound emotion. He smiled, gazed out the train's window as it sped through Switzerland, aware he was emotionally over his head. Instead, he focused on the challenge awaiting him in Berlin.

But as they reached the German border, the train slowed. He sensed a change as it chuffed into the station at Saint Marghreten and, when the carriage doors opened, it was impossible to ignore the ruthless chill behind the glassy blue eyes of the Gestapo officers that accompanied the customs officer.

They handed his passport from one to the other, and for a moment he wondered if they could see through him, read his true intentions behind the disinterested front of an American businessman.

Finally, after what seemed like hours, they handed him back the document with a polite smile. ''We wish you a pleasant stay in Germany, Herr Ward.'' A cold sweat broke out beneath his fine English suit as the carriage door closed and the train continued out of the station.

* * *

Dex registered into his usual suite at the Adlon, certain the rooms were bugged. Picking up the phone, he waited for the operator, knowing all calls would immediately be reported.

He called Truman Smith, the American military attaché with whom Bullitt had put him in touch, and arranged a lunch as expected. Then he set up an ostensible meeting with Max, taking time to discuss details that had already appeared in their correspondence and which should keep the Gestapo at bay.

Max met him in the lobby at twelve-thirty, shaking hands in a firm, businesslike manner, before taking him to a prominent restaurant frequented by high-ranking Gestapo members dressed in shiny top boots and black uniforms. They sent a shiver down his back, and he cringed inwardly when Max rose to chat with Herr Goebbels, Hitler's propaganda minister, to whom he was introduced.

"Are you enjoying our beautiful city, Herr Ward?" he asked, after the introductions. Dex replied politely, having mastered the disengaged air of one too busy to be worried about a war that didn't concern him.

To any outsider, Berlin seemed a serene, sophisticated center of well-dressed citizens having *kaffee und kuchen* in their favorite coffee shops and dancing into the night, as removed from war as Paris.

They spent time at Max's office discussing orders and patterns, a new line that depicted blond girls in dirndls and ruddy young men in lederhosen, kitsch examples of Hitler's German vision, to be reproduced for everyday eating purposes.

But on the third day, once they'd been well seen and recognized, they went for a walk in the *Tiergarten,* the only place they could secure some privacy. Signs with *Juden Verboten* filled him with rage, doubling his determination to transmit as much information as possible. He was horrified by the chilling undercurrent he sensed beneath the veneer, aware now of the great personal risk Max was incurring, and hoped that, when he returned to France, Sylvain would take his warnings more seriously.

"How long do you think it can last?" he asked softly.

"Not long," Max replied. "They're on the move. Troops are being transported to the Dutch border as we speak."

"I see. Business may become slow."

"Perhaps."

"Will Hitler fight?"

"Very soon. It is crazy to believe otherwise. The Italians will join in, too. It's mad. If Germany wins the war, God help us. The world as we know it will be lost."

They moved along a path and Dex smiled benignly at a *Kindermädchen*, proudly pushing a large perambulator, before continuing.

"How will we keep up the designs if the market wants the stuff you showed me yesterday?" Dex asked, worried. "Maybe we should execute some orders."

"Perhaps, but I think for the moment we are okay. I showed some samples to a visiting high-ranking member of the party the other day, and even offered him a dinner set." He gave a low, harsh laugh. "That should keep them at bay."

"Max, you certainly have balls. Please be careful," Dex murmured, watching warily as two figures in black leather coats appeared out of nowhere and walked toward them.

"As you can see, Herr Ward, we Berliners are lucky devils, blessed with the best," Max remarked, eyes glistening, waving his hands enthusiastically. "*Heil* Hitler." He nodded and jutted out his right arm smartly as the men passed.

"*Heil* Hitler."

Dex watched them leave and glanced at Max. "The more I see, the happier I am we're doing something about this. You're right, Max. It may not be long. I hope I can convince them of that back home."

26

Lausanne, Switzerland, 1938

Flora had counted the days until Dex's return like an excited schoolgirl concealed in the trappings of a grown woman.

But just as innocence in youth was charming, being untouched at her age seemed ridiculous. She wondered uncomfortably what he would say and do when he realized she was a virgin. Secretly she studied Geneviève's book, blushing at the pictures, yet burning with the desire for experience.

It was early December when they finally left Paris, driving northeast to Dijon and then into Switzerland via Pontalier.

The day was cold and sunny, Lake Geneva a shimmering pond where a single paddle steamer glided sedately into the pier at Rolle, the red and white cross of the flag billowing like a tiny dot at the stern.

They drove slowly, hand in hand, winding their way down the steep, narrow inclines, among the vineyards and the dried, gnarled roots of the vines battened down under the frost.

Flora gazed at the mountains, the lake, the tiny villages snuggled along their borders, and pinched herself to make sure it was real. She was really here, alone with Dexter Ward, whose mistress she was about to become. But it didn't feel tawdry and the word offended her. If anything, they were illicit lovers. Or would be.

Genny had pushed her to go, not hesitating an instant when, embarrassed, she'd poured out the whole story.

"Don't think twice, just go," she'd encouraged. Flora's only misgivings had surfaced the evening before, when they'd arrived in Beaunes, where they were to spend the night.

But to her surprise and relief, two rooms had been reserved. Dex had gone out of his way to make her feel at ease, chatting easily and holding her hand, as though determined not to rush her. They'd talked for hours, lingering over their wine, Dex as euphoric and enchanted as she.

This time, though, there were not two rooms but a large suite at the Beau Rivage Palace overlooking the lake and Flora gazed in awe through the bedroom door at the huge bed, the crisp white sheets and lace pillowcases. A frenzied new batch of misgivings made her move hastily to the window, where she drew back the lace curtains and gazed blindly at the gardens. Clasping her hands nervously, she opened the French doors and stepped onto the balcony, shivering, the rich scent of roasted chestnuts and sugarcoated almonds spiraling up from the vendors next to the water.

Dex followed, his arms closing about her, his cheek next to hers as he gazed out over her shoulder, swaying her gently.

"Happy?" he asked, drawing her hair gently back from her face and dropping a kiss on her neck. "Come back inside. It's cold." He took her hand and drew her into the room, eyes devouring her with a new hunger. "Don't be afraid," he murmured, drawing her into the circle of his arms. "I'll never harm you."

"Dex, I want to tell you something," she murmured into his shoulder.

"Shh." He placed a finger gently over her lips and smiled. "Not now, darling. Just let me love you."

"But—"

"Later."

He slipped a hand deftly behind her neck, kneading it until she could think of nothing but the desire in her heart and body, the longing she felt when he pressed her close. She let out a small gasp, feeling his need, the ache unbearable as he slipped off her wool dress, melting as his fingers caressed her skin. Sensations, hitherto undreamed of, wreaked havoc on her. Before she knew it, she was lying naked in his arms, with nothing but a string of pearls between them.

"Flora, my beautiful Flora," he whispered, watching her reverently, making each moment last a lifetime—the time he'd waited to make her his own. God, how he loved her. He needed every breath in her body to be his. He would never allow his brother to touch her ever again, no matter what he had to do. He gave himself up to the art of loving her, bewitching her, holding his own impulses in check to satisfy her every need, determined to make this moment so perfect she would never lie with his brother again.

She lay entranced, not ashamed any longer but welcoming his gaze, his caresses, the stubble on his chin that grazed the soft texture of her breasts. Each touch was imbued with a magic so unique, she knew deep within that she would never belong to another man as long as she lived. Finally, she was purging Gavin from her being. It wasn't a betrayal, merely a passing, and it was time.

It was dark as he lay down next to her, anxious to feel the closeness of her body.

Then she reached for him, tentatively at first then with more daring, causing delicious torture as he held back, his mind split between present and past, as mixed images grappled in his heart and mind.

She helped him undress, shirt falling to the floor as she wrenched it from his waistband. Then he lay over her, rejoicing in the feel of her skin on his, lips touching hers as his fingers drifted downward and he sought further.

To his surprise, she stiffened and he hesitated, confused at her reaction. It was that of a young virgin rather than a married woman. He kissed her again, tenderly, before easing his fingers inside her, wishing it were he and not his brother who'd possessed her first. But as he probed, her muscles tightened, her nails dug into his shoulders, and all at once he came to a sudden halt.

It wasn't possible, couldn't be. Yet the evidence was undeniable. The shock of discovery was such that he withdrew and sat up, bewildered, the primal thrill of possession quickly replaced by the knowledge that he could not—would not—take her under false pretenses. He rose from the bed, dragged his hand through his hair and gazed at the lake, torn between his conscience and desire.

A muffled sob made him turn, horrified to see Flora, her head buried among the pillows, sobbing. *My God,* he realized, anguished. *She believes I've rejected her.*

"Flo, darling, I'm sorry. I didn't mean—" He hastened back to her side and sat next to her, stroking her hair.

"Don't call me that," she burst out between sobs. "Never call me that again. I want to leave, to go back. *Now.* I—"

"Please, darling, let me explain."

"Th-there's nothing to explain," she whispered, the words catching. "I tried to tell you b-but you w-wouldn't—" She buried her head once more and all he could do was stroke her, desperate to tell her the truth. But after Berlin, he knew that was impossible. Damn Max, damn his commitments and the war that he knew was coming sooner or later. Damn the world that robbed him over and over of all he so desperately wanted.

He gazed down, his heart in tatters, wishing he could stop time and wake up where they'd begun. But too much had passed. Too much depended on Dexter Ward and the present and even now, as temptation to throw it all to the wind beckoned, discipline won. Perhaps, after all, it was better this way. Oh God, how it hurt. He reached for his underwear and shirt, aching with a pain he'd never known existed until this moment. What more would he have to give up, for God to forgive him, he wondered bitterly.

After a sleepless night, Dex left the room early to allow her to dress. She had told him she wanted to return on the train and he'd agreed, all his attempts and explanations coldly rebuffed. He walked sadly down the wide staircase knowing her well enough to know she'd retreated into her own world.

He drove her silently to the station then waited awkwardly on the platform for her carriages to arrive. Each minute dragged. Dex changed his mind constantly, feeling foolish one minute for not coming clean, then remembering the reasons for his silence; finally, the weight of responsibility was an iron yoke from which there was no escape.

You made your choices. Abide by them. Eugène's words rang through him like a death knell. By the time the train drew into the station and Flora climbed aboard, he was ready to drop from mental exhaustion and disappointment.

The goodbyes were formal and senseless, a world apart from the two lovers who only a day ago had been discovering one another for the first time, thinking only of the fulfillment of their longing.

As the train pulled out of the station, Dex thought his heart would break with pain too intense to stand. He lingered, gazing at the rails, knowing that he'd had his chance and failed utterly.

27

Paris, France, 1939

Paris was in a state of uncontrolled excitement, an eerie euphoria, laughing by day, dancing till dawn, drunk on the last drops of freedom, determined to empty the bottle dry.

Now that von Ribbentrop and Stalin had signed a nonaggression pact, war was inevitable. In a matter of weeks, perhaps days, the world around them would change, just as it had the last time. For the first time since Flora had left him at the station in Lausanne, Dex was thankful for the decision he'd made.

His first concern now was for Alix and their son. As he made his way home to Avenue Foch, he prayed she would finally listen to him and go back to America. He'd tried often enough to persuade her over the past year, but it was in vain.

In the end, it was Arianne who made the decision for her.

"You have to go, Alix. Dex is right, there's Scott to think of," she said sadly.

"Thank you, Arianne," Dex said. "Perhaps you can talk some sense into her. With any luck, it'll be a while before things heat up, but not necessarily. They're going ape-shit over at the embassy."

"The conscription notices are all over town. Paris already looks like a war zone." Arianne gazed pensively out the window. "This time next year, France will not be France anymore. Laval, Reynaud—the lot of them are a bunch of imbeciles, mouthing off about the wondrous Grande Armée."

"Then come with us," Alix urged. "What will you do here in a war, Arianne? She can't stay, can she, Dex?" Alix pleaded, turning to him for support.

"She's right, Arianne. I'll try and get passage on the first ship to New York for all of you."

"No." Arianne shook her head sorrowfully. "I'm sorry, Alix, but I cannot abandon my country in a time like this. If there is a war, then my place is here, in France."

"What nonsense!" Alix exclaimed. "Why are you so hardheaded? What earthly good could you do here? Now stop the heroics and let Dex get you a passage."

"If there still are any available," he warned. "It'll be difficult, but I've already set the process in motion. The *Athenia* sails on the third of September. If I'm lucky, you'll all be aboard."

"What about you?" Alix asked.

"Me?" He glanced at her, touched by her obvious concern. "I'll take care of myself. I made it through last time around."

"How long ago that seems," she said with a wan smile. "I'll never forget the day you and Johnny came home."

"I made it out alive then and I will now," he assured her, giving her arm an affectionate squeeze. "Don't worry about me, Alix, you have Scott to think about." He gave her a hug.

"I'll miss you, Dex," she said, stroking his cheek fondly. "Promise you'll come over?"

"As soon as I'm able. Scout's honor." He lowered his voice and leaned close. "Do you think she'll go?"

Alix shook her head, eyes brimming, and Dex sighed. He knew too well the anguish of separation caused by circumstances bigger than one's self.

"Arianne, please take this chance," he begged, in a last attempt to make her change her mind.

"Thanks, Dex *chéri*, but I can't. France is my home, my country. I cannot abandon it like that!" She snapped her fingers. "God knows, this place is already a chaos. Look at who we have to lead us. A bunch of dotards, the heroes of Verdun, men who should have retired twenty years ago.''

Dex agreed but said nothing. Now that it was upon them, there was little use criticizing.

"See if you can persuade Geneviève and Sylvain to leave," Arianne added. "They really do need to get out. God help *them* if the Germans should invade."

"Don't you think I've tried?" Dex dropped onto the sofa, tired. "Ever since I got back from Germany last November I've done little else but try and talk them into leaving. But Sylvain refuses. Like you, he says that if France goes to war, he's a Frenchman and he'll fight."

"What about her?"

"Same thing. Refuses to budge without him. Very laudable, I'm sure, but unrealistic. If half of what I've gleaned in Germany is true, I dread to think what might happen."

"I've tried, too," Alix said, shaking her head miserably, "but it's useless. Genny is determined to stay, and Sylvain seems more worried about the duchess's darn brooch than what's happening around him." She sighed and sat down next to him on the sofa. "What do you really think is going to happen, Dex?"

"Germany'll be on the march within a week. The Polish don't stand a chance. And if that happens, Britain will be forced to take a stand. France will follow suit. After that, who knows."

"What about the United States? Will they join in?"

"Not at present. Roosevelt will stick to his guns. Right now, he wouldn't have the support of the American public." All at once he recalled his conversation with Bill Donovan at the Plaza, and wondered what F.D.R.'s real agenda was.

He rose and switched on the wireless but the commentator was eulogizing the Grande Armée and its invincibility. He switched it off, irritated.

"I'd better get going. I'll be back later." Before leaving the apartment, he slipped into the nursery, where Scott lay sleeping, and stood gazing at his son, touching his small fist and marveling, as he always did, at the miracle of life.

* * *

On his way back to the embassy, he decided to make a last attempt at persuading Sylvain to leave, and grabbed a cab, directing the driver to the Place de l'Opéra. Then he walked the short distance to the Cour des Pages, where Madame de Rothberg was trying on a bracelet with two assistants hovering over her solicitously.

"Ah! Dexter." She smiled.

"*Madame.*" He bowed and kissed her hand.

"Tell me, what do you think of this bracelet, Dexter dear, and of all this rumpus going on."

"I think the bracelet is superb and the *rumpus,* as you call it, extremely serious."

She raised her wrist to the light. "I hope Sylvain had my brother Levi deliver the best stones." She squinted critically before lowering her hand, leaving him irritated. Could she be so blind to what was occurring?

"*Madame,* are you aware that we are on the brink of war? I came here today to plead with your son to leave the country before it's too late." He noticed the assistants had discreetly disappeared, and continued. "Don't you know what is going on in Germany?" he asked angrily, unable to contain himself. Couldn't they see what was happening under their damn noses? All at once, he remembered a scene he had witnessed during his last visit to Berlin that had left him cold—a child weeping in a doorway, a mother dragged away by the Gestapo police, then eerie silence in the street alive with unspoken fear.

Madame de Rothberg laid down the bracelet and looked at him. "Sit down, Dexter, and control yourself," she said as though addressing a small child. "I know you mean well, but what do you propose I should do? Run like a scared rabbit? Leave everything for those swine to enjoy, if they do come? I am a French citizen. It is up to the government to defend my rights."

"Should the Germans invade France, you would have no rights left to defend." He pulled up a blue velvet chair and sat down opposite her. "I came here to try and hammer some sense into your son."

The proud veil dropped, and her face looked suddenly drawn. "I wish you could persuade him. I am an old woman, Dexter, and it is different. The thought of starting a life somewhere else, of leaving all I am used to..." She shook her head sadly. "I'd rather take the risk. But them. They are so young." She cast him an anguished look.

"You should think of yourself, too. What about your daughters?"

"Rebecca is in London with her husband and Ruth is at home." She sighed. "I don't suppose she will find a husband now. If there is a war, all the men will go."

"That is hardly an issue right now."

"Perhaps not to you, but it is to me. My daughter is thirty-two."

"Madame de Rothberg," he said patiently. "We are on the verge of war. I have spoken to William Bullitt, the American ambassador. All American citizens who wish to return to the U.S. are being evacuated. I am certain that I could arrange for you and your daughters to leave. This may be your last chance. Go while you still can."

"I obviously have more faith in the French army than you do," she said with a wry smile. "For Sylvain and Geneviève, it is different. They are young. We have relations in New York. Plus, there is the family bank. But me," she shook her head, "I shall stay at home. What could they possibly want with an old woman and an old maid?"

Dex opened his mouth, then closed it. It was useless. They simply did not want to believe that what was now an everyday occurrence in Germany could just as easily happen here.

To Dex's relief, Alix, Scott and their nanny sailed from Cherbourg to Glasgow a few hours before Germany marched into Poland. He decided to stay in Paris where he could be in touch with Bullitt and the embassy staff. It would be impossible to communicate with Max for the moment; Dex didn't even know exactly where he was. The last drawings he'd received had spoken of imminent maneuvers, and his information had proven completely accurate.

In the early evening, he and Arianne took a long walk and

watched a barge sail down the Seine, while sirens blared in the distance and a dog barked. Dex was thankful that his family was on their way home, and Flora safe in Skye. He glanced at Arianne, noting the grief on her face, the lines etched within hours, knowing how she felt; his own longing and frustration were so acute that at times he felt physical pain.

They remained silent, buried in their thoughts. He glanced over at Notre-Dame, serene and stately, the regal witness of man's power and weaknesses for almost a thousand years.

A couple leaned on the parapet close to them, the boy dressed in a crisp new uniform, exchanging a long tender kiss followed by a ripple of youthful laughter. Oh God, it was happening all over again. The laughter followed by death and destruction, those memories that lurked and were never far from mind. He sighed, glad his son was young and hoping that by the time Scott grew up, the world might have more sense than it did now.

That night he and Arianne dined at Fouquet's on the Champs-Elysées, trying to fill in the void left by Alix and Scott's departure.

"Thank God they'll be safe," she commented wistfully as the champagne and caviar arrived at the table, a last gesture of defiance before the inevitable fall. "To a safe journey." They raised their glasses and sipped.

Dex nodded and smiled to passing acquaintances—people in diplomatic circles he had taken care to cultivate relationships with over the past few months—then turned his attention back to Arianne, worried about her, too.

"I want you to stay on at the apartment, Arianne."

"Thank you, Dex." She rested a hand on his. "I know this hasn't been easy for you. Me and Alix, I mean. Still," she added with a brave attempt at humor, "we had our moments."

"That we did." He glanced at her, half-amused, aware of the twinge of guilt he always experienced whenever he looked at his son. But now, in a strange way, they'd become a family unit.

On September third, they listened as a crackling voice came

over the wireless, announcing that Great Britain was at war. At five o'clock that same afternoon, France followed suit.

"Well. That's that," he remarked, standing at the window and watching the cars, their headlights painted black. A line of trucks, filled with young soldiers headed for the Maginot Line, rolled slowly up the avenue. There was an air of gaiety, of hope. Some young girls waved and blew kisses from the pavement and the soldiers laughed and waved back. He sighed. An old woman was standing under a tree, gazing at the trucks. She was not smiling and neither was he. It was all déjà vu. But this time, he would take care of things his way.

"Alix must be on the ship to America by now," Arianne remarked, joining him at the window. "What a relief it is to know they are safe."

"Do you regret not being with them?"

"Of course. But I couldn't. *C'est la vie.*" She gave a shrug and he pressed her hand. She returned the pressure, and for a moment they stood in silence.

That night, Dex was wakened by the sound of a telephone ringing. Glancing at the clock, he realizing it was well past midnight. He jumped out of bed and grabbed his dressing gown, filled with sudden foreboding. Reaching the hall, he seized the receiver.

"Ward speaking."

"Mr. Ward, this is Brooker, from the American embassy. The ambassador asked me to call you."

"What is it?"

"It's your wife, sir."

"My wife?" He looked up and saw Arianne, standing in her robe, hugging her arms, her face petrified.

"I'm afraid I have bad news, sir. The *Athenia* was torpedoed by a German submarine, two hundred fifty miles northwest of Ireland. She's sinking fast. We don't have much news yet. It's coming in on the ticker as we speak."

"My God," he whispered, his legs suddenly weak.

"She was hit midship at 9:00 p.m., sir. We don't know much more, except there are two British merchant ships in the area and a yacht. As soon as I have any further news, I'll call. I'm sorry.''

"Thank you," he replied numbly, replacing the receiver.

"What is it?" Arianne was shaking his arm wildly.

"The *Athenia* was torpedoed last night."

"And Alix? Is she all right?"

He shook his head. "They don't know. All we can do is wait. If they've been picked up, they'll be taken to Galway, I guess." He closed his eyes, willing God to make it okay. He'd tried so hard to avoid tragedy, yet here it was, knocking hard at the door. The war had been declared only hours before the ship was attacked and Dex was already crushed in its midst.

All day they waited for the telephone to ring, barely talking, both too shocked to do anything but hope and pray. At 11:00 p.m. the phone rang. They rushed to the hall and answered on the first bell.

"Dexter." Bullitt's voice made his heart sink.

"What is the news, Bill?"

"Not good, I'm afraid. Most of the passengers were saved, but—I'm afraid Alix didn't make it. I'm so sorry, Dex."

"My son?" he asked, his voice a thin whisper.

"The nanny saved his life. They've been put on a vessel to Canada. We're shipping as many kids out as possible. Hitler has broadcast that the attack was a mistake. Let's hope he means it."

"Thank you, Bill."

"If there's anything I can do…"

"I'll make arrangements for the body to be taken home."

"We'll do whatever we can to help cut through the red tape. I can get you onto the next ship out to New York."

"I'd be grateful."

When he turned, he saw Arianne huddled by the wall, tears pouring down her cheeks. "I knew she shouldn't have gone," she repeated over and over. Then she rose and rounded on him. "It's your fault. Why did you send her?" she shouted. "You killed her, *assassin*."

Dex moved swiftly, grabbing her arms and pinning them to

her body. "It's nobody's fault," he whispered hoarsely. "It's the goddamn war. Thank God Scott's okay."

Then he imagined Alix floundering, terrified, in the freezing water, trying desperately to grab on to something, her limbs turning numb, dragging her down, down... Arianne collapsed in his arms and they held one another. Every moment he'd known Alix, from the first time they'd met on the pier at Hoboken till the day she'd sailed, flashed before him.

He led Arianne gently to the drawing room and poured them each a stiff cognac.

"Do you want to come with me to New York?"

She gulped down the brandy and shook her head. "No. It is over. I cannot... *Je ne veux pas.*"

He nodded. "I understand. You need time to heal. I'll make arrangements for Scott, then I'll be back. This damn war may just need us."

"Why do you want to come back?" she asked, face ravaged and tear-stained. "This isn't your war. Stay where you belong. Why get involved? You don't need to."

"It's personal," he murmured, knowing that now it had truly become so.

28

Skye, Scotland, 1939

It was early October when Flora received the letter from Geneviève telling her that Alix was dead and Dexter had gone to the States. She looked out the window, past Angus trudging through the rain in his old shooting jacket puffing on a cigarette, seeing Dex's image, stark and vivid as ever.

When she'd returned to Paris after the fateful journey to Lausanne, it had been Genny who'd soothed her. She hadn't revealed everything that had happened, but she was too devastated to pretend all was well, too broken to feign happiness. She'd rushed home as soon as possible, to Strathaird and safety. It was her own fault for getting entangled with a man of the world, out to have a fling. Her fault entirely for making him into an updated version of Gavin, bestowing qualities on him that didn't exist. Now she was back in her cocoon, where she meditated, wrote and communicated with her own world. The fashionable dresses bought so enthusiastically months before were packed safely away in mothballs in the attic.

Angus stopped, lit another cigarette, then continued toward the castle. He would be off in a few days to join his old regiment in the south. Already his uniform lay, pressed and ready.

She closed her eyes. It was happening all over again. Suddenly she remembered the song she and Dex had danced to in

Paris, "Begin the Beguine." It seemed somehow appropriate. For although nothing had occurred yet, the pregnant silence on both sides boded ill. At any moment war could burst down upon them, as it had before, ripping families to shreds and leaving hearts in tatters.

Six months later, no action had taken place and the war became known as the Phoney War.

It's rather ridiculous, Geneviève wrote. *We are as gay in Paris as ever we were. Everyone is calling it* La Drôle de Guerre, *and the Germans cowards.*

Flora kept Genny's letters, taking them out from time to time and rereading them, always seeking news of Dex, searching between the lines of Genny's flourishing handwriting. Tante Hortense wrote occasionally, too, and once in a while Eugène. But from Dex she heard nothing. How could she expect to?

Then, in one of Geneviève's chatty letters, she learned that Dex had returned in April. Why, she wondered. Why return when he didn't have to? She put the letter away, determined to overcome her longing that still lingered, despite his rejection. Would she ever forget him? Those magical days in Paris seemed like a dream to her now, as she functioned with a skeleton staff in the castle, preparing for what she was sure would come. Yet deep inside, a tiny ray of inexplicable hope lingered. It was nonsense of course, but still. It made life bearable.

29

Limoges, France, 1940

After the first panic had passed, Max's correspondence picked up again and by November was well under way. German tank production, according to the messages Dex received, was up considerably. The French and British armies might be well-manned, he realized bitterly, but they were badly armed, and the German air force held definite superiority. After the Munich Conference in 1938 Roosevelt had switched the main U.S. defense policy from the navy to the army, in case of war. Since it was illegal to sell implements of war under the Neutrality Laws, the old fox used factories in Canada, a brilliant move that allowed him to sell to the British and French. It wouldn't be tomorrow, but Dex was certain that if the war went ahead, as he was sure it would, at some point America would be dragged in.

On May 10, Dex was sleeping soundly in the apartment in Paris when a sudden ring of the telephone made him leap up.

"Brooker, sir." The man spoke quickly. "Germany just invaded Belgium, Holland and Luxembourg. God knows how many troops there are, they're talking about over one hundred armored divisions rolling toward France as we speak. They say the front extends from the North Sea to the Swiss border. Good luck, sir."

"Good luck," he whispered.

So this was it. He went to the old-fashioned kitchen and fiddled about in the half-light looking for a cup, then something to boil water in, since he couldn't see a kettle. France didn't stand a chance against the German onslaught. It really was the end of the world as they knew it. As he'd predicted, German troops were heading past the Maginot Line, then would continue south. He sighed, thankful that Scott was in Connecticut. He found some coffee and lit the gas, glad once more that Flora was in Skye.

Should he have trusted her with the truth, despite the danger, he wondered, pouring the boiling water into a teapot and burning his finger in the process.

He picked up the tray and made his way to the study. No, he couldn't have told her. It wouldn't have been fair to put that burden of guilt on her shoulders. And living with Angus would have been impossible after he revealed himself. He thought of all the information Max had transmitted that he'd been able to pass on—vital statistics that could sway the balance of power—and knew that he'd been right, however high the price.

During the days that followed, he had little time to think. Men were leaving for the front, making it necessary to cut the workforce at the factory. His presence was required eighteen hours a day to organize matters with those leaving. But his main concern was for the la Vallières and Sylvain, who still refused to leave the country. He insisted instead that Colonel de Gaulle, who had fled to London, from where he planned to lead a free French army, needed faithful supporters inside France.

At Eugène's insistence, the family assembled a few days later at the Château de la Vallière. He had invited the Havilands to be present, their long-standing relationship making them an essential part of any decision making. Dex's presence was also requested, in the hopes that he might sway Sylvain and Geneviève.

The Germans were advancing toward Paris fast, encountering only slight resistance as they mowed their way through the countryside. The French government was to relocate in Tours at any moment and the embassies would follow.

"Everything is so calm," Arianne told Dex on the phone. "In Paris, there's no sense of reality." It was as though the Germans and their advancing tanks were a myth, and no real threat to their precarious world.

"We must take measures," Eugène insisted once they were assembled in the salon, waiting for Jean d'Albis, the youngest of the Havilands, to arrive and the Comtesse to appear.

"I wish you'd gone when I told you to," Dex remarked to Sylvain, seeing the couple exchange a quick glance.

"Colonel de Gaulle is forming a free army," Sylvain insisted, "and he will need loyal supporters here in France. I've heard that there are groups forming." He glanced at Dex. "They plan to join the Maquis."

"You mean Guingoin and his crew?"

Sylvain nodded, tight-lipped.

"I've heard about them." Dex remembered the comments about the guerilla fighters that he overheard at the furnaces, all picked up and registered for future reference. The Maquis was a Resistance group that fought from the hills.

"You don't mean to join them?" Eugène exclaimed, aghast.

"I'm damned if I'll be chased from my country by the Boches or be dragged off like a lamb to slaughter," Sylvain answered stubbornly.

"But you would be an outlaw. A price would be put on your head. It is unthinkable."

"It's useless trying to dissuade us, Eugène. We've made up our minds." Geneviève took Sylvain's hand. Not the capricious, stubborn Genny of her youth, Dex realized suddenly, but a woman who'd made up her mind to stand by her husband. The grim realization that this war was going to be different from the last dawned on him again. Technology and information would be the key.

He glanced at Genny, his heart full. Why did happiness always have to be so brief, so ephemeral? He sighed. There would be no more letters with news of Flora, which Genny carefully relayed, no more way of knowing what was happening in her life. There was still Angus, of course. Dex was buying MacLeod coal regularly and had established a friendly business relationship that might pay off in time. Right now, though, there were other priorities needing his attention.

He returned to the conversation, which had taken an emotional turn. Eugène was pacing the ancient parquet; his thin face had grown older in the past few days as he attended to the needs of his parishioners, some of whom remembered all too well what had happened last time.

"Have you both gone mad?" he was saying, facing the young couple then turning in despair to Dex. "This is outrageous. Genny, you cannot do this."

"I have to," she whispered, eyes alive with a new fervor.

"Don't you think you're making a hasty decision?" Dex countered. "It may be too late to turn back, if and when any fighting begins."

"We realize that."

"No, you don't," he exclaimed bitterly. "You have no goddamn idea what you're talking about."

"Perhaps not," Sylvain agreed with a glint of steel, "but we've decided anyway."

"If we die, we'll die together." Geneviève leaned closer to her husband. "My mother-in-law and Ruth refuse to move out of Paris, too."

The Comtesse entered the salon, obviously relieved to see her daughter. "I'm so glad you've come home, dear," she said fondly. "So much wiser, under the circumstances." She smiled gratefully at Sylvain, who glanced at Dex uncomfortably.

"I'm not staying, *Maman*. Sylvain and I are going to see what we can do to help the Free French—you know, the Maquis."

"What? Go into the countryside with a band of Communist savages? What an idea, Geneviève! I thought I had brought you up better. And you, Sylvain—" she turned on her son-in-law "—how can you dream of dragging your wife into such clandestine activities? I will not have it," she exclaimed haughtily, then sat down in her high-back chair. "Free French, indeed. We have one of the greatest armies in the world. Let them take care of the Germans. You shall see. Pétain will keep them at bay, teach them a well-deserved lesson. On the radio it is plainly stated that our troops are terrifying those cowards to death.''

Dex and Eugène exchanged a glance. "Of course, *Maman*," Eugène said, voice soothing. "But still… It is better to be prepared. Just in case.''

"I am sure there is nothing to worry about. Life in Paris continues as usual. I talked to my cousin Chantal this morning. She had a pleasant evening with friends entertaining the king of Albania. Certainly, some people have moved into the larger hotels. A mere precaution, which I'm sure will prove unnecessary.''

Realizing they were wasting precious time, Dex signaled to Sylvain and they crossed the room, leaving Sylvain's wife and mother-in-law in the midst of a long and arduous discussion. Eugène had gone to the door to receive Jean d'Albis, who had just arrived.

"You're sure you're making the right decision?" he asked, lowering his voice. "You'll be a marked man, Sylvain.''

"What choice is there?" He gazed angrily out the window at the flower beds, now in full bloom. "If I join the army, I'll probably be taken prisoner. Let's face it, Dex, you were right. The army is as unprepared as you said. When they discover I'm a Jew, they'll either send me into forced labor or kill me. I believe in de Gaulle and what he's doing. I know the factions here will be hard to handle, the Communists especially, but that's all the more reason to stay. Guingoin's a good man, even if he is a Commie. Plus, the location here is ideal to hide in. If we could set up a network allowing us to communicate with London, it would be terrific.''

Dex thought fast. "I may be able to help. No, not here." He gripped Sylvain's arm. "Make your arrangements, then contact me. And of course, no one—and I mean *no one,* not even Genny—can know. Have you made other arrangements, in case you have to escape?''

"Yes. Through my uncle. And others, in case that fails. I need to get going. We're wasting time quarreling with the

Comtesse. She'll never understand and can't be expected to,'' he added sadly.

"But what about Genny? You're not serious about letting her join you? You know what could happen to her if she were caught."

"I wish it were that easy," he exclaimed, anguished, "but she refuses to listen. Perhaps her brother will have better luck." They glanced at Eugène, trying to placate his mother and Geneviève, who were arguing.

"I doubt it. You can count on me for anything I can do. Times may get tough and I'm an American and for the moment, at least, neutral. That may come in useful."

Sylvain nodded. "Why are you getting involved? It's not your war."

"Arianne said the same thing. None of you appear to realize that I make my livelihood here."

"But it's more than that, isn't it?"

Dex hesitated, then nodded. "At some point, America will get involved. I'm too old to fight—in the conventional way, that is. But there are other ways, ways I believe that will win this war. Manpower will be the least of it. Information will be the secret."

"And you're discouraging me from doing my bit," Sylvain said with a wry smile.

"No. Never that. But I am in a privileged situation, a neutral in a war zone. You, on the other hand, are not."

"I am a Frenchman. I must defend my country as I see fit."

"Brave words, *mon ami.* I hope you'll not live to regret them." How innocent they were, how unprepared for what he sensed was to come.

"I would rather die like a man, defending what is mine, than run. I know where my loyalties lie."

"I know that." Dex gripped his arm reassuringly. "And though I think you're a damn fool, I admire you for it. It's only a matter of days before they march into Paris and then only God knows what will happen."

"Here comes Eugène," Sylvain murmured.

"Sylvain, you must persuade Genny to stay here with us,"

Eugène insisted. "It is unheard of that she take this foolish step. Do you think there is any chance the Germans might still be repelled?" he asked, hanging on to a last thread of hope.

"None, I'm afraid. We are being overrun as we speak."

"But what about the British? Surely the Channel will help."

"You're not reckoning in the air force," Dex countered. "The Germans are in much better shape. I'll be leaving for Paris later tonight, and I'll keep you informed. And Eugène, make sure you keep *your* channels open. A secretary to the bishop can move where others can't," Dex said, looking him straight in the eye.

"We'll miss you, Dex. Let's hope it all blows over fast." Geneviève linked her arm tenderly with her husband's.

The sight of them, so in love and unaware, left him cold. He swallowed, glanced across the room. "Let me say hello to Jean d'Albis. I suppose there will be a meeting of the Commission des Porcelaniers. I'd better find out when it is. Promise me you'll be careful, Genny, won't you?" He hugged her, suddenly remembering her in her pram, a little redheaded cherub, during that last summer of 1913 before all hell broke loose.

After arranging to meet with Jean d'Albis, who was the Swiss consul, Dex departed, leaving them to argue the issue of Geneviève among themselves. He returned quickly to the house then left for Paris.

Traffic was terrible as the population fled south, cars piled high with luggage and furniture, old carts filled with children, grandparents and anything they could carry with them. A long line of pedestrians trailed next to the vehicles, the young supporting the old, men and women with grim expressions seeking refuge wherever they could find it.

It was dark by the time he reached Paris, where the windows were shrouded in blackout and sandbags were piled everywhere, the street lamps painted a weird shade of bluish purple, which gave an eerie feeling to the silent city, all at once a ghost town.

He let himself into the apartment. There was no sign of Arianne and he managed to get a call through to Brooker, working nonstop at the embassy.

"The government's moving to Tours in the morning, except Bill and a skeleton staff, who are remaining here at the embassy to hand over the city."

"The French are on the run as usual?" he remarked dryly.

"So what's new?"

"It reminds me of last time," he murmured. "I'll be in touch. I'm sticking around."

"You could've stayed back home," Brooker remarked in a tired voice. "I don't know why the hell you want to be mixed up in all this, sir."

"Neither do I," he answered untruthfully. "Maybe it has to do with Alix."

"I understand. Good luck."

"You, too."

He went looking for Arianne among the busy tables at Aux Deux Magots, surprised to see extra seats crammed onto the busy pavement to accommodate the crowds, as though the war were nothing but a scary story. Even on the eve of surrender, Paris was living her last hours of freedom with gusto, those who'd decided to remain doing so in style, and with determined bravado.

He went inside and glimpsed Arianne through the brass railing that separated the leather benches. Dex squeezed onto the banquette, between a thin man who chain-smoked Gauloises and hadn't shaved in several days, and Arianne, looking pale and thinner. He glanced at her, worried. "Why haven't you left?"

She shrugged. "Where to? And what for? It's all over, isn't it?"

"Not necessarily," Dex answered.

"They say the Germans may be here in a few days. Perhaps even tomorrow."

"That doesn't mean the war is lost, just beginning."

"Same thing."

"Not at all. Listen, if we'd taken that attitude last time, we'd have been beaten to a pulp. Brace up, girl.'' He looked her firmly in the eye and saw her pale cheeks flush.

Then she shrugged again and took out a cigarette. ''Any news from the States? Is Scott well?''

''Wonderful. They're still in Connecticut. His nanny says the air suits him. I miss the little beggar, don't you?'' She nodded, eyes brimming, and he changed the subject.

After dinner they wandered through the streets, in a surreal atmosphere, the city extraordinarily peaceful as she awaited her conquerors.

''You'd better get out of Paris, Arianne,'' he said thoughtfully. ''God only knows what'll happen once they arrive. Why don't you come to Limoges? You can stay at the house.''

''*Merci*, Dex. Maybe I'll take you up on it.'' She made a moue, her smile more like her old self. ''But somehow I don't see myself *en province*.''

''We may see ourselves doing a lot we didn't imagine over the next few months—or years,'' he added dryly, remembering that last time the war was supposed to have ended when the leaves dropped. Instead, it ended four long years and more than twelve million dead later. How many would it take this time?

Less than two months later the French government signed the armistice at Rethondes, and in early July Maréchal Pétain established a headquarters in Vichy. On October 3, Jews were banned from certain branches of employment, and the next day Pétain and Hitler met at Montoire, marking the official beginning of a collaboration.

Sylvain and Genny had now permanently joined the Maquis and the family lived in daily terror. Limoges was part of occupied France but the la Vallières still hadn't received a visit from the Germans, perhaps because of the family's obvious importance in the area and Eugène's prestige through the Church. Dex, working long hours at the factory, wondered how long that would last when they learned Geneviève was married to a prominent Jew and that both had disappeared for several months. The radio he had hidden was functioning regularly now, manned by himself and two faithful Maquisards—workers in the factory and part of the Resistance, who took over when he traveled to Paris to meet with Brooker, who'd remained in the city.

Flora was never far from his thoughts, just as Alix seemed hauntingly present. He missed her more than he'd imagined. He missed Scott, too, but knowing he was safe and well cared for was more important right now.

He sat behind the large desk at Harcourt's and thought of Angus, based in the south of England. He'd learned this through MacDuff, who basically ran MacLeod's. To his relief, Flora had remained in Skye. He could visualize her in the dreamery or walking along the cliffs, the wind whipping her hair, the smell of the sea filling her nostrils as she made her way along the buttress, the cool, salty spray crashing below. Perhaps she would stop and listen, hearing things others didn't, which as a child he'd teased her about. Perhaps she still searched for Gavin's soul in the echoes coming down from the hills, whose peaks remained cloaked in mist even in summer. Strange, that at a time when he could barely think beyond the increasing daily demands of strategizing and playing his role of the American businessman more interested in making a buck than establishing who his buyers were, she should haunt him more than ever.

He sighed and got up, focused on the messages he needed to get through to London tonight. In a few hours the factory would be silent and he would make his way to the furnace where the radio still remained, carefully covered. Thank God he'd had the good sense to plan ahead. Already three sabotage operations had taken place and several cases of arms had been parachuted into the region surrounding Limoges, thanks to proper direction. They'd established a secret airfield and links with Colonel de Gaulle and the British. Sylvain made regular contact through one of the factory workers, Durand, a man they could trust, but danger was everywhere. The less any of them knew, the better. He didn't like the atmosphere in the factory, as regular disputes broke out between the Communist faction and the fascists.

Max had been drafted into the army but had managed to

retain an office post in Berlin that allowed him to keep up occasional contact. But business was slow and less regular, the post censored and sometimes the information was obsolete by the time it arrived. Some was relévant, though, and Dex knew the line had to be kept open at all cost. Ironically, Germany became one of his best markets, and the factory produced thousands of kitsch plates and mugs under the resentful gaze of his workforce. Yet those who worked there—mostly women, for the men had been drafted or sent to labor camps in Germany—were grateful for the jobs.

The Blitz left London bleeding, and Dex became increasingly afraid for Flora. What if things got worse and the Germans reached Scotland? It was bad enough having Sylvain and Genny to worry about. God, so much had changed. Arianne had joined the Resistance and was having an affair with a German major who spewed his guts onto her pillow every night. Thanks to her, several Jewish lives had been saved.

"One day I'll kill him," she told Dex as they sat in the Avenue Foch, "but not while he's still useful." She stubbed out a cigarette, her eyes glassy and cold.

"Be careful. If they have the least suspicion, you know what will happen."

"I know. But it's all I can do for France. At least we're becoming more organized, and the sabotage ops are more frequent. The *Boches* are more and more upset," she said gleefully.

"And the reprisals ever heavier," he answered wearily. "I don't know how effective the Resistance is."

"We have to sacrifice some for the good of all. They know it, even as they die."

"Would you?" he asked curiously, for she seemed so fanatical, a far cry from the woman who'd seduced his wife.

"I hope I would. I hope that, if the time comes, I will look death in the eye and know I did what I had to do."

"You're a brave woman." He smiled gently, took her hand and held it a minute.

"I'm not alone. I'm very well aware of what you're up to,

Dex.'' He looked up, startled, but said nothing. "And I admire you doubly because, as I've said, it's not your war.''

"I don't see how America can stay out of it for much longer. Dunkirk and the Blitz have left Britain hanging on by a thread.''

"I know. But we have de Gaulle. And Jean Moulin. The man is a wizard. He has finally managed to get the inside factions of the Resistance to agree, for once. How they expected to fight, quarreling among themselves, is beyond me.''

"That's France,'' he answered, smiling despite everything.

30

Brighton, England, 1941

By September of 1941, Flora knew she had to take part in the war effort and was posted to a recovery clinic in Brighton. Here she helped young officers, mostly wounded pilots and S.A.S. boys, to regroup and heal from the horrors they'd lived through. It helped to tell them of her own experiences, even mentioning her husband's experience with shell shock in the last war. She was glad she didn't have a son, and put all her care and love into helping them recover.

It was one of the pilots who told her about Pearl Harbor, as she was counting sheets. Putting them down, she rushed to the radio, which was surrounded by the injured men, all listening to the news.

"This'll change the picture," one of them commented. "Roosevelt won't be able to stay out of it now."

"About bloody time, too."

The conversation buzzed around her, but all Flora could think of was Dex. He'd be called up. Maybe he was too old to fight. Either way, he wouldn't be a neutral anymore. She closed her eyes, praying he was in America.

Rumors of the Resistance had reached them, and Geneviève's words in her last letter—"I shall be absent for a while"—made terrible sense. No wonder Tante Hortense wrote incoherently. The thought of Genny, hidden in the Maquis and fighting the Germans, was terrifying.

At the end of the year, excitement reigned, for the Americans finally entered the war. It was whispered that a brave *résistant,* Jean Moulin, had secretly been parachuted into France, where de Gaulle had given him the task of unifying the Resistance.

In early June she learned that the Jews in occupied France were now obliged to wear a yellow identification star, and wondered, horrified, what had happened to poor Baronne de Rothberg and her daughter Ruth. Would they be subjected to this indignity?

31

New York, U.S.A., 1941

In late November of 1941 Dex traveled to New York, then proceeded straight to Connecticut, thrilled to see Scott. A few weeks later, back at Sutton Place, he switched on the radio in John Sr.'s study and frowned when he realized all programs were interrupted. He sat down with a bang on the nearest chair as he learned that Pearl Harbor had been bombed. That meant America would fight.

He had two paths to choose, he realized, walking up the wide marble staircase to the hollow sound of his footsteps echoing through the empty house, so full of haunting memories. He could see if his old uniform would fit his forty-one-year-old frame, present himself to his former unit and probably be stuck in the States with an office job for the duration of the war, or he could get in touch with the one person he'd been carefully avoiding since their chance meeting at the Plaza some years before. He'd heard rumors about Bill Donovan. But by putting himself in Donovan's path he would be taking a great personal risk.

He passed a sleepless night, but by morning he knew what he had to do. He owed it to them all to take a stand—for Max, Sylvain and Genny, Eugène and the others who were risking their lives every day in the name of liberty.

At ten o'clock he picked up the phone in the study and made the call. Two days later, he was driving up to a discreet brownstone in Georgetown. He was surprised when Donovan himself opened the door with a broad, welcoming smile.

"Good to see you, Dex. Come on in."

He wished he could say the same and shifted uneasily, praying the step he was taking wouldn't ruin his life. Excitement and foreboding gripped his gut as he followed Donovan into the house, wondering where to begin. Brooker was still filtering information coming from either London or Germany—a rare thing of late, since Max had been sent to the front—to the Americans, giving them an edge that would be essential now that they were actively part of the war. He sat down in the chair offered to him and accepted a whiskey gladly, aware that if anyone had the clout to further what he'd already set in motion, Donovan was that man. Even Roosevelt didn't make a legal move without him.

Both men remained silent, each waiting for the other to make the first move.

Then Donovan smiled, his eyes sharp and intent. "I don't suppose you're here to pass the time of day, so why don't you tell me what brought you."

Choosing his words carefully, Dex filled him in selectively on the events of the past three years, feeling his way, gauging when the time to negotiate had arrived and holding back enough to give himself leverage.

"Phew! You've been busy. What makes you think I'd be interested?" Donovan's eyes narrowed.

"Past experience."

"Fair enough. But why did you come to me? Why not have Bullitt pursue this?"

"I've heard you're setting up something of your own."

"I see." He sipped thoughtfully, standing by the fireplace, sleeves rolled up to his elbows. "It's true that we're dependent on the Brits. Obviously, what you've set up is brilliant. Not to mention the cover." He gave Dex a speculative glance. "Never thought of going back to being your old self, Dex? I didn't think you seemed too happy to meet me that day at the Plaza."

"You're right." Dex hesitated. "I couldn't tell if you remembered."

"So what's the deal?"

"I go on being Dexter Ward. I supply information to you, some through the embassy staff as before, but the bulk comes to you directly. We'll need to set up codes and signals. For a while, I think I can keep coming and going. I've a good relationship with the German command—they believe I'm only interested in making as much money from the war as I can. Nobody's aware I'm connected with the Free French. They don't even know I speak the lingo."

"What about your cousin, Father de la Vallière?"

"How...?" Dex gazed at him, aghast, his tie too tight, breathing suddenly difficult.

"You didn't think I hadn't heard of all this before today, did you? Have you any idea how important the information you've gathered is? As soon as I heard a half-ass description of the man behind it, I knew it had to be you." He grinned. "I need you as badly as I did last time, Captain. I won't blow your cover."

Dex sighed, relieved. "I want your word," he said slowly, "that any records that may still exist, and your memory, will be wiped clean. Gavin MacLeod never existed."

"This could be turned the other way around. I could be the one blackmailing you," he murmured, swilling the whiskey, eyes locked with Dex's.

"Could, but won't. And I'm not blackmailing, I'm asking."

Donovan threw back his head and gave a hearty laugh. "I like your style, Ward. I'm in. You have my word. You're the man I need right now, and you couldn't have come at a better time. If you hadn't looked me up, I would've come ringing your doorbell." He held out his hand and they shook. "To the everlasting demise of Gavin MacLeod." He raised his glass and drank deeply.

"To victory," Dex replied, and sent up a thankful prayer.

32

Washington, D.C, 1943

The FBI's reaction, when Hoover learned the navy was taking over what he considered one of his departments, was anything but pleased. But Roosevelt handled him with his usual aplomb.

"Navy intelligence wasn't too happy either," Donovan sighed as he and Dex dined together in the brownstone, preferring the discretion it offered. "It's hard to keep everyone content without stepping on someone's precious ego. That said, Ward, I need your cooperation."

"I don't see how I can do more than I have. Information's hard to come by."

"I'm not referring to that. I'm very satisfied with all you've brought to the table. I'm thinking of a different line of work."

"What kind?" Dex eyed him, not liking the innocence of Donovan's smile.

"How are you feeling? In good shape?"

"Never felt better," he replied, mystified.

"Good."

Where was Donovan going with all this pussyfooting, he wondered. "I'm having a hard time following your train of thought, I'm afraid."

"I have a job for you. Something that requires you be in shape."

"You're not suggesting what I think you are?"

"You mean having you parachute into France to organize those buggers into some kind of proper resistance we can use? Well, of course I am. Who else would I ask?" He smiled benignly. "I don't know anyone who speaks French like you, or has the contacts you have, or knows the terrain as you do. You fit the role to perfection, Dexter, make no mistake about it."

"But I'm forty-three years old, for Christ's sake!" he exclaimed, rising abruptly and dragging a hand through his graying hair. "Hell, I'd be dealing with kids old enough to be mine. It's nonsense!"

"Dex, they're a brave bunch of men, women and kids, but half of them are Commies, the other half anarchists and the rest crazy. They need direction. We can't afford anymore single actions," Donovan added gravely. "We need well-planned, strategized targeting that will be firmly in place once we finally invade."

He was right, Dex realized, heart sinking. The manpower and will were there, but the execution of the Resistance movement was chaotic. He'd lived it, had all too often been privy to the brave but senseless acts that led to horrific reprisals and unnecessary loss of civilian life.

"First we'll need to get you into shape." Donovan looked him over critically. "It'll be back to the good old days. Nothing a few weeks up in Arisaig won't take care of."

"Jesus, that's where they're training the S.A.S." It wasn't too far from Skye, he realized with a sudden shudder.

"Damn right. I wouldn't want anything less for you, Dexter. I've already set it up with them." He rose, dropped his napkin on the table and gave him a jovial slap on the back. "A few weeks from now you'll be a new man, then we'll parachute you in behind the lines."

"Thanks a lot."

"Hey? Where's the Captain Ward who had to be restrained not to get himself killed?"

"He grew up." But as preposterous as it was, the proposal thrilled him.

"You sure about that?" Donovan raised a skeptical eyebrow. "Something tells me you haven't changed much."

Was it true? Perhaps, if he took a good look inside himself, some of the old impulses still remained. But there was Scott to think about, and Harcourt's to run. Before, he'd been so damn young he'd been unaware of what he would be leaving behind. Still, the more he thought about the prospect, the more challenging and appealing it became. He just hoped that physically he'd make it, thankful now that he'd kept up a rigorous exercise program over the years. He tightened his stomach muscles, glad there was no unseemly flab like some of his contemporaries had developed.

Again the thought of Skye, of perhaps seeing Flora and healing the rift, made his pulse beat faster. "When do I leave?"

"The day after tomorrow."

33

Skye, Scotland, 1943

Flora helped young Major Perkins limp across the lawn, glad that by putting Strathaird at the disposal of the recovering officers, she was able to use her nursing skills better than she had in Brighton. The idea had occurred to her after several of the men remarked how much they would like to get away for a true break from the war, which they'd heard could still be found across the Channel. Angus was too busy to do anything but agree; he was actually taking pride in the job he had been given, training young officers of his old regiment and preparing them for the psychological rigors of war.

But here in Skye, the war seemed far away, despite the injured soldiers reading in the drawing room or enjoying the sun and breeze, seated on the lawn. Most of them were sent here for the care she provided, for at Strathaird Flora was renowned for healing both body and soul.

"I'll sit on the bench for a little and rest, if I may." She caught the strained look in Major Perkins's eyes and smiled.

"Of course." They walked toward the wooden seat, and the major sat down, relieved. "I'm sure you have lots to do, Lady MacLeod. I can stay here. You should take a walk yourself. You never seem to get a break."

"Don't worry about me," she said, smiling down at him.

He couldn't be more than twenty-two or three, but already the worry was written on his face. His plane had been taken out twice and the last time he'd survived by a miracle.

It was true that she had little time for herself, but she really didn't mind. Quite the opposite. Filling her days with purpose was rewarding. But as Flora looked out over the lawn and down toward the sea, she felt a sudden urge to walk, breathe in the fresh summer air and think a little.

"Are you sure, Major Perkins?" she asked, laying a rug over his legs, knowing how badly shaken he was. His copilot and best friend had been killed, and it was pure chance that he'd been rescued before he froze to death in the Channel.

"I'll sit here and dream about when all this is over."

"So you should. You have your whole life ahead of you," she encouraged. "If you're sure you'll be all right, I'll take a short walk. Give a shout if you need me."

"Thanks. I will. Have a good walk."

She nodded, smiling, then went down the steps, wandering along the deserted cliff. She plucked some bluebells and watched the waves, lapping today rather than slashing the rocks as they so often did. In the distance, a fleet of naval vessels dotted the horizon, too far out to distinguish the flags. She wondered if they were British or American, then glanced up at the clouds, realizing the weather was about to break. The last days of summer were upon them and soon autumn would set in.

She walked on, enjoying the breeze ruffling her hair as she trod along the path, her thoughts wandering, as they always did when she had a minute, to her cousins, to France and Dexter Ward. She barely noticed a figure approaching, but when she did, she frowned. There was something familiar about that walk, the set of the approaching man's shoulders, and as he drew nearer she saw he wore an American naval uniform.

Flora stopped. A shudder ran through her and she gasped. It couldn't possibly be him. It was just another trick of her wild imagination. Then, as the distance closed between them, tears rushed to her eyes and she trembled, recognizing the handsome features, seeing the hope in his eyes as he reached her and they stood face-to-face.

"Dex," she whispered, trembling. "Is it really you?"

His eyes were bright blue and piercing, so mesmerizing and intense she could do nothing but gaze into them, heart racing, as he gently reached out and took her hands, the warmth and touch of his grasp leaving her dizzy.

"Please give me a chance," he begged, eyes pleading.

He was here before her, real and alive. Relief and longing overwhelmed her as she stood, unable to do anything but stare into his eyes. Then she was in his arms, feeling that same familiar warmth and scent, the wholeness she had longed for since the departure from Lausanne. The days of berating herself for having overreacted, for not allowing him to speak his mind, faded as their lips met and he held her tightly.

"My darling. My beautiful, wonderful girl. God, how I love you, Flo."

"I love you too, Dex. It's been such agony."

"I know." He kissed the top of her head, her forehead, grazed her cheek gently with his thumb, as Flora came slowly back to her senses.

"What are you doing here? I though you were in France or America."

"I've been posted to Britain. I'll tell you all about it. But first, let's go to Finnian's Loch up on the hill."

She looked at him, startled. "How do you know about the loch, Dex?"

"I'll tell you when we get there."

"Not there," she protested. "I can't go there. I—"

"Because it was where you and Gavin first kissed?" he asked tenderly.

She nodded, bewildered, as he took her hand and they began walking. How could he possibly know about the loch?

It was a short walk to the tiny loch that lay nestled at the foot of the hills, its banks sprinkled with white and amethyst heather. He gazed up at the Cullins, rising majestically in the distance, remembering, his eyes damp. Returning here was not nearly as easy as he'd believed. Each sniff of air, each glimpse of heather was a poignant part of the identity he'd left behind so casually, like a pair of discarded gloves.

He pressed Flora's hand. He wanted to tell her the truth, to be himself again, roll back time and begin where he'd left off. To forget Dexter Ward, and Harcourt's, and the life he'd built for himself.

He turned her gently toward him. She was as lovely as ever, the gray eyes deep and tender, the longing written starkly across her face. He gripped her shoulders. "It's me, Flo, darling," he whispered, and saw the flicker of confusion in her eyes. He stopped abruptly as Scott, Donovan, Harcourt's, Sylvain and Genny flashed before him in quick succession and caught his breath. He had no right to abandon them. He couldn't do it, nor could he risk her reaction.

"I know it's you, Dex, don't worry." She ran her fingers through his hair. "I'm over the past. I'll always love Gavin, but I've moved on. I'm not trying to substitute you for him, darling. I want to be yours because I love *you,* not a ghost."

"Just forgive me, Flo," he whispered, lowering her gently to the grass, torn between longing and guilt for not telling her the truth. Gently he trailed a finger down her throat, past the string of pearls to the plain neckline of her blue and white striped cotton dress. It made her look as young and innocent as she was. *God forgive me,* he begged as his lips came down, almost touching hers. "I'm sorry, Flo," he murmured in a low whisper, "but I can't change."

She smiled and shook her head, eyes misty, then slipped a hand behind his neck as his mouth closed hungrily on hers and his hands roamed as possessively as if he'd been loving her all his life. He flicked open the buttons of her dress, meeting no resistance, her need as urgent and avid as his. Soon they were lying naked, clothes strewn among the heather, reaching for one another, no longer taking time to caress but consumed by an overwhelming need to be a part of the other.

Time and space faded as at last he thrust deep, fulfilling his ultimate wish. He let out a groan of ecstasy when he heard her gasp. He tried to stop, not wanting to cause her pain, but gave way when her hips reached up, grinding, forcing him to possess her as he had in his most daring dreams. Her nails raked his shoulders as the desires held in check for a quarter of a century burst forth, and they reached past the point of no return as one.

They talked for hours, hidden in the shadows of the rocks by the deserted waters of the loch.

"How did you know about this place?" she asked, stroking his chest.

"You told me," he lied. "Don't you remember?"

"No." She shook her tired, happy head. "I don't remember anything except what happened here a few minutes ago," she murmured, lifting her lips for his kiss.

"I still can't believe your husband never made love to you." He slipped her head onto his shoulder and lay back, breathing in the scent of his youth blended with their lovemaking.

"Don't let's talk about any of that. It doesn't matter why. It had to do with the past. But it's all over now. What matters are the others. I'm so worried about Genny and Sylvain. Have you any news?"

He hesitated only an instant. "They're with the Maquis. Genny's helping whoever she can escape into Spain over the Pyrenees. Sylvain's organizing sabotage with the head chap running the Resistance in our area."

"So it's true what they say? There really is a force to be reckoned with inside France? But oh God, Dex. What if something awful happens to them?"

"We can't think like that," he replied, thinking suddenly of the mission that awaited him when he left her. "Remember last time? Attitude is everything."

"You're right," she answered with a sigh. "Where were you last time?"

"With the First Americans, just below Verdun. But that's not what I want to talk about right now." He pulled her on top of him, hands gliding to the curve of her buttocks. "I'm going to come and fetch you after the war," he said, making a sudden decision. If he couldn't assume his true identity, then why not take her to New York, where they could be legally married?

"But I couldn't just go," she whispered, troubled, remembering her promise to Angus many years before.

"Why not? You can get a divorce. I'm free to marry you."

"Poor Alix," she murmured, "and little Scott."

"We both need you, Flo."

"Don't. It's too fast, too sudden. And anyway, the war is still not over. God knows what will happen if—"

"We won't lose," he cut in, "but let's think about finding an answer for now. Can I come and stay at Strathaird? You could pretend I'm injured," he cajoled.

"Don't be silly, there's nothing injured about you. Look at you." She rolled off him and leaned on her elbow, feasting her eyes on his body in awe, submitting gladly when he took her into his arms once more. They made love again with all the care and tenderness lacking the first time.

"I suppose you could stay at the castle," she mused afterward. "We could say you had to come to Scotland and got a few days off. By the way, why *are* you here?"

"I had some work to do for the American navy," he answered glibly, knowing she'd figure out at once if he told her he'd been in Arisaig for several weeks.

"I'm sure Angus wouldn't mind if you stayed. He likes you," she added, turning bright pink. "Is that terribly disloyal?"

"Nothing between us will ever be disloyal, Flo. Remember that."

It was several hours and a lifetime later when they left the loch and wandered back to the ancient stronghold that was his heritage. Entering it as a stranger, he refused to acknowledge the chill of fear, the sudden pang of pain that stabbed his heart.

He stood in what had been his father's study, taking in the MacLeod lands—*his* lands—that stretched across the island. Watching the sea and its unique clarity, he sensed the wrath of his ancestors bearing down on him, truly aware for the first time of all he'd left behind. Someday, he realized, tearing his eyes away, there would be a reckoning. He shuddered, the picture of his mother and father in the silver frame on the mantelpiece making his heart bleed. How could he have been so callous? And why, he wondered bitterly, when he'd finally fulfilled a dream that left him happier than ever, did God see fit to burden him with this guilt? No, he resolved, he couldn't tell Flora the truth. Not now. Perhaps not ever. Perhaps he should just be glad for what he had, and let the rest go. But instinctively he knew that was impossible.

As fate would have it, Flora had offered him his old room. The sight of it brought tears to his eyes as he opened a drawer and found his old school tie still inside, along with a couple of letters from friends and two pairs of socks. It was as though he'd never left, he realized, sitting on the bed in awe, wondering how he would stand the strange, clawing nostalgia overtaking him.

That night, after he'd slipped back to his room from Flora's bed, he tossed fitfully, sleeping lightly then waking to voices calling his name. At one point he sat up, shivering, certain he could hear the soulful lament of the war pipes. He saw figures in Highland dress walking toward him, their faces angry and swords unsheathed, making him turn on the light, terrified. It was a while before the vision faded, and he sat, trembling, unable to believe it.

"I swear I will return," he whispered softly, placating the spirits he knew surrounded him. "I will return and take vengeance." A sudden pain seared through his heart, and for a terrible moment he thought he might be suffering a heart attack. He clutched his chest, fighting for breath, then finally fell back on the pillows and into a dead sleep.

The next two days flew by, and all too soon the American naval jeep he'd requested was in front of the door, where he and Flora took formal leave of one another, although they'd spent all night in each other's arms.

"God bless you, my love," she whispered. "And if you see Genny and Sylvain, tell them I love them both."

He nodded silently, shaking her hand and forcing himself to climb in the jeep before he kissed her and ruined their lives. He left her, staring blindly at the empty spot where minutes before he'd stood and wondering if the past two days were just another of her strange fantasies. But the ache in her thighs and muscles, the taste of his kiss, were as real as the strong north wind blowing in from Scandinavia. They were in for a storm, she thought abstractedly.

Flora walked toward the cliff, knowing she couldn't face anyone right now, not bothered by the first drops of September rain. She recalled each instant, each miraculous moment. Oh, but there was magic in the air. She hugged herself and watched the surge of the waves, closing her eyes as the summer rain caressed her well-loved skin, still feeling his touch, his life and soul now one with hers.

How simple Dex made life seem, as though now that they'd found each other, life would be a fairy tale. She sighed, tears catching at the thought of all the danger he was about to go into. He hadn't told her, but she knew perfectly well he was on a mission. That was the only reason he could possibly have been up here. To train. The feel of his muscles, the condition his body was in, and the cagey answers he'd given told her all she needed to know. *Oh God, please spare him,* she begged, knowing she wouldn't survive if he too were taken from her.

She didn't want to think about the problems that would arise when he did come back. They would deal with that then. But as she walked back to the castle, she knew there was no use pretending. She was not the same woman that had left Major Perkins on the bench two days earlier, and already she knew that Angus would be the victim.

34

France, 1943

As the Dakota left the English coast behind and flew through the night over the Channel, Dex sat in line between the radio operator and two French S.A.S., kids who reminded him of himself twenty-five years ago. They had that same intense look he remembered so well, that held none of the fear he felt now. He had so much to lose, and a life he desperately wanted to live. He had no idea where their destination lay, and would only be told shortly before they jumped. Thirty minutes later, a sealed envelope was handed down the line. When it reached him, he simply stared at it. Then, realizing the others were watching, Dex opened it.

This was it. In fifteen minutes he would be free-falling through the sky, praying that his parachute would open.

The young man next to him nudged him shyly. "If anything happens to me, I want you to have it," he shouted above the noise, pointing to the burgundy S.A.S. beret on his head.

Dex shook his hand. "Thanks. I'm very honored," he replied, touched. It was customary among the lads to choose a successor for their beret, a superstition that promised it wouldn't happen.

An hour later, he picked the hat up from the field where they'd landed. The kid's chute had failed to open. He paused, realizing he didn't even know the boy's name, then slipped it on. Perhaps he was too old for this job, too sentimental.

Swallowing his anger at the soldier's pointless death, he braced himself and, beckoning to the others, stealthily followed the *résistant* who'd met them. They walked in darkness for another twenty minutes, through brush and trees, and finally stopped, crouching in a field. As daybreak hovered, a grayish glimmer outlining poplars and a few straggling dwellings in the distance, they piled into a rattling truck.

"Let the show begin," he said, eyeing the three men with him, making sure they were okay and breaking the tension. "We'll get these bastards, whatever we have to do."

35

Skye, Scotland, 1943

Flora rushed down the corridor to the bathroom and leaned over the toilet bowl, retching. She waited but nothing happened. Soon the sensation passed and she resumed her usual activities, thinking she must have eaten something bad. But the next day it happened again, and after a week she went to see the doctor.

"There's a simple explanation, Lady MacLeod," the doctor, an elderly man who'd known her since childhood, responded after examining her. "You're expecting."

Flora looked at him blankly. "I'm afraid I don't understand. Am I ill? Expecting what?"

"A baby, my dear. I think you're pregnant. We shall have to wait a few more days to be absolutely sure, but all the signs are there." He beamed in a fatherly manner.

Flora sat down, aghast. This was a possibility that had never occurred to her. "Surely I'm too old? I'm forty-two, isn't that rather late?"

"Late but not impossible. We shall have to monitor the pregnancy carefully. If you need my help and advice, I'm always here, Lady MacLeod," he added with a kind, understanding smile.

Flora thanked him and left the office, stunned, driving slowly home across the island, wondering vaguely if her petrol ration would last. Instinct told her it was true that she was carrying Dex's baby. The thought both thrilled and horrified her, and she wondered how she could reach him, to tell him and share the joy.

Then the truth sank in further and she wondered unhappily what she would tell Angus. That she was having an illegitimate child? That she wanted to get divorced? How could she do this to him in the middle of the war? It would be bad enough in normal times, let alone now. Yet what, she asked herself as she turned into the drive, was she to do?

After helping one of the nurses carry a new patient to the room Dex had vacated only weeks earlier, she ran to the dreamery and curled up among the cushions, gently touching her belly, both happy and anguished. It might be months before a letter reached him. And her heart sank at the thought of Angus, due home on leave in a few days. She cringed, ashamed but unable to quench a new thrill. By the time she got in the car later that week to fetch Angus at the ferry in Ardvassar, she knew there was no way out; she must tell him the truth. If he shunned her, she would have to bear the shame and find a solution until Dex could be reached.

The ferry arrived punctually and Flora stood on the pier, trying desperately to look cheerful.

"His Lordship's aboard, I take it," an elderly man, who was also waiting, said jovially.

"Yes." She tried to infuse enthusiasm into her answer, waving as Angus descended the ramp with his duffel bag under his arm, looking better than he had for months. He was one person the war had done good, and he looked younger and healthier than he had in years. They hugged and he slipped an arm affectionately around her shoulders.

"Gosh, it's good to see you, Flo. Don't know what I'd do if you weren't here waiting for me." She smiled weakly, wondering how long she would be able to keep this up.

That evening after dinner, they sat before the fire in the study the way they used to, Angus in his old velvet smoking jacket and Flora fiddling with her tapestry, pretending to stitch. He sighed, sipped his Drambuie, then leaned back in the deep leather armchair. "It's wonderful to be home, Flo, and so good to see you. You look a little peaky, though," he added, frowning. "Is something wrong?"

"No. I'm fine." She smiled nervously.

"Are you sure? I know you pretty well, old girl. Never seen you like this before."

"Don't worry, I'll be all right. Just something I ate." *Coward! Why don't you tell him?* she asked herself, angry at her own weakness and trying to summon up courage.

"I'm glad to hear Dexter Ward took the time to come by and spend a couple of days here. I hope it did him good. He's a brave man. I learned the other day he's a top agent for the O.S.S., an intelligence equivalent of MI6 that the Americans have put together. I think he's flying missions into France." Her heart missed a beat and she stabbed her finger with the needle.

"He didn't mention that," she said, trying desperately to sound normal.

"No, he wouldn't. It's top secret."

"I see." Her voice sounded odd.

"Flo, is something the matter?" Angus frowned, watching her.

"It's nothing." She shook her head and looked down, trying desperately to concentrate on choosing the right shade of green thread for the leaf in her design.

"Is it that bad?" he asked kindly, leaning toward her, a new understanding in his manner that made her want to weep. "Nothing's so awful that I won't understand."

"I'm going to have a baby," she whispered, closing her eyes, waiting for the anger she was certain would follow.

But to her astonishment he joined her on the sofa and squeezed her hand.

"Don't be ashamed, Flo. I've been expecting something like this to happen for some time. It doesn't come as a surprise." He stroked her cheek gently, then rose and stared into the flames sadly. "I haven't been much of a husband to you, have

I? I wish I could have been, Flo, but Gavin's always stood between us like some kind of invisible barrier. I sense him everywhere. If I had...you know...made love to you, I don't think it would have worked. I would have felt I was betraying him, robbing him of something I had no right to.

"I don't want you to worry," he continued, staring into the fire, his expression fixed. "And there's no need to tell the father. Is he still here?" he asked, obviously assuming it was one of the young officers staying in the castle.

She went beet red and shook her head, unable to speak.

"How far along are you?" He turned and glanced at her.

"Just over a month," she whispered, praying he wouldn't associate Dexter's visit with the pregnancy.

"I hope it's a girl," he murmured, picking up the poker and nudging the coal. Flora sat up.

"You're truly not upset, Angus?"

"What right do I have to be upset, Flo? You've been a perfect wife, whom I've neglected all these years. I think you know I've had affairs, too."

"But Angus, don't you mind that the baby isn't yours?" she asked, rather astonished.

"Not really. I want you to be happy. It's the least I can do for you. You know, if you hadn't married me after Gavin died, I don't know what I would have done to myself."

"Angus, what if the baby's father...well, what I mean is..."

"That is the only thing I'm asking, Flo." He came over and took her hands, his eyes pleading. "I don't want to know who he is, and if you haven't told him, then please don't. These wartime flings happen, but it's hardly fair to put the burden on him, when we can keep the baby. I promise I'll do the best I can to be a good father." His voice held that same panic she remembered so well, and a tight, metal-like vise gripped her heart. What should she do? For a moment her head spun. She despised the thought of lies and pretenses. Yet she had no clue where to find Dex, and Angus was offering the child a name, love and security.

"I'll do anything, Flo," he begged, sensing her doubt. "Just please, never leave me."

36

Limoges, France, 1944

Eugène watched from the far side of the dining room of the Hôtel de la Paix as Dex circulated confidently among the tables, exchanging a polite wave with General Gleiniger, the commander in chief of the German forces in Limoges, whose headquarters were in the hotel. Then Dex came toward him, as relaxed as though he had not blown up a bridge twelve hours earlier.

"Good to see you, Father." They shook hands and he sat down, Eugène wishing God had given him Gavin's guts. He was as cool as a cucumber. What nerve, to wander in as though he owned the place, after organizing a large part of the Resistance with Jean Moulin. And when he wasn't sabotaging roads or stopping the German advance, he was back in England, strategizing with de Gaulle. Yet now he was exchanging pleasantries with Albert, the headwaiter, and waving to a couple of German officers sitting two tables away.

Eugène knew that he himself was a suspect. Not only was his sister married to a prominent Jew, but she and her husband had bounties on their heads. The fifth column was everywhere, and only his clerical robes and high standing within the Church had saved him from the inevitable visit to Gestapo headquarters.

Geneviève, about to have a baby, was in hiding with Madame Baudry, the la Vallières' retired housekeeper, whom they trusted implicitly. She lived with her husband in the quiet burg of Ouradour-sur-Glane, a market village on the Glane River, where no Resistance action had taken place and where the Germans rarely stopped.

Today Eugène wasn't worried about his sister, but the reports he'd heard that a division of the Waffen S.S., Das Reich, was headed toward Limoges. The Germans seemed to think that an invasion of France was imminent and were sending all their strength north, to Normandy. He'd just called to arrange this lunch—they always met in public spots to avoid suspicion—when he learned that several young Maquisards had been caught and shot summarily by the approaching tank division.

Dex eyed the room, making sure it was safe to speak. "We're okay, but be quick," he murmured, catching Albert's eye, counting on him to warn of any danger. "What's up?"

"The S.S. are sending a division this way. I think they're headed north but they shot several of our boys this morning. Apparently Sylvain's men are going wild."

Dex's mouth twitched angrily but otherwise he showed no reaction. "That's the last thing we need," he said in a half whisper, cutting off as General Gleiniger marched back into the dining room, flung his gloves down and began talking angrily in German with two fellow officers.

It didn't take long to learn what the conversation was about from Albert, who was ostensibly serving cognac.

"Some of Colonel Guingoin's men have kidnapped a high-ranking S.S. officer and are holding him for ransom," he whispered, pouring them each a snifter, then showing the bottle to Dex. He examined it carefully, swearing inwardly. The kidnapping couldn't have come at a worse moment. Sylvain's men should have had more sense than to commit an emotional act of bravura that would inevitably bring repercussions. But he betrayed none of his feelings.

Their conversation finished, the two men rose and took leave of one another, after arranging to communicate through Auguste, a boy who worked in the factory and helped in the church.

Only the knowledge that Geneviève was in the capable hands of Madame Baudry stopped the Comtesse from going to Ouradour immediately to help with the birth. It took much effort for Eugène to convince her that by going she would be endangering her daughter's and son-in-law's lives. When the news arrived via the Resistance that she'd safely delivered a boy, the family breathed easier. But the baby was small and Madame Baudry was worried, determined to take him to the doctor in Limoges as quickly as possible. It was suggested that perhaps Eugène could find an excuse to visit the village while Madame and her husband were away and slip in to see his sister.

"You must go," his mother insisted. "We don't know how she is. If only your father were alive, I'm sure he would have found a solution."

"I'll go, *Maman*. Don't worry, I'm sure she's all right," Eugène answered wearily.

"My poor darling daughter. I shall never forgive Sylvain for having led her astray."

"*Maman,* in all fairness, Genny never gave him a chance."

"I know, I know, but still. He should have been firmer."

"He wasn't able to get his mother to leave Paris and look what happened. She and Ruth have disappeared without a trace. I've tried everything to find out where they are. So has Sylvain's uncle. But it is too dangerous for him now. God help them both," he said, crossing himself.

As the tram rumbled through the countryside toward Ouradour, Eugène realized what a blessing it was that Monsieur and Madame Baudry lived in this quiet spot on the river Glane, a region with little Maquis activity. The Germans never bothered about the area. His heart went out to his sister. Having her baby in hiding, with only Madame Baudry and the midwife to assist, could not have been easy. But *Dieu merci,* at least she and the baby were safe. How thrilled Sylvain would be when he learned he had a son.

The tram came to a jolting stop in front of the station. Eugène and a number of other passengers alighted. But to his astonishment a German soldier stepped forward, barring their way.

"Weg Weg," he shouted, pointing his rifle. "Go away."

The passengers began to run, terrified. Some huddled into the tram, but when the soldier's back was turned, Eugène made a quick escape into a nearby field crouching among the high grass, then climbing the forested slope to where he could get a good view of the small burg below.

From his vantage point, he ascertained that the town was surrounded. He caught glimpses of soldiers patrolling the streets. Then he heard a drumroll.

One by one the inhabitants came out of their homes, from shops and cafés. The children were marched from the schools. It appeared to be an orderly identity check and he breathed easier, glancing at his watch, hoping they would be quick and that he would still have time to see Genny before taking the tram back to town.

By two-fifteen the town square was filled with men, women and children and surrounded by soldiers with leveled machine guns. Eugène shivered with sudden foreboding, trying desperately to distinguish his sister among the women, knowing instinctively she was there. But it was too far away to see their faces.

Time lingered on. At three o'clock, the men were separated from the women and children and another cold chill ran down his spine. An S.S. officer was talking to a man Eugène presumed was the mayor. They disappeared for a few minutes then reappeared, and four men, probably hostages, stepped forward. Their usual routine, he realized bitterly.

He sat down more comfortably on the grass and watched attentively. In twenty minutes or so they would be on their way and he could enter the town.

But almost forty minutes later, the men were split into separate groups and marched in different directions. He couldn't see where they were going but it looked as though they were being directed into barns. Several groups of soldiers with machine guns and ammunition stood about, smoking and chatting.

Eugène changed positions, wishing they'd get on with the ID check and leave. It was almost time to catch the tram home and he wouldn't see Genny at this rate.

At four o'clock sharp he jumped as a deafening explosion and the rumble of machine guns tore the air. What was happening? He struggled to his feet, shaking, watching the women and children being herded into the church in the silence that followed. Desperately he searched for his sister. Several buildings had caught fire and he gazed in horror as it spread rapidly from house to house. Letting out an anguished cry, he realized they had been shooting the men and that the survivors were being burned alive. He ran down the slope, tripped, and fell to his knees, eyes glued to the flames engulfing the homes, hearing the tortured shrieks of the wounded as he stumbled back to his feet. Searching through the smoky haze, he was relieved that the women and children were still in the church with the priest, where no harm could befall them.

Eugène tried to move but his limbs wouldn't carry him. Murmuring frantic prayers, he watched as two soldiers entered the church with a large chest then came back out, closing the doors tightly behind them.

Suddenly he heard new screams and stared, aghast, at smoke seeping from under the church's doors. They had placed dynamite within God's house, he realized, and were killing the women and children. Finally the door of the sanctuary gave way under the pressure of those pushing their way to freedom. But as soon as those imprisoned burst outside, they were gunned down in a resounding volley of bullets.

"*Arrêtez, je vous en prie!* Stop, I beg you," he shouted, running once more toward the village, certain Geneviève and the baby must be among the victims fighting for their lives. But as he stumbled through the trees, he was grabbed from behind, and a hand clapped over his mouth. He struggled wildly, then a voice spoke softly in his ear.

"It is too late, *mon père.* There is nothing we can do. They will only kill us as well."

By now the whole village was in flames and they watched in silent horror as a man getting out of the tram was shot and his body thrown into the Glane.

As evening set in, the soldiers plundered the village. Whatever they didn't take was burned or destroyed methodically, setting fire to any houses that remained unscathed, except one, where perhaps they planned to carouse that night.

The stranger, a middle-aged farmworker, touched Eugène's shaking arm. "Come. We must make haste."

Together they made their way through the fields, walking in stunned silence, pursued by the acrid scent of fear and burned flesh. They walked until they reached a hamlet some five kilometers away, where there seemed to be no German soldiers, and headed for the church.

When the *curé* opened the door, Eugène sank to his knees and fainted.

As soon as news of the savagery committed at Ouradour reached Dex, he drove to la Vallière, thinking of Genny as he'd seen her happiest—on her wedding day, when Flora had returned to his life. How devastated she would be when she learned of her cousin's horrible fate.

He reached the château, sadness enveloping him as he strode up the steps, the black ribbon covering the knocker making his eyes tear once more. Poor little Genny, the baby of them all.

Madame Baudry opened the front door, her face pale and drawn.

"Thank God you're safe, *madame*," Dex exclaimed, clutching her hand. "And the baby?"

"Safe, *Dieu merci*. My husband and I had taken him to Limoges, to the doctor. He was running late so we missed the tram back to Ouradour."

"Where are the family?"

She indicated the salon and he crossed the hall, hearing the murmur of voices broken by tears.

As he entered, Eugène rose and Dex realized in shock that he'd aged ten years in only days. Another priest stood at the Comtesse's side, while two women whom he didn't know huddled nearby, dabbing their eyes. They embraced silently. There was nothing to say. The sight of a photograph of Genny, smiling, confident and radiant, was too much to bear.

It took him a few minutes but he pulled himself together, knowing he must remain calm if he was to be of any help. There were decisions to be made. The baby's safety was a problem. The first place the Germans would look if they found out about him was the Château de la Vallière.

"Where is the baby hidden?" he asked Eugène.

"At Jean Luc's farm."

"I don't think that's safe. The S.S. may be on the lookout." He lowered his voice. "I heard they're blaming Sylvain and Guingoin for the kidnapping of a high-ranking S.S. officer. God help us if they learn of the baby. You know they'll go to any lengths to smoke Sylvain out."

He realized Eugène was mumbling to himself in an undertone. Dex touched his arm and the priest started. "I should have gone down to the village. Perhaps I could have impeded the massacre, perhaps as a priest I could have—"

"There was nothing you could have done," Dex interrupted firmly. "They would merely have killed you as well. But I need you to concentrate, Eugène. We must take precautions. If possible, we must remove the baby from the area."

"What? Oh, the baby. Yes, of course," he answered vaguely. "It was my idea to send her to Ouradour, you know. It was one of the quietest places in the region. The Germans never went there."

"You must stop blaming yourself. It wasn't your fault. And now we owe it to Genny and Sylvain to take care of their child."

The arrival of the d'Albis family, there to pay their respects, stopped him for a moment.

"I am so sorry, Eugène. So deeply sorry." Jean embraced his friend and shook hands with Dex. As Swiss consul, Jean d'Albis had made a formal complaint against the atrocity. "I have seen General Gleiniger. He is horrified by what has occurred."

"So he goddamn well should be," Dex barked.

"He is. And worried. He advised me that a new Gestapo man, Sharenberg, has been appointed to the area to flush out the Maquisards. But they don't know how long it will take for him to arrive. I am told he is a cold-blooded bastard."

"Enough. I will hear no more. I shall go myself to the general and make a formal complaint," Eugène exclaimed, trembling.

"We must remain calm," Jean insisted. "Have you any news of Sylvain?"

"No. And the silence is deafening," Dex murmured, worried about the baby. "We must get the child out of here, Jean. God help Sylvain if they find it."

"How could this have happened?" Eugène raged bitterly. "For the first time I questioned my faith," he said, eyes glazed. "How could God allow such a thing to happen?"

"Eugène, we must concentrate on getting that child out of here before he becomes a tool in the hands of the Gestapo."

"There is a possible solution, but I have no idea how it could be pulled off," Jean murmured thoughtfully.

"Shoot."

"Didn't you mention to me that your cousin Flora is expecting a baby, Eugène?"

"A baby?" Dex interjected, stunned. "Flora? What kind of a baby?"

"The usual kind, I suppose."

Dex's pulse doubled and he sat down with a thud. He did some quick arithmetic. The baby must have been conceived in those few blissful days, he realized, tears of joy battling with grief.

Jean continued. "Then I suggest we ship the baby to Flora. When is she due?"

"According to my mother, very shortly."

"She never told me," Dex murmured.

"Told you?"

"About the baby. The line got cut off and we weren't able to finish the conversation."

"You saw her?" Eugène stiffened.

"Yes."

"Excuse us one moment." Eugène turned to Jean, who left them to talk privately.

"Is it yours?"

"Yes."

"How could you?" he whispered, shaking his head sadly. "What a mess." Eugène closed his eyes.

"That will have to be dealt with later. We have other priorities right now. Jean's right. If we could get the baby to Flora, she could pretend it was hers and it would be safe."

"You mean *they* pretend it is *theirs*. Angus is aware that his wife is having a baby," Eugène said dryly. "If my mother is to be believed, he is thrilled at the news."

"But that's absurd. The child is mine. I—"

"What did you expect her to do? Pack her bags and run all over the country looking for you? Cause a scandal and endanger her health and her home? My God, you can be idiotic at times," he ended.

"He knows the baby isn't his. Flora was a virgin," he whispered.

"Then Angus has assumed the child, and knows that Flora had an affair."

"The child is mine, just as she is, and as soon as this damn mess is over I'm going to fetch them. She can get a divorce."

"She can't. She is Catholic. It is out of the question that they be divorced."

"But the marriage was never consummated."

"This is not the time or the place to be discussing such a delicate matter," Eugène responded, exhausted. "As you pointed out, the baby is what we must worry about. I don't see how it could be done. It would be impossible to leave France with the child."

"I'll see what I can do through my connections. I think we might be able to swing it," Dex answered, forcing himself to stop thinking about the pregnancy and concentrate.

"Very well. Keep me posted."

Jean returned, catching the end of the conversation. "But who would take care of the baby during the trip to Scotland?" he asked, straightening his bow tie.

"I've no idea. All that's detail. The boys at H.Q. will manage somehow. The main difficulty I see will be getting it to the airfield."

There was a long moment's silence as they pondered the matter.

Then Jean cleared his throat. "I have an idea," he said, his voice barely a whisper. "Does Monsieur Baudry still have that old Renault of his? What the Americans would call a jalopy."

"I believe so," Eugène murmured blankly.

"It was a popular model that has a hidden compartment in the trunk. You can only find it if you take the back part to pieces. It usually contains a spare wheel and the necessary tools for a tire change."

"You mean to fit the baby in there?" Eugène clarified.

"But what if it cries?" Dex asked.

"Madame Baudry can give it some valerian to make sure it sleeps."

"It's risky, but feasible," Dex admitted. "What if Baudry is stopped and they search the car?"

"I can arrange a pass from Kapitän Stoll," Jean supplied.

"Then let's see if it can be arranged as soon as possible, Dex said. "I have to go. I'll begin making plans at once."

It was after six o'clock the next day when Dex got to the factory, but still not all the workers had left. He glanced out of his office and down the hall. Tourbet, the chief accountant, was still at his desk, sleeves rolled up. There was something he didn't like about the man, something his gut told him to be wary of. What the hell could he possibly be doing here at this time?

Dex popped his head around the door of the accounting department and smiled. "Still working, Tourbet? With our reduced orders, I wouldn't think there was that much to do. Just goes to show, doesn't it?"

"I was getting last month's stock straightened out. Since Pierre and Marcel left for the *travails forcés* in Germany we have been understaffed." He shook his head. "It is terrible all these young men forced to go and work for *les Boches*."

Dex agreed, but he had his own suspicions why Marcel and Pierre had been sent off to forced labor in Germany. He would bet his last dollar that Tourbet had something to do with it.

"I'm leaving. Can I drop you off somewhere?" he asked casually.

"*Non, non, m'sieur.* You are too kind. I can still catch the tram."

They left together, Tourbet locking up carefully behind them. Dex waved goodbye and drove the Packard out of the front gates, watching in the rear mirror as Tourbet headed toward Route de Toulouse and the tram. Dex drove off in the direction of home, then turned into a side street, made a U-turn and returned slowly, coming in the back way through a dilapidated gate covered in weeds and shrubs. He parked behind one of the old factory buildings that was now out of use.

Dex slipped out of the car and into the ancient building, stopping to make sure he was alone before walking down the long stretch to the last furnace. His steps echoed despite his efforts to move quietly. He stopped again, tense, and turned back to make sure he wasn't being followed, before removing the old boxes of broken chinaware that lay sprawled carelessly at the foot of the kiln. After another quick glance around, he opened the iron door of the huge oven and reached inside, feeling for the flashlight he'd left there. Finding it, he switched it on and looked up at the radio. Thank God for foresight. After seeing *Casablanca,* he'd baptized the radio Ingrid and his communiqués began with *You must remember this.* Suddenly he wished there was a radio at Strathaird so he could tell Flora how happy and proud he was that they were having a child.

Snapping back to the present, Dex concentrated on the task at hand. Sylvain's baby had to leave France as soon as possible. The Gestapo were capable of killing hundreds with such chilling detachment; torturing a baby in front of its father, to make him betray his comrades, would be child's play.

Knowing the men were probably waiting outside for his signal, he climbed up to the platform where the radio sat and switched the flashlight off and on three times up the chimney,

Then, putting the headphones on, he plugged in, hearing the familiar crackle and fine-tuning to pick up the right frequency.

There were numerous messages and he listened carefully in case there was anything for him. After several minutes he heard *Salesforce heading for Casablanca, repeat, Salesforce headed for Casablanca.* Dex replied—*You must remember this*—repeating it twice then waited anxiously. Soon *A sigh is just a sigh* came in and he exhaled, relieved. Salesman, the British agent with whom he operated, had landed safely and would be waiting at Drouot's farm later tonight.

He switched the radio off and waited. Soon footsteps echoed below and he climbed down from the platform, wiping the grime from his clothes and straightening his jacket. He always dressed formally in Limoges after he'd realized the Nazis, who showed great deference for hierarchy and order, were easily impressed. Well-decked-out and expensive meant he was okay—for the army at least. The Gestapo was a different matter. That reminded him of Jean's earlier comment concerning the new *Kommandant,* Sharenberg. The name was familiar.

He spied Louis, a young baker from Bergerac, and Robert, his gardener, in the shadows by the door. Putting the crates carefully back in position, he eradicated all trace of his visit, then made his way hurriedly toward them, the German name still ringing eerily in his memory.

Louis was driving an old truck tonight and Dex climbed in the back with Robert, hastily removing his clothes, donning an old pair of gray pants and a worn shirt and beret they'd provided for him.

"He's coming," he said, referring to Salesman.

"Thank God. Anyone else?"

"Hercules," Dex referred to Sylvain by his code name, "and the Colonel." He didn't mention the baby to Robert. Plans were kept secret until the last minute, revealed to as few as possible. It was not that he doubted the man's loyalty, but in case of capture and torture, it was better he knew less.

It took them almost two hours on winding bumpy roads, driving far into the forest to avoid checkpoints, but finally they reached the desolate farmhouse that was the central meeting point.

They entered the kitchen and sat at the gnarled wooden table placed in the center of the low-beamed room. A single gas lamp stood propped in the corner of the uneven brick floor, flickering eerily as the three men waited in tense silence.

They didn't have to wait long before the muffled sound of an engine and footsteps had them on their feet, Robert close to the door, pistol ready, and Dex and Louis positioned to shoot. They waited for tonight's code word, tapped out in Morse code.

It came. The knocks, though soft, sounded earsplitting in the tense silence.

Slowly Robert unbolted the door, his gun cocked. The tension eased when Salesman—Major Staunton—entered, followed closely by Troy—a man he'd worked with before—and Sylvain. Dex was horrified at the grim lines on his face and his glazed expression as silently they gripped hands, for no words could assuage the pain of emptiness caused by Genny's murder, her sparkling youth and beauty dimmed, transformed forever into charred, unidentifiable remains. The Gestapo had returned the next day to finish their dirty work, burning the bodies of the women and children who'd suffocated in the church, stripping the population of Ouradour of the right to claim their dead, buried now in common graves.

The men sat at the old pine table and drank some wine. Dex listened carefully to what they had to say, relieved to learn Sylvain's men were not involved with the kidnapping of the S.S. officer. But it was perhaps to avenge his disappearance that Ouradour had occurred. No matter what had truly happened, the consequences if the baby were found would be catastrophic.

"It could be an ace for the Gestapo," Salesman commented.

Troy nodded and Sylvain gripped his glass, knuckles taut, his thoughts a million miles away.

"We have very little time and must act at once," Dex continued, wincing at the agony etched in Sylvain's features.

"I'll see what can be done, but your boys are the right people for this. Bogart," Salesman replied, using Dex's code name, "you can land a B17 or 25 at Framboise." He referred to their landing field, thirty kilometers south of Limoges.

"I'll get through later tonight. I'll need to reach the factory before dawn and talk to London."

"Right. We'd better be on the move." Salesman rose, catching his eye. "I need a quick word with you."

They left by the kitchen door and stood in the moonlight, surrounded by a hint of thyme and rosemary and the hum of crickets. Dex saw Salesman pass a hand fleetingly over his eyes, then straighten his shoulders.

"If the operation fails, I'm afraid Hercules will have to be taken out," Salesman said in a half whisper. "The risk if he's caught could blow everything we've taken years to build." Dex shuddered, aghast. Salesman continued. "No man could resist seeing his baby tortured and not give way, old chap. You know as well as I do that's the first thing those swine would do— *and* take pleasure in it," he added, the only sign of emotion a nervous twitch to the left of his mouth and the bitterness in his tone. "I'm sorry."

In the seconds that followed, a thousand scenarios for Sylvain's escape fleeted before him. But deep down he knew that Salesman was right. Too many lives were at stake, and perhaps even the outcome of the war. They'd received news of the Allied invasion and knew that General Patton's troops were advancing south as they spoke. It wasn't over yet, though, and there was still a strong German offensive to be dealt with.

"We'd better make damn sure it works," he said dryly.

"Right. You're certain this Baudry chap is one of us?"

"Of course. He and his wife have worked for the la Vallières all their lives. They lost their entire family at Ouradour. Jean d'Albis says he can get us a pass via Captain Stoll. Gleiniger and his top command were appalled at what happened at Ouradour."

"Good. Send him word through the priest. It's the safest route. We'll name it Operation Tinker Bell. Good luck. I hope to God it succeeds."

They shook hands. Dex braced himself.

"If I get the okay for tomorrow or the day after, are you prepared?"

"Yes. Framboise, that would be best," he said. "By the way, I hear you Yanks are rolling through Normandy. Patton's drinking every ounce of petrol he can lay his hands on."

"About fucking time."

They went back inside. Sylvain was sitting exactly as they'd left him. Troy—who'd taken out five Gestapo officers single-handedly and blown up half the tracks from here to Bordeaux—was cleaning his revolver, and Robert and Louis sat silent except for a grunt here and there.

They said quick goodbyes. Dex gave Sylvain a quick hard squeeze. The operation must succeed.

Operation Tinker Bell was put together with the speed of lightning, and once again Dex gave thanks for American courage and efficiency. Nobody he contacted questioned the necessity of risking their lives to fly in and pick up "a package."

At eleven o'clock the next night, Dex and Robert reached la Vallière by a secret route that Dex remembered from his childhood days. Eugène let them in by the back door. There was no time to waste. He had received his answer at dawn. *Three raspberries for Tinker Bell.* That meant 3:00 a.m. at Framboise— the French word for raspberry—airfield.

Madame Baudry and the Comtesse wept as they handed him the sleeping baby. The women had given the infant valerian to keep him from crying. He held the child in his arms, looking into the miniature face, a knot in his throat as he tucked it among the pillows in the secret compartment of Monsieur Baudry's Renault.

"Father."

"What is it?" Eugène turned nervously as Madame Baudry pulled his sleeve.

"The child is not baptized. What if... Oh, *mon Dieu!*" She clapped a hand over her lips, trembling.

"It can't be helped," Dex interrupted in a firm whisper. "We haven't got time."

"But the child cannot travel without being baptized. If anything should happen, his soul might be damned."

"If I get a glass of water, can you do it?" he hissed to Eugène.

He nodded. Robert rushed into the house, grabbed a glass of water from the kitchen and came hurrying out. He handed it to Eugène who leaned carefully over the sleeping baby, swaddled in the trunk.

"Au nom du Père, du Fils, et du Saint-Esprit," he muttered, *"je te baptise—"* he looked up inquiringly. No one had thought of a name.

"David Jonathan. That is what they wanted," the Comtesse whispered, voice breaking.

Eugène touched the child's forehead and finished quickly, crossing himself. Handing the glass to Madame Baudry, he gripped Dex's hand. *"Que Dieu vous garde."*

Dex nodded. He prayed none of them would learn the consequences if they didn't succeed. The thought of Sylvain being captured was too dreadful to even contemplate.

Monsieur Baudry would go ahead in the Renault with the pass that Jean had extracted from Captain Stoll, along the main road to Angoulême and through the checkpoint. The pass said he was visiting his ailing mother in a nearby village. Dex and Robert would follow, taking the back roads, until they reached the Framboise landing field.

"We've got two hours," he said, glancing at his watch. "We'd better step on it. *Bon courage!*" he said, gripping Monsieur Baudry's callused hand.

"On y arrivera," he replied, putting on his cap. *"Ils ne nous auront pas tous*—they won't get us all."

Dex got in next to Robert, who was driving the Peugot, and they followed Monsieur Baudry out the back driveway.

As they drove off, Dex looked back. The Comtesse stood on the steps, a solitary fragile figure. She raised her hand and gave them a regal nod, sending them on their way. He waved back, gripped by a premonition that this was the last time he would see her.

They drove an hour and a half before disappearing onto dirt

tracks that would lead them to a vantage from which they could see the checkpoint below. Leaving the car, they crawled through the bushes, watching as Monsieur Baudry's car approached the checkpoint at Roussac.

"Why are all those searchlights on?" Dex whispered, his pulse racing, eyes narrowed. Instinctively he felt in the waistband of the old gray pants for his .38.

"They must be doing a special search. *Merde alors!*"

"Shit. Why? I don't like it."

"Baudry should be okay. He has Gleiniger's pass."

But fear rushed through Dex as he watched the soldiers, dogs sniffing, stop every vehicle.

"I don't like it," he repeated uneasily, each second dragging as Monsieur Baudry's little black Renault edged its way to the front of the line. The cars in front of him had been stopped, the drivers hauled out, papers scanned. The S.S. officers were checking everything, the atmosphere strangely tense.

"They're looking for a clue to the Kämpf kidnapping," he whispered. "That has to be it. Damn it!" Dex said, almost to himself, eyes glued to the soldier as he looked over the papers Baudry had presented him. Willing them to let him go, Dex's heart beat faster when an S.S. officer took the papers from the soldier's hand, inspecting them closely. It seemed interminable, and he could imagine poor Baudry's tension, not knowing whether he would be allowed to move forward or not, praying the baby wouldn't wake up and cry. Then, to his shock, the officer indicated that Baudry should pull the car over.

"*Merde!* Come on, Robert." They hastened back to the car and began driving. "There is no time to stay. We must go to Framboise and get word to Salesman to wait. There's nothing we can do about Baudry."

They drove the last few miles in tense silence, through the back roads lit by a full moon, slowing when they approached an old stone farmhouse.

Robert flashed a signal with the headlights. The response came immediately and he drove down the rough road and straight into the grange. Jumping out, they stealthily slipped around the back of the barn and down into the wine cellar. Dex knocked three times, stopped, then knocked again.

The lookout had allowed them past. Now the wine cellar door opened a fraction, then let them in. To Dex's surprise, Salesman and Troy were seated on casks under the brick *vôutes* of the cellar. The room was rampant with tension.

"What happened?"

"Hercules," Salesman replied, voice bitter. "He and some of Guingoin's men have kidnapped the new S.S. Commandant. Someone overheard them discussing their plans and passed the information on."

"My God." Dex slammed his fist down on a cask, trembling. "Doesn't the fool know we're trying to save his son, for Christ's sake? They're checking Baudry now. He's down there at the checkpoint. My boys will be landing at three at Framboise." Dex leaned against the curved brick wall next to Troy.

"Are the S.S. there?" Salesman asked.

"In full force. Why did it occur to Syl—Hercules to do this? Where did it happen?" He clenched his teeth.

"About ten miles down the road. Sharenberg was driving with only two *motards* and another chap. Sylvain deviated the road signs just outside Bellac. I suppose they headed right into the bush. You know what'll happen. The S.S. will begin shooting hostages if Sharenberg's not handed over. The usual scenario."

"Was Guingoin a party to this?"

"No. I think this was out of his control."

"Sylvain must have lost his mind." He shook his head. "Doesn't he know his son is in the trunk of the goddamn car and that this insubordination threatens his life?"

Salesman handed him a bottle of cognac. Dex took a long gulp, then another.

All at once, Troy went to the door, listening. They waited as the far-off rumble of an engine broke the silence. Dex exchanged a look with Salesman.

"Mercedes," Troy whispered. "And a jeep."

They took their positions silently. In the quiet, they heard the car doors opening, the muffled whispers, then heavy boots descending the steps of the cellar. Troy flattened his back against the wall by the door, a knife raised in his right hand. Salesman, Robert and Dex had their weapons pointed directly at the door.

Then the knock came. Once. Twice. It stopped and then resumed. The same knock Robert had used. They exchanged worried glances.

"It's Hercules. Open up. I have the pigs well secured." They heard the deadening crack of a bone, followed by a groan. Salesman lowered his weapon, indicating for them to keep him covered, and edged his way to the door.

"Pass code," he whispered.

"En passant par la Lorraine."

An old French nursery rhyme, Dex realized, struck, despite the tension, by the irony that tonight's password was a nursery rhyme.

Salesman opened the door and Sylvain entered, pushing a tall, blond officer, eyes covered, mouth gagged. He crumpled to the floor. His nose had been broken, blood soaking the cloth covering his mouth. His hands were bound behind his back.

Dex stared as Sylvain spat at his prisoner, eyes wild and glazed. Two other Germans were brought in, bound and gagged, and thrown in the corner by their companion.

"I'm going to kill you slowly," Sylvain threw at him. *"Langsam ganz langsam.* And when you're half-dead but conscious enough to feel the pain, I'll put you on fire, watch you sizzle, burn you to a crisp like you burned my wife." He gave the man a savage kick before Salesman restrained him.

"Enough!" The sharp command made Sylvain turn. "Get his gag off, Bogart."

Dex unknotted the cloth from the man's mouth and unbound his eyes. He retched, blood and saliva pouring from his lips. Salesman eyed him coldly. "Are you Sharenberg?"

"Yes, I am." The words were pronounced painfully, but his English, though clipped, was perfect.

"You speak English?" Salesman asked, eyes narrowing, his voice a monotone, devoid of emotion.

"My mother was half-English," he whispered, trying to wipe his mouth on his shoulder unsuccessfully.

Dex gazed at him, pulse racing. He was young, no more than twenty-six. He studied him, the room spinning as Greta's eyes returned his stare. For a terrible moment he thought he would faint, but he held on by a thread, needing to know.

"Who was your mother?" he asked, his voice harsh, unable to take his eyes off the man.

"Who cares who sired the pig," Sylvain hurled angrily, shaking off Salesman's grip.

"My mother was Greta von Ritter." The effort made him close his eyes.

Dex sank trembling onto a wine cask. Greta sprang before him: Annenberg, the snow-covered fir trees and love-filled moments of that perfect winter... He reached for the bottle, watching Salesman questioning the Nazis methodically. Perhaps if he'd returned sooner, found Greta and married her, the boy might have been fighting with them now, a hero instead of a gruesome executioner.

"If I am not returned right away there will be immediate repercussions," Sharenberg was saying, voice thick with blood. "They will shoot batches of ten hostages every hour."

"Shut your fucking mouth." Sylvain tried to kick him but was stopped by Salesman.

"*Don't.*" Salesman grabbed him roughly by the arm, and Dex pulled him out of earshot.

"Your son is in the back of Baudry's car at the checkpoint," he said carefully, letting the words sink in. "The S.S. have stopped him. If we don't get the baby to Framboise now, there'll be no hope left. If the baby cries, they'll end up getting both you and Baudry. You can figure out the rest. Especially after this." He glanced at Sharenberg, swaying on his knees, struck suddenly by his hands, tied before him as though in prayer. Long and slim, they were hauntingly familiar.

He frowned, gasping as he caught a glimpse of the left hand and clearly recognized the kidney-shaped birthmark above the inner edge of the thumb. As Sylvain continued talking to him, all he could do was stare. Then, slowly, he twisted his wrist,

and stared down numbly at his own hand. They were identical.
Blood draining from his face, the room spun as he sank to the
nearest wine cask, holding on by a thread. Sharenberg was his
son. His eyes flew to the man's face. How hadn't he seen it at
once? The nose, the lips, so like his own, the high cheekbones
and heavy eyebrows, though blond—the resemblance was undeniable.

A pain so sharp he could hardly breathe caught in his chest,
seconds marked by the burden of a lifetime, as pictures of a
small child replaced the man before him. *God, have mercy
upon my soul.*

Dex followed orders blindly as they pushed Sharenberg and
his cohorts, eyes covered once more, outside and back into the
cars. Slowly the small convoy made its way to the hill above
the checkpoint.

"One of us will have to negotiate," Salesman whispered.
Cars were still being stopped, the drivers and passengers herded
against a wall, rifles pointed at them.

"We can't just bid for Baudry," Dex said, trying to think,
terrified that at any moment the Maquisards might lose control
and kill the prisoners. "If we do they'll know something's up."

"We negotiate Sharenberg. On the condition they let everyone go." Salesman's lips were thin, his face stark.

"I'll go," Dex volunteered, welcoming the danger, hoping
he could ease his conscience.

"No, we need you too much later. Troy had better go."

"Won't it expose him?"

"Yes, but we can't help that. He'll go with his face covered." He produced an old balaclava. "My lucky charm," he
murmured. "It's kept me safe. I hope it will do the same for
him."

"Let's get on with it. We haven't much time," Dex said.

All at once he glanced back at Sylvain, gazing glassy-eyed
at the cars below, unaware that Dex's son was being traded for
his.

Taking Troy aside, they explained the terms: Sharenberg and
his two men would be handed over one hour after all the hostages had been liberated. That would give them time to get

Baudry to Framboise. The night was clouding over now, and perhaps the weather would delay the incoming plane a few minutes.

"Baudry will know what to do. And for Christ's sake, don't kill anyone," Salesman commanded, handing him the balaclava and a white handkerchief. "This is our only chance. I repeat, *only.*"

Troy nodded silently. They shook hands and he pocketed his knife, then disappeared into the night with the stealth of a wild animal who knew every inch of the terrain. Sylvain followed with their prisoners, ready to offer proof to the S.S. officers. A few minutes later they heard shouts and movement. Soldiers were pointing to a white handkerchief extended on a long stick waved a hundred feet away from the checkpoint, glimmering in the glare of the searchlight.

Two S.S. officers talked for a minute among themselves then one of them advanced toward the flag. A loud voice wrenched the air.

"Drop your arms." It was Troy.

They watched with bated breath as the officer turned and instructed the men to lower their arms and throw them in a heap on the ground. Then Troy dropped his own revolver and advanced, arms held high above his head. Sylvain's tired eyes stayed glued to the Renault, squeezed among the cars.

Dex and Salesman watched, tense, as the S.S. officer reached the spot where the handkerchief protruded from the brush at the side of the road.

A few minutes passed, then he turned and walked quickly back to the checkpoint, where he consorted with the others.

Then everything happened at once. Orders were shouted and passengers were told to return to their vehicles. The soldiers began organizing the traffic.

"We did it," Salesman exclaimed jubilantly, grabbing Dex's shoulder. "Come on, there's not a minute to lose. I think Baudry can just make it."

"He *must* make it," Dex whispered, voice raw.

The cars filed slowly through the checkpoint one by one, then picked up speed and went on their way, the sound of the hastily revved engines expressing better than words the heartfelt relief of the passengers.

Dex turned, relieved. The mission would succeed and his son would live. But it was impossible to grasp that this man, who bore his blood, was a monster who tortured and killed.

"Stop."

Dex froze. Out of the shadows he saw Sharenberg come forward, holding a revolver to Sylvain's head. He rolled into the brush, dragging Salesman down with him.

"It's over," Sharenberg shouted to his kidnappers. "Come forward before I blow this Jewish *schwein*'s brains out."

"Careful, Bogart," Salesman whispered, gripping his weapon. "Not too soon or we'll blow it. You're better placed than I am, you shoot."

Palms sweating, he cocked the gun, like an automaton acting by remote control, as Sylvain's head was yanked back. The revolver at his temple and Sharenberg's bloodstained face flickered in the moonlight, a grotesque Halloween mask.

God forgive me, he whispered, shaking, as the shot echoed through the night like a thunderbolt. The gun trembled in his hand and Sharenberg crumpled to the ground at Sylvain's feet.

Dex rose as if in a dream and ran to where the body lay, limp and warm. Falling on his knees, tears bathing his cheeks, he gazed at the boy he'd never known and, reaching out, gently closed his eyes.

"Murdering pig," Sylvain hissed, about to shoot at the body.

"Don't, you fool," Salesman ordered. "That one shot may already have given us away. We must get out of here as fast as we can. We've got exactly twenty-eight minutes to make it. I know a back route that will take us to Framboise."

"What about the others? We should kill them now."

"No. It'll just mean more reprisals. Leave them with Robert. Come on, Bogart."

Dex took one last look, then rose unsteadily.

"Come on, we can't waste any more time." Salesman gave him a curious glance.

He went blindly to the jeep. Sylvain barely gave them time to jump in before the vehicle raced off through the undergrowth, down the earth road, skidding down small lanes as they rushed through the night to the rendezvous.

Dex sat in the back, unable to think, hear or speak, the shock of his discovery too great to bear. Twenty minutes later they slowed, turned left and followed a dirt track for several miles until they reached a stile. Far above, the sound of incoming aircraft hummed.

"It's them." Salesman jumped out and pushed open the gate. Then the jeep was hurtling across rough terrain to the airfield where torches were being lit, preparing for the landing.

They reached the spot where the Renault stood waiting. A Maquisard was flashing his quick signal to the plane. Dex followed Sylvain, who ran to where Monsieur Baudry stood holding a tiny bundle in his arms, and watched as Sylvain's face softened for the first time in days. Gently he lifted the soft cloth shrouding the baby's face, tears glistening as he gazed in wonder at his son. Tears fell from Dex's eyes as well. Tears for the son he'd never known, lying dead in the middle of nowhere, and for the child who was about to be carried to safety.

"He's beautiful," Sylvain whispered, awed. "Dex, if anything happens to me, promise that you and Flora will take care of him. Won't you?"

Dex nodded, unable to utter a sound as Sylvain glanced up at the incoming plane. "Here, hold him a moment." He handed Dex the baby, then drew a thick-banded gold watch from his arm. Uncovering the baby's leg, he slipped it up his thigh and secured the clasp, before carefully taking him back in his arms.

"Eugène baptized him David Jonathan. The Comtesse said that was the name you'd chosen," Dex shouted above the roar of the plane.

"David Jonathan," Sylvain murmured reverently as the plane, a U.S. Navy B17, came to a standstill. He held the baby close, protecting it from the sudden rush of wind caused by the running engines, as a young copilot jumped to the ground and hastened toward them.

"*Shalom,*" Sylvain whispered, giving his son a last kiss.

"Sh'elohim yishmor alecha." God watch over you and keep you safe.

Then he handed him to the young American pilot. "Take good care of him, I beg of you."

"I sure will, sir," the boy replied, receiving the bundle awkwardly, clearly more frightened of holding anything so small, alive and precious, than facing an enemy squadron.

They stood in silence watching as the plane took flight, a silent group of men to whom death and violence had become an everyday matter. Yet to each of them, the fragile bundle of hope disappearing on the horizon represented everything they were fighting for. And as the predawn sky grew light and they turned back to the jeep and harsh reality, there were tears in all their eyes.

At 5:00 a.m., Dex climbed up to the radio and tuned in, exhausted. Ten minutes later he heard what he was listening for. *Tinker Bell's raspberries delivered.*

37

Skye, Scotland, 1944

If it was a girl, she would name her Nathalie; if it was a boy, Gavin. All afternoon Flora sat on the lawn sleepily, feeling the baby move, the soft summer breeze and the trace of North Sea brine caressing her cheeks. Dex's child. The fruit of their love.

She glanced at the astrological chart she was working on, unable to complete it until the baby was born. He or she would be a Gemini. The ascendant would depend on the time of birth, which she was certain would occur within a couple of days.

She heaved herself out of the faded striped deck chair, hands securing her lower back, and made her way toward the castle, hearing the phone ring in the distance as she climbed the steps. She hoped Margaret would hear it, for she had no intention of skidding down the passage.

Soon Margaret came pattering through the great hall and into the drawing room. "It's a call fer ye', m'lady. His Lordship, from London."

"Thank you, Margaret." She smiled at the ruddy-cheeked girl and went down the passage to the large black telephone reposing on an old chest.

"Angus?"

"Hello, darling." He'd become very tender ever since she

told him about the baby, acting as though it really were his. Yet the tenderness made her feel guilty and fear for the future.

"How are you?" she asked.

"I—there is a somewhat unusual situation going on. I can't talk over the phone. Suffice it to say that I'll be arriving tomorrow at dawn at the usual place." They never mentioned names, but she knew he meant the airfield the Americans had been built on the far side of the island. "Just ask Duncan to be there."

"Is everything all right?" She frowned. Angus sounded worried.

"Fine. I'll explain when I get there. Just make sure Duncan's there."

"Of course. I think the baby may come very soon."

"Thank God for that."

She smiled at his evident relief. "It can't be that bad—after all, women have babies all the time."

"Yes, yes, of course," he replied absently. "I'll see you tomorrow. And Flo..."

"Yes?"

"No, sorry. Nothing. I'll tell you tomorrow. Goodbye."

The line went dead and she put down the receiver with a shrug, content. Her only worry was Dex's whereabouts. She wished he were here for the birth, knowing she wanted the impossible. She had decided from the beginning of her pregnancy not to dwell on matters that could cause her unhappiness and perhaps harm the baby. She laid a hand on her belly and wandered back to the drawing room where shortly Margaret would bring in tea and scones.

But as she reached the door she stopped abruptly, gripped by a sudden premonition. She closed her eyes and listened, hearing a voice as clearly as though it were next to her. It was a woman's voice. She clutched the back of a chair, swaying to and fro. *My God, it was Genny, calling her.* Flora opened her eyes, aware of a presence, a hazy figure extending her arms, handing her something. She tried desperately to hold the vision, but it faded, leaving her shaken. Her cousin had suffered some harm and was trying to tell her something, asking something of her. She collapsed in the nearest armchair, trembling.

That night she lay restlessly, her dreams agitated, and at 3:00 a.m. awoke in a cold sweat, seeing flames surrounding Genny's contorted face and hearing screams. The dream left her weak and shaking. Then she heard the far-off sound of a car and remembered that Angus was arriving.

Putting on her dressing gown and slippers, she descended the ancient staircase to the great hall and unbolted the front door, shivering on the steps, still haunted by the dream.

Dawn was breaking when Duncan's old van finally drove up to the castle. Angus got out. He was holding something carefully, and as she approached, her heart leaped.

"What is that?" she asked, kissing him on the cheek.

"Let's go inside," he replied anxiously.

She waved goodbye to Duncan and followed Angus into the castle just as he uncovered the face of a tiny baby. She rushed forward, then stopped in her tracks as Genny's pleading face appeared before her once more.

"Oh my God. No!"

"It's Genny and Sylvain's baby. They managed to get it out of France. The chap who contacted me said an American agent did it. I'm sure it was Ward."

"Genny?" she asked, taking the baby in her arms, tears pouring down her cheeks.

"I'm afraid she's dead, darling."

"She came to me yesterday afternoon, I saw her. Now I understand. She was asking me to take care of her baby..."

"There's something else, Flo. We must get the baby upstairs at once and keep him hidden until ours is born. It's imperative we pretend the child is ours. They're terrified that if the Gestapo finds out Sylvain has a son...well, I don't need to paint you a picture."

"What's his name?" she asked, peering through her tears at the sleeping child.

"David Jonathan."

"David Jonathan," she whispered, raising her eyes to the

shadow hovering next to her. "I'll love him as my own," she whispered. "Don't worry."

They were hastening upstairs when suddenly Flora gasped, gripped by an unexpected pain.

"What is it, Flo, are you all right?"

"I think it's the baby. Oh God, hold David."

Angus took hold of the baby and placed him on the bed, then helped her to lie down next to the bundle.

"You must call Moira, the midwife," she said breathlessly. "I've left her number next to the phone."

"Will you be all right?" Angus hovered, uncertain of what to do.

"Just go, dear, or it'll be too late."

The next day, the villagers celebrated with a free round of drinks at the pub. Lady MacLeod had delivered twins. A fine boy and a girl, named David and Nathalie. Duncan MacRae made a speech and they raised their glasses to the health and future of the MacLeods of Strathaird, happy the succession was now secured.

38

London, England, 1944

It was mid-June by the time Dex reached England. On arrival, he reported immediately to Major Remington, a soft-spoken, middle-aged Englishman. He was the last person Dex would have imagined would be in charge of covert operations, but he'd learned long ago not to ask questions. This was not a business for ID checks. It came as a shock when Major Remington told him he was being given leave.

"Why?" he asked, annoyed. He'd hope to be posted on another operation immediately, sick of hovering around Limoges, gathering information and keeping up his cover. He wanted action, something that would help keep his mind from wandering to Flora and the babies, frustrated that he couldn't claim them as his.

But on the twentieth he received a call from Donovan at the sprawling, stately manor in Sussex used by their operation asking to meet with him. Asking was a polite way of commanding.

On his way to the appointment, in the car Donovan had sent, Dex was surprised to see the driver heading west. They were not going to London, as he'd believed. After an hour, the jeep passed through the imposing gates of a country estate and up a long driveway to the house.

He was shown into the library by a young major, and was

taken aback when he recognized the people already in the room. Nonchalantly Donovan introduced him to Winston Churchill, seated in a wing chair smoking a cigar, and to Charles de Gaulle, standing, thin and erect, by the fireplace.

"This is Major Ward, Prime Minister, the man I've mentioned. Charles, I believe you and Dexter already know one another?"

"We've met in Paris." De Gaulle gave a small bow and a stiff smile.

"Sit down and have a drink," Churchill rejoined. "We have some questions that perhaps you can help answer."

Dex sat down and accepted the whiskey Donovan handed him, flattered at being summoned to an important strategy meeting.

"We know the Maquis have been raising all hell in your area," Churchill began. "They seem to be gaining a lot of ground. The question for us is whether we arm them or not. This Guingoin fellow seems up to snuff, but it's the damn Communists we're worried about. If we drop arms to the Free French and they get into the wrong hands, it could make things more difficult than they are already."

"It's a risk," Dex said slowly, catching de Gaulle's eye. "On the other hand, if they don't have the means to fight they won't be able to do their job. They need boots, as well as weapons. Ammo's a problem, too. And better training is required—more fellows in there organizing the rank and file."

"And there must be French agents accompanying them," de Gaulle insisted.

"Of course," Churchill murmured.

"And doctors," Dex continued, glad to have the chance to get the Resistance's message through to the top. "They need a French doctor who can operate an aid station in each area, and set up some way of taking the severely wounded to a safe hospital. It's hard to get men to go into action if they think they'll be left behind to be tortured or killed."

Donovan nodded. "Reports say the guerrillas are staying too long in the same place, that the Germans keep close tabs on food shortages. The minute they hear of one, they figure the population are feeding the *résistants*. It's a tough call," he mused. "The groups have to stay dispersed, but close enough to be quickly assembled for action."

"Things are better now that more of the French army has joined them. They're disciplined, easier to train." Dex heard de Gaulle grunt and watched Churchill drawing slowly on his fat cigar, realizing this was the moment to push his point home. "But as I said, the ammo's as important as the weapons. We've had ambushes fail because our guns have stopped firing."

"Good point. What do you feel about the command relationship?" Churchill asked. De Gaulle stiffened.

"It's fundamental they go on reporting directly to their own leaders," Dex replied carefully, aware of the tension. "In my sector, that's Colonel Guingoin. It would be hopeless if we tried to take over their operations. We need to stick to planning and supplying. They'll take our advice as long as we don't step on their toes. They're highly competent, courageous men," he added, seeing de Gaulle relax again.

There was a moment of silence, then Churchill looked up. "I say we go for it, gentlemen. We're preparing a mass invasion. If we don't ready our men or give them the proper means to fight, it could fail. These fellows are all we've got. We'll have to trust them and hope for the best."

"I agree, and I speak for General Eisenhower, too." Donovan glanced at de Gaulle.

"*Il était temps,*" he replied with a sniff.

"Dex, you and Salesman had better be in charge of this one. Is your radio still in shape?"

"Ingrid works like a dream, sir."

"Ingrid?" Churchill queried.

"Ward's radio," Donovan supplied, grinning. "He had the foresight to install a top-of-the-line set in one of the broken chimneys of his china factory in Limoges before the war."

"Brilliant." Churchill smiled, impressed. "Wish we'd all had that forethought. Now, if you'll excuse me, I think I'll take a quick snooze," he said, balancing on the edge of the armchair with surprising agility for a man so large. "Good luck, Ward. And keep me posted, Donovan. This should make for some interesting reading."

39

Limoges, France, 1944

Now that the top brass had decided to furnish arms to Sylvain and Guingoin's area, Dex waited in excited anticipation for the orders to come through.

On June 26, Operation Zebra parachuted over the Limousin by day, dropping over two thousand containers of arms into the area.

At 22h.45, two planes left Keevil airport. One held thirteen S.A.S., all Frenchmen who had joined the elite British commando force. Captain Charles Brown of the American army, two French officers of the Forces Françaises Combatantes, Captain Viguier and Lieutenant Chevalier, and Dex flew in the other, along with ten more S.A.S. It was a silent flight, each man aware of the gravity of the mission's purpose: the liberation of southwestern France.

As the plane crossed the Channel, Dex dreamed of victory, of leaving the painful past behind and beginning a future with Flora and his kids. He must be getting old, he realized, to be yearning for domesticity. Yet at forty-four, he was as fit as any of the boys in the line next to him.

It was almost time to jump. This was the harrowing part, exiting through the hatch without a reserve parachute.

Dex jumped with Brown and Viguier into the predawn darkness, three kilometers from the lights. Attached to Brown's leg was a pouch that held the pieces of the Jed radio.

Dex watched, worried, as Brown slid forward in the harness. He wished the pilot had dropped them a bit lower. Eight hundred feet was too damn high, in his opinion.

Brown landed close to him. "Shit," he exclaimed, seeing that some of the radio pieces had smashed on landing.

"We'll deal with it," Dex answered, searching for Viguier, who had drifted off to the left. After twenty minutes a local farm boy appeared. They followed him for several minutes until they came into a clearing. All at once he recognized Jean Luc's farmhouse through the trees and forced his eyes away from the spot he'd killed Sharenberg—it was easier to think of him as that. He tried to control his trembling hands, knowing he should have been prepared for this. They would be meeting with Salesman in a nearby village, a remote area some thirty kilometers south of Limoges that was ideal for their base.

Salesman and Dex shook hands with the camaraderie of two men who have skimmed death together. Then Brown and Viguier joined them and they set about contacting London. Thank God the radio was working, despite the damaged parts. It would be vital throughout the operation.

For the next seven weeks they remained in hiding, helping organize French operations. Now that they were properly armed, the *résistants* were gaining ground. A lot of time was spent strategizing with Colonel Guingoin and his men.

Dex saw little of Sylvain, for he was usually embroiled in the most dangerous tasks, as though seeking danger to alleviate the pain. He learned sadly that René had been killed in North Africa, and was not surprised when, two weeks later, the Comtesse died quietly in her sleep. All of this was transmitted by Troy, who kept the link with Limoges. Going to the funeral was out of the question, for the risk of being recognized was too great.

It was August seventeenth when they finally got word that the Milice—the French collaborating army—had left Limoges and that more German troops were approaching from the south.

"That's all we bloody needed," Salesman exclaimed, poring over a map of the city with the garrisons colored in red. "There are five German garrisons in Limoges already." He looked up, eyed Dex and frowned. "I'm afraid I'll have to give London word to bomb the city," he said regretfully.

"But that's unthinkable. Think of the civilian losses."

"I know. But what can we do? If the Germans take over the town, we're done for."

"Let me talk to Colonel Guingoin," Dex pleaded. "At least give me twenty-four hours to see what can be done."

Salesman hesitated. "Very well. But we can't leave it any longer than that, I'm afraid."

It took him a while to locate Guingoin, but Dex finally got an answer to his message, via a small boy, saying the colonel was waiting to meet in a nearby barn. Dex followed the child, nerves on edge. The disaster had to be avoided at all cost. Worst of all, the Communist faction would probably welcome the bombing, so they could move in triumphantly afterward.

But Colonel Guingoin was French, first and foremost, and chief of the Maquis in the area. Dex had faith in his clout, knowing that his patriotism came before politics.

When he reached the barn, he found Guingoin in pitched battle with three Communist members and waited, disgusted, as they argued back and forth, admiring Guingoin's firm stance.

The reports of Limoges were confused. On the one hand, rumor stated that the Germans were preparing to flee the town; on the other, that troops from the south were hurrying to join them.

"Sit down," Guingoin invited with a tired smile.

"Thanks." Dex pulled up a chair and proceeded to explain Salesman's concerns and his decision to authorize an Allied bombing if a solution wasn't found immediately. Dex and Guingoin stayed up all night, desperately searching for an alternative, but by morning none could be found. There was nothing Dex could do but tell Salesman he'd failed.

* * *

The bombing was to take place on August 21.

"There must be a way," Dex murmured to himself, counting the hours in agony, still praying for a solution to avoid a tragedy of immense proportion.

It was in the late-afternoon heat that a messenger arrived, agitated, at the farm. Five Maquisards had been caught in a guerrilla operation and were being held by the Gestapo at the prison in Ambazac. Their chief was Sylvain.

Salesman, Dex and Guingoin, who had joined them, sat in horrified silence. The Germans had made it clear that, even if they left Ambazac, they would kill as many Maquisards as possible and leave the jails clean.

"There is little we can do to help them without compromising our position," Guingoin said, shaking his head sadly. "Our first duty is to try and save the town."

Dex looked up as one of the men motioned to him.

"A message for you from the priest."

The man whispered in his ear and he got up. "Perhaps there's a solution after all," he exclaimed, excited despite the horrifying news of Sylvain's capture. "General Gleiniger has expressed his desire to negotiate with the Allies. The message comes from my friend Jean d'Albis, the Swiss consul in Limoges."

Colonel Guingoin took off his glasses and wiped them, eyes alight and tense. "So our tactic of tightening our offensive and stepping up the pressure has finally worked. They think they're trapped. We may just be able to pull it off and save Limoges! Bogart, this is it. Get out there and see what can be done. Salesman, stop the bombing, please—at least for a few hours— and let d'Albis see what they want. In the meantime, we'll attack as planned and keep up the pressure."

When Eugène received the go-ahead, he grabbed his bicycle—petrol was scarce—and pedaled up the steep hill to Joutenx, the d'Albis residence, which stood in a beautiful park above the city. The day was as stifling as the tension in the town, and he sat down gratefully on the terrace, glad for the glass of lemonade offered him by Jean's mother.

"Guingoin says for you to send word to the Germans. He will meet us at St. Paul and give us a written text for Gleiniger."

"But who will present it? You can't," Jean exclaimed. "The *communistes* would never negotiate with a Catholic priest. And Guingoin can't go either—Gleiniger would never sit down with guerrillas."

"Then I'm afraid you'll have to go, Jean. You're the only acceptable party."

"I suppose I am." It was not an easy task. For all he knew, the Germans might shoot him on sight.

The next day, after arranging a time with the German High Command and advising the mayor of what was about to occur, Eugène watched anxiously from the street corner as Jean made his way toward the Hôtel de la Paix, which housed German headquarters.

Jean neared the guards at the hotel entrance. Then, all at once, he turned around and hesitated.

A gendarme stepped forward. "*Eh bien,* Monsieur d'Albis, are we going or not?"

Jean gave a quick nod. Gleiniger must have foreseen his reluctance and sent the man to prod him. He smiled nervously and, straightening his shoulders, made his way into the hotel.

Half an hour later he emerged from the building and walked calmly to the end of the street where Eugène was waiting.

"Well? What happened?" he asked impatiently as they made their way toward Joutenx.

"I thought they might grab me," he remarked with a relieved laugh, "but it was quite the opposite. They received me as an ambassador. All very formal, of course. General Gleiniger says Guingoin's conditions are impossible. I have asked him to consider meeting at my house with an Allied delegation consisting of one Brit, two Americans—Dex and Brown, probably, he's U.S. Army—and one French Free Forces representative. Joutenx would be considered neutral ground, as I am the Swiss representative."

"And did he agree?"

"Gleiniger asked me if I thought it would be a disagreeable

situation. I said no, I didn't believe so, as the meeting would take place at my home.''

"And he's accepted?" Eugène could barely contain his excitement.

"Yes. We'll meet at four tomorrow afternoon. What do you think?"

"Think? I think it's a miracle. *Incroyable.* You may just have saved the town from being destroyed!" he exclaimed, thanking God for the thousands of lives he prayed would be spared. "Now we must make sure Salesman has called off the bombing definitively."

The Allied delegation arrived at Joutenx furnished with a special safe-pass from the general, at three-thirty the next afternoon. They stood nervously in the dining room, discussing what could be done to rescue Sylvain and anxiously awaiting the Germans.

"Do you think we should offer them tea?" Jean's American mother, Renée Haviland d'Albis asked doubtfully. "It's rather an awkward situation."

"I don't think so, *Maman,* I don't think it would be suitable," Jean answered absently, glancing at his watch. It was four o'clock and there was no sign of the Germans, who were notoriously punctual.

"Remember that we cannot allow our feelings to get involved," he repeated. "This is a diplomatic meeting, and very formal," he insisted, glancing at Guingoin. "There can be no emotional displays, no cross talk, no breaches of etiquette."

Guingoin paid no attention, rubbing his glasses and pacing nervously. Staunton calmly lit his pipe and Dex drummed the shiny mahogany table at which Brown sat.

Finally, at ten past four, the sound of wheels on the gravel announced their arrival. The Allies assembled to the right of the dining table, while Jean ushered in the Germans, headed by General Gleiniger. After saluting punctiliously and excusing themselves for their tardy arrival, they sat down on the opposite side of the table. The general, a powerful man with a determined gaze, sat in the middle, Kapitän Stoll, who'd given Jean the pass for Baudry, at his right.

Jean, the moderator, cleared his throat and asked Salesman to speak first. As soon as he began reading the Allied statement, General Gleiniger interrupted.

"It's totally unacceptable. I don't want to hear this. All I want is for my troops to leave the town unharassed."

"Perhaps if you read the document, General, we could discuss the matter more easily," Jean insisted politely.

As cool as a cucumber, Dex realized, admiring Jean's smooth handling of the situation.

Grudgingly the general conceded. Finally, thanks to Jean's implications that the town was surrounded by Maquisards, he reluctantly accepted: The German troops would put down their arms and give themselves up to the Maquis. The general would turn himself over to an Allied delegation.

Dex gave a sigh of relief and Salesman nudged him under the table.

"Would the political troops be made prisoner, too?" the general questioned.

"We can't do that," Salesman replied. "Only uniformed troops can be taken prisoner."

"That includes the S.S.," Jean put in hastily, immediately recognizing the general's real question.

"In that case..." The general seemed relieved. Since Ouradour, Gleiniger had become disgusted at the S.S. killings. He'd talked to the mayor after the slaughter, telling him how truly sorry and ashamed he was. Gleiniger knew how such violence reflected on the German army, and he was also aware that few people knew the difference between the Wehrmacht and the S.S. In truth, Gleiniger was not a Nazi but a military man sent by Hitler to Limoges in disgrace. Now he wanted to make sure the S.S. wouldn't get away unscathed. Dex sympathized. He would have wanted the bastards nailed, too. The man was a true general, thinking now only of his men, for having survived Stalingrad he knew the name of the game. It was finally agreed the officers would keep their cars for this last evening; Gleiniger requested that the signing of the capitulation be delayed until 9:00 p.m.

Then they all rose and took formal leave. Jean accompanied the general outside.

"Thank you for all your help, Monsieur d'Albis. I must go and give some orders before we meet again tonight." He saluted briskly.

Jean murmured goodbye and the cars drove out of the gates.

"I believe it is all arranged," he said to the others, straightening his bow tie. "Perhaps a glass of champagne would be in order."

A couple of bottles of vintage champagne were brought in by the butler. Already they could hear rockets going off in the town.

"Congratulations, gentlemen. Well done," Salesman remarked, raising his glass.

"Damn right," Dex agreed, clinking glass with Guingoin who was avoiding the Vichy representative. "But now we must see what we can do for Sylvain."

"We'll try and set up a raid later on tonight, once the Germans have signed," Guingoin declared. "I hope it won't be too late."

Dex closed his eyes. It was surreal that this moment of triumph should by shadowed by Sylvain's capture. But there was little they could do except wait until after nine. Then they would act.

Later that evening, they took an Allied jeep that Salesman had uncovered and decorated it with the five Allied flags. By the time they reached the German H.Q., the news had spread and the town was delirious with happiness.

"No way the Gestapo are blind to this," Guingoin remarked to Dex in a bitter undertone as they entered the hotel and went upstairs, realizing the place had been sacked. "I just hope it won't be too late. We owe it to Hercules to get him out of there."

But when they reached the general's apartments there was no sign of him.

"Don't tell me he's not going to keep his word, *nom de bleu!*" Guingoin exclaimed.

At that moment the door opened and Kapitän Stoll came forward, face tense, stripped of the impassive mask he'd worn earlier.

"What is wrong?" Jean asked, concerned. There was still no sign of the general.

"The S.S. have kidnapped him," Stoll replied.

"This will put a stop to everything," Dex murmured, not wanting to believe what had happened.

Stoll looked up. "I will sign for the general," he said, recouping some of his former dignity. "We shall keep our word."

Dex watched as Stoll, head held high, handed his dagger to Jean. He passed it to Salesman, who then handed it back to Stoll. Dex realized that, thanks to Jean's insistence on protocol, the whole event had maintained tremendous dignity.

But the war still wasn't over, and Sylvain's life remained in danger. As soon as they left the hotel they separated, Salesman, Guingoin and Dex driving in the direction of Ambazac. Perhaps, if they were lucky, there would still be time.

There were ten men with him in the cell, battered and dirty, waiting to know their fate. Some were fearful, the others resigned, too exhausted to care anymore whether they lived or died. Caught in an idiotic ambush that should have been obvious, Sylvain felt doubly angry. At himself. How could he have let himself be nabbed in such a ridiculous fashion?

He stood nervously, close to the bars, trying to distract himself from the pain in the arm they'd broken by listening, his slight knowledge of Yiddish allowing him to pick up a few similar German words the guards were saying.

A woman walked in with a basket under her arm. Sylvain glanced at her, then looked more closely. It was Françoise, the barmaid who'd had an affair with René de la Vallière, he realized as she sidled up to one of the guards. Bitch, collaborator...or maybe not. Suddenly he remembered a remark Dex had made a while back, about Françoise and her involvement with the Maquis and steadied his hand enough to reach for the gold Star of David that was hidden beneath his shirt. The guards were talking fast and seemed agitated and he wondered how he could attract her attention.

Then she turned and looked at the cell, eyes filled with fear and pity. *My God,* he realized, freezing. *They're going to shoot us.*

He felt for his pendant again, his mind made up. Lifting his arm, he made a slight signal to her. She glanced warily at the guards, who were arguing to her left, then to his relief made her way stealthily toward him. When she was close enough to hear, he whispered.

"Will you give this to Father de la Vallière?" Glancing in the direction of the guards, he stretched his hand through the bars. She snatched the star and slipped it into her décolleté, moving quickly back to where she'd been standing.

Two hours later, Sylvain stood as the guards opened the door, rifles leveled. Together with the other prisoners, he was marched from the cell and thrown against the wall of the prison courtyard, the man next to him shaking with fear.

"It was worth it," he said as the soldiers leveled their rifles and he took a deep breath. As they pulled their triggers his last thought was for David. *"Shalom,"* he whispered. "Until we meet again."

When Dex and Colonel Guingoin's men entered Ambazac, the town was deserted, the streets ominously quiet as they drove toward the prison.

The place was in chaos. Abandoned desks were covered with papers and cups of stale black coffee, bottles of beer and half-eaten sandwiches. Dex and Guingoin hurried through the damp building, fearing the worst as they passed empty cells, and rushed toward the courtyard. They stopped, horrified, at the sight of the bodies lying at the foot of the dirty wall.

"No, goddamn it," Dex shouted, angry tears burning as he recognized the men. Then he crouched, gently turned Sylvain's body over, took his head in his arms and gazed into his face. The tears were uncontrollable as he gazed into his friend's face, still beautiful and sensitive despite the pain, the lines and the suffering. He remembered the days in Paris before the war, with Genny and Flora, so many happy, carefree times that would never come again. What a waste, he raged, hands trembling as he smoothed the hair from Sylvain's cold forehead. What an utter waste.

Yet he looked strangely peaceful, as though in death he'd found some measure of tranquillity. Perhaps he had. Perhaps all he'd wanted was to join Genny and leave this mess behind.

But what about the baby?

Guingoin kneeled next to him as Dex looked through Sylvain's pockets to make sure there was nothing of value that should be kept for the child in memory of his father. But there were only a few francs, some stray bullets and a crumpled photo of Genny. He smoothed it tenderly, then gently laid Sylvain on the ground. They waited for the men to carry him, with the others, to a nearby cemetery.

"He was the best," Guingoin said sadly, taking off his beret and wiping his glasses. "I couldn't have asked for a better friend or companion."

Dex nodded. "God bless you," he whispered, rising as Sylvain was carried reverently by his companions to the cemetery, where a grave had been dug.

Then he exclaimed suddenly, "No, over there." He pointed to the la Vallière plot, where his uncle and aunt and the previous generations were buried and where two plaques, in memory of Genny and René, had been placed. "He must be buried with his family."

Guingoin motioned to the men, who quickly began digging. There was no time for caskets, but Dex vowed he would see to it later. As the last shovel of earth was piled upon the grave, they stood to attention, eyes wet, and, saluting, sang the "Marseillaise."

"Goodbye," he whispered, staring down at the mound of fresh earth where Guingoin had placed a wildflower. "Go in peace, my friend. I swear I'll take care of yours, as I will my own." Then he turned and didn't look back. There was work to be done, and Sylvain would have been the first to want him to go.

40

The next few months were a mixture of relief and horror, and the knock on his office door made Eugène look up with a sigh. There had been too many knocks of late—too many demands, too much injustice and indignity. People were revolted at those whom they believed had collaborated with the Germans and the Vichy government, and condemnations, with no eye to justice, were rampant. He had pleaded with the authorities for reason, but it was in vain. One judge he knew agreed with him, but he was told by his colleagues, "You are not to judge but to condemn." It was a sad state of affairs, one Eugène prayed would pass soon. The demarcation during the war had not been black or white, but gray. True, there were the cases like Ouradour, where Germans had murdered in cold blood. But he could never allow personal feelings to interfere with evaluating what was right or wrong. What he was seeing of late was mayhem.

"Come in," he said after a few seconds, removing his glasses. His hair was thinning, his eyesight was worse, and sometimes he felt old, even though he was only in his forties. The weight and pain of experience and sorrow had marked him as nothing else could.

"*Mon père,* you must come quickly." His aide, Father Jê-rome, looked agitated.

"What is it this time?" he asked, sighing.

"Another condemnation. A woman. She says she is from Ambazac and has begged to be allowed to see you. I believe it has something to do with your deceased brother."

"Very well. Where are they holding her?"

"In the street. They have shaved her head and are champing at the bit to carry out the sentence," the young priest remarked, disgusted. "I think we should be quick, *mon père,* or it will be too late."

They drove as fast as they could until they reached the spot where the savage retribution was taking place. Men and women, stripped of their dignity, were barely allowed to defend themselves before they were shot like rabbits. "It has gone too far," Eugène murmured as they left the car and elbowed their way through the shouting crowd.

"What is her name?" he asked.

"Françoise Dumont."

Eugène walked determinedly through the angry human mass until he reached the door of the house where the prisoners had been herded, to avoid being lynched on the spot.

"Who is in charge?" he demanded.

"I am." A small, beady-eyed fanatic in a beret came forward, his expression grim and satisfied.

"I have come to see a parishioner of mine, Françoise Dumont."

"She is sentenced to death. The executions will be carried out within the hour."

"Nevertheless, she is my parishioner and has the right to confession."

"She's already confessed." There were some laughs.

"You have seen fit to judge the living. But just as you have judged, God will judge you. One day you will pay for all this." Eugène waved an angry hand at the house.

The man shifted uncomfortably under Eugène's severe gaze. He was imposing, had authority and was a renowned figure in the community.

"Very well," he said reluctantly. "Pascal, get the woman, the one who was caught fucking the S.S. guard. Put her somewhere she can talk to her priest. She wants to cleanse her soul," he added with a snicker, for the crowd's benefit.

Eugène followed the man into the house. The hall was dark and dingy, reeking of sweat and fear. Several men and women stood huddled, some crying, others silent, faces haggard.

"This is she." The man gave a woman sitting crouched on the floor, a kick. "Get up, *putain.* Your priest is here. Take the chance and confess your sins. It's the last you'll get."

Eugène touched the woman's arm.

"You asked to see me, Françoise. I am here to help you."

Slowly she raised her fear-filled, anguished eyes, enormous now under her shorn head. Gently he helped her rise.

"Don't be long," the man muttered. "We've got another lot to deal with after this."

Eugène supported her into the next room where she collapsed onto a wooden chair. He sat next to her, holding her hand, afraid she would faint.

"What can I do for you, Françoise? I would try and get the sentence commuted but I fear there is little hope."

"*Mon père,* I have wanted to find you, to give you something…and to ask you something."

Eugène nodded, uncertain of what the young woman wanted.

"I met your brother-in-law, Sylvain de Rothberg, before his death. He asked me to give you this." Her hand quivering, Françoise dropped a Star of David into his palm. Eugène started with recognition. It was the necklace Sylvain had designed and worn always.

"*Mon enfant,* there are no words that could show you my thanks. And what is it you wished to ask me?"

"I have a son," she whispered. "His name is Armand. He is the son of your brother René. My parents are dead, and after this, no one will want him. He is a good boy."

He remembered the rumor about his brother, never doubting that she was telling the truth. Only a desperate mother would go to these lengths at such a time.

"I will do all I can for him, have no fear."

"Thank you, *mon père*. There is one other thing."

"Yes?"

"I would like to leave my son a letter. For later. I—something to tell him how much I loved him."

He nodded, took out the pen and notebook he always carried with him and laid it on the table.

Trembling, Françoise picked up the pen and wrote in a shaking hand, tears glistening as she signed her name with an effort. "Please. When he is eighteen. Not before. Please kiss him for me," she whispered, voice cracking.

"I will keep it in a sealed envelope in my safe. Do you wish to confess, my child?" He glanced at the door, hearing the crowd outside grow impatient.

She shook her head. "I have done what I had to do. If God wishes to forgive me, he will." She shrugged and closed her eyes.

"Come on in there," the man shouted through the door.

"We are coming," Eugène replied. "God bless you, *mon enfant*. I will try and talk to them, see what I can do," he whispered, helping her rise. But her eyes were glazed now, as though she barely heard him.

"I love him, you know. René would have loved him too…perhaps."

The door burst open and the man snatched her arm.

"*Allez, putain*, enough. It's time to meet your maker, like the other poor bastards you denounced," he said, pushing her forward.

Eugène made a last attempt to intercept him, but the crowd rushed in, flattening him against the wall as they dragged the victims into the jeering angry street. Shortly afterward a rattle of gunfire told him it was over. How long, he wondered, devastated, before France came to terms with the immeasurable schism bequeathed by the last four years of occupation? He took the forlorn note, folded it and placed it carefully in his pocket along with the necklace.

Back at the *évêché* he put the note in an envelope, melted a few drops of red wax and sealed it with his ring and the la

Vallière family crest. For a moment he hesitated, then he wrote in stark black letters:

Armand de la Vallière.

After the Allied landing in southern France, Dex and Salesman headed south to assist local *résistant* groups. House-to-house fighting was brutal and bloody, and Dex saved his skin and that of several others over and over. But one day, in the midst of one such fight, he was shot in the thigh, in the same vulnerable spot he'd been hit during the First World War.

"It's time we got you out of here," Salesman ordered.

"I'll be fine," Dex murmured, lying faint from loss of blood in a barn that had been converted into an aid station.

"No. You've done your share, Bogart. Don't bloody well push it too far."

He had little choice, for his condition worsened in the night, and he was barely conscious by the time he was carried onto an R.A.F. bomber and flown back to England.

Little by little, his leg and the strain of the past months began to heal. The war finally came to an end and he directed his energies toward the future, thinking of his children and Flora. There were other battles ahead before he fulfilled his dream and life with Flora finally began.

41

Skye, Scotland, 1946

Flora laid David lovingly back in his cot, where he gave a satisfied gurgle before sticking his thumb in his mouth and closing his eyes. That was one dealt with. She sighed, smiled and turned her attention to Nathalie, who had just woken. It was the nanny's day off and she had little time to do more than run from one baby to the other.

She lifted her tiny daughter tenderly, feeling the damp nappy, awed as always by this miracle of life. Motherhood had come to her as naturally as seeing spirits, and she thrived on the babies, lavishing her love and attention, caring for them, enjoying each moment spent with them.

Downstairs the phone rang and someone answered. It was probably Angus, calling to say what time he would be arriving from Edinburgh. His dedication to the children was touching, and his new attitude toward life amazing, as though the babies had given his existence meaning. For the first time, he and Flora enjoyed true complicity, sitting before the fire, the babies gurgling in their playpen. The only shadow marring her happiness was the knowledge that certain facts had to be faced, and that one day soon decisions would have to be made.

News of Sylvain's death had come as a shock. But when

Angus proposed that they continue assuming David as their own child, it had seemed right.

But Dex's last letter burned a hole in her pocket. Oh, how she loved him and wished everything was different. She dropped the wet nappy into a clothes basket. He seemed incapable of understanding how difficult all he was asking was. To simply leave Angus, pick up the babies and go with him to America was something she could barely conceive. Perhaps he wasn't aware of how much the children filled her existence, in a new and different way. She smiled down at her daughter, her heart torn, as Dex's bright blue eyes twinkled back at her.

And there was Angus. His whole life was focused on her and the children. He was determined to sort out his affairs and begin a new life. Did she have the right to put an end to that? To destroy the one chance he had?

Flora wiped the baby carefully, then dried and powdered her before slipping on the new nappy and pinning it adeptly. If only things could just go on as they were, she sighed.

She laid Nathalie back in her cot and glanced at David, quietly asleep. What right did she have to uproot them? Was love a good enough reason? She would always cherish Dex, yet she realized, with a shock, that he had no place in this new reality.

But I promised him, she argued, closing the door of the nursery gently before slipping upstairs to the dreamery and reading the letter one more time:

> At last we shall be together. There should be no difficulty about the divorce. I have made inquiries, and as far as the Church is concerned, the nonconsummation of the marriage should be grounds enough.

She let the pages drop to her lap and stared out the window. Did he believe that life was that simple? That the dream they'd shared before and during the war could exist in the world they lived in now? Surely he must realize it was impossible to put the children—and Angus—through such pain.

She looked out to sea, miserable, torn between duty and desire. After staring for a while at the waves crashing onto the

rocks below, she realized the only solution was to meet Dex
and discuss it. Perhaps he would see reason and realize that,
for now, leaving would be impossible.

Three weeks later, Flora entered the lounge of the North
British Hotel in Edinburgh, wearing the Chanel suit she'd
bought with Genny back in 1938 and hoping she would not be
recognized.

But before she had time to breathe, he was next to her, lifting
her fingers to his lips, mesmerizing her with his gaze, her heart
a turmoil of agony and joy. His mere presence was a cruel
temptation. He wore a dark navy suit, white shirt and striped
silk tie, handsome as always. A little older, perhaps, his hair a
little grayer, and there were thin lines around his mouth that
hadn't been there before the war. But he was as lithe and vital
as ever, as though he still had a world to conquer and not
enough time to do it.

"At last," he whispered, drawing her into his arms.

To her horror she realized he was about to kiss her, and she
stepped hastily back.

"Hello...Dex," she said, casting a rapid glance around the
lobby, thankfully empty except for an old gentleman with a
pug dog, engrossed in his paper, and two women, their heads
together, chatting over coffee. She sighed, relieved. The last
thing they needed was a scandal.

"Perhaps we should sit down," she suggested. "Over
there," she added, heading to the far corner of the inner lounge
close to the fire, where she sat down quickly with her back to
the foyer.

He frowned and sat next to her. "Is something wrong, Flo?
You seem nervous. Aren't you happy?" He leaned forward and
took her hand. She tried nervously to take it back. "I can't
believe we're finally together. Are you going to come away at
once or will you need a couple of weeks? I've made all the
arrangements," he said, leaning back, his eyes as blue as his
tie, his handsome, beloved face so close she longed to touch,
caress it. Oh, how could she resist? How could she make him

understand? And how could she live with the pain of not having him close to her, now that she'd finally found him?

"…and we'll sail at the end of the month to New York," he was saying, full of wild plans and projects. "You'll love it. Scott will love you. I can't wait to see Nathalie, hold her in my arms." He reached over and squeezed her hand. For a moment she closed her eyes, wanting so badly to let him whisk her off her feet.

"Dex, it's not quite as simple as you make it sound."

"Of course it is." He gave a low laugh that sent shivers down her spine. "I know you have qualms, honey, I understand, but they'll pass. You'll see, darling, it'll be wonderful, marvelous. You'll love Connecticut, the house in New York—"

"Darling, I don't think you understand. I can't just take the children and leave."

"Why on earth not?"

"For one thing, poor Sylvain is dead." She glanced at him hesitantly. "We—we've decided to go on pretending—that is, assuming—David as our own child. We love him so, and I know that is what Genny would have wanted. She came to me, you see, and I gave her my word."

"We?" he asked, eyes narrowing.

"That is, Angus and I…feel that it is the right thing to do," she said, flustered under his scrutiny.

"I see." She saw a facial muscle twitch. "You didn't see fit to consult me first?"

"How could I?"

"No. I suppose you couldn't." He smiled again, not letting go of her hand. "I have no problem with that. I'll bring him up as my own. I'll—"

"But you don't understand." Flora clasped his hand desperately. "They're not *things* that you can wrap up and take, they're children. I can't uproot them, leave Angus by himself, I—"

"Ah! Now we're getting to the crux of the matter. It's him this is all about, isn't it?" He drew away, anger glistening where before there'd been longing.

"No, of course not." She looked away, knowing she didn't sound convincing.

"Don't worry about Angus. I'll deal with him. If he causes any trouble, I'll call in the notes."

"Notes?" She frowned. "What notes?"

"The debt on Strathaird. I'm holding the notes. If he so much as squeaks, I'll bankrupt him."

"What are you talking about?" Flora gazed at him, horrified. "How could you dream of such a thing? And how did you get those notes in the first place? It's simply appalling!"

"No, it's not. It's life. He should have done a better job running MacLeod's."

"But you can't hurt Angus," she said in an anguished whisper.

"No? I will, if he gets in my way. I won't let you stay with him, Flo." His voice had become low and dangerous and she felt a sudden shudder as he gazed at her possessively.

"Stop it," she exclaimed. "I refuse to be coerced, by you or anybody. It's not fair."

"But you promised. You said—"

"How could I have guessed then that I would have two babies to love and care for? Oh, can't you understand, Dex, dear? See beyond yourself?"

"You mean you don't want to come with me?" he asked, amazed.

"I—oh dearest, dearest, I want to so badly it hurts. I love you so dearly, but how can I? Strathaird and the babies and— well, it's my whole life you're asking me to leave!"

"You'd rather stay with him."

"No! That has nothing to do with it. I have commitments, obligations. Life isn't just what we want, when we want it."

"Why are you so worried about him?" he asked, eyes alive with jealousy.

She looked down and sighed before answering. "Because he loves the children. They've changed his life."

"How touching. And just where does that leave me?" he asked, mouth tight with anger.

She looked away, unable to answer.

"I see." He leaned back into the red velvet cushions and stared at her, face hardening. "I can't believe it, Flo. That you could do this to *us*. Now, after all this time, all these years of waiting and wanting you—my God! I swear if you don't come to me I'll ruin him."

"Are you blackmailing me?" she asked, shocked.

"No! Of course not. But I can't live without you. I love you, you're mine and so are the babies. I'll pay whatever price."

"I'm not a chattel and neither are the children," she responded, trembling. "How can you speak to me like this?"

"Because I love you. And I'm warning you. If you don't come with me, I'll ruin him."

"Too bad. Ruin him. You'll be ruining me and the children too."

"I'll claim paternity. I'll go to court and prove that Nathalie's mine, I'll—"

"Will you stop talking rubbish?" she exclaimed angrily. "I can't believe this is the same man I loved. If you so much as attempt to hurt Angus or the children, I will never see you again, *ever*. And as for claiming paternity, I'll deny every word, in court or anywhere else. You have no right to do this."

"My God, that's rich," he exclaimed, his voice rising.

"Hush, we're in public. Please, Dex, don't be so difficult," she pleaded, anger diminishing. He was childlike in his anguish. It was so like him to breeze in and think he could take over. "Please be patient, and let some time go by," she pleaded, reaching for his hand. "You'll realize I'm right."

"No, I won't." He stared coldly at her. "I spent half the damn war dreaming of this moment. I kept myself alive for the time I'd take you in my arms and we'd begin a new life together. And I was fool enough to think that was your dream, too. My mistake."

"Of course I want that, too!" she wailed. "But don't you see that I can't? We're not alone in the world, Dex."

"I'm not going to argue. I'll give you two weeks to make your mind up, Flo. Perhaps *you'll* think differently in a few days. It would be far more damaging for Angus to be ruined financially than to lose you to me. Believe me. I would make certain of that.''

She shook her head, bewildered, and rose. ''You don't even sound like yourself. You have no right to do this.''

''I have every right and you know it. You're mine, Flo, and so is my child,'' he said, towering above her now, eyes blazing.

''As long as you continue thinking in this selfish manner, you have no right to anything, Dexter. I love you. I'll always love you, but I'm not destroying the world around me to satisfy your ego.''

''*My* ego?'' He gave a harsh laugh. ''I love you. That's the only reason I'm determined to make you see clearly. And you love me. You're just blinded by that whining piece of—''

''*Don't.* Stop it, before you say something we'll both regret forever.''

''I'm warning you, Flo.''

''I will not be threatened, Dex, and neither will my children. If that's the kind of man you are, then I'm glad I found out now, for they deserve better. Goodbye.''

She turned on her heel, trembling, and rushed through the hall of the hotel, tears blinding her as she stepped onto the pavement. How could he act like this?

''A cab, madam?'' the doorman asked.

''Please.'' She nodded, trying to hide her anguish, praying he wouldn't follow her, her heart in shreds as the taxi drove up to the curb.

For one moment, as she opened the door she hesitated, wanting desperately to turn back, rush into his arms and let him have his way.

But she couldn't.

As the cab drove down Prince's Street she saw him standing on the pavement, a tall solitary figure, fists clenched and gaze bitter. She turned away, her heart bleeding and soul shattered, the sacrifice almost too much to bear, knowing she would love him forever.

42

Lassuade, Scotland, 1947

Angus waited nervously for the car to draw up in front of the old Victorian house that was his office and had been his father's before him. It was grimy from coal and soot, standing among the pits and miners' dwellings, its only claim to beauty the rose garden at the front that brightened it.

Today Dexter Ward was coming to visit the pits. They had been trying to arrange the visit for some time. There was even talk of an exclusive partnership between Harcourt's and MacLeod's. Angus hoped that might be possible. He liked Ward, knew he was a much better businessman than Angus himself, and hoped the visit would be a success.

At the sound of the approaching vehicle, he stepped into the hall and straightened his tie, determined to make a good impression. He hadn't told Flora. It would be a wonderful surprise if things worked out, and if they didn't, then so be it. He'd find another way of sorting things out, without worrying her to no purpose.

Dexter Ward stepped out of the Rolls and glanced about the familiar surroundings. How often he'd come here as a child with his father and gone down into the pits, although he didn't like being underground. He saw Angus open the door and come out onto the step with a welcoming smile. Dex walked up the path, still bothered by the slight limp that would probably remain for life. They shook hands, then stepped inside.

Angus looked well. Too damn healthy. Well, that wouldn't last, not after he'd brought the ax down as he planned to later in the meeting. Let him believe for a while that Dexter Ward was his savior, that his problems were at an end and that happily-ever-after was the name of the game. It would make the fall harder.

"Would you like to visit the pits first?" Angus asked.

"Why not?" He smiled broadly and followed his host across the road to the entrance of the collieries, where they were handed helmets before climbing into the lift that would take them underground.

It was a strange sensation to be back among the grime-covered faces, the smell of coal as familiar to him as his own name. As the lift came to a halt, the miner secured the lever and the door opened.

"This way, please." Angus went ahead and he followed down the dark, low corridors hewed inside the earth, alongside the trolleys that carried the coal on rails to the entrance. There it was hauled up to ground level, then transported to several parts of Europe.

An old miner named Beatty accompanied them, and Angus explained what they were seeing, describing the different stages of how the coal was processed. It was stuff Dex knew by heart and he could have taught Angus a thing or two, but he patiently followed in his twin's footsteps until they reached the ledge that opened up onto the old mine, which reached down several hundred feet.

A railing had been erected to avoid accidents, but it still looked dangerous from where he stood. He'd never liked coming here; the place had always given him the creeps, as it did now.

At a discreet signal from Angus, Beatty moved away and the two men gazed at the shaft below.

"This was the first mine. The rest are all additions that came later, about the beginning of the century. My father was very innovative," Angus remarked, stretching his hand out and touching one of the metal crossbeams that supported the structure. "All our support is in metal. Before, it used to be wood and caused far too many accidents. This is still fairly modern. Of course, they've nationalized most of the coal now, but I'm still negotiating with the government."

"Then why would you want me on board?" Dex asked curiously. "If you're cutting a deal with the government, you don't need a partner."

"Well, that's the thing, you see." Angus shifted uncomfortably. "Unfortunately, there's rather a lot of debt to contend with."

"Find a good bank to back you. You must have collateral."

"There again, things are somewhat tricky."

"You mean you've blown the lot?"

The words rang harsh and hard, echoing in the dark silence. Angus's head shot up as though slapped in the face.

"I—"

"You've done what you've always done, you coward, and allowed the company and everything else you own to go down the drain."

"I don't understand, I—" Angus paled, breathless all of a sudden. There was something hauntingly dangerous and familiar about the man next to him, something that brought back distant memories. He shivered, trying to pull himself together. "I'm afraid I don't understand why you're taking this attitude."

"Because it's true." Dex leaned against the parapet and studied him, enjoying the trapped-rabbit expression on his brother's face. He relished each second, each horror-stricken gasp, each panicked blink.

"I'm not interested in your coal but in your wife, MacLeod. You hadn't guessed? Well, they say the husband is always the last to know. Nathalie? She's my daughter. And I plan to have them all living under my roof and my protection."

"This is outrageous, scandalous," Angus whispered, reaching for the railing in shock.

"But true." Dex never took his eyes from his face. "You never thought I'd come back to haunt you, did you?" he whis-

pered, seeing his brother go ashen. "You never had the insight
to perceive that it was I, in the guise of another. No, I didn't
die where you left me, Angus, and now I'm back to take what's
mine. Every last little piece of it."

"Gavin." The name echoed, hurtled, reverberated.

"Yes. It's me." He moved closer until his face was only
inches away. "I'm going to make you go through hell and
back, just as you made me. Oh, don't give me that crap about
shell shock." He raised a hand as Angus tried to speak, his
eyes pleading and cheeks gray. "We both know it was a good
story. But not good enough. I'm here to stay, brother."

"Why? Why didn't you return until now?" he whispered.

"Because it wasn't the right moment." He glanced down
the corridor to make sure Beatty wasn't coming. "Now it is
right. Now you're up against the wall, with nowhere to run,
just like I was in that trench. There's no one to help you,
Angus, no one to give you a helping hand. You're going to
sink in the mud, just like I did, and you'll have to drag yourself
out of it by yourself. Except," he added, pulling back, "you
never will. You'll writhe and squirm a little and then you'll let
it suck you in."

"Please, if it really is you, Gavin, then listen. I beg of
you—"

"*You* listen," he interrupted icily. "I hold the notes to every
debt you ever acquired. I own you, your wife, your children
who aren't even sired by you. Flora is mine. You weren't even
man enough to fuck your own wife," he threw out, disgusted.
"If you're lucky, I'll leave you enough to eat with and a place
to live. Now come on. I'm going up. I hate it down here."

He turned and saw Beatty coming toward them, then plastered the smile he'd worn earlier back on his face. "Most interesting," he murmured, heading back down the tunnel. Beatty
followed him.

"Careful of your head, sir, there's a low ledge there."

"Thanks."

A loud crash made them turn suddenly and look back. There
was no sign of Angus.

"Good God!" Beatty rushed back toward the ledge and Dex

followed, suddenly gripped by fear. They reached the railing and leaned over but it was too dark to see. There was no sign of Angus anywhere.

"His Lordship's fallen," Beatty cried, shouting for help. Soon others came running, heads lowered against the ledge.

"Fetch the ropes," the foreman shouted as the men squinted into the hole that loomed, deep and hollow, below.

Dex stood back and loosened his tie, trembling. Had he caused this to happen? Had he pushed his brother to do this? This wasn't how it was meant to play out. He pulled the strings, not Angus. He'd intended to ruin him, to cause every unhappiness he could, but this... He found a cigarette but stopped before lighting it, knowing he couldn't down here, and gasped for air. It was too late. He'd pulled the plug and the water had run out, and now he was left dry.

Part Four

1962–1998

A double blessing is a double grace.

—William Shakespeare
Hamlet

43

Limoges, France, 1962

As always, Flora felt sad on the anniversary of Angus's death. She was glad she wasn't at Strathaird, where she would inevitably wander down to the graveyard. It was so strange that, like Gavin, his body had never been found. The pit he had fallen into had proven too deep and narrow to enter. Now both brothers' names were engraved on the old granite headstone, under which neither of them lay.

After the accident, she'd been certain Dex had something to do with his death, but witnessing his utter desolation and distress had finally convinced her. As if to prove his remorse to her, he had destroyed the notes he held against Angus, returning Strathaird to her name.

They were married at La Renardière in an informal service with their closest friends and family. Eugène, although he'd never seemed very thrilled at the thought of her marrying Dexter, had conducted the service. After fifteen years, she still wondered about Eugène's reservations. Both their cousins were dead and Dexter was a close friend, but still there was an odd feeling she was unable to explain.

It was cooler now. July afternoons could be sweltering, even out here on the terrace. She got up from the wicker chair, plumped the colorful striped cushions and picked up the basket she'd placed on the balustrade earlier. A walk in the garden before evening would do her good, and the house needed fresh flowers.

She ambled down the shallow stone steps to the flower beds, laid out years before by Tilly Harcourt. The children would be back in half an hour or so from their tennis match, she thought, eyeing a hortensia, then deciding it looked too lovely where it was and opting for the lilac bush next to it. Scott was so good with the little ones. She shook her head at herself. Little ones, indeed. The twins—as even she thought of them—had turned eighteen last month. In the autumn David would be going to university and Nathalie to finishing school in Switzerland. Scott was grown up and had a master's degree in political science, much to Dex's regret. But, as she'd pointed out, you couldn't expect your children to be exactly what you wanted. They had their own lives to lead. Scott was a sensitive, intelligent, warm human being who loved causes, not porcelain, and seemed to have inherited his mother's intellectual bent. David, on the other hand, who had neither of their blood, was fascinated by the porcelain business, thrilled to be spending the summer working at the factory.

Life had smiled on them over the past few years, and at sixty-one she was happy and content. Dex had opened up a new world to her, taking her places, showing her things she never would have known had he not come into her life. When she thought of Gavin, it was as a beautiful yet poignant memory, part of youth now left behind. For Angus she carried a latent sadness. And even now, there were moments—very occasionally, when she was particularly cross with Dex—that she wondered. Had he really had nothing to do with Angus's death? She'd learned over the years how formidable he could be.

Stretching across the dahlias, she snipped a rosebud and slipped it into the basket, careful not to prick her finger with its sharp thorns. Now that he was older, he was mellower than the man she'd first met at Genny's wedding in 1938, but the vitality, that power and energy, still remained.

Her basket was almost full as she headed back to the sprawling, fantastical pile John Harcourt had built. There was a man she regretted not having met. Over the years, Flora made certain that pictures of Alix and the Harcourts graced the piano and the shelves, encouraging Scott to ask about his mother and grandparents and sharing the memories with the other children. She wished she could do the same for David, knowing it was impossible.

She and Dex had discussed the matter before the twins' eighteenth birthday, when they'd decided to give him Sylvain's watch. Should they tell him who he really was?

"They've got enough to cope with as it is," Dex pointed out. "The boy already has one stepfather to deal with. He believes Angus was his father. I know he considers me his dad, but I think it would be crazy to confuse him even more. And there's Natty to think about, too. It would shatter her world to pieces if she thought David wasn't really her twin. You know how sensitive she is."

It was true. Nathalie was the sweetest, kindest, most loving child she'd ever dreamed of and the apple of Dex's eye. He spoiled her rotten, of course, but Natty was a being that no amount of spoiling could ruin. She appreciated each gesture, cherished each gift, each tiny detail. Flora was thankful she was outgrowing the asthma she'd been prone to as a child. Flora couldn't imagine where she'd gotten that from; the only person she remembered having it in his youth was Gavin, but that, of course, could have nothing whatsoever to do with the matter.

She went to the pantry and put the flowers in water in the sink before wiping her hands and going upstairs. Bill Hunter, Scott's best friend from Princeton, was staying with them, and the children were having friends over for dinner tonight. Julie, the cook, was preparing an American-style barbecue. She was wondering, as she changed her dress, about the obvious attraction that Natty and Bill seemed to be developing, when the door opened.

"Hi, darling." Dex came across the room, dropped a tender kiss on her neck and stared over her gray head into the mirror, smiling. If anything, age had enhanced him. His hair was thick and gray, his eyes still as sharp and blue as ever, and he got up every morning to play several sets of tennis with the boys, keeping them on their toes. She sighed, slipped a hand up to her shoulder and touched his fingers tenderly.

"I was thinking about Natty."

"Oh?" He frowned. "What about her? She's not sick again?"

"Oh no, nothing like that. But have you noticed how she and Bill seem to be getting along?"

He straightened, and pulled off his tie with a grimace. "It's too darned hot for a tie these days. Whoever invented the damn things was a lunatic. No, actually, I hadn't paid attention. But what's wrong with that? He's a fine young man from a good family. You know I'd love to keep her locked up in a glass bottle for the rest of her life, but that's not about to happen—not with her looks and nature. It'll be a lucky man who marries our daughter, Flo, and Bill's not a bad candidate."

"Dex! That's ridiculous. She's barely eighteen. I wasn't thinking on those lines. I was merely remarking on the attraction between them, that's all. Plus, he's a lot older than she is. I think perhaps that's what's worrying me."

"He's only twenty-four. That's a healthy age difference. I'd rather have Natty be with a boy like Bill than hanging around beatniks. Be thankful she's attracted to someone respectable, and a friend of the family."

"I give up." Flora smiled, laid down the brush and spun the stool, watching him undress, his strong muscular body as attractive as ever. How unfair it was that men got riper with age and women withered, she reflected. He could probably find himself a twenty-year-old if he wanted, with that physique. She went over and hugged him. "I love you, you know. You're the handsomest man I've ever met, and the worst part is you know it."

He pulled in his tummy, arched an eyebrow then dropped a fond kiss on her lips. "I have the loveliest wife in Christendom, so we're even. What time's the barbecue?" he asked, a sudden gleam in his eye, his hands wandering down her back hopefully.

"In half an hour."

"Shucks."

"Another time, perhaps," she said, taking his face in her hands and kissing him full on the lips. "We need your services out there, so don't be long. Julie's got everything under control in the kitchen."

"Can't even make love to my own wife," he grumbled as she headed, laughing, to the door. "I'll be downstairs in ten."

From the noise outside, she could tell the children were back, and took a peek onto the terrace. Scott was organizing the food with Julie, David had three girls drooling over him, and Nathalie and Bill were on the swing under the arbor, in earnest conversation. She sighed, watching her daughter. It wasn't surprising Bill was enchanted with her, for Nathalie was perfectly lovely. Long, silky chestnut hair that flowed over her soft, tanned shoulders contrasted with the white of her tennis dress. Her father's bright blue eyes were as misty as Flora's own, and her long brown legs never seemed to end. What young man wouldn't be mesmerized by her, she recognized. Bill wasn't bad himself. Tall, well-built and athletic, with a pair of laughing brown eyes and hair that reminded her of Gavin's.

How young they were, how full of life. She drew away from the French door, reminded of Sylvain and Genny, wondering what they would have thought of their son. David was so like Sylvain it hurt. Yet those were Genny's eyes laughing mischievously at the coquettish blonde who was reaching up to straighten his collar. Gosh, how pushy these girls were. She would never have dreamed of doing anything of that nature in her day.

"Jealous?" Dex slipped up behind her, amused to see her disapproval. "Do I take it one of your chickens is being attacked by a member of the opposite sex, my love?"

"Don't be silly." She leaned her back against his chest. "I just wish this could go on forever, that I could wave a wand and make it all stay exactly as it is. Soon they'll be bringing someone home, getting engaged and married." She gave a tiny shrug. "It's selfish, I know, but I love them so."

"Stop worrying, we've a long time ahead before that happens."

"Really? Take a look at your daughter," she said tartly, nodding at the window. "I'm beginning to think you're right, and that Bill and she are more serious than even I believed."

Dex moved to the window, watched as Bill took Natty's hand in his and felt a sudden pang of jealousy. "Hmm. Maybe we'd better keep our eyes open. I'll have a word with Scott later—it's better to be on the safe side."

"I thought *I* was the worrier."

"Bill's a nice guy, but she's still my baby."

"Why am I not surprised," Flora murmured, taking his arm and ignoring the dark look he sent her. "Come on. You can help David entertain the girls," she added, laughing.

By midsummer Nathalie and Bill were inseparable, David was dating a Danish au pair girl, whom Flora found in his bed one morning when she entered the room early by mistake, while Scott sought safety in numbers, filling his new M.G. with Limoges' loveliest debutantes.

"I didn't have a clue what to say," Flora exclaimed, embarrassed, as Dex roared with laughter. "I mean, what does one say in a situation like that? Good morning, do you take tea or coffee? I mean, really, Dex, David should know better."

"Remember Sylvain, dear. There was a never-ending trail of women in and about that apartment before he fell for Genny. I figure David will be exactly the same. When we least expect it, he'll fall head over heels, just like I did for you."

Flora sighed, passed him the coffee and agreed. "You're probably right. Have you seen Natty today? She's supposed to be going with me to the American women's flower association, something Renée d'Albis came up with."

"I doubt you'll be seeing Nathalie for the rest of the day. She's gone sight-seeing with Bill and that young man with his hair around his collar, who thinks he's going to save the world. You know, Scott really picks up some weird friends," he said, lowering the paper. "They're not exactly the kind of people I can talk to."

"I thought you liked talking to Bill."

"When does anyone get to talk to Bill lately? He's as smitten with Natty as I was with you, Beautiful."

"Well, I'd better go to Renée's do with or without Natty. What are you up to today?"

"Oh, the usual. Factory in the morning, a round of golf with His Eminence in the afternoon. You know, I still can't believe Eugène made it to cardinal. Not that he lets me forget it," he added with a touch of bitterness. Flora frowned. It was several years since she'd seen him look at all bitter. They rarely mentioned the war, having agreed to remember Genny and Sylvain as the lovely exuberant couple they'd known, and not perpetuate the pain that had followed, as much for the children's sakes as their own. They couldn't live in the past and build their future.

They kissed, and Dex watched her go to her Jaguar. She was as lovely in his eyes as ever. God, he was lucky. The perfect wife, the perfect family. After all that suffering, life had finally given him a chance at true happiness. He even forgot Gavin, except when Eugène reminded him. Angus's death at times tormented his dreams, but he'd learned to live with it, to compartmentalize and let go of the past, instead moving on with his life.

The screech of wheels on the gravel made him take his glasses off and peer through the window. He got up as Natty jumped out of her Mini and came running into the house, hair flying, tears pouring down her cheeks.

"What on earth's the matter, baby?" he asked, disconcerted.

"Nothing," she sobbed, then rushed past him up the stairs and slammed the door to her room. He stood helplessly in the hall, gazing up the stairs and wondering what to do, wishing Flora were home. Should he go up? Leave her be? Girls weren't simple, he'd discovered.

Moments later, another vehicle pulled up and Bill came in, running an agitated hand through his hair. "Is she okay?" he asked anxiously, passing a hand over his mouth.

"What's going on?" Dex asked, frowning. Something was obviously very amiss between these two. "Why don't you come into the study, son?"

Bill hesitated, then nodded and followed him across the hall to the study, which was as untidy and chaotic now as it always had been.

"Sit down and tell me what's going on. It's early, but do you want a drink?"

"No. Thanks." He dropped onto the sofa and stared at the carpet. "It's all my fault, sir. I—gee, I'd do anything for this not to be happening."

"Shoot."

"I don't know where to start. It's this girl back home in Connecticut. We—well, she and I were dating back in the spring. Then in June she came to Princeton for one weekend and…well…"

"You slept with her."

"That's right. I guess it was wrong, but she wanted to stay with me and—"

"Look, I'm not your confessor. We've all had our affairs in our time, and I understand. But don't tell me you went and told Natty? Women can be darn sensitive about these things."

"If it were just that." Bill swallowed and clasped his hands. "Sir, I love your daughter. I didn't think things like this could happen. I mean, I've known Natty several years. She's my best friend's sister, and then all of a sudden it was as if I'd never seen her before. I've never known a girl like her. She's beautiful, sensitive, intelligent."

"Give it some time. She'll come around."

"I'm afraid that won't be possible."

"Why not?" Dex leaned back, threw his leg over the other knee and listened sympathetically.

"Because Cheryll's pregnant."

"Cheryll?"

"The girl I told you about. She's almost two months pregnant and she say I'm the father. I'm going to have to marry her," he ended, voice cracking.

"How do you know you're the father?" Dex inquired, eyes narrowed.

"Because she was a virgin," he said, closing his eyes for an instant before taking a deep breath. "I have to do the right thing, sir. I—well, I had to tell Natty why I have to leave. If I hadn't told her now, she'd have found out sooner or later. I didn't want her to think it was anything to do with her. Quite the opposite. I'd do anything to change things," he finished in an anguished whisper.

There was not much to say. "I'm sorry, son. Really sorry. I was beginning to think we might see you as part of the family."

"I—I was thinking of waiting until she'd finished school in Switzerland before asking you, sir. The truth is, I love her and…God, what a mess."

"There's no way out?"

"No. She's told her parents and I've told her I'll do the right thing. I just wish Natty didn't have to suffer because of a mistake I made."

"So do I. But that's life. Sooner or later we all get hurt, one way or another," he answered, biting back the anger and staying reasonable, despite his pain for Natty. "You'll always be welcome here, Bill."

"Thank you, sir." They rose and shook hands, two men who understood values and the need to abide by them.

Leaving Bill, Dex went upstairs and knocked on the door of Natty's room, but there was no answer. He opened it tentatively, wanting to fold her in his arms, to kiss away the pain and make everything all right, the way he used to when she was little. But there was no sign of her. The bed was made and the room in perfect order. He hadn't seen her go out, but she might have slipped out the back door. Maybe she needed time alone.

He went downstairs and checked the garage. Her bicycle was gone. Maybe the ride would do her good, poor baby. It was hard to see his child's heart breaking for the first time. He frowned, blotting out the blond, green-eyed image that flashed through his mind, and went back into the study, deciding to wait around, see Bill off and be here when Nathalie returned.

An hour passed. Scott popped his head in, then went sadly upstairs to help his friend pack. It was too bad this had happened; Bill would have been the perfect addition to the family.

By one o'clock, Nathalie still hadn't returned and Dex began to worry. Perhaps he should take a spin in the car, see if she was on the road someplace, and bring her home.

David came down the stairs just as Dex was walking out the front door. "Have you seen Natty?" he asked.

"No. Not since she and Bill left this morning. Is something wrong, Dad?" He ran down the last few steps.

"Come with me. I'll explain on the way." David would be the best person to help her. They really were like twins, these two, sharing everything.

"I'll drive, Dad." He threw the boy the keys and got into the passenger's seat of the Alfa Romeo. "What happened?" David turned on the ignition and shifted gears.

"It's Bill and her. There's a problem. Bill's knocked some girl up back home and now he has to marry her. He found out last night. He's pretty cut up, and Natty was crying her eyes out last time I saw her. What a damn mess," he exclaimed, genuinely worried that there was no sign of her.

"That's terrible," David said, shocked. He drove slowly, turning left onto the Route de Toulouse, both of them scouring the road for a glimpse of her. After several minutes of driving they headed down a lane where she liked to bike, relieved to see a solitary figure pedaling fifty feet ahead.

Stopping alongside her, Dex jumped out of the car. "Baby, put the bike in the car and come home."

She slowed the bike, steadied her feet on the ground and nodded silently. Her eyes were red and her face tear-stained, and at that moment Dex hated Cheryll for ruining Bill and Natty's possible happiness. He went to her and helped her with the bike, while David got out and slipped his arm around her.

"I'm sorry, Nata." He hugged her close, using the nickname he'd called her when they were children. "It'll all work out, you'll see. Maybe when he gets home they'll figure something out and it'll be okay." He helped her into the back of the car, while Dex closed the trunk with the bicycle protruding.

In five minutes they were home. Dex held her close as they walked up the steps and into the house. "Come and sit with me in the sitting room," he said, stroking her hair, wishing she'd say something and get it out, instead of holding it all inside. He pulled her next to him onto the sofa while David went to fetch a jug of lemonade.

"Whatever happens, this summer will always be a beautiful memory for both of you," he said softly, gently stroking her hair, hurting for them as he'd never believed he could hurt again. "You'll see. You'll get over it. In two months you won't remember him except as the way you used to, as Scott's best friend."

"No, Daddy, you don't understand," she exclaimed suddenly, clutching his sleeve, her eyes wild. "I've always loved him. Ever since he came home with Scott the first time. All I've ever lived for were the summers here and...and... se-seeing him again. And now he *really* saw me for the f-first time and I thought...I thought he really loved me, too and—"

"He does love you, baby. But this is bigger than him. Let him go home and see if he can figure something out. It's a tough one, though, and he's a gentleman. Don't, baby," Dex begged as the tears poured once more and he drew her into his arms, letting her cry into his shoulder. "There, there, my darling, don't worry." He wanted to say, *Daddy will sort it out;* instead, he rocked her, eyes closed, as she sobbed.

Then all at once he felt her body stiffen, caught the sudden gasp and pulled away, horrified.

"Natty? Natty!" She was wheezing, eyes panicked and he clutched her, terrified. "My God. David," he shouted, unable to move her as she fought for breath. "She's having an asthma attack."

The door flew open and David rushed in, followed by Scott and Bill.

"What on earth? My God!"

"Get her medication," Dex shouted to David, while Scott rushed to the phone and dialed emergency.

He shook her, then forced breath into her mouth, but as David raced back with the medication she slumped in his arms. They placed the inhaler rapidly into her mouth and pumped her body, willing her to breathe.

He knew at once when it was over, the familiar aura of death clawing like an unseen shadow as he propelled air into her silent lungs. Folding her in his arms and rocking her as he'd always rocked her, he was oblivious to the boys and to Flora, who'd entered the room and stood trembling several feet away. His Natty, his beautiful baby girl, the child born of love and hope. He gazed into her childlike face, serene and innocent, still unwilling to believe. Not another, dear God, not his own beloved angel. Anything rather than this.

David knelt and took his twin from Dex's arms, still trying to revive her, refusing to face the truth, while Bill wept by the window. Scott held his mother as she moved, dazed, toward them.

When he became aware of her presence, he read the anguish, the tragedy written once more in those beloved eyes. Where was God at a time like this? God was a joke, never there when they needed him, an absentee referee who blew his whistle relentlessly. Where was God when Genny and all the other poor souls at Ouradour had been cruelly murdered? When Sylvain was shot, or when he'd tried to find Greta, only to learn years later the monster lying dead by Dex's hand was his son? Where? He screamed silently, holding his daughter's head to his heart. How much did it take? What was the final price he had to pay? Would God be satisfied, now that he'd stripped him of his most precious treasure?

The ambulance arrived. Looking into Natty's face one last time, he kissed her forehead tenderly. "Forgive me, my love," Dex whispered, tears flowing as they lifted her body from his arms and Flora stroked her face, hands trembling.

"Don't let them do an autopsy," she whispered. "I couldn't bear it."

They carried her out, David walking next to her, weeping silently.

"It's over," Dex murmured. Flora reached for his hand, clutching it. "She was born of such intense love. Why, Flo? Why?" He glanced at her, pale and silent next to him. "Why her? An innocent, the consequence of an act of love so great—" His voice broke and he stared into the empty fireplace. "Where is God?" he asked bitterly. "Where is he hiding when we need him most?"

"I don't know," she whispered. "I wish, oh, how I wish I did. Oh, Natty." She sobbed silently. With an effort, he moved to her and held her, exhausted, drained, unable to see anything but Natty lying dead in his arms. There was no escaping the death and devastation that followed him, no reprieve, he realized, now or ever.

44

London, England, 1987

Bradley Harcourt Ward was a man who'd learned to be independent and assume responsibility early in life. When no one was at Heathrow to meet him in international arrivals, he shrugged, lifted his Vuitton garment bag from the trolley and headed to the tube station.

He got off at Sloane Square and walked the rest of the way to his grandfather's apartment, glad of the exercise.

London in summertime was hot and clammy but he was happy to be here. He'd graduated from Yale a month earlier and was ready now to get his teeth into the real world. Not that he wasn't familiar with Harcourt's dealings. He'd spent the better part of his childhood, since his mother's death from cancer when he was five, with his grandfather, Dex, who'd seen to that. He was very close to his grandparents, who had cared for him when his father, Scott's, career as a political activist took him away.

He turned the corner on Eaton Square, wondering who would be at the flat. Colin, Uncle David and Aunt Penn's son, was at summer camp in Vermont, that much he knew, but God only knew where their daughter, Charlotte, was. Last time he'd seen her was two years earlier, when the entire family had assembled at the chalet in Gstaad for Christmas.

He turned into Chester Square, past St. Michael's Church and the gardens, and mounted the steps of the building, hoping someone would be home. He'd forgotten the key in New York. Oh well, he resolved, he could always ring his uncle. He pressed the buzzer and waited.

"Who is it?" a young female voice inquired.

"Bradley Ward."

"Brad? I'll open up."

He arched an eyebrow, wondering who it was. The voice sounded too old to be Charlotte's; then again, she must be seventeen now. He felt suddenly guilty that he hadn't paid much attention to his cousins these past two years, but with studies, trips, helping Uncle David in New York and keeping up with Dex—as his grandfather preferred to be called—he'd had very little time. He imagined her coming down in the elevator, a skinny little thing with red hair and braces.

Brad was a patient man and he waited calmly. If it *was* Charlotte, she'd probably mislaid the keys or tripped on the carpet on the way out. She was, as his grandmother liked to term it, "spontaneous."

The door opened, and for a moment Brad wondered if he needed his eyesight checked. Before him stood a tall, slim, titian-haired beauty that had nothing whatsoever to do with the Charlotte he remembered.

"What on earth happened to you?" he asked as she flung her arms around his neck, making him stagger. "Whoa, wait a minute, we'll fall down the steps."

"I *do* look different, don't I? It's so great to see you, cuz." She stepped back, cast him a brilliant smile that to his dismay sent a red-hot poker jab of lust shooting through him.

"That's an understatement. *Metamorphosis* would be more appropriate," he murmured, following her into the narrow main hall.

"Grandpa's arriving next week, Mum went back to Skye yesterday because Granny wasn't feeling well, and Daddy's at their flat." They squeezed into the old-fashioned elevator. Brad reeled as a whiff of Diorissimo and a brilliant, bright-eyed smile sent another shaft of desire to every part of his body. By the time they reached the third floor, he was breathless.

"Mum said to ask if you mind sleeping in the blue room,

because Grandpa left all his golf gear in yours and she didn't have time to clear the cupboard." She twirled, her tiny white T-shirt barely reaching her belly, a pair of tight stonewashed jeans lying on her perfect hips, revealing a neat waist.

"That's fine. I'll sleep anywhere."

"Really?" She arched a mischievous eyebrow, leaving him floored. He followed her to the bedroom, studying her feminine walk, the mass of hair falling down her back. Her butt was the cutest thing he'd seen in ages, and her legs, well, her legs were never-ending. He stopped himself abruptly. This was *Charlotte,* his baby cousin, he was staring at. The thought was sobering. He must get an immediate grip on himself.

He laid the garment bag on the blue brocade bedcover, then took off his blazer and hung it in the closet before pulling his passport and some loose change from the pocket. Plunking it on the bed table next to the lamp, he gave himself time to regroup.

"So. What brings you to London, brat?" he asked, pulling the curtain and switching on the light.

"I've decided to be a model. What do you think?" She twirled like a ballet dancer and he noted she wasn't wearing a bra.

"Not bad. You're tall enough. A bit scraggy in the arms, perhaps, but I suppose that's good if you plan to do pictures." He studied her critically for a moment.

"Scraggy?" Charlotte exclaimed, eyes blazing, "I'm not scraggy!"

"Okay, skinny then." What amazing eyes she had. How come he'd never noticed their color before? A violet hue he didn't think he remembered seeing before.

"Don't be beastly, Brad. The director says I have the perfect figure and that I'll be a hit."

He was inclined to agree but shrugged instead. "Could be right, I guess. Got anything to drink around? Coke?"

"There's a bottle of champagne chilling in the fridge," she said with an injured sniff. "Not that you deserve it," she remarked darkly, more the little girl he remembered.

"Don't get into a huff, Charlie," he teased, determined to get her back into perspective. "We can't all drool over you."

"Gosh, you're horrid," she said over her shoulder, heading

for the kitchen. "God help your girlfriend." She turned on the light and went to the fridge while Brad opened the cupboard and took out two flutes.

"Any cashews?"

"Yup, second shelf to your right. Mum bought them especially for you. So, *do* you have a girlfriend?" she asked, her manner conversational, exchanging the flutes for the bottle and waiting with them extended while he unwrapped the foil then popped the cork silently.

"Should you be drinking?" He squinted at her doubtfully. "Are you sure Uncle David would allow this?"

"Do stop being such a twerp." She scowled as the champagne frothed. "I'm not a baby any longer, I'm a grown woman."

"No kidding," he murmured, watching, amused, as she flounced into the drawing room, flopped onto the deep yellow cushioned couch and flung her legs onto the ottoman. He followed her, startled at the picture she created, the Waterford vase of fresh lilies forming the perfect backdrop for her heart-shaped face and titian mane. He raised his glass. "To your future career."

"Thanks. I really am going to model, you know, I'm not just kidding. In fact—" she took a long sip, smiled like a Cheshire cat "—I've just got a job."

"Congratulations. Who with?"

"Peter Rogers."

He nearly choked as she pronounced the name of erotica's most renowned photographer. "You have to be kidding."

"No, I'm not," she answered, unaware of his reaction. "I went to his studio today and we took several pictures, and he said that—"

"I don't give a flying fuck what he said. You're not going back there, Charlotte."

"Excuse me?" Her glass hit the table next to her with a bang.

"You heard me."

"Who the hell do you think you are?" she retorted, astonished.

"Your cousin, and several years your elder."

"Well, that's a good one. You don't even bother to send me

a postcard for two years and now you walk in here, as cool as
you please, and start telling me how to run my life? What a
bloody nerve.'' She swung her legs onto the floor and rose.

"I know, you're right. I'm sorry.'' He ran his fingers through
his thick chestnut hair, streaked with gold after two weeks of
surfing in Malibu, and tried to think straight. "But you can't
take a job with that man. What did he make you do?''

"Well, pose, of course. What an idiotic question.''

"Pose for what?''

"I don't know, Brad, some magazine, I suppose. I didn't
ask. I'm just thrilled to have the job.''

"Have you told Uncle David?'' he asked, resorting to a different tactic.

"I was planning on telling him when he comes back from
Cap Ferrat.'' She leaned down, picked up the discarded glass
and sipped nonchalantly.

"Why not now?'' he asked smoothly, eyeing her carefully,
pouncing when she hesitated. "You're not telling your father
because you know damn well he'd lay you across his knee and
spank the hell out of you—which is, I'm warning you, exactly
what I'll do if you even think of taking a job with that man.''

"How dare you,'' Charlotte seethed, her cheeks flaming.
"I'll do whatever I damn well like and there's nothing you or
anybody can do about it.''

"Want to bet on it?'' he said evenly. "You so much as step
into that man's studio and I promise you'll be in a finishing
school in Switzerland so fast you won't know how you got
there.''

"You wouldn't,'' she whispered, stepping forward.

"Don't try me.''

"I'd never forgive you.''

"In a couple of years you'd be thanking me profusely.''

"But he said I was so good. You're spoiling my chances.''

"Of what? Becoming a porn star?'' He threw her a sneer.

"How dare you!'' The slap caught him full on the cheek
and he winced, rubbing it ruefully, aware he'd pushed her too
far.

"Oh gosh, Brad, I'm so sorry, I didn't mean to do that, but
you—''

"It's okay. I'm interfering in something that, as you pointed out very clearly—'' he clenched his jaw ''—is none of my business.''

She lifted her fingers to his cheek, bit her lip. ''Your cheek is all red. I'm so sorry, Brad,'' she whispered, eyes swimming.

He looked away, the touch of her hand on his skin sending goose bumps up his spine, knowing that if one tear spilled he was done for. ''Charlie, I'm not saying you shouldn't model if you want to, but do it with a respectable agency. Rogers is a porno photographer, he'll stick your face on a nude body and splash you in every male magazine from here to Copenhagen. Is that really what you want?'' He turned, looked her in the eye and saw her blush. ''You didn't take your clothes off, did you?'' Anger simmered as she blushed redder. ''Charlie, tell me you didn't do it?'' He snagged her wrist in an iron grip.

''Just my T-shirt,'' she whispered, lips quivering. ''He made it seem so normal. I wanted to look professional, so I—''

''Yes?''

''When he told me to take off my T-shirt and pose, I did,'' she murmured, a tear plopping onto his shirtfront as she leaned forward, her bent head reaching his shoulder.

''I should do what I said and give you the hiding of a lifetime,'' he murmured through clenched teeth, pulling her close and letting her sob into his shirt while rubbing her back. Ignoring his body's reactions, he thought about how to go about retrieving the pictures before any damage was done. ''Don't worry about it, baby, I'll deal with him. Just be more careful next time and don't get carried away.'' He raised her chin, dragged his thumb softly over her cheeks and wiped the tears, looking her over critically. ''With a face like that you won't lack opportunities, believe me. But next time, pass it by me.''

It cost him fifty grand to buy the photos and negatives but it was worth every penny, Brad concluded the next day. Throwing the envelope on the bed, he glanced at it, suddenly tempted.

What was wrong with him, acting like a wet-dreaming adolescent? He picked up the envelope and threw it angrily into the top drawer of the dresser. He was as bad as Rogers. The thought of the smarmy English photographer made him shud-

der. Thank God he'd gotten her out of this scrape. He just
hoped in the future she'd have more wisdom.

Three weeks passed. Dex came and went, passing through
on his way to Cap Ferrat with Uncle David and Aunt Penn,
leaving him to hold the fort at Harcourt's offices in Piccadilly,
which meant twelve-hour days and no lunch break. He'd barely
seen Charlie since the night of his arrival, except to tell her the
photos had been recouped. After that, she'd avoided him.

Finishing his last memo one Friday, Brad caught sight of his
Breitling watch, astonished at how late it was, although it was
still daylight.

He pushed back the black leather chair and rose from the
long teak and metal desk. Going to the window of the gener-
ously proportioned modern office, he looked out over Picadilly,
watching the evening traffic—the number-eight double-decker
buses and black cabs—weaving their way to a standstill.

After three weeks of nonstop work he could use a break, he
realized, running his fingers through his hair, loosening his tie
and unbuttoning his shirt collar. Perhaps he'd go home and
have a shower, then grab a bite somewhere and take in a movie.

He picked up his briefcase and locked the door behind him.
As he'd expected, there was no sign of life, the secretarial pool
empty as he padded down the long carpeted corridor to the
private elevator and pressed garage. As he took out the keys
to his grandfather's new red Porsche, he wondered who, among
several girls he dated, might be in town at this time of year.
None, he concluded ruefully, enjoying the power of the engine
as he drove smoothly up the ramp and joined the traffic.

Charlotte sat on the arm of the sofa swinging her leg, the
phone squeezed between her ear and shoulder as she filed her
nails and decided whether or not to go out on a date with
Jimmy Castairs tonight or not. He'd become rather boring and
didn't kiss very well. Lately she'd been experimenting with
kissing. A late bloomer, she needed to catch up to where her
girlfriends had already trodden. The school dance had been her
first experiment, but the mere thought of Jimmy slobbering
over her made her shiver.

She looked up at the sound of the front door. Brad walked

in, waved and threw his briefcase on a chair in the hall before going into the kitchen.

She canceled her date, got off the phone and stuck the nail file in the back pocket of her black Chanel miniskirt. Leaning against the doorjamb, she watched as he opened a beer.

He'd always been handsome, but of late Brad had filled out, seemed so much older and more mature than before. Or was it just that she looked at him differently? His back was turned and she studied him, tall, broad-shouldered, muscles rippling under the rolled-up sleeves of his white oxford shirt. The rest of him was scrummy, too, she realized, biting her lip, knowing he would turn around any second.

As though sensing her presence, he looked over his shoulder and smiled, those piercing blue eyes just like Grandpa's flashing against his tan, still visible after three weeks stuck in an office.

"How are you doing, brat?" He glugged down the rest of the beer and smacked his lips. "Boy, did I need that."

"Long week?" She ignored the brat bit, determined to set their relationship on a new footing.

"Yep. Too darn long. Think I'll take a shower then get a bite to eat."

"What would you like?" She sidled into the kitchen. Remembering a scene in the movie she'd watched the week before, she copied the smile, the gesture and the script, which had impressed her as very feminine. "Go take a shower," she purred. "I'll whip you up a superb omelette."

He arched a skeptical eyebrow. "You cook?"

"Sort of," she admitted, wishing it had come over better.

"How about I take you to dinner?"

"Really?" Her heart beat faster. "I'd love to."

"Good. I'll see you in twenty. Don't take hours fixing your face, you look great." He picked up the paper he'd laid on the counter.

"I do?"

"What?"

"Look great?" She crossed her leg, toe pointed at the ground the way she and her friend Liz had practiced at school, and bit her lip suggestively, annoyed when he surveyed her critically.

"Not bad."

She vowed she'd leave him hungry, then decided against it when he grinned and made an irresistible suggestion. "Would you like to go to Annabelle's?"

"Oh, Brad, that would be simply wonderful!" She hurled herself at him, gave him an excited hug. "I've been *dying* to go. All the girls at school have been, and I'm the only one who hasn't. Are you a member?"

"No, but Dex lent me his card. Now go put something respectable on, or they may not let you in."

"Anything you say," she murmured obediently.

"When you say things like that it makes my skin crawl," he remarked, pinching her cheek. "Get going, brat, I'm ravenous."

An hour later they were seated at Annabelle's in Berkley Square, dining on green asparagus, followed by Dover sole.

"I didn't think it would be so dark in here," she remarked. "Let's dance afterward."

"Your wishes are my command, my lady." He lifted her hand, eyes brimming with laughter, sending a tingle through her she'd never felt before, not even when she watched old movies of Alain Delon.

"Have you found a job?" They didn't refer to the photo incident.

"I have a couple of things in sight," she replied vaguely. "Mummy still insists I go to Château d'Oex in September. Brad, can't you talk her into letting me stay in London? I don't want to go to finishing school in Switzerland. It's so silly and old-fashioned. I mean, no one goes to finishing school nowadays."

"What do they finish?" he asked, lifting his glass, savoring a sip of Pouilly-Fuissé.

"That's the point, they don't. You learn French—which obviously I already know, since we spend practically every summer in Limoges and Cap Ferrat—and teach you a bunch of idiotic things like sewing and cooking. It's just a way of keeping me out of trouble. Or that's what they think," she added gloomily, spearing a new potato with her fork.

"They may have a point," he murmured, slipping a hand over hers and laughing low, making her swallow. "Just kidding, Princess. If you think you'll hate it, I'll talk to Uncle David, see what I can do. But you'd better come up with a proper job or something to do that will convince them."

She returned the pressure of his fingers and smiled. "Thanks, Brad. That's jolly decent of you."

After crème brûlée and coffee they moved from the restaurant into the discotheque, which seemed even darker than the restaurant.

"Want to dance?" he asked after ordering a bottle of Krug, enjoying her company more than he'd expected. They'd chatted of this and that, and he'd listened, surprised at how intelligent, pertinent and sensitive many of her views were. Not just a pretty face, he realized. "Ever thought of going to university?" he asked as they joined the other dancers on the floor and his hands slipped around her waist, a sharp shudder racing when her fingers touched his shoulders and they swayed gently.

"Me? I'm no good at that sort of thing."

"You're bright enough. Why not give it a chance?"

"No. Too much work. I like drawing and making things, but I can't stand exams." The dance floor was filling up, forcing them closer. He tightened his hold. When her hands glided up the back of his neck, her breasts skimming his lapel, he made a halfhearted attempt to withdraw, knowing he should take her home. Instead he drew her closer until her head lay snuggled on his shoulder. He closed his eyes, the feel of her, the scent of her freshly washed hair, and the music intoxicating, all the while persuading himself it was nothing but a friendly, cousinly dance.

But there was nothing cousinly about the way Charlotte's fingers played with his hair, or her smile when she raised her head. He was foolish enough to look into those huge, mesmerizing violet pools, wondering if he was crazy. Even though he was only loosely related to Charlotte—their fathers had been raised together as step-brothers but were not connected by blood—he should still act responsibly toward her. Christ, she was only a teenager. What his grandfather and uncle would say if they knew. Have him certified, most likely, he realized, brushing his lips on her temple, desire searing at her quick intake of breath.

The music ended and sanity returned. He took her hand and led her back to the table, wondering what had come over him. He wasn't attracted to very young girls, preferring more experienced women. He'd even had an affair with one of his female professors, twelve years his elder. Yet here he was, at Annabelle's, of all places, bowled over by his seventeen-year-old cousin. Perhaps he *should* be certified, he concluded, picking up her flute and handing it to her, sharp arrows piercing his body when their fingers touched.

"Maybe we'd better get going," he remarked, trying to sound casual. The sooner they got out of here, the better. He signaled the waiter and paid the check, leaving the bottle of champagne half-full.

Charlotte leaned into the corner of the Porsche and watched him drive, loving everything about him—the way his long fingers gripped the wheel, the outline of his face in the dark. The fact that he was obviously finding it difficult to resist her was also extremely flattering.

She'd never kissed an older man before and wondered what it would be like. Not that Brad was old, of course, but he must be at least twenty-two, which put him in a very different league to the three sweaty-palmed adolescents who constituted her previous experience. As they approached Chester Square, she made up her mind. Brad would be her first. After all, she was the only virgin left in the group. Everyone else had been to bed with someone, and here she was, seventeen last month and barely kissed.

The scent of Brad's cologne and the thoughts he evoked made her feel funny. Good funny, but funny all the same. She shifted and crossed her legs, the short skirt of her simple white dress riding upward. She didn't pull it down.

Charlotte unlocked the door and Brad held it for her. She pressed the elevator button. He slipped an arm around her as they reached the front door of the apartment. But all the determination he'd mustered during the drive home vanished when she spun round and snaked her arms behind his neck, lips parted.

"Let's get inside," he murmured, a splinter of common

sense prevailing until, stumbling in the dark, they reached the sofa. Aware that he was acting like an oversexed adolescent, nonetheless Brad was unable to stop when she dragged him down with her among the cushions.

It was a ragged kiss that shattered every part of his body, and when he came up for breath it was to make sure he didn't explode there and then. He rolled away, then leaned over and kissed her once more, amazed by the way their mouths melted, his hands gliding up her taut silky legs, stroking her thighs. She felt like nothing he'd ever experienced.

"Do you never wear a bra?" he murmured, kissing her throat, then on down to the swell of her small, taut breasts, nibbling her nipples, hard as acorns, through the thin film of silk.

He found the zipper, pulled it and she arched, the dress slipping off easily, tongues and bodies melding now in a frenzied hurricane, all reason forgotten. He gasped, tried to stop her when she unbuttoned his shirt relentlessly, tugged at his belt buckle. Then he groaned as her fingers deftly unhooked his waistband, and relented as skin met skin, the feel of her exquisitely unique, as though she were made exclusively for him.

The shrill ring of the telephone brought him back to earth with a hard bang.

"Leave it," she whispered, trying to stop him from rising and answering. He hesitated, let it ring again, then reached over and grabbed the receiver.

David's voice on the other end sent desire hurtling out the window. He sat up, dragged a hand through his mussed hair and got a hold on himself.

"Charlotte? No, she's out," he lied, horrified that he'd been on the verge of seducing his uncle's teenage daughter. He replied automatically to David's questions, while trying to focus, aware the situation had gotten totally out of hand. How could he have allowed it to happen? He was the adult and responsible. She was nothing but a kid.

Shivers ran down his spine. He hung up the phone and reached for his shirt, lying crumpled on the rug, not looking at her, afraid that if he did he might give in. Never in his life had he felt such empathy, such charismatic energy. It felt so damn right it hurt.

But it wasn't. "I'm sorry, Charlie. I should never have allowed this to happen." He pulled his shirt on, buttoned it up fast then reached for his briefs.

"Why not?" She sat up, switched on the lamp, hair falling about her in a fiery waterfall, leaving only a glimpse of her small, upturned breasts.

"This is crazy." He rose, pulled on his pants and fumbled for his belt, trying not to look at her. "Here, get dressed." He picked up her dress, held it out silently.

Charlotte stared at him, wide-eyed, then rose slowly and stood before him, feeling a strange, delicious mixture of shyness and power, exhilaration and fear. She looked up, slipped her arms around his neck, suddenly angry when he didn't respond, annoyed when she kissed him and his lips stayed firmly closed. He was not going to send her away or treat her like a child.

"Brad, darling, please," she begged, reaching up in another attempt to pry his lips open, furious when methodically he unclasped her arms from around his neck and stepped back, reading the determination in his eyes, enraged at being thwarted.

"We'll discuss it when you get dressed," he said, moving to the window, running a hand through his hair. She gazed after him, livid, then grabbed her panties and pulled her dress on haphazardly.

"How dare you do this to me?" she cried at his stiff back, seeing his hand slip to the back of his neck, working out the kinks. "How can you just stand there and say nothing?" she said, angry tears welling. "What a wimp you are, Brad Ward. And what an idiot I was to want you to be the first. You're a coward and a hypocrite. You're scared of *Daddy*," she mimicked, glad when he turned and she saw his lips tighten.

"I'm sorry. It's my fault. I never should have allowed this to happen," he said, contrite.

"What do you mean, *allowed?* As if I don't have a will and the choice was just yours. You're so damn full of yourself. I hate you!" She stumbled into her high heels, grabbed her bag. "And for your 411," she snapped, tears burning, "though you may not want to fuck me, there are a number of guys out there who'd give their right arm to." She derived some satisfaction when his eyes darkened and her hands clenched, then she ran out and slammed the door behind her.

He went to the window, watched, worried, as she flounced down the street, then sighed as she stalked round the corner, knowing she'd go to her parents' place. God, why had he let this happen? He'd have given anything to turn back the clock to the moment when they were in the kitchen. What had inspired him to ask her out to dinner in the first place? And to a nightclub, of all places.

He turned out the lamp and went to bed, unable to get her out of his mind, the taste of her lips and the incredible feel of her body leaving him tossing with longing for her, and anger at himself for being a fool.

He didn't see her the next day or the day after that. When he came home on Monday evening he noticed her things were gone from the other guest room. Leaning against the doorjamb, he gazed into space, then made a decision. If he stayed in London he'd end up seeking her out, for the past seventy-two hours had been hell to deal with. As soon as his uncle returned, he'd make up an excuse and get the hell out of Dodge.

For both their sakes.

45

New York, U.S.A., 1987

That autumn, Scott surprised the family with an unexpected announcement. After seventeen years of widowerhood, he'd fallen in love with a political journalist, Dolores de la Fuente, twenty-five years his junior. The couple were married in a small private ceremony in Washington. The bride's parents, the Uruguayan billionaire Diego de la Fuente and his wife, were present; Brad and Dex acted as witnesses; and Scott's old friend, Bill Hunter, was best man. Flora wasn't well enough to come and Dex hastened back to Strathaird after the ceremony, worried. At eighty-five she was becoming very frail.

Brad worked hard, throwing himself into work at Harcourt's and dated a number of different girls in a determined attempt to forget Charlotte. But her lips seemed uncannily irreplaceable; the memory of her melting under him, and her soft tiny moans as he'd caressed her kept getting in the way.

The thought of her perhaps experiencing these same things with another man tortured him, to the point that he had to stop himself from flying to London, where she'd persuaded her parents to allow her to stay and model.

In November he received a phone call from his dad, telling him they were expecting twins. What would it be like to have baby brothers or sisters, he wondered, happy that his father had finally found someone as delightful as Dolores.

By April he'd decided that he would wait to see Charlotte until the summer, when they would inevitably meet either in Limoges or at Cap Ferrat.

Todd and Rick were born in early July, one dark and black-eyed like Dolores, the other blond and blue-eyed with a look of the Wards.

"I thought they were supposed to look the same," he murmured, gazing with awe at his half brothers. As he left the hospital he stopped at a newsstand and picked up the *Wall Street Journal,* then stopped dead. Surely that couldn't be Charlotte on the front of *Hello* magazine?

He picked it up and flipped open the magazine. It was her, all right. Three full damn pages of her and the new British movie star John Drummond. He hesitated, then bought the magazine, taking the subway to give him time to read the article. Consumed by jealousy, he devoured the pictures of the couple, embracing in Paris, stretched on a yacht in Majorca. He threw it into the trash can and walked to Sutton Place in a blinding rage. Damn Charlotte for growing up. Damn her for being beautiful, and damn her for haunting him and feeling the way she had in his arms.

That night he called Veronica, a sexy Venezuelan he dated from time to time, and enjoyed a healthy bout of what should have been satisfying sex. But he woke up the next morning as mad as he was the night before.

Two weeks later, with no clear idea of what he was hoping to achieve, he boarded a plane to Paris. He'd learned from his uncle that Charlotte was going to Limoges with her mother and their grandparents.

He reached La Renardière in the late afternoon and went straight to see his grandmother. She kissed him, smiling in that faraway manner he loved so well, and immediately asked what was wrong.

"Nothing," he lied, head turning abruptly when he heard voices in the distance. He was sure one of them was Charlotte's.

After a few minutes he excused himself, went back downstairs and out onto the terrace where the rest of the family were assembled. He was shocked when he saw her. She looked pale and sad, with none of the vivacious sparkle of the previous year. They kissed formally, his eyes closing an instant when their cheeks touched. At least she was treating him as though nothing had happened. But gone was the suppressed vitality, that subtle energy and vibrancy. He would rather have seen her furious, as he had last in London, than silently biting her fingernails.

As he chatted with his aunt and grandfather, he wondered what was wrong. He longed to take her in his arms, soothe away her frown and see laughter spring into her eyes. Instead, he drew her into conversation, determined to reestablish their friendship, if nothing else, and to find out the cause of her unhappiness.

It took him several days of gentle perseverance for her to finally give way, sitting on the grass after a tennis match. He listened, horrified, as hesitantly she opened up, plucking the string of her racket nervously, looking anywhere but at him.

"I never thought I'd get pregnant. It just never occurred to me," she said, biting her lip. "I don't know what to do, Brad. I can't possibly tell John. It wasn't that kind of relationship. I mean, I'm sure he never dreamed of anything like this. It seems so unfair to him." She looked down and a tear plopped on her cheek.

"If you're expecting his baby, he has to know," Brad answered smoothly, masking his shock with an effort.

"But it's not his fault," she insisted. "I should've been more careful, taken the Pill." She sniffed, then wiped the back of her hand across her cheeks like a little girl. He handed her a large white handkerchief and waited while she blew her nose, wishing John Drummond were here so he could find a plausible excuse to break his balls.

"You're such a good egg, Brad. After the way I walked out that day. And I know now you were just being decent." She smiled and took his hand. "I feel so much better now that I've told someone. Having a friend like you is wonderful."

He winced but nodded, realizing his feelings were secondary at this point and would have to remain closeted. She needed help and guidance and he'd elected to give it.

"The first thing you must do is tell John."

"But what if he doesn't like the idea? It might hurt his career."

"Charlie, this isn't an idea you like or dislike. It's a baby who in—" He stopped, raised a questioning eyebrow.

"Seven months," she murmured.

"Who in seven months will be here to stay. It takes two to tango, babe. You're not alone in this," he insisted, keeping his temper under wraps.

"But—"

"No buts. You're getting on the phone and telling him *now*."

She hesitated, fiddling with a strand of her gorgeous hair that glinted in the sun. He looked away.

"What if he doesn't want to get married?" she asked in a small voice. "Mummy and Oncle Eugène would have a fit if I had an abortion. Dad's a bit more broad-minded, but what about Granny and Grandpa?"

"Do you want one?"

She shook her head, eyes filling once more.

"Then don't worry about any of that right now," he said, relieved. "One step at a time. First, give John a chance."

She stayed silent and plucked a daisy, hands unsteady, pulling out the tiny white petals one by one.

"I'll speak to him. Where will you be later on?" she asked in an uncertain tone.

"At the factory." He helped her rise, held her arm as she wiped the grass off her tennis dress, then handed her the racket. "You shouldn't be playing tennis," he remarked. Right now he would gladly have murdered John Drummond. For doing this to her, but also for having taken what he considered his in the most casual of manners.

"I'll call you later, then." She linked an arm in his in a cousinly fashion. "Do you always work yourself to death,

Brad? You never stop. You should have more fun, find a date. Do you have a girlfriend hidden away somewhere?''

"Tons of 'em.'' He flung his arm around her, wishing he could pull her head onto his shoulder, the soft scent of her hair, grass and Guerlain leaving him dizzy. From the tension in her limbs he could tell how wired she was.

"Are you sure you don't want me to stay?'' he asked softly when they reached the house.

"No. Thanks, but this is something I need to do myself. I'll give you a buzz once I've talked to him.''

"Okay.'' He gave her a peck on the cheek and a quick hug. "Get on with it. The sooner you're in the clear, the better.''

She smiled bravely and nodded. "And Brad—''

"Yes?'' He turned expectantly, car keys dangling in his right hand.

"Oh, nothing. Just, thanks for being such a brick.''

"Anytime,'' he answered, turning quickly, squeezing his eyes tight to smother the pain as he walked around the house to the car.

Arriving at the factory, he went straight to Dex's office, sat in the old leather chair and stared at dusty porcelain, old 38's and an S.A.S. beret, thinking. What if John really didn't want to marry her? Should he marry her himself? The thought made him sit up. What would it be like to raise another man's baby? He gazed at the faded photographs of La Vallière, of people he'd never met but had heard about all his life, realizing he didn't give a damn. If she needed him, he'd be there and would love the baby as his own. He leaned his head on his hands then fiddled impatiently with the inkstand, picked up an old photo. *May 1938* was written in faded brown ink on the back. He flipped it and frowned, astonished to see a replica of Charlotte smiling up from the picture. The man with her seemed familiar too, but he couldn't place him.

"Who is this?'' he asked Dex when he walked in a few minutes later, fresh from a game of golf. At eighty-eight, he was as healthy as ever and as mentally agile.

"That's Geneviève, Oncle Eugène's younger sister whom

you've heard us speak of, and her husband, Sylvain de Rothberg.''

''Funny,'' he remarked. ''She looks exactly like Charlotte.''

Dex took the picture from him and frowned. It was true. Charlotte's resemblance to her paternal grandmother was staggering. He put the photograph on a shelf, half covering it with a book before glancing at his grandson. Brad was staring out the window, miles away, he realized with a frown.

''They were good days,'' Dex said, coming over to the desk. ''Genny was a lovely girl and Sylvain one of my closest friends. You've heard the story dozens of times,'' he said wistfully, then sat down opposite the boy, wondering what was bothering him. ''Are you happy with the Taiwan deal?'' he asked. Dex sought Brad's opinions more and more, anxious to let him make decisions so that when the time came for David and Brad to take over completely, he'd be prepared.

''It's pretty well tied up. Just a few details to polish, but essentially it's a done deal.''

''I think it'll make Harcourt's grow in Asia. I may not be around to see it, but I'll bet the stock market will skyrocket in the nineties.'' Dex never thought about dying, or about the future. After all, the MacLeod name was safe and the secret of David's parentage would be buried with Eugène, Flora and him.

Dex watched Brad's fingers drumming the desk and arched a thick, white brow when the phone rang and Brad pounced. He was shocked when he heard the boy's next words.

''Look, if he won't marry you, I will.'' There was a pause as the woman on the other end spoke. ''We'll discuss it later. I'll be back in half an hour. Just stop worrying—it might hurt the baby,'' he said, lowering his voice, suddenly aware that his grandfather was looking at him oddly. People got the impression that because he was old Dex was old-fashioned, but Brad knew this was far from being the case. On the contrary, Dex was one of the most levelheaded, open-minded beings he'd ever encountered.

He laid down the receiver and met Dex's gaze full on. ''It's Charlie. She's pregnant.''

"So I gather. What have you got to do with it?"

"Nothing."

"Then why were you offering to marry her?" he said evenly.

"There's a possibility the father may not come through," he replied, biting off his words and scrunching an old memo in his fist.

"That's not your problem," Dex pointed out. "She may be my granddaughter and I love her dearly, but I'll be damned if I'll see your life screwed up because of her stupidity."

Their eyes locked as the phone rang once more. This time Dex grabbed it. "Hello, Charlotte. Yes, I'll pass him to you." He handed Brad the receiver, lips drawn in a thin line.

"I can't find him anywhere. At his agent's they say he'll only be back next month. Maybe he has another girlfriend by now."

"I'll be there in ten. Just wait," he said, hanging up. "I can't leave her out to dry, Dex. I just can't do it."

"Please think, before you do something stupid that you'll have to live with the rest of your life," Dex begged. "I'm coming with you," he added, getting up. "David's flying in tonight. What a mess."

They drove home in silence. When they reached the house, Brad bounded up the stairs and knocked on the door of her room.

"Come in." She was sitting on the edge of the bed, looking suddenly childlike, vulnerable and afraid. He sat next to her, slipped an arm around her shoulders and hugged her. "Your father's coming in tonight."

"I know. I suppose I'll have to tell them," she whispered in a tiny voice.

"I think so. The sooner you do, the better."

"I feel so awful. They'll be so disappointed in me," she whispered, voice breaking.

"I'll be there. Stop worrying." He squeezed her tight and dropped a kiss on the top of her head, then winced when she turned and buried her head in his chest.

* * *

Dex held Flora's hand as Charlotte finished, her eyes glued to the ground.

"Where the hell is this bastard?" David burst out.

"Calm down, dear." Penelope reached out a restraining arm to her husband's arm. She was a charming woman, with well-cut, chin-length blond hair that framed an understanding smile. Her hazel eyes usually sparkled with humor, but just as quickly could turn compassionate. "I'm so glad you've told us, darling," she murmured to Charlotte, eyes bright. "Whatever happens, you know we'll always support you in any decision."

"Oh, Mum." Charlotte threw herself into her mother's arms and wept.

"I'll murder the bugger," David exclaimed. "Does he know?"

"Not yet. He's filming on some remote island," Brad supplied.

"What if he doesn't want to marry her?"

"She won't be the first person to bring up a child by herself." Penelope raised her head and gave him a firm look. "There's no need to make a drama out of this, David. Things like this happen every day."

"Not in my family they don't."

"I don't want an abortion, Daddy."

"Good God, of course not. That's not what I meant." He dragged a hand across his forehead.

"If John doesn't come through for her," Brad said, "Charlie and I can get married."

Sudden silence reigned in the room.

David turned, eyeing him with new respect.

"Which I think is a very bad idea," Dex cut in from the sofa, where he and Flora sat quietly observing the drama.

"Dex, this is my life and I run it my way," Brad snapped. "Charlie knows I won't let her down if she needs me."

Penelope looked at him, tears swimming in her lovely gray eyes. "Thank you," she murmured softly. "But neither of you should marry for all the wrong reasons."

"I already told him I won't." Charlotte gulped. "Oh, Brad, you're so wonderful!" She got up and hugged him. Dex read the tension in Brad as he quickly withdrew and felt a jolt. He loves her, Dex realized, shocked, listening to the far-off ring of the telephone. "Someone get the damn phone," he exclaimed irritated.

David went quickly to the hall, then returned, his mouth set. "It's for you," he told his daughter severely. "From some damn place I can't pronounce."

Charlotte glanced up, her eyes suddenly excited. "It must be John." She rushed into the hall, and the family waited.

After several minutes she returned, transformed. "You were right, darling," she exclaimed to Brad, the word slicing his heart. "John wasn't upset at all. Quite the opposite. He's just off to make sure with his agent that this is the right move for his career. Isn't it great? And I owe it all to you." She reached up and kissed him on the cheek.

"His agent?"

"Yes. You know, to see if it's the right publicity move and so on. Isn't it perfect? And thanks for saying you'd marry me, Brad, you're such a brick."

"Anytime," he murmured dryly.

"I *do* hope he says yes. John thinks it will come at about the right time to tie in with the promotion of his new film. Isn't that lucky?"

"Very," he responded, meeting his uncle's gaze over her head, feeling numb and strangely disappointed although he knew he should be relieved. Catching his grandfather's piercing frown, he looked away.

As it turned out, John's agent considered it *fabulous* timing. Couldn't be better, in fact. They would delay the release of the movie to coincide with the baby's birth. He was already dealing with press coverage, deciding whether it would be better to announce the engagement or the baby first.

"Isn't it customary to have the wedding first?" Brad asked, unable to keep the sarcasm out of his tone.

"Oh yes, you're right. Of course." Charlotte's eyes sparkled, her old self once more, oblivious of the pain she was causing. "I'm so happy, Brad." She threw herself into his arms and he held her, feeling the beat of her heart against his chest, wondering how he was going to stand it.

During the next few weeks life became a hectic sequence of wedding preparations. Brad flew back to France from London, where he'd returned after Charlotte's engagement was announced, agreed in mid-August to attend the wedding. Reluctantly he agreed to be an usher, along with his cousin Colin, now nineteen and attending UCLA, and Armand de la Vallière, Oncle Eugène's rather enigmatic nephew whom David assured him had tried to steal his watch when they were boys.

Colin joined Brad at the church, his freckled face breaking into a grin. "I can't believe Charlie's actually marrying John Drummond. You've no idea what it's done for my stock. All the girls flock around me now, in the hopes of getting a photo with him. Have to capitalize," he added, winking.

The press was there en masse, cameras flashing, journalists poised outside Limoges Cathedral as the bride entered the church on her father's arm. Brad stood with the other ushers at the back of the church, watching in disgust as John posed, making sure they got his best angle. Then a hush followed and Mendelssohn's wedding march echoed through the packed church.

Charlotte floated down the aisle, a vision in white tulle, more beautiful than he'd ever imagined any bride could be. He swallowed the regret as John, not he, took her hand and they kneeled before the cardinal.

Halfway through the service he could stand it no longer. He slipped out of the pew, and edged toward the back of the church. Outside, a burst of sunlight hit him, and a reporter rushed up to him, questions rippling off her tongue.

"Get lost," he said curtly, shoving his way through the crowd and finally reaching his Porsche. He threw his top hat and gloves angrily into the back, damned if he was going to the reception. On impulse he headed to the family home to change before the bridal party returned. Glancing scathingly at the shimmering silver and magnificent flower arrangements, he headed upstairs, determined to be out of there before they arrived.

An hour later he was headed for Paris. The sooner he put distance between Charlotte and himself, the better. He wanted nothing more to do with her. She was married to someone else and about to have a baby and there was no room for him in that threesome.

46

Skye, Scotland, 1993

The twins were growing so fast they could barely keep up, Dex realized, watching as they stood near the edge of the pond and threw in the fishing line. He was ninety-three and Flora ninety-two. A ripe old age, it was called. Yet he didn't feel old. Perhaps it was because of his excellent health. Flora worried him, for each year she became frailer and was often unable to leave her room. They had transformed the dreamery for her, building a bathroom next door and placing her bed by the window where she could look out over the sea and the garden she loved so dearly.

Almost a century had passed since that day at Midfield when he'd taken her into his arms and given her, by today's standards, a very chaste kiss. He smiled and glanced at the twins, regretting that he wouldn't see them grown. That reminded him to add another addendum to the trust he'd set up. You never knew when the time would come to hit the road.

Todd was getting twisted in the line. "No, not like that," Dex exclaimed, rising from his deck chair with an agility that belied his age.

"It's Todd, Grandpa. He's doing it wrong again, look." Rick pointed to the line that by now was entangled in the bushes.

"I tried, Grandpa," Todd murmured, his big blue eyes and the shock of blond hair a contrast to Rick's dark looks.

"Now, hang in there, both of you, while we straighten this thing out."

Patiently he unraveled the twine and showed them how to wind the reel, putting an end to the argument as to who would be the first to have a turn.

When they'd settled again, he leaned back and watched them, brushing away the flies with his straw hat. Hearing the telephone ring back at the house, he wondered if it was Brad. Maybe he'd come up to Skye for a few days after all. The boy never stopped and he needed a break from Harcourt's, where he was now vice president. David was president and Dex still presided as CEO, attending board meetings and going regularly to the office, but also enjoying the time he could spend with the little ones, whose parents seemed to be permanently on the road. He sighed. It wasn't his affair, but women didn't seem to pay much attention to their offspring nowadays. Not that he had anything against women working and being active.

"Mr. Ward." He heard Aisla, the housekeeper, calling and saw her running across the lawn, apron flying. "Mr. Ward, the telephone." She handed him the portable—a magic invention that meant you didn't have to get up every five minutes. What with remote-control television and computers, they'd have little use for their bodies in a few years, he reckoned, accepting the receiver. "Thanks. Perhaps the kids should have tea soon. Ward speaking," he said into the cordless wonder.

"Mr. Ward, this is Pat Macfee from the State Department."

"What can I do for you? Are you sure it's not my son, Scott, you want to speak to? He's the State Department Ward in this family."

There was a moment's silence. "I'm afraid I have bad news, sir."

He stiffened. All at once, Brooker, from the Embassy in Paris, flashed before him and he shivered. The voice on the phone was filled with that same familiar tone of regret, as though taught to impart tragedy.

"What is it?" he said harshly, his heart racing, breathing difficult.

"We've had a call from Beijing, sir."

He closed his eyes, filled with sudden foreboding. *Not Scott,* he begged silently. *Please, not my boy. Let me go first, Lord, I've been around too long as it is.*

"Mr. Ward?"

But he couldn't hear, for he'd collapsed in the deck chair while the children fished on happily.

Aisla discovered him ten minutes later, when she came to fetch the children for tea.

Scott and Dolores's plane had crashed on its way to Manchuria. None of the U.S. Commission had survived. After suffering a minor heart attack, Dex was prohibited from attending the memorial service.

Brad and David stood next to Diego de la Fuente, Dolores's father, who was recently widowed, surrounded by hundreds of mourners. Both Scott and Dolores had been well loved and admired.

Brad shook hands dutifully, unable to register that his father was dead. The lack of a coffin and remains made it seem unreal. After meeting with lawyers and taking care of the estate, he flew to Scotland with Diego to take part in the decisions about the twins, orphaned at the age of five. Like he had been, Brad mused. Except he'd only lost his mother, not both his parents.

For the first time, his grandfather looked frail. Granny rarely left the dreamery now and he'd go up later, after settling Diego, who was overwhelmed by grief at the loss of his wife only six months earlier and now his only daughter. David sat close to his father, and Penelope handed round drinks. Aunt Penn had taken charge, as usual, making sure the children were unaware of the pain surrounding them.

A crash on the stairs had Brad jumping up. He found Todd picking himself up, dolefully rubbing his elbow. He crouched next to the little boy, inspecting the arm, realizing all at once that he'd have to assume an active role in their lives now that

Dad and Dolores were gone. Diego was incapable of taking care of them, and it was out of the question for the twins to live with Dex and Flora. He knew Aunt Penn and Uncle David would offer, but that wasn't fair either. As their brother the responsibility was his. He smiled, pulled Todd's sleeve down and winked. "You'll live."

"He can't jump three steps but I can," Rick declared smugly, determined not to be outdone in attention. Brad saw his grandfather standing in the doorway watching, smiling sadly, and listening patiently as the kids rushed over to him, entering into a long, confused description regarding stairs and jumps.

No, he realized, watching. This was no place for little kids.

After a while the boys headed off to the kitchen in search of chocolate cookies and milk.

"What are we going to do about the *niños?*" Diego had followed them into the great hall and was leaning against the newel post, dejected.

"I'll keep them here," Dex answered.

Diego raised doubtful eyes to Brad, clearly too tired to think in English.

"Why don't I take them back to New York with me?" Brad suggested. "They'd go on with their routine, not have to change schools."

"But you are a young man," Diego murmured. "You cannot be expected to take care of two young children. You have your own life to live."

"They're my brothers. I owe it to Dad and Dolores to bring them up right." He glanced at Dex. "You guys did the same for me. You're welcome to visit whenever," he said with a tired smile. The past few days had been traumatic.

"Thank you, you are too kind," Diego said. "I must say it is perhaps the best thing for the little ones. They should be with happy, young people, not old folks like us." He gave Dex a sad smile.

Brad looked up. "I'll never be able to replace Dad and Dolores but I'll do my best."

* * *

Three weeks later, Brad left the office on Park Avenue, exhausted. He'd barely had time to grieve for his father when the twins had developed measles and a major crisis in the factory in Taiwan demanded his presence. Thank God for Uncle David's untiring support. He pulled off his tie and poured himself a whiskey in the back of the limo before glancing over a report that needed to be faxed out by the time he reached the house.

Twenty-eight, unmarried, with no social life and the responsibilities of a fifty-year-old. Great. Yet he didn't complain. He looked up from the fax, worried. David had rung earlier telling him that Charlotte and her family had suffered a bad car accident up in Skye over the weekend. Charlotte had apparently been driving. He'd never seen Charlotte's daughter, having found an excuse to not attend the christening. He hoped she was all right, and that Charlie was okay.

Four months later, the Taiwan business matter was still pending. Leaving the twins in the nanny's safe care, Brad boarded a Concorde to London to discuss the matter with David in person. As the plane approached Heathrow, he wondered where Charlotte was and what she was feeling, wishing he could reach out and be with her, knowing that was ridiculous.

After several hours at the office, a final decision was made around midnight. He declined David's offer of a lift home and walked back to Chester Square, glad of the breath of air after being cooped up all day.

Back at the flat he sank onto the couch, switched on the television and remembered he wasn't in the States when the screen went fuzzy.

Time to hit the sack, he concluded, yawning. As he got up, he noticed the light blinking on the answering machine and automatically pressed the message button.

"Hi, this is Charlotte." His heart jerked. "Dad said you were flying in today. Give me a call in the morning."

He replayed it just to hear the sound of her melodious voice then jotted down the number.

Next morning he fiddled with the phone before finally dialing. He was surprised when she answered promptly, and his heart lurched at how sad her voice sounded.

"Brad! What a wonderful surprise. Won't you come over for dinner? John and I would love to have you. I can't wait to see you."

He spent a frustrating day, pleased he'd called, then angry with himself for feeding his longing. *Fool, idiot, loser,* he repeated as he walked up the front steps of the house in Notting Hill and rang the bell. What if…? But then the door burst open and Charlotte threw her arms around him.

"Brad, darling. It's been such ages. How super of you to come." She tugged him inside, through a hall filled with odds and ends, artwork and Asian buddhas, to the drawing room, a brightly decorated space filled with colorful cushions, throws and exotic knickknacks, so totally Charlotte he couldn't have imagined it otherwise.

While she busied herself with the drinks, he absorbed each detail of her person, each subtle change. It took him only seconds to read the lurking sadness behind the bright smile, the forced gaiety that replaced her natural effervescence of old.

"John should be home in a little," she said, casting a nervous glance at her watch. "They're getting ready for the next shoot, so everyone's hectic."

"What about your daughter?" he asked.

"Genny? She'll be back in a minute. She went to a painting class with her nanny. We're quite an artsy family. I design jewelry now and—" She cut the sentence off, head flying up as the front door opened. He heard a child's voice. Charlotte rose anxiously. "Genny," she called. "Come in here, darling. We have someone I want you to meet."

Brad rose as a little redheaded girl entered the room, dragging her right leg. *My God, the accident,* he realized shocked, glancing at Charlotte, reading the suffering, the suppressed agony as she embraced the child, lifting her into her arms. "This is Genny. Genny, this is Brad. My cousin, and a good friend. Isn't he handsome?"

Genny nodded shyly then hid her face in her mother's lovely hair, reminding him of a Madonna and child. Then she ran back to her nanny and they sat down again.

In a while, he found himself talking more openly than he

had in ages—about the loss of his father, the responsibility of bringing up the twins, his concerns for their grandparents, now very old and frail after his father's death. The only thing he didn't mention was himself, preferring to listen to her anecdotes. Their conversation was interrupted when the door burst open.

"Charlotte, where's the bloody key to the Ferrari? You haven't lost it again, have you? You know I don't want you driving it, after the accident." John marched in, irritated, tight leather pants and a white silk shirt setting off his muscled figure. He glanced at Brad indifferently.

"Do you remember my cousin Brad, darling? He was at our wedding," Charlotte said hurriedly.

John plastered on his gleaming Colgate smile. "Of course. Great to see you again. What studio are you with?"

"Harcourt's," Brad answered, tongue-in-cheek, seeing Charlotte bite her lip as John gushed and promoted himself.

"I won't be back for dinner. We have to get the final shoot wrapped. There's a problem with the angle of the cameras. I don't like the way they make me look." He frowned, concentrating on the problem.

"But Brad's staying for dinner, couldn't you—"

"Good. You won't be by yourself then, will you? Ta-ta."

"Say good-night to Daddy, darling." Charlotte pushed Genny, who'd come back into the room, toward her father. Brad frowned, noticing how reluctantly she went, wincing at John's obvious indifference and the repulsion on his face before he kissed her dutifully.

His eyes flew to Charlotte, seeing the set smile, anger and pity jostling as he read her determination to make the best out of a bad situation.

After John departed and Genny went upstairs, they had dinner in the eclectic, casual-chic dining room. He listened, watching her in the glimmer of the candlelight, staying on neutral subjects, making determinedly positive remarks whenever John's name came up. Whatever the deal was, she seemed determined to see it through. And he admired her, even though his heart yearned.

"How did it happen?" he asked when she referred to the accident.

"I don't really remember. We'd driven up from London and I was whacked. I told John we should stop off somewhere for the night, but he thought we should push on. I must have swapped places with him shortly before the accident—we'd been doing that most of the way. I was knocked out, and when the police arrived John realized that I'd driven off the road."

"It's not your fault," he said protectively, hearing the guilt in her tone.

"Yes, it is. And if Genny's leg doesn't get better, I'll never forgive myself," she whispered.

"Give it time."

She nodded. "I'm taking her to a specialist Daddy found in New York."

"If there's anything I can do?"

"Thanks." Their eyes met in a warm, understanding exchange.

"How come you called her Genny?" he asked, smiling, searching for a change of subject, something that wouldn't pain her quite so much.

"It was Granny who suggested I call her Geneviève, after Oncle Eugène's sister, the one who was killed at Ouradour-sur-Glane during the war. She says I remind her of her. It suits Genny, don't you think?"

"Definitely," he murmured, remembering the photograph in Dex's office.

It was past ten by the time he left, heart heavy, soul too weary for sleep. It was so goddamn unfair. All of it. And like his grandfather, he questioned a God who deprived the twins of their parents, killed in their prime, and allowed little Genny to suffer an accident that could leave her deformed for life.

After half an hour he picked up a cab and sat morosely in the back, watching the traffic crawl past Marble Arch, wondering what he could do to help. By the time he reached the flat, he realized the answer was nothing. It wasn't his place to interfere, particularly when she'd made it abundantly clear she was in for the long haul.

Two days later he returned to New York, but Charlotte's image remained in the back of his mind, unable to blot out the sadness in her eyes.

47

Skye, Scotland, 1997

Dex was walking again and even taking an interest in the news. But he tired easily, nodding off in his chair for several minutes at a time. Flora's awareness came and went. Some days she was there, others she lived far away in a world of her own. Dex spent long hours next to her in the dreamery, holding her hand, remembering the past.

Often his mind turned to Angus, to the times when they were young, the old memories more vivid each day. There were his dreams, too. But all that was part of a life left behind many years ago. Now he sat impatiently in the sitting room, waiting anxiously for Brad and the children to arrive. They should already be here, he remarked, drumming his cane softly on the carpet.

The twins were nine now, and Brad was doing a fine job of educating them. He sighed. Not much of a life, poor lad. He wondered if he was still in love with Charlotte, whether that was the reason he'd never married, or if it was just plain lack of time.

Dex was wondering whether to make the journey to Limoges this year, but the idea of leaving Flora concerned him. Still, he wanted to see Eugène. What for? A swan song? he asked himself, giving a short laugh that ended in a cough.

After Brad and the children had spent a week in Skye, it was decided that Dex would accompany them to Limoges. Two days after his arrival he was driven to La Vallière, the past vivid as the car went up the drive, and the chauffeur parked in the same spot where they had placed baby David in the back of the Renault so many years ago.

Eugène met him at the foot of the steps. Dex made a sly reference to his red sash, the same one he'd been working toward for thirty years, and together they entered the house.

"It all seems so near nowadays," Dex said. "The past, I mean. Sometimes I remember things that happened during the war more easily than I do yesterday. Natty seems awfully present at times."

"It's true of us all. How is Flora doing?"

"Up and down. Scott's death was a shock." He looked sadly at the pictures on the piano. "I can't believe I lost them all, Eugène. The one I never knew, the one I loved more than life itself, and the one I knew and cared for the most. You know, often I wonder if we were right to hide the past from David." He sighed.

"Let bygones be bygones," Eugène said. "There's no room left in what little time remains for any of that. Soon we'll all be history and the past will be forgotten. Nobody will know the truth and they'll be none the worse for it."

"That sounds odd coming from you," Dex remarked with a spark of his old humor.

Eugène spread his hands in a gesture of defeat. "What's the use? I've learned a lot too over these many years."

"You're probably right," he conceded, not convinced, noticing now how his cousin had aged. A few sparse hairs protruded from under his skull cap, and his cheeks were hollow and withered, like a leaf left out in the sun too long. Yet his eyes still held that same fervent gaze that Dex remembered in him even as a child.

"God's given us several good innings," Dex remarked, shoulders shaking as they walked slowly out onto the terrace. "We can't complain. I suppose I even got my own back on Angus in the end, though not as I'd have planned."

"Did you really have nothing to with his death?" Eugène eyed him skeptically. "I've always found that one hard to swallow, you know. Do you realize I've been dealing with your antics for almost a century?"

"It's too long for anybody to live, isn't it?" Dex laughed, avoiding the former question, and sat in one of the garden chairs, wiggling the arms. "Why don't you buy some new chairs? These ones have been around since the thirties and they're hellishly uncomfortable."

"I see nothing wrong with them."

"No, you wouldn't. Your trouble is you're not a modern man, Eugène. You need to move with the times. Have you heard of this newfangled thing they call the Internet? It's a revolution in communication."

"I hope you'll be around to enjoy it."

"That'll be up to him, won't it?" He pointed his cane skyward. "When does he ever do what we think he will?"

"Never," Eugène answered. And believed it.

48

London, England, 1997

"How's Genny?" Brad asked as he and David sat down for lunch at Simpson's on the Strand, knowing she'd been operated on several days before. He'd had flowers sent to the hospital and a huge box of chocolates from him and the twins. Last summer they'd spent more time together during the summer, and the children had hit it off.

"As good as can be, under the circumstances. I'm sorry for Charlotte, though. She has too much to cope with. At least this jewelry designing keeps her entertained. She's really very good, you know. I didn't realize until I saw some of her work the other day how talented she really is. Funny how one's inclined to underestimate one's own children. How are the twins doing?"

"Growing. They've started Little League baseball. Dex is pleased because they play for the Yankees this season. I try to be there as often as possible. I saw Dex and Granny the other day in Skye. I was up for the weekend."

"Dad's amazing. Poor Mum's getting very out of it, though." He sighed. Brad thought he looked older this past year, his dark hair almost all gray, a tired look in his eyes. "I miss your father," he remarked with a sad smile. "We had so many good times together growing up. I remember the old days in Limoges. It was Scott that got Dad to back me when I wanted to race cars, you know. He was the most altruistic person I think I've ever met.''

Brad nodded. ''We had a strange but close relationship. Not really like father and son. Dex was more of a dad to me. But I loved my father.''

''I know. Scott was never the same after Nathalie died. And then, of course, there was your mother. That was the last straw. He was very much in love with her.''

''I remember her a little. There's a perfume I've smelled sometimes at parties. I'm sure it's the one she wore. I never wanted to ask Dad—he hated talking about her. I think it hurt him too much.''

''Joy de Patou. She always wore it.''

''Thanks. I'll remember. If I ever find a woman I feel like marrying, I'll buy it for her,'' he said, thinking of Charlotte.

The waiter brought the carving trolley and the conversation turned to Harcourt's and business.

49

Skye, Scotland, 1998

Flora awoke one crisp February morning aware it was her ninety-seventh birthday, more alert than she had been in ages. So much went on in her other world that it was difficult at times to keep abreast with this one. But today she felt a keen awareness. She wondered if Dex's cold was better and if the children would come as they hoped, weather permitting.

She climbed slowly out of bed and stepped hesitantly toward the window, her limbs stiff and unsteady. She frowned at the strange purple hue covering the loch, the hills looming heavily. A few errant rays of sunlight pierced the clouds, and on the lawn the first snowdrops and crocuses were poking their heads aboveground.

There was an eerie quality she noticed, shivering, an all-too-familiar feeling that she recognized and dreaded even now. She watched the wind pick up and heard the windows rattling in their ancient sockets, then saw the sun flee as the gale picked up strength, tossing three small crafts that were bobbing out in the bay. The sky darkened and the gulls flew low, squawking, their shrill calls echoing as the sea turned to murky lead, the spray-tipped waves shrouding the rocks, the first raindrops pattering against the panes. She turned away and blinked as vivid images pranced impishly. Gavin, Scott and Nathalie, Dexter.

Always Dexter and Gavin, merging into one, Angus falling down and down, wounds too deep to heal, still festering.

Charlotte had been very present in Flora's dreams the past few days. She was unhappy. Perhaps John Drummond was flaunting his mistresses again. She thought of Brad all of a sudden and sighed. How did you measure pain, she wondered sadly, knowing he carried a broken heart.

The wind blew harder and the windows rattled. The electricity suddenly went out. Flora sank into the cushions of her window seat and listened. To the words of the wind, to the chant of the waves, trying to understand, to hear what they were telling her. She shivered again and hoped Mary would be up soon with her morning tea. She could tell by the swell of the waves, the murmuring voices in the distance, that something was afoot.

She sat, eyes closed, listening to Celtic voices that spoke in ancient tongues. All at once she glanced up at the fairy emblem of the MacLeods fluttering over the east turret, and clutched a cushion as it appeared to her at half-mast.

She swayed gently back and forth as hazy images floated before her, old-fashioned kilted figures advancing in battle dress. MacLeods, she realized fearfully, recognizing the tartan, rising to claim their rights.

The door opened.

"Good morning, m'lady, and a happy birthday to ye'." Mary's cheerful voice brought her back. She smiled as the girl brought the tea over to her, setting it on the small table next to the window seat, and poured the steaming brew into the fine Haviland cup.

"Are the children here?" she asked, unsure of the time.

"They're expected within the hour, his lordship says." Mary could not be brought to understand that Dex was not "his lordship" but Mr. Ward. Never mind. She sipped slowly, her mind busy with the eerie sensations of moments earlier. Why, after all these years, would the MacLeods seek to stake a claim?

Mary helped her dress, brushed her fine white hair, which covered her shoulders gracefully, with the same silver brush that had lain on the dressing table for almost a century, then assisted Flora to the old cage elevator that still chugged and jerked its way down to the great hall. Dex had wanted to install a new one but she had begged him not to, preferring the old one, even though it got stuck more often than not.

"His Lordship'll be pleased to see ye' downstairs, m'lady, and so will the children when they arrive." Mary beamed at her from a round, florid face.

When they reached the sitting room, Dex was nowhere to be seen. Mary helped her sit on the sofa, placed a stool beneath her legs and covered them carefully with a cashmere rug, before leaving in search of his lordship.

Flora gazed into the fire and suddenly the room swayed. She held the arm of the sofa, and all at once she saw Geneviève, followed by Sylvain.

"Geneviève," she whispered, reaching out.

"Granny?"

Charlotte's voice penetrated the haze and she turned. But it was Geneviève standing there. "Geneviève? Have you come for David? Please, not yet," she murmured.

"Granny?" Charlotte crossed the room, worried, and took her grandmother's hand.

"Oh, it's you, dear. For a moment I thought you were someone else."

"Geneviève?" she asked curiously.

"That's right. I could have sworn that she and Sylvain were here. But then, you and she are so like one another that sometimes I get mixed up," she murmured, closing her eyes as Charlotte stroked her fingers and frowned at the strangeness of her words. She shook her head. Granny was very confused of late. But it was good to see her up for her birthday.

"Happy birthday, Granny," she whispered, giving the soft cheek a kiss. "Little Genny and I have a present for you, haven't we, darling?" She beckoned to her daughter, standing in the doorway.

"How lovely." Flora smiled as the child limped across the room. "Come here, Gennykins, and let Granny see you," she said, smiling. "My, how you've grown up. Soon you'll be wearing lipstick."

"This is for you, Granny," Genny said, proudly handing her a small flat package. "If you like, I'll help you open it," she added hopefully. "Mummy made it."

"Why don't you open it for me."

"All right." Carefully she unwrapped the pink and white wrapping paper and showed her a flat blue velvet box.

"That is like Rothberg's boxes used to be," Flora murmured.

"Rothberg's? You mean Sylvain's jewelry store in Paris."

"That's right."

"He's my favorite," Charlotte said with a sigh. "Of all the jewelers of that period, he was the best. I wonder whatever happened to all his collection?"

"I don't know, dear. Nobody does. Poor Sylvain." Then, seeing Genny was impatient to open the box, she smiled. "Open it, will you, dear? I can't wait to see what's inside."

Genny lifted the lid proudly, displaying an amethyst pendant shaped like a heart embedded in white gold, a tiny bright diamond shining up at her.

"Oh my goodness," she exclaimed. "It's perfectly lovely. Did you really make that, Charlotte dear?"

"Yes, she did." Genny beamed proudly at her mother. "Put it on, Granny."

"You'll have to help me."

Genny laid the box down and picked up the pendant, placing it around her great-grandmother's neck and carefully clasping it at the back. "There. Mummy, we should get a mirror for Granny to see."

"Oh, yes, please."

"There's one in the powder room," Charlotte remarked.

"I'll get it." Genny limped off excitedly to get the mirror while Charlotte sat next to her grandmother, who was gently touching the jewel at her throat.

"What a beautiful gift, my love. So thoughtful and kind. I wonder what Sylvain would have said if he knew."

"Knew what?"

"That you design jewelry, too."

"I don't know." Granny seemed far away again, and she shook her head, uncomprehending.

All at once the door burst open and the twins came bouncing in, followed by Brad, her father and mother, Colin and her grandfather. Charlotte rose to greet them, hugging Brad and the twins, whom she hadn't seen since the previous summer. "Gosh, you're enormous," she exclaimed, ruffling Todd's blond hair and Rick's black mane.

They gave Flora presents, chatted, drank champagne and celebrated. Dex was in good form, thrilled to see his wife up and enjoying the day, and David was happy to see his mother so well.

"When are you off to Chamonix?" Charlotte asked her brother.

"Tomorrow. I'm off at dawn," Colin replied. He'd finished at Cirencester and was getting more and more involved with running the MacLeod estate.

"I wish you weren't going," Flora remarked all of a sudden.

Colin looked up and smiled. "Don't worry, Granny. You know I'm a good skier."

"I know. Just being silly, I suppose."

Charlotte frowned uneasily at her brother then glanced at Brad, who happened to be looking her way. They exchanged a long smile.

John hadn't bothered to come. He was shooting a movie in Monte Carlo. Or so he'd said, but Charlotte wondered. There were constant rumors, which she'd scotched. For some reason, the sight of Brad across the table made her feel doubly abandoned.

That night, after they'd taken Granny up to the dreamery and the children were playing video games in the nursery, Brad and Charlotte sat in the sitting room in front of the fireplace, talking. Colin popped in and whistled to Rufus, his dog. "Come on, old boy, time for a walk. See you two later," he said with a smile.

"Colin has a new girlfriend," she remarked.

"Do you like her?"

"Not much."

"Any special reason?"

She laughed. Brad and she were always on the same wavelength. "Just sisterly jealousy, I suppose. Actually, I think she's all right. A bit too sophisticated for Colin, though. He's a farmer at heart. Loves the estate, the land. You couldn't pry him off Skye if you tried."

"It's not a bad place to be."

"Pretty deadly at this time of year," she remarked, wrinkling her nose.

"That depends whom you're here with," he teased. "I, for instance, am having a very good time in Skye right now."

"Really?" She arched an eyebrow.

"Yes, ma'am."

"Can I improve on it by offering you a glass of whiskey? I don't think I could bear more champagne."

"I'll get it." He rose, poured them each two fingers of single malt from the decanter on the silver tray behind the sofa and handed it to her. A shudder rippled through her when their fingers touched, suddenly remembering his mouth on hers all those years ago. He hadn't changed. Just become more handsome, more mature, more the kind of man any woman in her right mind would die for.

"How's your love life?" she asked, half teasing.

"Great."

"What does that mean?"

"Charlotte, when exactly do you think I can squeeze a love life into my already hectic existence?" he asked, laughing.

"Don't give me that, Bradley Ward. A man like you must have tons of women lining up in the wings."

"Right. I'm not as popular as you seem to believe. Remember, I come with baggage."

"And a huge bank account," she scoffed.

"Thanks. I can think of better reasons for liking a guy. I keep it simple." He took a long sip of whiskey and met her eyes.

"Which means?"

"Why are you so interested?"

"No reason." She shrugged, then laughed and looked at the flames. "It just strikes me as odd that you've been alone all these years."

"I'm not gay, if that's what you're thinking."

"Oh, don't be silly." She hurled a cushion, missing the flowers by an inch. He caught it deftly.

"Be careful, I played football in college. And to satisfy your rampant curiosity, I have a few selected young ladies whom I date from time to time. Since I don't live alone, I end those nights—note I said nights, not evenings—at what used to be Dex and my great-uncle Johnny Harcourt's bachelor pad on Fifth. Satisfied?"

"Yes." She sent him a bright smile. Trust him to have a neat solution to everything.

"How's your husband?" He watched as she took a quick sip before answering.

"Fine, doing lots of work. Never stops. In fact, I should phone him shortly. He'll want to know how today went."

Will he, Brad wondered skeptically as she rose and poked the fire. The last he'd heard, John Drummond was fucking his costar and had no qualms about letting it be publicly known.

Colin left for Chamonix early next morning. Brad planned to stay on a few days, at least over the weekend, after which he was headed back to New York, then on to Hong Kong.

The weather was bad for the next couple of days and the children quickly became antsy. When the rain stopped and a hint of sunshine appeared on Saturday, they were all relieved.

"Better get them out," Penelope remarked to Charlotte over breakfast.

"Yes, or we'll all go mad."

"Brad, what about a walk this afternoon?"

"Sure. Sounds good. The kids want to ride."

"I hope the ground's not too wet," Penelope murmured. "I worry about Genny."

"She'll be fine, Mum."

Brad noted the slight irritation in Charlotte's tone and glanced from one to the other. Aunt Penn said nothing, but he wondered how much she knew. It must be painful to see your child suffering, he realized, knowing it was bad enough for him to see Charlotte miserable.

"That's the phone again," Penelope exclaimed, getting up. "It hasn't stopped all morning. By the way, pop in to Mrs. Bane's and pick up the cake, will you, darling?" She hastened to the hall to pick up the receiver.

"If you want, I'll get the kids out of your hair," Brad offered. Charlotte seemed nervous this morning. "Did you sleep okay?"

"I'm fine, thanks. I'm still feeling the effect of all that champagne the other day. Don't bother about the kids. I'll deal with them."

"It's no bother, Charlie," he said softly, wishing she would let him in, if only a tiny bit.

"I know. I—" Her eyes suddenly filled with tears.

With difficulty, he restrained himself from taking three strides around the table and enveloping her in his arms. "What's wrong, babe?"

She shook her head and brushed away the tears. "Sorry, just being silly."

"No, you're not—"

The door burst open and Penelope stood in the doorway, trembling.

"Mummy, what is it?" Charlotte jumped up, shocked, and Brad followed.

"Where's your father?" she whispered hoarsely.

"I don't know. Mummy, what on earth is it?" Charlotte clutched her mother's arm, gripped with fear.

"There's been an avalanche."

"No." Charlotte gasped and Brad grabbed her as she stepped back, horrified.

"Seven people are still missing," Penelope continued, as though reciting something. "Including Colin."

"What's being done?" Brad asked, aghast.

"Everything. The teams are still searching."

"I'll go find Uncle David," Brad murmured, leaving them

holding one another while he rushed to the garage, where he believed his uncle was fixing the engine of his vintage Rolls.

By midday there was still no news. David was preparing to leave immediately.

"I'll go with you," Brad offered.

"No. Stay here and hold the fort, Brad. If—oh God." He closed his eyes, blotting out the fearful image of his boy buried under rocks and snow. "There may yet be hope, though after forty-eight hours in such low temperatures, smothered by the snow and rocks, it is almost impossible for them to be alive."

Dex got up. "Why is God determined to rob me of those I love?" he asked querulously. "I can't lose him, too."

He couldn't believe what was happening, imagining the avalanche sweeping Colin into its relentless arms, a mighty white tidal wave leaving nothing in its wake but devastation. They sat for several hours, listening to the news on television, the Paris office keeping them regularly updated with the latest reports.

At 3:00 p.m. the news finally came. The bodies had been recovered and were being brought down to the village of Chamonix at that very moment. Colin was among them.

Dex sat in the corner of the sofa in shattered, bleary-eyed silence. He was weary of pain, worn with waiting and wondering, with piecing together the broken remains over and over, only to have them shatter, this time beyond repair. Flora, who'd risen from her bed and joined them downstairs, sat next to him, aware that her premonition had been justified. Poor darling Colin. She sighed unhappily, aching for David and Penn, for Charlotte, standing white and forlorn near the fireplace, where Brad was leaning over to hear her whispered words, features taut with sadness. Her husband hadn't bothered to return her call.

Flora slipped her hand into Dex's, feeling how it shook, aware of all the implications Colin's death held for them. Losing him was bad enough, but losing the last heir to Strathaird was a tragedy as well. She wondered if David and Penn and Charlotte had realized that yet, or if they were too besieged by grief to have thought further than the moment. Her eyes remained pinned on Brad and she shook her head as images floated once more before her eyes. She turned, saw how pale Dex looked and gently stroked his fingers.

"Do you realize what this means?" she murmured, leaning forward and wiping the tear that coursed down his cheek.

He nodded silently. "The MacLeods," he whispered, shivering. "They'll not rest until their blood is reinstated. I can feel it. I have denied it all these years, Flora, and Colin has paid the price." He gazed at her in horror.

"What do you mean? That isn't your fault, dearest," she murmured, squeezing his hand a little harder.

"Oh yes, it is," he replied bitterly.

Charlotte sat on her brother's bed, holding the watch her father had given him on his eighteenth birthday. So many memories flew through her head—the times they'd shared, the ones she'd cherish, the ones she wished she could change. But there was no room left for that anymore. Colin was gone.

She stared once more at the watch then gently slipped it onto her wrist. There was some story behind it but Granny had never wanted to talk about it. Something to do with the war and the sad death of Aunt Geneviève, after whom she'd named Genny. Now she understood better why. Losing someone you loved dearly was the hardest thing that could happen. The sheer finality of it was shattering. She studied the watch as a tear plopped onto her cheek. *Rothberg.* Geneviève's husband, killed in the Resistance, a man she admired as the greatest jeweler of all. She clasped the watch, feeling a strange current, as though Colin, and Uncle Sylvain, whom she'd never known, and Aunt Geneviève were all connected to her through it. It was strangely comforting.

She turned and saw Rufus, Colin's Labrador, his tail and ears drooping, next to her and stroked him gently, determined not to start crying again. She needed to be there for the others—her mother and father, who had lost their only son. Dex was having people in from Edinburgh to talk about the estate and to see if the male line of the entail could be altered. If it couldn't, it meant that someday, when her father died, some long-lost MacLeod would become the next laird, taking Colin's place. She stared out the window rebelling at the thought. Strathaird was theirs, their home, their life. How could they conceive of one day perhaps conceding it to a stranger? She cared about that for herself but much more for Daddy, Mummy and her grandparents. After all, Strathaird meant everything to them. It was a part of them, a sanctuary, the haven where all ills were cured, all problems resolved and hearts healed. It was here she'd come running after they'd had the accident and Genny had suffered the damage to her leg, here she'd learned to come to terms with her daughter's handicap, and that she'd received the love and understanding necessary for her to go on.

She swallowed, patted the dog once more and glanced at the photos next to Colin's bed, some of them taken only weeks before. It would be a long time before she could actually believe he wasn't coming back. There was one with Brad taken last summer in the States. She picked it up, lips quivering. Thank God for Brad. Thank God he was here to help them. She rose, her back aching from the strain of the past few days and smoothed the bedspread gently.

"Goodbye, Col," she whispered softly. Then she turned and quickly left the room.

Dex was thankful when Eugène arrived. He had brought Colin's body back from France with David and would conduct the funeral services in the small chapel where Dex himself had a headstone. The thought made him shudder. He was tortured since Colin's death, alternately acknowledging then denying the hand of fate. But he sensed it. He knew the MacLeods wouldn't rest until the wrong was righted.

"What must I do to satisfy them?" he asked Eugène as they sat in the study together, two old men too used to death, too accustomed to burying those whom they should have predeceased.

"You ask me? You, who never want advice. Can't you see it for yourself, Gavin?" Eugène murmured, hands folded over the knob of his cane, his eyes turning to his cousin sadly.

"Surely you can see that there has been enough sacrifice in the name of this farce that you chose to make us all live with?" His voice grew angry. "Oh, don't tell me. I know you don't relate one thing to the other, simply because it doesn't suit you, *mon cousin*. But I see it loud and clear. There's a pattern. They have all died, all been sacrificed. All had to disappear to clear the way, leaving you with no choice but to face the truth. Others have paid the price for your choices, Gavin. And what a high price it has been," he added bitterly.

"Are you saying I am to blame for all that has happened? For Colin's death? You talk nonsense, Eugène. How can I be responsible for the boy dying in an avalanche?" He muttered something under his breath, then thumped the arm of the sofa, frustrated. "The trouble with you is that the Church has warped your mind."

"Think whatever you like," he snapped, "but I'm telling you to beware, or once again your silence will put others in danger. The Church has not warped my mind to the extent that I can't see what's before me."

"And what is that, pray?" Dex asked uncomfortably, trying to push the images from his mind.

"The MacLeods have no heir any longer. You'll be obliged to go scouring the planet for some distant relation to take over when David dies. Penn, Charlotte, Genny, all of them—should they outlive David—will be ousted from their home, and all because you are too proud, too selfish to admit the truth. Instead, you slither out of facing your duty once again. Brad is the heir to Strathaird and you know it. And a better heir would be hard to find," he added crossly, the pressure of the past few days and Dex's blind selfishness getting him down. "If I hadn't pledged my secrecy all those years ago, I swear I would tell them myself."

Dex looked at him, shocked, then let his eyes wander to the rug, blindly tracing the faded tree of life with his walking stick. It was true. As Gavin MacLeod's only grandson, Brad was the rightful heir, though he'd never allowed himself to think like that. Was Colin's death God's way of demanding reparation for his abandonment? He followed the stitches of the branches at his feet slowly. And all at once he knew. The MacLeods would never rest until the true heir returned. He'd said it to Flora and Eugène without really believing his own words. Now he knew they were the truth.

Time and tide wait for no man, he reflected bitterly, and neither did God. He leaned back and sagged in the armchair, exhausted, overwhelmed by an ache so great he could hardly bear its weight. All at once he experienced a longing stronger than any he'd felt since he'd departed almost a century before. Oh, if only he could turn back the clock, say the same words differently, taken those few moments of reflection that could have changed a lifetime. Now it was too late. The dice were thrown and too many fates sealed. There was no course open to him but to succumb, no alternative but to bow to their strength, to their demands, for until he did they would continue to demand more sacrifice until he conceded.

He looked up at the portraits on the wall, meeting his ancestors' eyes. "You've won," he whispered.

He looked out the window where the sky had darkened and a storm was brewing. How would he tell her, he wondered. How would he tell his Flora the truth? And Brad, the boy who would become the heir to Strathaird. No. Not the boy, he realized, smiling for the first time in days, the man. A man who assumed his responsibilities, whom Dex had brought up to be the image of what he himself should have been. If anyone was true to the MacLeod tradition it was Brad, with his deep sense of loyalty and duty, his nobility of spirit peppered with wit, wisdom and humor. Yet, he wondered, seeing Eugène had nodded off, did he have the right to burden him with more than he already carried? After all, he was young, the vice president of a huge international enterprise that demanded his all. And as though that wasn't enough, Brad had his brothers to bring up, acting as surrogate father. Why, the boy had no social life to speak of, no wife—probably some mistresses, he conceded. All at once he wondered if Brad still had feelings for Charlotte. Well, that was neither here nor there in this particular matter. The point was whether he could ask him to bear the weight of the MacLeod heritage as well. He glanced once more at the pictures. A sudden flash of lightning zigzagged in front of the window illuminating their faces and he knew the answer.

Outside, the rain poured endlessly, a monotonous flow down the windowpanes, a never-ending cycle of birth, life, death and sometimes rebirth. Dex and Flora sat silently together in the library. It was time, he realized—had been time long ago. Yet he'd fled from the truth, always thinking he could manage it his way. And look at the result. Another had paid in his place. Life came around, back to wherever it wanted. However far or hard he ran, there was no escape. He leaned back for a moment, still trying to assimilate the pain of Colin's death. Then, all at once, he knew it was time.

"Flora, I need to speak to you," he said suddenly, rising unsteadily. Leaning on his cane, he stepped nervously toward the mantelpiece, his heart trembling. But it was too late for fear, too late for regret. There was only one way out and he must face it. He raised his white head and gazed across the room at her. "I should have told you from the beginning," he whispered. "I know you'll never forgive me but please, if you can, believe I did what I thought best at the time, what I—" He stopped, shook his head and muttered. The door opened gently and Brad stood in the doorway.

"Come in, my boy. You too must hear what I have to say. Then we'll decide about the rest of them." He swallowed and watched his grandson sit silently next to his grandmother on the sofa, eyebrows knit, concerned. Dex didn't need to tell him what was about to be revealed, Brad just sensed it was something important. Dex sighed, wishing he could spare the boy more responsibility and his beloved Flora the pain. But Eugène was right. It was time to come to terms with the truth. A sudden surge of panic gripped him as Flora and Brad gazed at him expectantly.

"What I'm about to tell you is a strange tale. But it's true and you have to believe it," Dex began, concentrating on the silver knob of his cane. "I am not doing this out of choice but out of necessity."

Brad watched his grandfather shift uneasily before the fire, as if what he was about to say was hard to get out. He frowned, barely concentrating, his mind still taken up with the horror of Colin's death and Uncle David, Aunt Penn and Charlotte's misery. But as Dex began, he forced himself to listen, realizing that it must be something momentous for him to be speaking at such a difficult time.

"It goes back to 1917, to the war. All wars are stupid but the '14-'18 beat the lot of 'em. None of us knew why we were fighting, why our youth was being destroyed. The death toll was absurd, the conditions horrific and it wiped out the flower of our generation."

Brad suddenly paid attention, aware of the intensity, the new inflection in Dex's voice and his grandmother's quiet look of expectation.

"Go on, Dex, dear," she murmured when he hesitated.

"Life in the trenches was boring, stagnant," he continued, "except when we went on a raid behind the German lines. That was fun. But that's not what I want to talk about," he said, coming back on track, fixing Brad with a piercing look. "Brad, I wish I didn't have to tell you this, didn't have to burden you with more than you already carry. But I have no choice. The life and well-being of too many depends on my telling you the truth about who I really am."

"What do you mean, who you really are?" he murmured, bewildered. Was Dex suffering from delayed shock after Colin's death? He touched his grandmother's arm but she merely shook her head.

"Go on, Dex," she whispered.

"Dexter Ward was a dead captain in the New York Sixty-ninth whose identity I assumed at the end of the war. We won't get into that now. Suffice it to say that I decided to become Dexter Ward, to forgo my true identity, and make a life for myself in America."

"Hold it." Brad rose, passed a worried hand through his hair and tried to register this information. "You're telling us you're not who you are?"

"That's right. I am Gavin. Gavin MacLeod, heir to the MacLeods of Strathaird. Not Dex," he whispered hoarsely, ramming his cane into the Persian rug, his voice rising and his eyes seeking Flora's. "Flo, your Gavin, whom you believed dead all these years, was me. I deceived you, lied to you, made you believe for all this while that Dexter Ward existed, and that the man you truly loved died in the Somme, because I was too much of a damn coward to tell you that I'd left, abandoned you to a fate you had no wish for."

"But why?" Flora reached up, eyes bright and glistening with unshed tears. "Why, my darling, didn't you tell me?"

"Because I read the announcement."

"The announcement?"

"Your wedding announcement in the *Times,* telling of your marriage to Angus, and my father's death. When I read that Angus had taken my place, even as your husband, I—I decided to assume the identity of the American officer whose uniform I'd been given at the end of the war, when I joined the New York Sixty-ninth."

"Wait," Brad interrupted, sitting down again with a thud. "You'll have to explain this better. Are you saying that you're Great-uncle Angus's twin?"

"Yes. But he chose to leave me to die in a trench. Unfortunately, I didn't oblige. I survived, was taken prisoner and escaped from a German POW hospital near Frieburg with a couple of other officers. I made it back to France eventually and met up with Bill Donovan and the New York Sixty-ninth. Then at the armistice I was in a bar in Rheims. By mistake I got caught up in a fight and woke up on board the *Mauritania,* sailing for New York. When I told them who I was, nobody believed me. They thought I was suffering from shell shock."

"So what happened?" Brad asked, fascinated despite himself.

"I made friends with Johnny Harcourt on the boat. He took me home with him, and the family ended up adopting me, so to speak. They believed I was from Oklahoma and that my family were all dead. Johnny hated the porcelain business, but because of my experience in Oncle Eustace's factory in Limoges, I knew a lot about it and loved it. Your great-grandfather and I developed a wonderful relationship." He paused, eyes suddenly far away. "After I'd studied at Columbia and Johnny died, I joined Harcourt's and married Alix."

"This is incredible," Brad murmured, wondering how his grandmother was bearing up. "But what do you propose to do by telling us now?"

"Establish you as the rightful heir to Strathaird. While Colin was alive that wasn't necessary. Now I'm afraid that's changed."

"What?" Brad jumped up and they faced one another. "I can't become the heir to Strathaird. That's ridiculous. I'm an American, for Christ's sake. What's it got to do with me?"

"Don't you see?" Dex said gently. "You're my grandson, Brad, my next of kin. The MacLeod blood runs in your veins, boy, and you're the legal heir to the title and the lands of Strathaird."

"No. Wait a minute. I'm a Ward. I run Harcourt's and I have kids to bring up—"

"Who are MacLeods as well."

"Whatever. I don't care who you were or who you decided to become, but you can't just march in here and pick up people's lives like pieces on a chessboard and place them wherever the hell you want. I'm sorry, Dex, but this time you've gone too far and I'm not playing. All my life, I've been the son Dad wasn't. I've taken on every challenge and responsibility you sent my way, assuming his obligation and a number of yours. But enough is enough. I won't be a part of your schemes. You should have thought this one out a while back. Not now, when it's too late."

Their eyes locked and tension ripped the air. Then slowly Dex laid an arm on his grandson's sleeve and his voice softened. "I can't force you to do anything, my boy. But I have to ask you. Strathaird needs you, the family need you. If you don't accept, some long-lost relation we've never met will inherit when David dies. That means that Charlotte and Genny—Penn, too, if she is alive—would be thrown out of here."

"Don't play that card, Dex." He felt anger rise once more at the way his grandfather ruthlessly manipulated them all.

"Don't you see, boy? I've tried to escape the pull, tried to run as far as I could, but even now, at the last chapter of my life, I still can't escape. There has to be a reckoning, Brad, and I'm afraid that reckoning is you.''

"This is crazy, totally absurd.'' He threw up his hands, refusing to concede.

"I know that it must seem so,'' Dex sighed, his voice frail.

Brad glanced at him, astonished to see a different expression than he'd ever seen before. Even the tone of his voice had changed. Gone was the manipulative pride, the arrogant authority that automatically expected obedience. Instead, he saw an old man weary of his burdens, pleading with him to pick up the slack one last time. "If you don't do it for me, then do it for her.''

The words hit him, making him writhe inwardly. So his grandfather knew that he still loved Charlotte. Dex would, of course, being him. And expected him to do this for a woman who was married to another man and whom he should be trying his best to forget.

He turned away, passed a hand over his face. Then he met his grandmother's eyes, read the silent plea there, and let out a long breath. He stepped over to where she sat silently listening. "If this is what you want,'' he said, taking her hand in his, "then I'll do it.''

"It is what has to be,'' she whispered, drawing him down next to her, a tiny smile quivering on her lips as he slid onto the sofa next to her. Dex gazed at her silently, his face white, the hand on his cane shaking slightly. Brad rose hastily and took his arm. He seemed so frail and fragile all of a sudden, as though the strength and power had been seeped from his being.

"It is too much to beg for forgiveness, Flo. I know that now,'' he whispered, leaning heavily on Brad's arm.

Flora raised her hand gently, her eyes locked in his. "Hush,'' she murmured. "Not all is as it appears. Now I understand why they've come. Why for several years now I've seen you both merging as one—you and Gavin, Gavin and you—all the time. I should have known, should have felt it. Just like the moment I first saw you across the room at Geneviève and Sylvain's reception.''

Brad watched in silent awe as the tensions and feelings of almost a hundred years churned around him, interlacing, weaving their way across the room as their eyes rested in one another's. He felt Dex tremble and wanted to help him sit down, but knew he mustn't. It was a moment the man needed to live on his own. But as tears began pouring down his grandfather's withered cheeks, he led him gently and seated him in the armchair where he collapsed in a heap.

"How can you ever forgive me, Flo?" He leaned forward. "What have I done? Oh, what have I done?" he muttered in a strangled whisper.

"What you've always done, my love," she murmured, sighing as the images melded into one. She gazed at him, not surprised, merely relieved to have it explained, to acknowledge the truth that had been lurking for so long, her heart suddenly light despite her sorrow over Colin. "You've come back," she whispered, stretching her hand across the small distance separating them. "You've come back, Gavin, as you always promised you would."

Brad saw his grandfather try to rise and helped him up, then stood aside as Dex stepped hesitantly forward, and watched, astonished, as he fell to his knees, buried his head in his grandmother's lap and sobbed. Then quietly he turned away and closed the door behind him, realizing there was no room there for anyone but the two of them—their past, their present and their dreams.

Several hours later, Dex and Flora faced the ravaged family. Dex had wanted to tell the whole truth—about himself, about Sylvain, about David. But Flora had soothed him, and Eugène had gently persuaded him not to. The MacLeods were one thing. The truth had to be told. But David had borne enough losing his son. How would he react to learning that he was not whom he believed himself to be? That his parents were people he'd seen from time to time in pictures and heard of in stories? No, Flora insisted, shaking her white head while gently stroking his, let the past remain tucked away where it would harm no one. Perhaps Sylvain and Genny wanted it that way, she realized, remembering their image that had appeared on the morning of Colin's death. The MacLeods would be quieted now that Gavin had returned, now that he could name Brad as his heir after David. And if he had no son, there were the twins to follow.

Brad tramped over the moor with Colin's dog, Rufus, close to heel, oblivious of the rain, trying to assimilate all that had passed in the past few hours and what it implied. Dex's story was amazing. But so like him, he realized wryly. Trust the old man to have an adventure hidden up his sleeve until the last moment. He smiled sadly, thinking of poor Colin. It seemed so damn unfair. His own new destiny stood strangely outlined before him. Not that it changed much for now, but it might one day.

He stopped when he reached the edge of the lawn and gazed over toward the sea with new eyes. There was something to be said about knowing you belonged to a place. It was stupid, perhaps, but knowing his true heritage changed the way he viewed everything. The air had become suddenly sharper, the wind whipping his face felt familiar, and the rain wasn't just rain anymore but smelled fresh, hopeful, like the snowdrops sprouting near the path, filling his heart and soul with longings long put aside. He closed his eyes and thought of his father, of Colin and then, as always, of Charlotte. The thought made him smile and he stood for a while longer, glancing over at the still waters of the loch that shrouded secrets, the subtle tremors on the surface a contrast to the swelling surf that crashed inland, determined to rule the rocks below the cliffs. Gusts of wind mussed his hair and he turned to face the oncoming gale, welcoming the sheer force of nature battling in her glory, a challenge he was willing to face.

Rufus barked and he opened his eyes, seeing a figure leave the castle and walk in his general direction. He knew at once it was Charlotte and headed toward the spot in the path that formed a crossroads. They reached it at the same moment from opposite directions, stood silently for a moment, then fell into step with one another, heading toward the sea, the dog trotting sadly alongside, as though he knew his master would never return and was already seeking a new one.

When they reached the edge of the cliff, the gale was full-blown. Charlotte stared out into nowhere, her titian hair flying, her tear-stained face so sad he thought his heart would break. A strong gust of wind had him grabbing her arm, pulling her away from the sheer ledge, gripped by sudden fear that yet another sacrifice would be demanded.

He slipped his arm around her, smelling the wind and the heather in her hair, feeling her snuggle close for comfort. And he vowed, staring up into the angry clouds that there would be no more death, no more pain. Whatever the gods wanted, he was prepared to pay, as long as they spared her.

Charlotte stopped and looked toward the castle where the faerie flag flew at half-mast and Brad tightened his grip.

"Is it really true what Dex told us?" she murmured.

"Yes. It's incredible. But then, Dex is incredible. Always has been, always will be."

"Do you realize this may all be yours one day?"

"No. I'm going to talk to Uncle David once things are more settled. There must be a way of breaking the entail, of having the property come to you."

"That wouldn't be right. As Granny would say, the Mac-Leods wouldn't like it. We must just accept the way it is, Brad." She turned in his arms, looked up at him tenderly. "Poor Col," she whispered. "I miss him so much. I don't know how I'll survive without him. He was always there. Always such a dear. I love him so much." Her voice caught on a sob.

He drew her into his arms, held her tight against the front of his worn shooting jacket and sighed. "For what it's worth, I'll always be there, Charlie. You can count on that."

Then he lowered his head to hear the muffled response whispered against the wind.

"I know."

For a moment they stood locked in each other's arms. Then

all at once the rain cleared, as suddenly as it had begun. The clouds picked up speed, the gulls began their low constant chatter and the air engulfed them with the sweet smell of wet grass, brine and hope. And, hand in hand, they headed back to Strathaird.

Flora and Gavin side by side stood at the window of the dreamery. Two figures were walking up the path. And as the light dwindled and the evening shadows reached out over the east turret, they watched the faerie flag of the MacLeods being lowered over their lives. Gavin slipped an arm around his love and glanced toward the heavens. Here was where it had all begun, where so much was ending, and where so much was perhaps still yet to be. And as the sun set in the west and he watched Brad and Charlotte reach the lawn, he sighed and tightened his arm around Flora, wondering what destiny Strathaird and the MacLeods had waiting for them.

New York Times **Bestselling Author**

REBECCA BRANDEWYNE

DESTINY'S DAUGHTER

Determined to track down her father's killers, Bryony St. Blaze travels to England to find Hamish Neville, the one man who knows about her father's research of a secret order known as the Abbey of the Divine.

But after an attempt is made on Bryony's life, the two are forced to go into hiding, dependent on one another for their very survival. Piece by piece, they assemble the puzzle to locate the lost book her father was murdered for. But time is running out. Can they unlock the secrets of the hidden treasure before the mysterious and deadly order catches up with them?

> "I have been reading and enjoying Rebecca Brandewyne for years. She is a wonderful writer."
> —Jude Deveraux

On sale December 2001 wherever paperbacks are sold!

New York Times Bestselling Author

JAYNE ANN KRENTZ

The Wedding Night

Owen Sutherland's whirlwind courtship has left Angie Townsend breathless and in love—and hopeful that the fierce rivalry that had divided their powerful families would finally end. But now, nestled in their honeymoon suite, Angie suspects she may also be a fool. A sudden, hushed phone call warns her of the terrible truth: her marriage is a sham, nothing more than a clever corporate raid orchestrated by her powerful new husband. The very husband reaching out to lead her to their wedding bed...

Is Owen Sutherland a calculating stranger...or the man she's married for better or for worse? Until Angie knows for certain, her wedding night is on hold...indefinitely.

"A master of the genre—nobody does it better!"
—*Romantic Times*

*Available the first week
of December 2001
wherever paperbacks are sold!*